YOUR ATTENTION, PLEASE

"We have laid a number of explosive charges on the gondola lift and on the Number One chair-lift. We can detonate this explosive from anywhere within a radius of ten miles by radio control. We are heavily armed and we are holding hostages in the gondola base . . ."

From the heights of the loftiest snow-capped peak to the depths of a hellish sudden death, Silky and Jake were just about to pull off the perfect heist . . .

THE MILLION DOLLAR LIFT!

RICHARD CRIGHTON

THE MILLION DOLLAR LIFT

AVON
PUBLISHERS OF BARD, CAMELOT AND DISCUS BOOKS

THE MILLION DOLLAR LIFT is an original publication of Avon Books. This work has never before appeared in book form.

AVON BOOKS
A division of
The Hearst Corporation
959 Eighth Avenue
New York, New York 10019

Copyright © 1981 by Richard Crighton
Published by arrangement with the author
Library of Congress Catalog Card Number: 80-68414
ISBN: 0-380-76604-3

First Avon Printing, January, 1981

To skiers everywhere.
Especially to Keitha,
    who gave me my first lesson.

CHAPTER ONE

SILKY AMBLER sat down at the bar of the Red Onion in Aspen, ordered a Vodka Collins, and surveyed the room. He studied the people without much enthusiasm. There were a few hard cases, real skiers, but, as always, a lot of the Red Onion crowd was strictly après-ski; a fashion parade of great-looking ski clothes that never saw the light of day until martini time.

He was relaxed, pacing himself, nice and quiet. Ski-bumming had a mystique to it. It had to be savored. You did not play it fast, push it, or make a goddam noise. You did not rush at the ski bunnies, get stoned, or stay up all night. You just let it all happen, and mainly you skied.

Jake would happen; it was a foregone conclusion. But, until he caught up with him, he wasn't going to bust a gut. Right now, he was in a mood to indulge himself. He had been dreaming of this trip all the way through his tour of duty. When the gooks started shooting, it was the fear of never skiing again, not the fear of dying, that made him scratch a little deeper in his foxhole.

Looking for Jake gave his one-man ski tour a sense of purpose; it kept him on the move and stopped him from getting hung up too long in one spot, with a chick or something.

He had called Jake's place in Boise over a month ago. The lady said that he had gone skiing. No, she didn't know where or for how long. She sounded a bit miffed.

Just like Jake. At any rate he was alive and kicking.

Silky had promptly rolled out his wheels and headed for Snowbird. It was a new area, built since he'd been away, and he had heard that they had a good early snowfall. Then he had skied a day each at Alta and Park City, getting limbered up. But he'd known, on reflection, that Jake would not be in Utah; the liquor laws were too archaic. He would be in Colorado. And the place to pick up the scent was the Red Onion.

He planned to spend a few days in Aspen, whether he turned Jake up or not. It was ritualistic, a sentimental journey—visions of wide, sweeping turns on the Big Burn and a plunging schuss through the powder of Aspen Highlands.

He picked up his check and paid it, ready to go.

"Silky!" A big red-bearded man punched him on the shoulder. "Long time no see."

He stared at him, then the penny dropped. "Christ, Jerry Cusack! Man, with all that fuzz on your face, I couldn't recognize you."

"You kidding? I was standing over there for ten minutes, trying to figure how I knew this black-bearded guy at the bar. Couldn't figure if you were a friend of mine, or someone I had picked a fight with."

They slapped hands. Silky ordered another round.

"What's new?" Jerry asked.

"I just got out of the army. I was in 'Nam."

"Me too. What outfit?"

"Special Forces."

"Shit, I was in the air corps. Fighters. How long you been in town?"

"Came in this afternoon."

"Staying long? You looking for work here?"

"No. I figure to stay a day or two. Actually I'm looking for Jake Snyder. Seen him?"

Cusack scratched his beard, crinkled his eyes. "No. But I think I heard his name mentioned. Some guys who came in from Steamboat."

"It's not critical."

"Got a pad?"

"I'm at the Holiday Inn at Buttermilk."

"Shit, man, you're welcome to crash at my place. Got a sleeping bag?"

2

"Sure. Thanks, Jerry. I've got money. The groceries are my treat for the week, and you're on."

"Done! Great! Where you figure to ski tomorrow?"

"Highlands, I guess."

"I'm working at Snowmass."

"Got a car?"

"No. There's a bus," Jerry shrugged.

"Screw the bus. I've got wheels. I'll drive you and ski there tomorrow."

Casually, just like that, which was the whole joy of it, they traded what they had to offer. It was the way Silky liked things to happen, without fuss and effusion. He had a pad and a place to ski; anything else would have been superfluous.

He stayed three days with Jerry. He ran the Big Burn fast and wide, just as he had dreamed of it, then moved up in search of the mogul freaks. Jerry took the day off on Thursday and they skied the deep powder at Aspen Highlands, after a nine-inch snowstorm.

Friday he dropped Jerry off at Snowmass, packed his gear, left a case of beer on the kitchen table with a big THANKS scrawled across it, and took off for Steamboat Springs.

It was snowing gently as he hit the open road, so he kept it nice and easy, listening to the radio. He had all day and was not going to get any skiing done anyway. He was relaxed, muscles toned, mind free of tension.

He mulled over the plan as he drove, considering how to present it to Jake. Not that Jake was the kind who wanted a whole lot of preliminaries, a load of bullshit, to suck him into a deal, but it was going to sound a bit strange the first time he heard it. Jake was impulsive and, if he got the wrong first impression, then it might take a lot of selling to get him back on track.

Silky didn't want that. He did not want to sell it. He wanted to lay it out quietly and carefully, the way he had thought it out, and just watch Jake's cold gray eyes sizing it up and laughing, for the joy and beauty of it.

He had lived with the project for nearly two years. Two years almost permanently behind the enemy lines, with nothing to think about except death, explosives—and skiing.

The idea had kind of drifted into his mind, while he

was lying in the scrub brush outside Sam Thong. They had been ambushed with heavy casualties, and he had to leave some of the wounded behind, some of his friends. He did not want to go, but he had been ordered back to cover the retreat of the Meo mercenaries. He was full of hate and revenge that day, another pinch of violence in his soul.

He set up a stack of claymores spread strategically around the bunkers and waited for the enemy to over-run the observation post. He proposed to let the advance V.C. patrols filter through, draw the second line into the captured bunkers, and then blow their little yellow balls off.

It was a long wait, well past midnight before he got the first alert. Alone with his thoughts, he had been picturing himself swinging up the chairlift at Winter Park when the seed of the idea first drifted into his mind.

It did not hit him with any particular force. It just sauntered around the outskirts of his brain, then wafted away again, as he forced his concentration back to the job in hand.

But it came back. It stayed with him through the long defense of Lon Chieng, like a poisonous root nurturing in the manure of violence and death that lay in his subconscious mind. Gradually, imperceptibly it blossomed into a plan; and still he was not fully aware of its presence.

Then one day, waiting for the chopper to take him in on "Fishhook," the ill-starred Cambodian adventure, he deliberately dragged it out of the recess of his brain and took a long, cold, hard look at it. And he knew it would work.

If he got back from this one, he told himself, he would do it.

From then on, it became an obsession with him. Every job he did, every trick he learned, every risk he took had a new meaning and purpose.

And now he was ready to pull it off. All he needed was one guy he could trust. And that guy was Jake Snyder.

The snow was coming down steadily by the time he finally pulled up outside the Village Inn. He got out of the car and stood for a few moments, like a man enjoying the exhilaration of a cold shower, letting the snowflakes spill over his tousled black hair, his shoulders, his beard, his outstretched hands. Sucking great gulps of the knife-edged air through his nostrils until they were numb with pain, he flushed out the last stink—and the last memory of the stink—of the sweat and the blood and the death of Vietnam.

It was a crisp, sunny morning. Silky walked across from the hotel to the gondola base, his skis and poles slung over his shoulder. There was something predatory about the way he moved, a swagger, a defiant swing of the shoulders, a warning to the world not to provoke him. He was a compact man of medium height, his black beard trimmed to a point, not bushy. His pale blue eyes were the eyes of a loner, sad eyes that had seen a lot of pain.

Two girls got in the cab with him, pretty young things. He sat opposite them, staring out of the window, not wanting to talk to them yet feeling an obligation. He sensed their scrutiny, innocent kittens sizing up a baleful dog.

"Been here long?" It was the best he could do.

They both answered at once, then giggled in embarrassment. "Only two days," the one in the yellow jacket finally answered for them. The other one in the pale blue outfit picked it up from there. "Lovely place, isn't it?"

"One of the best," he smiled. He felt better now. He had done his part, relieved the tension. The rest was up to them.

"Where are you going to ski?" the yellow one asked when they disembarked.

"I'm going up to the top," Silky said.

"Oh," she said with a hint of disappointment, "that's too advanced for us. Perhaps we'll see you around."

"Perhaps," Silky answered. "Have a good day."

He was halfway up the chair lift when he spotted Jake, a tiny figure coming straight down the fall line, spewing up little fountains of powder snow in his wake, as he bashed from mogul to mogul. There was an awesome grandeur to it, a lone man dancing on the scaly back of an angry mountain.

They had been close friends at school, he and Jake.

5

Jake's parents owned the best motel in Boise, Idaho, complete with dining room and lounge bar. As the only child of a relatively well-to-do family, Jake had an upbringing that was more worldly in environment, and more liberal in opportunity than Silky's. A ham radio enthusiast, he had his own transmitter at the age of thirteen. His own car, as soon as he was entitled to a licence, and plenty of money in his jeans qualified him as one of the most popular boys in the school.

He was a bright, imaginative student who made good grades with the minimum of effort. He was athletic without being tough, the kind of quarterback who "stayed in the pocket" and did not like to be trapped with the ball. A carefree perspective of life lent him a cheerful, fun-loving attitude and an easy charm. Jake had changed little since his school days. He had a round baby face with a soft, girlish complexion. He was clean-shaven by default, his vain attempt to grow a beard in the Navy having resulted in a dismal patchwork of soft down, making him look like a half-plucked chicken.

He had a long scar running horizontally from below the outside of his right eye to the edge of his nose. The tightened skin on this side of his face had the effect of lifting the corner of his mouth into a permanent roguish smile. Rather than marring his looks, at least as far as the girls were concerned, the blemish gave him a puckish appearance, of which he took full advantage by allowing the assumption that it was a war wound.

Actually, the scar was a souvenir of a crazy "chicken" driving contest during his last summer at school. Half the students had come out to watch as Jake and Shag Butler took their cars out to the Birdwell road for a head-on joust in the swirling dust.

Jake had won the first leg in a breeze when Shag chickened out a good fifty feet from the collision point. But you could tell from the way he glared at the jeering spectators, especially Betty Stacey, that Shag was set to come barrelling straight through next time and to hell with the consequences.

Jake had still given him a good run for his money. They weren't six feet apart when he'd swerved out, giving his brake a quick pump to help the slide. If Shag had just had the sense to shift a few inches—no more than a twitch—they would have cleared.

The impact had rolled Shag's old jalopy, busting both his legs. Jake had cracked his face on the steering wheel but he'd still managed to get his wheels under control. Betty Stacey had come running over to Jake and when she'd seen the blood and lacerated flesh she'd thrown up in the middle of the road.

Silky watched Jake flash by, out of shouting distance. Disembarking at the top, he decided to run part way down and wait to see whether Jake returned on the same chair.

Sure enough, he spotted him coming up. Waiting until he was abreast of him, he yelled out "Hey, sailor! How's your sea legs?"

Jake recognized him at once, even though it was nearly four years since they had last met.

"Jesus, Silky! You sonafabitch! Wait right there!"

Silky watched the small figure make a jump turn at the top, then come hurtling toward him, bumping and wiggling from mogul to mogul like a man with rubber legs. He pulled up with a flourish, squirting a plume of snow over Silky.

They slapped gloved hands. "Man, am I glad to see you." Jake laughed, frozen snow in his blond hair like a busted custard pie. "What the hell brought you here? You on leave or out?"

"I'm discharged."

"Man! When I heard you were in Special Forces, I wrote you off for dead. Jesus, what a fluke running into you!"

"It's no fluke. I've been looking for you."

"Really? Why?"

"Old time's sake. And other things."

"Great, man!" Jake's eyes twinkled with genuine pleasure. "Let's not stand here beating our gums. Let's ski. Then we'll talk."

With that, Jake shoved off, skating over the first bump for acceleration, full tilt down the slope. Reacting at once, Silky was off the mark in a split second, following close in his tracks. For almost three hours, they frisked in the snow, twisting, running, jumping, exuberant with high spirits, two magnificent exponents in unison.

7

They continued to the point of exhaustion, an unspoken challenge standing between them as to who would be first to call for a break. Finally Jake pointed down, running a headlong schuss, maybe seventy miles an hour, straight down Buddy's Run to the bottom. They braked together in a long slow roll, kicked off their skis, and headed into a saloon on Ski Times Square for a beer.

They had a lot to catch up on. Silky, as usual the quieter one, allowed Jake to rap on about his adventures in the Navy. It was typical of Jake that he only seemed to remember the funny parts.

Finally it was Silky's turn. He shrugged helplessly. "It was just a long load of shit." He did not have an amusing collection of anecdotes to match Jake's and he did not want to exaggerate the dangers and discomfort of his experiences.

"Come on, man. What was it *like?*"

"Like death rammed right up your nose." Silky bit the retort off with a grimace.

Jake looked at him in surprise, appraising him. "It sure toughened you."

"It did that," Silky concurred wryly.

Jake had noticed Silky's right forefinger, but had meant not to say anything. Not yet anyway. It was amputated above the first knuckle.

Silky spotted him glancing at it. "It could have been my prick," he said, wiggling the helpless little stump and they both burst into laughter.

The commotion brought the waitress back to their table. They ordered sandwiches and coffee. They wanted to do some more skiing in the afternoon, and neither of them believed in mixing his all-out approach to the sport with too much lunchtime beer. Their war reminiscences exhausted, their conversation drifted to matters of more immediate concern.

"Got any plans? A job or anything?" Jake asked.

"Hell no! Just skiing. At leats till the end of the season. After that I have some ideas. Nothing firm."

"You mean you're loose right now? Just ski-bumming?"

"That's right."

"Beautiful. That makes two of us. How are you fixed for bread?"

8

"No sweat."

Jake slapped his thigh, beaming with anticipation. "Oh, Silky baby, what a winter this is going to be! Are we going to have ourselves a good time!"

"What's new with you then? I heard your mother passed away. Your dad still running the old place?"

"Well, not quite. It's a long story."

Jake recounted the highlights with cynical humor. His mother had been the strong character in the family and it had been her brains, industry, and shrewdness that had made the motel a success. After his mother's death, his father had turned a good part of his energy toward drinking up the bar profits and feeling sorry for himself. Glad for a chance to escape his father's moroseness, Jake had joined the Navy as a radio technician, eventually being posted to an aircraft carrier in the Far East.

Within a year of Jake's overseas posting his father had married one of the bar waitresses, an event which Jake had accepted good-naturedly, remarking that it proved that there was a surprising load of spunk in the old man yet. However, the reserve was obviously limited, because he was buried five months later having, presumably, screwed himself to death; which, in Jake's opinion, was a hell of a nice way to go.

Returning home to find a new young stepmother, a little coarse but anxious to please him, he had taken it all in stride. He did not want to settle down to run the motel yet, anyway. His old man had left him a nice pile of cash, and he had the run of the place when he was there. The bar profits, in fact the whole business, had taken a turn for the better in the absence of his father, leaving him little cause for complaint. The order of things had changed, but, as he saw it, the new arrangement did nothing that called for any deviation from his merry approach to life. "So, when the first good snow report came in from Colorado, I packed my gear and two new pairs of skis in my step-ma's Pinto and took off for Steamboat Springs. I've been here about three weeks and was just beginning to get bored when you stepped back into my life."

Silky shook his head, laughing. "Well, that's you, Jake. Always landing on your feet." Jake had never really known what problems were. He either solved them without concern or brushed them aside. "Are we going to ski or shoot the shit?"

"Let's go."

Jake paid the bill, pinched the waitress's ass, and clomped over to the ski rack, boots still unbuckled. They found their equipment and moved into the line-up for the gondola.

As they waited to go inside the gondola base, they watched a couple of hang-gliders floating around above them, like multicolored bats. One of them swooped down low over them, yelling a greeting to Jake.

"Get your bird shit out of here!" Jake shouted back, with a laugh.

The gondola was not too crowded, since many people were still stretching out the lunch hour. They got a cab to themselves for the ten minute ride to the top.

"I'm going to try that hang-gliding act," Jake announced. "They say it's a fantastic trip."

"Not me," Silky stated firmly.

"Come on, man. It's the newest kick." Jake was surprised at Silky's negative stand.

"Listen, Jake," Silky was suddenly very serious, "I have been real busy, day and night, for more than two years, trying to stay alive. Believe me, it wasn't easy. The one thing in the world I wanted to live for was to ski again. Well, I made it. And there's no way I am going to risk my neck up there when I can stay down here and ski."

"Christ, man. It could be fun. They say it's a hell of a thrill."

"So is flying around in a chopper in a hail of ground fire. You go ahead. I don't need it."

"You've changed, man, you've changed."

"Yes, I have. I'm used to risking my life. But I don't do it for kicks anymore. From now on, I do it for money."

"What have you got in mind? Being a mercenary?"

"Not really. I'm tired of fighting other people's wars. If I do any more fighting, it's going to be in my *own* little war."

"What do you mean? Have you got something cooking, a plan or something?"

Silky took a long time to answer. They were getting near the top anyway. Not yet, he decided.

"Yeah. I plan to ski. I don't plan to fly."

Jake shrugged. "Well, who gives a shit? Now that you've shown up, the skiing has improved 100 percent anyway."

They stayed on the top, using the chair lifts and working on the steep stuff, White-Out, Shadows, and Twilight. Jake knew a lot of the crowd up there and was familiar with the terrain. It was the best afternoon of skiing that Silky could remember; ideal conditions, expert company, and a magnificent challenge. When they skidded out the last, wide sweep at the bottom, six of them together, he felt that great feeling of physical triumph, every fiber in his body spent.

They took aboard a couple of bourbons with beer chasers, just to ease their muscles—keyed all afternoon to split-second alertness—back to elbow-lifting speed. Then they checked Silky out of the Village Inn and moved his stuff into Jake's twin-bedded room at the Iron Horse.

After their exertions of the day, they wound the tempo right down, loafing in the bathtub, finishing Jake's bottle of bourbon, and dragging on some casual clothes.

They ate two huge steaks in the dining room, then walked over to the Yampa Station Pub to celebrate their reunion in earnest.

The pub was bursting at the seams with noisy, healthy, happy young people, most of whom seemed to know Jake. They spotted some of the guys with whom they had been skiing. One of them moved his girl over to his knee, making room for Jake, while Silky stood, watching his opportunity to grab a chair. Finally, he spotted a man getting up to go to the john and whisked his seat away, almost before he had taken his first step. He was only just in time to beat another man with the same idea.

There were a dozen of them in the group and they had a standing order with the waiter to keep three jugs of draft beer on the table at all times. The two hang-glider nuts were there and they started in on Jake, so Silky parked his chair at the other end with the skiers.

Silky just sat and savored the atmosphere. It was the

world he loved, peopled by the kind of crowd he enjoyed and admired. Christ, he was glad he had make it back!

By the time they left, Silky was so full of beer, it felt like his tonsils were awash. He and Jake rolled back to the Iron Horse, propping each other up, and fell into bed without bothering to get undressed.

Next morning they were awake around seven-thirty, little the worse for wear. It was surprising that their bladders, overextended with a gallon of beer apiece, allowed them to sleep that late.

Jake switched on the radio to the local station, thumping out a country and western program. He kept it low until the news came on, then turned up the volume to get the weather forecast.

They listened with desultory interest to news of an assassination of a minor Latin American general, a plane hijacking, and a bank robbery. The escalating Watergate scandal was the lead item.

"That's a dumb thing to do," Silky commented, "hijacking an airplane. If anyone calls their bluff, the hijackers are caught in their own trap. If they shoot the pilot, they go down with the plane."

"Well, it's not bad pay. What's the ransom demand? Three hundred grand? That's a lot of spending money."

"Yeah. If they ever get to spend it. But they have to find somewhere to land, where there aren't a million cops ready to pick them up or plug them as soon as they step off the plane. What's the use of all that cash if you're going to spend the rest of your life cutting sugarcane in Cuba?"

Jake did not respond. He was listening to the forecast: sunshine today, clouding over tonight, followed by six-to-eight inches of snow. That was the limit of his interest in world affairs.

Silky considered pressing his point home. He could have explained the advantages of his plan so easily. But the timing was not right yet. There was still a thin veneer of strangeness between them, born of four years spent growing up in different worlds. He had to wait until it wore away.

He flung off the bedclothes and opened the curtains,

letting the sun flood into the room. "Come on, you lazy bastard. I'm hungry."

They were in line when the gondola opened and so were most of the group from their table of the night before. In their state of health, a skin full of beer did not slow them down very much. All the same, they decided to cruise for a while on the easier terrain around High Noon, picking the chairs with the least lineup.

Steamboat Springs was a friendly place on a sunny morning. "Have a good day, now," said the cute girl who placed the chair under Silky's butt. And again, on the next chair, this time a big handsome man, "Have a good day, now." Steamboat was famous for the friendly ways of their handpicked staff, all neat but casual in their navy blue cowboy hats. It was said that more than a thousand young people applied for the fifty available jobs every year.

One of the joys of ski-bumming was making plans on the spur of the moment. Sitting on the chair lift, thinking about the snow forecast, Silky suddenly got the idea of Arapahoe Basin, the highest ski area in the United States. "Hey, if it snows tonight, the deep powder at Arapahoe will be out of this world tomorrow," he exclaimed to Jake.

"Fantastic idea. Let's go."

"After lunch, right? Before the snow starts, or we will never get through the pass."

"Right."

As soon as the lift lines began to crowd up, they grabbed a quick sandwich, checked out, packed the cars, and called ahead for a bed in the dormitory.

They took both cars as far as Keystone, parking Jake's Pinto in the parking lot there. They intended to pick it up on their way back, ski a day or two there, and then move on to Copper Mountain.

They drove over the Loveland Pass and arrived at Arapahoe Basin around five o'clock. A group of fellows were drinking in the dormitory, so Jake unloaded a case of beer and they joined the party.

Around seven, the whole gang went over to the cafeteria for a meal. Arapahoe Basin did not cater to the heavy-duty swingers and après-ski was not on the curriculum. They ate steak and french fries at a long tall

13

wooden table, swigged down big mugs of coffee, and told tales—mostly, of course, about skiing.

They were all in bed by ten. They were up early in the morning, no late risers. Everyone was there when the lift opened.

Plunging through deep powder up to their hips at thirteen thousand feet, gasping for breath in the thin air, they pushed themselves to the limit enjoying the dry taste of fear and the supreme satisfaction of winning against themselves.

Three of the crowd in the dormitory were pretty good freestylers, able to give Silky and Jake some good tips. After lunch, they built a jump lower down on the packed snow, and worked out on flips, forward and reverse, taking a few spills, fortunately more spectacular than serious.

They were dead beat when they got down at the end of the day.

Up early again next morning, they worked on their "wheelies," leaning back on the bumps, like contortionists, and bursting off the exploding snow in twisting midair turns.

By noon they had had enough of the celibate atmosphere of Arapahoe Basin. They packed the car and headed for the Ski Tip Ranch at Keystone. They talked of tail as they drove, like a couple of diabetics who had missed their insulin shots. "Nearly two weeks," said Jake in mock alarm, "it's enough to give a guy the bends."

Silky chuckled. They were relaxed now, completely in tune. It was time to get on with it.

"That gondola lift at Steamboat," he led in cautiously. "How many cars do you figure? Forty or fifty, something like that?"

Jake seemed taken aback by the sudden switch in the conversation. He considered for a moment. "Forty maybe. No more."

"That's a lot of people floating through the air together. What's your guess?"

"Hundred-and-fifty."

"Yeah about that. A hundred-and-fifty happy skiers . . . until it stops. I mean, if you stopped it, just like that" —he took his right hand off the steering wheel and

14

snapped his fingers for emphasis "—you would suddenly have a hundred-and-fifty helpless people."

"That doesn't happen very often. They take goddam good care that it doesn't. They nurse a baby like that pretty good."

Silky continued. "And if you left them up there for an hour or two, you would have a hundred-and-fifty very frightened people, don't you think?"

"Yes, but it wouldn't happen. They would rescue them with ladders from the grooming vehicles."

"But say we *made* it happen? What then?"

Jake frowned. "What the fuck are you driving at? What do you mean, we *made* it happen?"

"Like I said. We walk into the base. Press the emergency button and stop the whole goddam works. What then?"

"You're crazy! A bunch of guys will grab you and jump on your face. That's what. You will probably finish up in jail. What's the point?"

"A hijack," Silky said simply. "Nobody jumps on my face. Because I've got a submachine gun."

"What's the matter with you, Silky? Are you kidding or are you serious? Walking into the base with a sub-machine gun," he scoffed. "Christ, you would get lynched!"

"On the contrary," Silky continued very calmly, "anyone who touched me would get dead."

"But, Jesus, Silky, you can't just walk around a ski area with a submachine gun under your arm. It's incredible!"

"Exactly. It's the last thing anyone would expect. Everyone is concentrating on his own routine. No one is looking for any weapons. There is no security. I bet you could assemble a howitzer in the middle of Buddy's Run and tell them it was a new kind of snow-making machine. With a little bit of planning, I could bring a whole ski area to its knees in sixty seconds."

Jake stared at Silky. "You're nuts!"

"I'm serious." Silky stared straight ahead. He had expected an initial shock from Jake. After all, you could not expect to lay an idea like this on a man, however close a friend, and not create a certain amount of

15

surprise. "Now, shut up a minute and I'll lay it out for you."

"But for Christ's sake . . ."

"But nothing. Listen." Silky spoke very quietly, precisely. "You lay explosive around a few towers. That's easy; just dig it down under the snow. You set it to blow by radio, from inside the gondola base. You walk into the base a few minutes before closing. You wear ski masks. You press the emergency button, fire a few rounds into the wall and you take everyone in the base hostage. What's wrong with that?"

"What for? What's the point?"

"Ransom. That's the point. You've got one hundred and fifty people in the air. Just like the airplane hijacking, *except* that you are not up there with them. You are flying this show from down on the ground. You have maybe ten or twenty hostages in the base. Say between one hundred-and-fifty and two hundred people, absolutely at your mercy. What can the area do except pay your demands?"

Jake shook his head and laughed. "Jeeze . . . it's a hell of an idea . . . crazy, mind you . . . but smart. Probably a hundred flaws in it . . . but it's something to think about."

"Well, I'm going to do it, man. It's just a question of are you in or out."

They picked up Jake's car at Keystone and checked in at the Ski Tip Ranch.

They took a table in the corner of the bar, drinking bourbon and water. Jake shook his head again and again in disbelief. "You crazy bastard," he said at last, "you've got me thinking seriously about this thing. But we sure need a better reading on a lot of unanswered questions. For instance, how much ransom could we ask? And what is the maximum amount they could assemble in a hurry?"

Silky nodded. "Listen. I didn't ask you along just for the ride. There are two main parts to this caper. The physical operations; that's my department. And the planning, that's yours. You've always been the brains in our partnership."

They sat silently again for a few minutes. Silky didn't

16

have to push it anymore. Jake was slowly sucking himself in, without any help, fascinated by the logistical problems.

Jake swallowed his drink and leaned across the table. "Listen. One thing is certain. We don't pull this stunt this season. There's six months of detailed planning to get the thing into shape. Stuff to buy that cannot be traced, alibis to set up, training, rehearsals. Got to consider the weather, even the phase of the moon. I'll lay it all out for you, but let's agree on one thing for a start. The earliest we're going to do this is somewhere around Christmas, one year from now. O.K.?"

"Agreed," nodded Silky, noting with satisfaction that Jake had already graduated to using the word "we."

"Another thing. Where were you going to pull it?"

Silky knew more than to interrupt; he waited for Jake to continue.

"Now, how much you get depends on where you go. For instance, you hold up old Joe Jankowski at Arapahoe Basin and all you're going to get is the canteen receipts and what Joe's got in his pants' pocket. Maybe a hundred bucks. And I'm not looking at this for a hundred . . . or," he looked at Silky, "a hundred thousand." He paused. "A million, Silky, a million for each of us. And I know where."

Silky just smiled, taking a pull at his cheroot.

"Now we can't stand around all day waiting for them to get the money together. The more time you give them, the more chance they have to think. You know that, man, from your search-and-destroy missions in 'Nam. You have to be in and out before they recover from their surprise. Right?"

"Right." Silky was enjoying this.

"Two hours is the maximum for the whole caper, I reckon." He paused to let this sink in. "Now, where do you figure anyone could get two million dollars together in two hours?"

Silky had his own ideas, but he had not nailed them down. It had to be one of the big resorts, for sure. "Where?" he asked.

"Nevada, baby. Nevada. Lake Tahoe to be precise. They not only have banks, they also have all those lovely casinos. Oodles, but oodles of nice, pretty cash in

17

unmarked bills. Hell, there's probably half-a-million dollars just sitting there, on the green beize cloth, at any time, twenty-four hours a day."

Silky nodded approval. This was going just the way he had hoped. But there was no need to settle it all tonight. He wanted to steer Jake away from a flood of spontaneous ideas, give him time for more mature thought. He changed the subject. "Let's get back to more immediate problems. Like tail, for instance."

They didn't get lucky that night. It was not until they moved to Copper Mountain, three days later, that they struck oil. And then it was pay dirt, two ski bunnies with their own condominium apartment. They holed up with the girls until after New Year. It was a ball, a kind of embarkation leave before they went operational.

It was a glorious interlude. They were both in peak condition, skiing with a brash confidence, pushing each other faster and steeper, outwardly impervious to danger, but still relishing its constant piquancy.

Jake was in his element. The only flaw in his self-indulgent life had been the lack of a partner to share it with. Most of his Boise contemporaries seemed to have drifted off in search of careers or settled down into the petty, stereotyped roles of suburbanism.

Fun was synergetic. It had to be shared, recounted, relished, and chuckled over. Even skiing, that consummate sport, took on a new dimension when there was someone along to compete with, to admire, to dare and be dared.

Jake needed Silky more than Silky needed him and he realized it. Silky was a loner with a mission and, in the final analysis, Jake was just a role-player in that mission. It wasn't that Silky didn't value their friendship: it was just that Silky had a self-sufficiency which Jake lacked. He could take it or leave it.

It annoyed Jake sometimes to admit to himself that, but for the hijack project, this close comradeship would probably dissipate quickly. Why the hell couldn't they just dump the whole caper with its stupid risks and settle down to some good old-fashioned, aimless, unembroidered ski-bumming?

He put it to Silky one afternoon in the bar at Copper,

when their legs were stretched out and there was a bucket of beer between them. It had been a special day, sunshine and deep powder, and their mood was euphoric. "D'you ever consider the consequences if we get caught, Silky?" Jake asked. He kept his tone casual as if it was just a passing thought.

Silky eyed him carefully. He'd been prepared for this and he knew how to get to Jake. "Why? You want to chicken out?"

"Of course not," Jake bridled. "But, you know." He hesitated. "It's criminal what we're planning to do. I mean, breaking the law—that's something to think about. If we get caught, it's ten or fifteen years in jail. Ever think about that?"

"Not much," Silky replied evenly. He drew his legs up from the empty chair opposite him and straightened his back, looking down on Jake. "Listen," he said. "I think about getting caught, yes. I think and think and think about what the other guy is going to do to try and catch me. That's why I'm still alive. I'm fucking careful. But I don't think about the consequences of getting caught. I don't try to figure whether the fucking gooks are going to stick a poker up my ass, or squash my balls, or smash my skull. That's a contingent liability. I can't control that. All I can control is whether I get caught or not. And that's what I concentrate on."

Jake shrugged. He wanted to have it out, but no way was Silky going to assail his guts. He reached lazily for his beermug, consciously maintaining his pose of nonchalance. "Keep your shirt on, Silky." He smiled. "All I'm saying is that we've got it made right now. I mean, we've got the pad and the broads—the beer, the wheels, the cash, and the mountains. We've got our friendship. What else do we need? Why risk exchanging it for ten years in the cooler?"

Silky could have launched into a diatribe. He could have told Jake how he didn't really care to fritter his life away being a playboy. And how his old man didn't leave him a motel with a dame to look after it and a wad of cash to live on. But it wasn't Silky's motives that were in question.

Silky had played this kind of scene before. It was

19

always the brainy guys. They didn't lack courage but they had too much imagination—they brooded about insignificant details which sapped their resolve. He went for the jugular again, challenging Jake's spunk. "If you want to cop out, man, just say so. Nobody's twisting your arm."

"C'mon, Silky." Jake looked pained. "Don't give me that crap. You know I'm not yellow. All I'm doing is trying to put this whole thing in perspective."

Silky didn't persist. He finished his beer and stood up. "Let's get back to the condo," he said. "I'm hungry." He knew his man too well to waste time coaxing him. Jake would come round, but he had to do it in his own time. This caper called for volunteers, not conscripts.

Next day, Jake announced he was going hang-gliding. It was his way of getting one up on Silky—settling just which of the two of them was chicken. He was full of it after his first solo flight—the soft silence as he soared on his blue and gold wings, the sense of power, the loneliness, the challenge to mind and muscle, the exquisite blend of hazard and beauty. The girls listened to him in awe, while Silky reacted with smug satisfaction. He could read Jake's message better than Jake could. No way Jake was going to bale out of the hijack caper. It was a hell of a motive for a guy embarking on a life of crime, but, as Silky had known all along, there wasn't anything that Jake wouldn't do to avoid the imputation of cowardice.

Silky was in high spirits now that the job was a go. He was not the kind of person to be comfortable living with unresolved intentions. The promise of action, the threat of danger, the isolation of secrecy, the challenge of confrontation, these were the heady things on which he thrived.

Three years in Special Forces in Vietnam had developed in Silky an acute sense of self-preservation. At the slightest provocation he was ready to strike. But he took care never to provoke.

There was a new swagger to him now, an imperceptible sense of physical superiority and defiance. His body was trained to kill and he sat serenely inside it, like a man in a fort, secure in the knowledge of his superior firepower.

20

Best of all, he was running the show, not some fat-ass general in Seoul.

They had agreed to move over to Squaw Valley soon and reconnoiter Lake Tahoe from there. Silky knew that Jake was waiting for him to give the word, and he held back purposely, enjoying the tension of anticipation.

Then, abruptly, Silky announced at breakfast that they were pulling out. It was kind of a test of discipline. Jake got a charge out of it, watching Silky taking command, but the girls were hopping mad, then utterly dejected. They argued and they pleaded, but once Silky had given the orders, there was no going back.

Driving to Squaw, they reviewed the overall plan and catalogued the jobs to be done on this first assignment. The main thing, of course, was to select the target. They had laid out a number of criteria for this.

Silky wanted a gondola lift. A chair lift was too exposed; they didn't want their hostages freezing to death. It would put unnecessary blood on their hands and act counter to their objective, which was to ransom as many live people as possible. A tramway was equally unsuitable, too concentrated. If someone figured a method of escape—a rope ladder or something—then the whole contingent would get out. A gondola was ideal, forty or fifty separate groups spread out from the top of the mountain to the bottom.

Getaway was critical. Distance from the gondola base to a road where the vehicle would be parked. Turnoffs, crossroads, alternative escape routes. Vulnerability of the base to police snipers. Everything had to be checked and weighed.

Another subject for extended discussion was the possibility of accomplices. Both were against it in principle. They considered various candidates, but it always came back to the same conclusion; the more people in the party, the greater the risk. Yet doing it by themselves meant that one had to carry the holdup alone, while the other drove the getaway car.

"Let it ride," Silky concluded. There was too much at stake to start mustering new recruits out of thin air. "We'll get back to it when we're closer to going operational. Right now, let's stick to picking the target."

21

CHAPTER TWO

SILKY was beginning to tire of Jake's mulish obstinacy. So far, they had checked out three of Tahoe's ski areas and Jake had found fault with all of them. He began to suspect that maybe Jake was getting cold feet again.

Accustomed to being directed to a target because of its strategic importance, not its vulnerability, Silky found Jake's attitude ridiculously uncompromising. "Jesus Christ, man, you can't expect them to build to our specifications."

"No," Jake answered stubbornly, "but there's no point in taking stupid risks."

They pulled into the parking lot at Mount Casino. It was already crowded, but Silky found a space at the far end, opposite the gondola base.

They both spotted it at the same time. An exit, presumably a service door, in the middle of the gondola base, opening directly onto the parking area. The distance between the door and the nearest parked car was not thirty feet.

"Perfect." Silky's eyes lit up. "This is it."

"Not bad," Jake replied cautiously. "Let's go take a look around."

Leaving their skis in the rooftop ski rack, they strolled over to inspect the base more closely. Jake took half-a-dozen photographs of it from various angles.

Satisfied for the moment, they doubled back across

the parking lot and entered the ski lodge through the main entrance.

They checked the layout of the building carefully. There was a basement area containing the ski shop and locker rooms and an upper floor of executive offices; practically the whole of the main floor, other than lobby and ticket office, was occupied by a huge cafeteria, leading off to a bar at the far end. The entire front of the vast restaurant was glass from floor to ceiling, offering a magnificent view of the mountain.

They picked up a trail map from the desk, grabbed some coffee and sat in the sun on the big deck outside the cafeteria. From there, they had a good view of the skiers coming down Thunderbolt, the main lower trail. Two chair lifts, one just beside the lodge and one farther over toward the hotel, were winding their human cargo up to the mid-stations. Over to their right, the bright red gondola cars were gliding serenely up and out of sight to the 9,000-foot level, glinting now and then in the sparkling sunshine.

Jake took some more shots of the gondola base, using his telescopic lens. He was gratified to note that there were no ground-level windows, only the one solid door through which the flow of skiers was moving. Checking along the roof line of the lodge, he could see no line of sight for a sniper to pick off a man who might be standing at floor level in the base. So far, so good.

Silky drank his coffee in silence, watching Jake. He hadn't said anything negative yet, which was a welcome change. "It's promising," was the most that Jake finally conceded.

Silky heaved a sigh of resignation. "For fuck's sake, what more do we need? The place is a pushover."

"Maybe," Jake replied levelly. "Let's go and check."

They went back to collect their skis and rode the gondola lift a couple of times, making a preliminary inspection. If things checked out, they would make a more detailed survey later.

The loading routine was standard. Skiers entered the base through the side door and filed into four roped-off aisles. Silky noted the location of the emergency cutoff switch, easily accessible from the outside aisle. There were two men loading the passengers.

Jake stepped out of the line and moved to the service door, trying the handle.

"Hey, man!" One of the attendants yelled at him. "What are you doing?"

"I want to get my camera from the car," Jake replied coolly.

"Not through there, you don't. You'll have to go right around."

"Forget it," Jake retorted. "If you can't use it, what's the goddam door there for in the first place?"

"Emergency. In case there's an accident. The rest of the time it's locked."

Giving the man a pleasant smile, Jake returned to his place in the lineup.

After lunch they skied all over the base area, taking time out from serious reconnaissance to enjoy themselves. Jake posed Silky for a series of photographs in front of each of the gondola towers, making sure to include the big white numbers conveniently painted on each one.

Their last stop was at the base garage to look at the grooming fleet, eight big soft-tracked vehicles, neatly parked in a semicircle for their viewing.

The weather had changed capriciously during the afternoon. By the time the survey was completed, it was snowing steadily, with a sharp accompanying wind. They were glad to retreat to the cozy, convivial atmosphere of the bar.

"Well what's the verdict?" Silky asked, blowing on his hands. Christ, if Jake didn't buy this place, then he would pull the job alone. He had a gnawing suspicion that he had miscalculated Jake's guts after all.

"The best we've seen," Jake conceded. "If nothing else tops it, it will do."

Silky was sarcastic. "You mean you are on? You're actually ready to pull the job here? Well, thank Christ for that!"

"That's not what I said," replied Jake evenly. "I said it's O.K., if nothing better shows up."

"Oh, bullshit," Silky said firmly. "This is it. And that's final. Christ, it has everything, even its own casino. This is the target." He banged his fist on the table. "Look, man, you're either in or out. Make up your fucking mind."

Jake gazed at Silky thoughtfully for a long moment, then gradually his features relaxed into the old roguish smile. "O.K., this is the target, then."

Silky could hardly believe it. They were through with procrastination at last. He stuck out his hand and Jake took it. "Done," he said emphatically. "This calls for a drink."

The tension that had built up between them over the past week evaporated. In a way it had been a test of their partnership, a weighing of their conflicting personalities. Their respect for each other had hardened.

It was snowing heavily as they drove back to Squaw Valley. The radio forecast an overnight accumulation of more than twenty inches.

Both in better humor now, they resumed discussion of the getaway, the only point left undecided between them. Silky felt that if they took half-a-dozen hostages with them in a van, they could keep the police at bay. They would park another car somewhere on the outskirts of town and switch to it, probably keeping two of the hostages until they were clear away. Maybe they would even double back around the lake on cross-country skis. Jake dismissed these plans as too risky, but was unable to come up with a better alternative. The more he thought about it, the more he inclined to the view that they would need at least one more accomplice.

Silky still would not hear of adding to the team. "It isn't worth it," he argued. "You add one more guy to screw things up and possibly get himself caught. You have to split up the proceeds three ways. And all you save is maybe sixty seconds."

"Those sixty seconds could make or break the whole caper." Jake was adamant. "I don't like it the way it is."

"My God, you are a negative bastard, Jake. All you do is criticize. Why don't you come up with something better, then?"

"I will," Jake assured him for the tenth time. "Just give me time to think."

Silky sighed. Well, at least they had settled the target. And he had to admit that Jake's obstinacy had paid off in the final selection. There was no question that Mount Casino was far more suitable than any of the other areas that they had inspected. Let Jake think, then.

They arrived back at Squaw in good spirits. Now that they had a target, the whole operation had taken on a new perspective. But there was still one subject which Silky wanted to bring out in the open before he could feel that the job had moved from fantasy to stark reality. He gave Jake a couple of hours to relax over steak and beer, then hit him with it cold turkey. "We need to discuss killing," he said flatly.

"Killing?" Jake almost choked on his beer in astonishment. "What do you mean?"

"I mean this." Silky laid it out without any frills. "Our whole bargaining position is based on our threat to the lives of our hostages—in the base and on the gondola. Right?"

"Yeah," Jake said, listening carefully. They were talking about murder.

"Whether we get paid or caught depends on whether the other side believes our threat."

"That's right," Jake agreed.

"Well, I don't think that they will."

"You don't?" Jake was taken aback. "Why not? How can they afford not to?"

Silky spelled it out carefully, taking pains to emphasize every word. "I'm not saying they won't give it a lot of serious consideration. They aren't going to do anything rash like charging in like the fucking cavalry with guns blazing. But deep down inside," he paused to let it sink in, "they aren't going to believe us."

"Why not?" Jake was mystified.

"Because they know as well as we do that no one really wants to kill anyone in cold blood. Other than a sadist or a maniac."

Jake took a long pull at his beer, waiting for Silky to continue.

"Their tactic," Silky went on, "will be to play for time. They will go on feeding us excuses for not killing our victims, until they figure it's safe to call our bluff."

Jake had to agree. There were plenty of case histories to support Silky's contention that few kidnappers ever carried out their threats unless they were desperate. "So?" he said guardedly. "What are you getting at?"

"Just this." Silky looked him hard in the eye. "Are *we* bluffing or are we serious? What do you say?"

26

Jake ducked the direct question. "You're talking about killing innocent people. That's not so easy."

"Innocence and guilt have nothing to do with it," Silky retorted icily. "They are either in the strike zone or not, regardless of how they got there. We're not going out on a bird shoot."

"I guess you're right," Jake said reluctantly. "Go ahead and spell it out."

"O.K.," Silky said grimly. "This is the way I see it coming down. First, we set things up at the start so that the other side has no way to communicate with us. We'll send all our instructions out by tape. That way, they don't have any opportunity to try to wear us down."

"That's good," said Jake. "I like it."

"Second," he drew this out real slow so that Jake got every word, "we are both committed to kill as and when necessary to meet our objective." He paused looking for Jake's reaction. "Third, I'm in command. I give the kill orders. And they get carried out without question." Their eyes met again. "Unless you buy that," Silky continued, "this caper is not going to come off."

Jake felt himself being backed into a corner. He counterpunched, trying to sound flip. "You sound like you enjoy killing."

Silky grabbed Jake's collar across the table, knocking his beer into his lap. "Don't you ever say that," he snarled. "Don't even think it again. This isn't a fucking party. It's a kill-or-get-killed operation, you stupid bastard!"

"For Christ's sake, man!" Jake drew back, trying to shake Silky's grip. People were staring at them.

"If you haven't got the guts to kill without compunction," Silky hissed, "then you're a dead man before you start. I'm talking from experience."

"Jesus, Silky," Jake grumbled. "Let go of me, will you? Why're you so goddam touchy all of a sudden?"

"Because I don't need a dead man for a partner. That's why." Silky relaxed his grip on Jake's ski jacket. "Don't you question my motives, man. Consider your own."

The waiter came over to wipe up the mess. Jake borrowed a cloth to mop his pants and ordered a couple more beers.

It was not the first time that Silky had had to explain the facts of death to a raw recruit. They usually took a bit of time to get straightened out. "It's all or nothing, Jake. Otherwise you're going to get us both killed. Take it or leave it."

"O.K.," Jake answered with a shrug. "I guess you're right."

"That's not good enough," Silky pressed his point home. "No guessing. Either you are committed or you aren't."

Jake grimaced in resignation. "Alright. I'm committed. Now let's drop it. It may never happen."

"It will, man." Silky would not accept any concessions. "Wait and see."

Nick Diamado accompanied the five men to the main entrance to the Mount Casino Hotel and watched them embark in the big black Cadillac. He was a dark, stocky young man, handsome in a swarthy way, immaculately dressed in a pale gray suit.

Sol Leopold, the family's chief accountant, shook Nick's hand perfunctorily and stepped in, stretching himself out on the rear seat behind the tinted, bullet-proof glass. One of his assistants flipped up the jump seats and the other young man followed him in, both sitting awkwardly in front of Sol, facing ahead. The burly chauffeur slammed the door and took his place at the wheel beside the sallow bodyguard. The car roared off with a squeal of tires.

Nick was glad to see them go. They came every month to check the books, both sets. Sol's main job was to pick up all the money that had been skimmed off the top of the business. He had established standard accounting procedures for each of the profit centers—the hotel, the ski area, and the casino—designed to generate a supply of cash which was never disclosed in the official balance sheet. Despite the fat bundles of bills which Nick dutifully handed over from the wall safe in his office, Sol was never satisfied with his contributions.

He always had to go through all the records himself, invariably uncovering a few more dollars here and there. Not only that, the more he taught Nick the tricks of fraudulent accounting, the more openly he displayed his suspicion that Nick was probably dipping into the till himself

Nick was expected to dance attendance on Sol for the entire five days of the audit. Salvatore Diamado, Nick's father, insisted on it. Sol was to be shown the proper respect.

Respect. It was Salvatore's version of noblesse oblige. According to an unwritten protocol, each level of the Mafia commanded its due proportion. Sol's quota was high, because he was the personal representative of Nick's father.

Respect. Fear, really. Just as there was in the Nazi hierarchy, so here was there fear of another man's power to kill.

Nick found it all rather melodramatic and tasteless. As the youngest of Salvatore's three sons, he had very little to do with the seamy side of the family business. It had been Salvatore's decision, his acknowledgment of changing times, that Nick should go to college and work at a legitimate trade.

Nick often wondered what would have happened had Salvatore elected to move him into the drug or the prostitution operations. Respect again—respect for his father would have demanded that he do as he was bid.

Nick despised the whole Mafia scenario with its phony code of ethics, its silk-suited muscle, its self-importance, its obsession with intrigue, its stupid reverence of a spaghetti culture.

Two birthrights, however, he accepted without complaint, money and power. He felt that he could have acquired both on his own merits, but was not sorry that he was not forced to waste half his life putting this to the test. The important thing was to put these assets to good use, to acquire elegant tastes, and to run a business efficiently.

Nick had managed the gambling operation at Mount Casino since he was twenty-four; and he ran a tight outfit. Mount Casino, true to its name, was the only ski area in Lake Tahoe with its own casino. It had been built by Salvatore seven years before and was one of the most ambitious ski complexes in North America.

Needless to say, Salvatore Diamado did not appear as the registered owner. The deeds showed the three major shareholders as Paul Ruben, Dominick Abel, and Alfredo Costa. The first two were Los Angeles lawyers, holding 75 percent of the equity; they were Salvatore's front. Alfredo Costa, on the other hand, owned 10 percent in his own right. Alfredo had acquired his shares in a complicated deal in which the Diamado family had taken over his successful chain of pizza restaurants. Alfredo's business, built up from thirty years of hard work, was entirely legitimate—which was what made it attractive to Salvatore when it became family policy to dilute the criminal side of their holdings.

Alfredo Costa, and even more so his wife Pat, had developed an insatiable appetite for skiing over the years, so that he had been only too delighted to accept Diamado's offer to sell out his business in exchange for the presidency of and a minor ownership position in the new resort project. Of course there were a few special conditions about the accounting procedures, but these were discreetly handled by Sol Leopold; all Alfredo was asked to do was to turn a blind eye and keep his mouth shut.

A six-hundred-bed hotel was the heart of the Mount Casino complex. The entire first floor, except for a small lobby, was occupied by a vast casino with bars, discotheques and intimate dining rooms along both sides of the gambling area.

Attached to the hotel was the sports arena, boasting six indoor and eight clay tennis courts, with adjacent indoor and outdoor swimming pools.

The ski area offered thirty-one separate trails, accessible by ten double chair lifts and one gondola lift equipped with four-passenger cars.

Mount Casino could rival the biggest and best resort areas in the world.

Nick turned back into the casino and walked the center aisle. He enjoyed the nervous glances of the croupiers, the extra concentration that they affected, the tentative smiles of the blackjack dealers, the watchful eyes of the security men, the accentuated bustle of the cocktail waitresses. *Respect*. There was more of Salvatore in him than he realized.

He climbed the few steps up to his private office—set cantilevered over the gambling area—and closed the door behind him, shutting out the cacophony of thumping fruit machines, ringing bells, and cascading silver. Switching on his tape deck, he stood at the huge one-way mirror watching the action below. Business was good for this time of the afternoon. He knew the profit capacity of the room so intimately that he could estimate at a glance the turnover at any moment of the day.

He walked over to his desk and riffled through the in-basket; there was nothing that could not wait till tomorrow.

He looked at his watch, knowing damn well that it was about four-thirty.

Rena. She would probably stop at the Whi-ski bar with some of the other ski pros before she went home. The ski-tows were just closing now. His subconscious mind had planned this rendezvous all afternoon. Acting like a man who was making a spur-of-the-moment decision, he left the casino and walked briskly over to the ski area base lodge. The snow had picked up a lot in the past half hour. He turned up his collar and wished that he had worn overshoes.

He did not see her at first. The instructors were sitting at their usual table, maybe a dozen of them, but Rena was not there. He hesitated. If he joined the party and she did not show up, he would be stuck for an unnecessary round of drinks and a wasted half-hour. On the other hand, if he were already sitting there with the rest of the crowd when she appeared, then the encounter would seem more accidental.

His decision was made for him. Pat Costa caught his eye and waved him into an empty chair at her side. He had no call to rebuff the president's wife.

The rest of them were running a tab and he ordered a Scotch and soda. He knew them all well because he skied with them much of the time, when they were not giving lessons. He liked to run with the pros just to prove that he was at least as good as they were. He could beat most of them in a slalom race.

Pepi Mueller, the ski school director, was sitting on Pat Costa's left, exuding lazy charm. He did not talk much, just lounged back looking like the beautiful, blond Austrian he was, watching Pat with his cynical blue eyes. Pat was always two-timing Alfredo but Nick had not realized that Pepi was her latest target. If she had been Nick's, he

31

would have given her a good slapping, but Alfredo always appeared determined to remain oblivious of his wife's affairs.

"Hi, Nick. Got rid of the Gestapo?" It was Jim O'Malley, the mountain manager.

Nick looked through him. Christ knew why Alfredo put up with the insolent sonofabitch. His goddam Irish-American sense of humor was going to get him a couple of broken legs one of these days.

They were all in stitches. Nick heard Rena's laugh a half-tone above the others. Before he recovered himself, Jim had offered her his chair and pulled one up beside her.

"Hullo, Rena," Nick said. "How was the skiing?"

"Fine," she answered.

He wanted her to say more. Her voice, with its soft German accent, went right to his balls.

"Did you have a class?"

"No. I was skiing with Jim. Pat and Pepi were with us too."

The sound was delicious, but the message deflated him.

"It was lovely," she added. "You should have been with us, Nick."

"I wish I had been." He brightened up. "How about tomorrow?" Tonight was what he really wanted, but he was not going to risk being turned down in front of this crowd.

"Sure, Nick," she smiled with those funny, widely spaced teeth that he thought made her look impish.

Nick fiddled nervously with the frame of his spectacles. They were prescription, but he did not like to admit it. He always wore dark glasses—owned sixteen different pairs—and liked to pretend that they were an affectation, not a necessity.

"After lunch tomorrow then." He felt better, and perplexed at the same time. Why did this girl, blonde hair pinned in careless wisps, move him so strangely? Women to Nick were like good clothes. He could afford them and he acquired the best he could get. But they were accoutrements, casual possessions, never to be taken too seriously.

She was talking to Jim now. There was something private and intimate about their informal friendliness. Nick's right hand reached instinctively to squeeze the frame of

32

his glasses. He felt a surge of unreasoning anger, though he would never have admitted that it was jealousy.

"Doing anything tonight, Rena?" he blurted out, breaking his earlier resolution. Everyone seemed to be hanging on the answer.

"Yes," she said.

He smiled, feeling all eyes on him, making his smile say that he couldn't care less. He wanted to leave now. It would only take one quick phone call to get Gloria up to his room. But he owed it to himself, his image, to stick around, to underline that he was there to drink with the crowd, the people with whom he liked to ski, not just because of her.

Then, abruptly, she got up. "See you tomorrow," she said to everyone, not just to him.

Jim stood up with her. Nick scowled. I have to talk to Alfredo about this bastard, he thought.

"Bye for now, love," Jim said—so goddam nonchalantly, as if it didn't matter a damn to him if she left or stayed.

Nick decided to escape quickly. Maybe he could catch her on the way out. "Back to work," he murmured apologetically as he moved off.

She was nowhere to be seen. He considered waiting outside the ladies' room in the hope of intercepting her.

To hell with it. After five days with Sol Leopold he needed to get laid. Better call Gloria and leave the serious courting till tomorrow.

Jim stayed for one more drink, then excused himself. He did not want the bother of eating in the hotel and the lodge cafeteria closed an hour after the lifts. "It looks like it's going to be a long night," he said. "They are forecasting a twelve-inch storm. I'm going to starve if I don't get to the cafeteria before they close."

Barely making the deadline, he was forced to do some serious coaxing to get a big rare steak out of the cook. The place was nearly empty and she had already turned off her grill. "If only I was the marrying kind," he grinned, blue eyes twinkling with gratitude.

At thirty-three Jim O'Malley was a handsome, curly-haired fellow, his soft-spoken voice and gentle manners belying his six-foot-four frame.

During the winter season, the weather dictated much of Jim's life. When and where he slept and ate, the length of his working hours, his health, his humor, all were subject to the whims of the weather. He was like a farmer running a huge ranch, but his crop was snow. When the snow came, he had to harvest it, and when the wind or the rain or the sun or the frost came, he had to defend his domain against their depredations.

He never yielded to the weather. He respected it, but he fought it every inch of the way. He did not attack the weather impulsively, fists flailing in Irish temper. It took patience, experience, cunning, and ingenuity to beat the elements.

The backbone of Jim's defense system was his "Strategy Bank." Mavis Owen, Jim's secretary, was in charge of the records section, a meticulous computerized register of daily weather conditions for past years. Mavis was a slender, serious girl, with a halo of short brown hair, who peered intently through oversized spectacles.

Based on Mavis's data, the IBM system 33 computed the predictable effects of almost any combination of weather characteristics for each run on the mountain. Every trail had a different reaction to varying conditions, depending on the direction it faced, its steepness, its width, and the degree of protection provided by the surrounding trees.

Using these calculations, he had documented the preferred grooming strategy for every individual run on the mountain for almost any potential weather scenario.

Jim's army was highly mechanized: bulldozers for cleaning the parking lot, grooming vehicles for cosmetic work on the runs and lift lines, cannons for avalanche control. Since lack of snow was rarely a problem, he had not, so far, been able to justify the need for snow-making equipment, although, as a perfectionist, he would have liked to have this added dimension of flexibility.

Mechanization, of course, brought its own problems. Training and keeping drivers, for instance; a machine was only as good as the man who handled it and maintained it. Good drivers, who cared about their vehicles, were hard to come by and even harder to retain. The work was demanding and dangerous, the conditions lonely, noisy, and cold, and the working hours irregular and long, often all night. The ski areas abounded with

34

jockeys, happy-go-lucky ski-bums who would do anything for free tow tickets and a few dollars. But Jim would rather leave his fleet in the garage than turn it over to a bunch of irresponsible kids. It was too easy to wreck a machine, by taking unnecessary chances, by overworking it.

Mechanics were another headache. A vehicle broken down could "cost" a hundred skiers. Skiers were fickle, especially the intermediates; they were generally afraid of moguls and unable to handle deep powder. If the runs were not groomed to their taste, they would not come back.

Despite these problems, Jim had a pretty good crew, because he worked at it. His key lieutenant was Greg Fraser, the operations manager, responsible for all the vehicles and lifts. Greg was experienced, reliable, and thorough. He never took short cuts, believed in the importance of preventive maintenance. As a plodder and a pessimist, he offered good balance to Jim's more creative, optimistic approach to problems.

Then there was Hans in the garage, a dedicated craftsman with the disciplined mind of an ex-Luftwaffe sergeant-mechanic. He loved his vehicles, nursed them, and talked to them as if they were petulant children.

Having finished his steak, Jim climbed the stairs to his office and switched on the radio for the latest weather forecast. He would not leave the lodge until the storm was over.

He looked forward to the ensuing battle with the elements. A man with a balanced philosophy, he took his job at Mount Casino extremely seriously because he loved it; the rest of his life he took supremely casually, because he loved it too.

At twenty-four Charlie Potts was the number one driver of the Mount Casino grooming fleet. A lanky, loose-limbed farm boy from Montana, he had an abiding love for anything mechanical. His boyhood ambition had been to serve as a tank commander in the swaggering Afrika Corps; despite the traitorous implications of such an aspiration, he felt a secret compatability with their cold-blooded arrogance. Anyway, the Tiger tanks were the best machines.

The defeat of the Nazis having snuffed out his dreams, he contented himself with a black leather swastika-stencilled jacket and squat German helmet, which he wore when rampaging around the countryside on his motorcycle.

His recklessness suited Charlie to his job. He had a good feel for a grooming vehicle and enjoyed the inherent element of danger. Like a good racing driver, he knew the limits of his machine, had confidence in his own reflexes, and enjoyed putting both to the ultimate test.

As top driver, Charlie had the responsibility to groom the steepest slopes and he had the pick of the fleet to do it. The vehicle mix consisted of four Thiokol Packmasters, three Sprytes and a brand-new Bombadier-Skidozer. Charlie laid claim to the big yellow Bombadier—more because of the challenge of subduing its capricious temperament than because of the extra comfort of its roomy cab.

It was normal for the drivers to work all night, in two shifts, seven days a week. The snowstorm meant the cancellation of the first shift; the second shift got a bonus rest period, sleeping in the employee lounge until the visibility improved.

It was just after three o'clock in the morning when Charlie led the fleet in Indian file up to the top of the mountain.

Following a council of war between Jim O'Malley and Charlie, it had been decided to furrow the most exposed slopes. This meant compressing the snow with a heavy roller, leaving a ridge between each run. This maneuver left a good portion of the precious snow in the vertical rows of shallow windbreaks, thus preserving it on the slopes and preventing the swirling powder from dissipating in the adjacent woods.

But it meant double the work. Once the wind died down, they would have to go over the same ground again to flatten the furrows before the skiers arrived.

Charlie was on his fourth pass, going downhill, when he felt the vehicle hit a patch of ice. Before he could do a thing, he was hurtling down the mountain gathering speed to maybe fifty miles an hour. Slide!

The snow was so soft on top that the tracks had sunk

through to bare ice on the steep pitch. He had no traction, the heavy machine was charging headlong down the mountain, out of control. He pushed the steering levers forward so they would not create any braking action and, holding his breath, put his foot hard down on the accelerator. Coolly he let the machine have its head until he reached the short stretch of flatter ground between him and the woods which bounded the trail. His only hope was that, as the level terrain slowed his velocity, the churning tracks would catch up with themselves and regain control.

If he was ever going to recover traction, it had better be now. He eased back gingerly on the steering levers, afraid of locking his tracks and rolling the vehicle over.

He decelerated slightly, pulling gently back on the levers as he did so. He felt the vehicle shudder and bump, but it began to slow down. He had it under control now. He took his foot off the accelerator and pulled himself gradually across the fall line of the hill.

With one hand he pulled a cigarette from his pocket, flicked his throwaway lighter, and took a deep drag. Then he laughed. He knew he had ridden it out beautifully, and he realized that, in a way, he had enjoyed it. He'd have made a hell of a tank commander. He knew it.

For a while, Rena did not think she was going to make it to work. She had parked the sporty Mercedes at the bottom of the Ferguson's long driveway to give herself a good chance of getting away. She did not want to wait for the snowplow to show up. He could be hours late after a big snowstorm like this.

Despite her precautions she still had to go back to the garage for a shovel and broom to dig the few feet to the highway and sweep off the two foot cocoon of snow.

Well, she was no stranger to winter driving. She had been born in Lenzerheide, a Swiss ski resort, not one of the fashionable spots frequented by the tourist crowd, but the more exclusive because of its largely local clientele.

Her present hosts in Lake Tahoe, the Fergusons, had always enjoyed exploring off the beaten track. They had first stayed at the hotel, which Rena's father owned, eight years ago and the two families had been firm friends ever since.

Rena had taught skiing at Lenzerheide until her mother died. After that, she spread her wings a bit and did consecutive seasons at Klosters and Saint Moritz.

It was at Saint Moritz that she had met Pierre Dalmain, the French playboy racing driver. Completely swept off her feet, she had married him at twenty-one and plunged eagerly into the whirlwind round of parties and races that made up the hectic Grand Prix circuit.

Pierre's fiery death at Nuburgring in the eighth month of their marriage had left her prostrate. All her youth and enthusiasm for life died with him. Bitter and reclusive, she had returned to Lenzerheide to help her father, the only person whom she would allow to share her grief.

Now at twenty-seven, she was alone again. Her father had died the previous summer, and her brother Kurt, who had trained for ten years in the Hilton chain, had resigned his job to take over the family hotel. Kurt's Belgian wife made it clear from the outset that she would be his only assistant and that Rena's involvement in the management was no longer welcome. Feeling like excess baggage, Rena had seized in desperation on a long-standing invitation from the Fergusons and invested part of her small inheritance in this extended vacation.

As luck would have it, the Fergusons were very close friends of the Costas. Nellie Ferguson, anxious to restore Rena to the mainstream of life, had hit upon a scheme to surround her with people of her own age and interests: an invitation from Alfredo Costa to join the ski school at Mount Casino.

Despite the fact that she found it painful, Rena had been too polite to refuse. There was only a month's skiing left in the season, so she went along.

Still somewhat detached and aloof, she unconsciously thrived on Nellie's prescription, so much so in fact that she realized that she had become attached to the place, gladly accepting an offer from Pepi to return on permanent staff the following season.

Too exhausted from her digging to climb back up to the garage, she stood the broom and shovel in the snow where they could be seen from the living-room windows of the house. She started the car and, smoking a cigarette, waited a few minutes for the heater to melt the crust of ice from the windshield.

Patiently creeping a few feet forward, a few feet back, she finally reached the plowed highway and headed for Mount Casino. She was half-an-hour late.

Alfredo Costa, a sleek, well-preserved man in his late fifties, was never in his office later than eight o'clock in the morning. Today was no exception, other than that he had walked through the parking lot first to inspect the snow crew's work. They always missed the important little things, like entrances to doorways.

Of course, he never had a shoveling problem himself to threaten his punctuality. The Costas lived in a house set in its own grounds beside the hotel and their driveway was cleaned by the hotel plow at six o'clock every morning.

At nine o'clock sharp he took his position at the picture window of his office. As usual, he adjusted his watch to the morning radio time signal.

From his vantage point he could see both chair lifts and the gondola. He nodded in silent approval. They were all in operation. He had to admit it; he could not remember the last occasion on which they had started up late. At least he had taught them that much.

Then he scowled. There was only a handful of passengers on the Number One chair lift and he could see empty snow-covered chairs running up the mountain. The operators were supposed to sweep every chair clean on the first run through, before anyone was allowed to board.

Simmering, he turned on his heel and marched on an impulse down to the basement level. As he had suspected, the ski shop was still closed. He had caught her before. The damned woman who ran the shop as a concession never seemed to be able to cope with a snowstorm. A divorcée who lived alone, she did not have a man to shovel her driveway. A lame excuse. A woman who aspired to run a business should have enough intelligence to arrange to get to work on time.

Returning to his office, he dialed Jim O'Malley on the intercom. Mavis answered the second ring.

"Mr. O'Malley, please." His Italian inflection lent an icy tone to his voice.

"He just went home, Mr. Costa," Mavis said. "He was up all night."

39

"Then get through to him and tell him to phone me back," he said peremptorily.

He banged the phone back on its cradle. Jim O'Malley was a damned good man. But good men only stayed that way if you kept needling them, pushing them to excel. He had probably had five or six hours' sleep anyway, catnapping in his office. He should not have left his post without attending to the important minor details. Alfredo's secretary brought in his coffee as he sat stiffly at his desk letting his anger subside.

It was not the money, the profitability of the operation, which drove him. God knew, with the phony accounting system which Salvatore had foisted on him, he could hardly tell whether the operation was profitable or not. Not in the normal sense, anyway.

It was pride that motivated Alfredo. He had come up from Hell's Kitchen in New York and he had achieved his position by honest hard work. He loved this place, and was obsessed with making it the best ski area in North America, the best in the world. In response to this challenge he was ready to drive others to the limit.

He was pragmatic too, prepared to make concessions. In fact he would have been quite content if only Salvatore had kept his son, Nick, out of the operation. Nick was not a bad kid, so long as he stuck to his own side of the business. One thing Alfredo would simply not tolerate was Nick poking his nose into the ski operation. Alfredo was going to have that out with Salvatore at their next meeting, no punches pulled.

Alfredo had a faculty for making concessions in order to possess the things that he wanted most in life—like his wife, Pat, for instance. Fifteen years younger than he and daughter of an upper-crust San Francisco stockbroker, she had moved in a circle to which Alfredo once never dared to aspire.

But he had won her, not as the owner of a chain of pizza restaurants, but as the president-elect of a magnificent new resort complex. He had Salvatore to thank for that, too.

Of course she enjoyed the attention of other men. It was a natural trait in an intelligent, beautiful woman of her age. But there was one supreme love that she shared with Alfredo, the love of Mount Casino. He was convinced, despite her coquetry, that, as long as he maintained his position as president, she would never desert him.

His coffee was cold. He buzzed for another cup.

The weather, as though ashamed of its overnight excesses, forced a penitent smile. From behind wispy cobwebs of cloud, the sun burst out bravely. The huge mountain, puffed in its fresh white mantle, was ready to meet its new challengers.

It was the beginning of another day at Mount Casino.

CHAPTER THREE

JIM O'MALLEY woke to the sound of the alarm at a quarter-to-five and wasted no time getting out of bed. He was used to rising early during the ski season.

He dressed quickly, glancing outside as he did so. He had no qualms; the forecast was for a brilliant spring day and one look at the flickering dawn confirmed it. There was going to be a big crowd.

The Professional Freestyle Championship was the last major event of the Mount Casino ski season. After that, it was just a matter of winding down and closing off the operation when the lack of snow or the lack of people dictated it—probably no more than ten days at the outside.

Jim had a lot to do. Of course, all the runs to be used in the championship had been prepared, but he wanted to make a final check before the first event, the ballet competition, at ten o'clock. And he had a breakfast date with the sponsor's representative at seven-thirty in the cafeteria.

The subject of freestyle skiing had become a controversial one in the industry. Last year two freestylers had been permanently paralyzed from injuries suffered while doing aerial flips. Herschorn had smashed up at Steamboat, then Magrino was injured at Vail. Under pressure from their insurance brokers, a number of ski areas had placed an absolute ban on freestyle, considering it altogether too dangerous and bad for the overall image of the sport.

Other areas contented themselves with a prohibition of aerial flips.

Alfredo Costa's attitude was characteristic. So long as the lawyers could ensure that he was protected from being sued by an injured competitor, and so long as his insurance premium and coverage remained unaffected, he did not care who risked his neck at Mount Casino. The acid test was whether it brought publicity to the area and whether it drew the crowds. His approach was not totally callous. He argued that you could not put the clock back; these crazy kids were going to do it anyway. Trying to ban freestyle was akin to trying to outlaw the old biplane barnstormers.

Control of the sport, Alfredo argued, should come from within, not from denying them access to the terrain. This was in the process of happening, with the International Freestyle Skiers Association establishing basic safety rules, conditions of entry, and standardization of jumps and judging.

The sponsor's representative arrived about half-an-hour late, looking anxious and towing two Association officials in his wake. They went through the whole program in detail with Jim as they ate. By the time they were through, the cafeteria was filling up with early skiers.

After breakfast, Jim collected his skis. It felt quite strange for him to squeeze into his ski boots. A lot of people assumed that a mountain manager spent most of his life on skis, but this was far from the truth. If his total recreational skiing amounted to one week in a full season, he was having a good time.

The longest stretch of skiing that he had in any one season was when he took his annual busman's holiday. Every year for the past five years he had joined Skip Langdon's exclusive European ski tour.

Skip Langdon, now in his forties, had been in at the beginning of the postwar United States ski boom and had managed to make a dollar out of almost every facet of it. He had been on the Olympic team in '56 and had done a stint instructing at Stowe and then a couple of years in area management at Mount Tremblant in Canada. After that, he had branched out into writing articles for the ski magazines and then making exotic ski movies in virgin terrain. Now, with money inherited from his second wife, who had died in a plane crash during a trip to the Andes, he kept himself busy as the owner-editor of a ski trade magazine and as an occasional tour operator.

Every year, Skip took a group of about thirty people to one or the other of Europe's famous resorts. It did not take much effort. He had a man in Zurich who lined up all the hotel space and he usually had an oversupply of applicants, simply by word-of-mouth. In return he enjoyed being able to select his companions for a free holiday and there was a certain satisfaction in being one of the doyens of the industry.

Jim liked to go with Skip because he had a knack for picking the right people and the right places; not only that, he gave Jim a special rate to act as second-in-command. Skip knew Europe well from his ski movie days and he picked the small intimate hotels with character—the places where the discriminating natives went.

Jim and Skip had become good friends over the years. Skip owned a small house about seven miles down the lake. He skied Mount Casino sometimes, and now and then he and Jim played tennis or golf together. He was sure to be over today to do a story on the freestyle event; as soon as it was put to bed, they were taking off for Kitzbühel. For next year, Skip had already made arrangements to go to Klosters in Switzerland.

Stepping into his bindings, he joined the rest of the party at the Number One chair lift and they went up together to inspect the various courses.

The meet required considerable organization. The men's aerials and the ladies' ballet were to be covered by TV. The Mount Casino Public Relations Director and his group were responsible for the production problems. They had set the cameras up on the rear deck of the Bombadier grooming vehicle and the sound and camera crews were busy checking their equipment.

Each of the courses was lined with temporary snow fencing for spectator control and field telephones were strung between the start, finish, control, and judging points. The ballet was to take place at the bottom of Thunderbolt, the aerials at the top, and the mogul skiing on Blackjack.

The ballet course was in good shape, having been meticulously groomed by the vehicles on the morning shift.

Spectators were already milling around and some of the competitors were limbering up.

Satisfied, Jim and his group took the gondola to the top to inspect the aerial jumps. These had been constructed of snow to the specifications of the Association. There were two jumps in direct line, about five hundred feet apart.

From there they went on up to the top of the mountain by chair lift. There was really nothing to prepare, of course, on the mogul run; in fact the bumpier and tougher the shape of the hill, the better the competitors liked it. It was just a question of ensuring that everyone was familiar with the start and finish positions and judges' placement and of establishing that the fencing was in place. They skied down the run together. Jim made no attempt at "bashing" the hill in the manner of the freestylers. He was a straightforward, strong, hard skier with a conventional style and no desire to indulge in acid-rock antics.

He enjoyed the run immensely, feeling the old exhilaration, and decided to have a couple more, purely for fun. He went up again on the chair, took the narrow Twenty-one trail, then swung over to Interstate, circling the mountain wide and coming out at the bottom of Thunderbolt on the far side, away from the ballet course. From there he took Number Two chair up again and, feeling loose and confident, ran Pokerface flat out down to the bottom again.

The ballet competition was just getting under way when he arrived. He had really not been much exposed to this relatively new technique, and watched these graceful balletomanes perform their pirouettes and prances with great panache. A slender girl, spinning sinuously over the slippery snow to the strains of *Les Sylphides*, left him open-mouthed.

Silky and Jake watched the ballet event with little interest. There was no doubt that the performers were highly skilled—some of the waltzing maneuvers were almost unbelievable—but it just was not their style.

They were both deeply tanned, with strange white circles around their eyes where the skin was protected by anti-glare goggles. Spring skiing, unencumbered by warm-up clothing, was the zenith of the ski experience. Their tempo was slower, skiing hard for two hours in the

45

morning while the going was still fast from overnight frost, then loafing around the sundecks drinking beer and girl-watching in the afternoon.

This was their last outing. It had been a great, care-free season and they hated to see it come to an end. But they had had the best of it.

They had other matters to attend to and they had made up their minds to drive East on a buying trip. Their first objective was to acquire the necessary explosives, guns, and ammunition for the coming operation. Silky had an ex-army buddy in New York who had the right contacts.

After that, they planned to cruise around New England picking up the rest of their gear. Everything that was to be used in the actual hijack would be purchased as far away as possible from the scene of the crime.

"Let's go," Silky jerked his head, "before the crowd hits the lifts. I want to get a good spot for the aerials, near the second jump."

There was already quite a long lineup for the Number One chair, but it was too pleasant a day to start getting fractious. The wait gave them time to review the assembled talent, and by silent pact they split for the run to the top, each riding with an unattached girl.

Silky's was a really cute ski instructress, a blonde pixie type. He had seen her around quite a bit, admired her fluid, unpretentious ski style.

"Lovely day," Silky opened. He was not adept at small talk.

"Yes," she replied. Apparently she was no blabber-mouth either.

"Where did you learn to ski so well?" Silky ventured.

She turned to stare at him. "In Switzerland," she said. "I was born there."

She had a German accent which Silky found very at-tractive. At the same time it put him on the defensive. She seemed more worldly and sophisticated than the usual run-of-the-mill ski bunny.

"Going to watch the aerials?" he asked.

"Yes."

Silky gave up. They were getting near the top any-way. This girl was out of his class. "Have a good day, then," he said brightly, mimicking the Steamboat lift crews.

Jake was waiting for him at the top. His gal was standing with him, looking as if she were already connected to him by an invisible string. "How did you make out?" Jake said.

"I didn't," Silky replied.

Jake grinned. Silky had never been any good at pickups. It was always Jake who had to make the first advance.

Silky could not care less. He had come up to see the show. "Let's move," he said, "and get a good spot to see the action."

"Rena!" It was Nick's voice. She could hear him shouting from the direction of the judges' stand.

She hesitated, checking the group from the corner of her eye. Jim O'Malley was there. She always felt at ease with Jim. He was friendly, did not seem to have one eye on her pants all the time.

She skied across the course to join the group. Alfredo was there, in his element as father of the feast, issuing last-minute orders. She saw Pat Costa too, with Pepi in close attendance.

Searching the rest of the VIP group, she spotted Nellie Ferguson. Waving to Nick as she slipped by him, she joined Nellie and Stan a little farther down the slope, near the second jump. She noticed the dark, bearded man with whom she had ridden the lift, catching his eye for a moment and smiling at him involuntarily.

Jim O'Malley appeared close beside her. Nellie and Stan Ferguson greeted him as an old friend. Jim was very popular; he seemed to know everyone in Lake Tahoe.

The announcer was explaining the rules. Each competitor was to do two jumps of his choice, filing a "flight plan" with the judges before takeoff. Points were awarded, in the manner of a high diving competition, for the execution as well as the difficulty of the chosen maneuver. The two jumps were taken separately, the competitor being allowed to regroup after the first jump.

The first competitor was announced. The crowd watched in silence as he hurtled into the first jump, landed a little unsteadily, fought to hold his balance, then sailed off the second jump, curled himself into a somersaulting ball, and landed gently, flexing his knees, in perfect control. A burst of applause brought a happy grin to the young man's face.

The next one down immediately eclipsed his predecessor by doing a double back flip and then a back moebius, a back somersault accompanied by a full twist.

Fifteen of them went through their paces, without any major disaster. Their confident expertise made their astonishing acrobatics seem easy, divesting the spectacle of some of its thrill: it would take one of them crashing down on his back to demonstrate the split-second timing, nerve, control, and balance on which their safety depended.

Jim watched Alfredo presenting the prizes in front of the TV cameras and chatting spiritedly with the announcer, no doubt plugging the magnificent amenities of Mount Casino. The old rogue had gotten away with it once more, an excellent crowd, coast-to-coast publicity, and an incident-free performance. The other ski areas, many of them waiting stubbornly for another ghastly injury to confirm the wisdom of their freestyle moratorium, had been upstaged again.

You had to hand it to the old bastard, Jim admitted to himself. He was a natural showman who understood the morbid machinations of the human mind. The risk of death was a popular attraction, and, in the tradition of the great impresarios, he gave the public what it wanted.

The party for the freestyle competitors was at the home of a wealthy lift manufacturer, a lavish Swiss chalet on a hill overlooking the lake. Everybody who was anybody was there, and there was enough booze to keep the affair afloat for a couple of days.

It was a fitting blowout for their last night in town. Silky had wangled an invitation for them through a couple of old buddies among the competitors—not that it would have been a tough place to crash, since half the guests did not appear to know the host and hostess.

Everyone was tanned and animated and the women were all gorgeous, some in ski or après-ski fashions, others in off-the-shoulder evening gowns.

Jake was towing the girl he had picked up on the chair lift and looked well set for a night in the sack. It was a perfect scenario, squiring her to buffet and booze at someone else's expense.

The party was running on three levels; discotheque in the basement playroom, general conversation on the main floor, and necking and other serious occupations on the mezzanine and in adjoining bedrooms. The sweet smell of dope mixed with the pungent aroma of expensive perfume and tobacco.

Jake moved down to the disco to give his date a chance to loosen up her muscles for the ensuing event, while Silky sat comfortably people-watching halfway up the staircase.

He spotted Skip Langdon and moved to renew an old acquaintance. A few years back, when he was just out of school, Silky had fluked into one of Langdon's movies, glacier skiing in the Bugaboos. Silky was friends with one of the helicopter pilots and he had just happened to be on the spot when one of the regulars in the ski group dropped out with a broken ankle.

Skip seemed pleased enough to see him once he got Silky placed in his memory.

"Still doing movies?" Silky asked. That trip to the Bugaboos had been one of the most thrilling experiences in his life and he hankered after a return engagement.

"Nothing lately." Skip shrugged in resignation. "I'm getting a bit too sedentary these days. But I plan something in Chile—maybe next year. Want to sign on, if it goes?"

"Sure thing."

Skip pulled a visiting card out of his wallet and handed it to Silky. Call me next fall—about October. Maybe I can use you. I remember your style. First class in deep powder. Still not that many Americans who can handle it."

Silky put the card away carefully. The season in Chile was much later than in the United States. He planned to be at a loose end by then.

Skip seemed to know everyone at the party and he wasn't the sort whose attention you could monopolize for too long. "Thanks," Silky said. "Count me in." As Skip turned his attention to a tall blonde in his entourage, Silky made his way back to his vantage point on the staircase.

"Hello." Silky looked up, surprised to see the blonde

with the German accent smiling up at him. There was something about her grin that made him feel protective. She was in a flimsy, pale blue jersey dress which clung to her in the right places.

From where he stood above her, he could see right down the cleavage between her bra-less breasts. It embarrassed him. He blushed. "Can I get you a drink?" he blurted.

She hesitated. "Alright."

"Keep me a place, then." He pointed to an empty spot next to her on the stairs.

Again, she seemed uncertain, so he left her to make up her mind on her own. When he got back, she was sitting there, with the same childish smile, almost apologetically. He squeezed in beside her.

"You alone?" he asked.

"Sort of. Nick Diamado brought me but . . . well." She gave a funny little shrug. "I don't belong to anyone."

"And he thinks you do?"

"That's right." She seemed relieved that he understood her situation.

"Do you live here in Tahoe?" Silky asked. He did not mean the question to be loaded. He was not thinking of a session at her apartment. He just did not classify her as potential tail.

"Oh, no," she answered. "I am staying with friends. A vacation. I am going back to Switzerland soon."

There was something about the way she said it that surprised him, as though she was not looking forward to going home at all. Maybe she was just sorry that the skiing was over.

"I reckon it's time to call it quits. My buddy and I have been skiing all over Colorado and California since last November. We're starting a leisurely drive East tomorrow."

"East?"

"Yeah. New York."

Now she was surprised. "All that way? Driving? How long will it take you?"

Silky shrugged. "Six, seven days. Maybe longer. We're not in any hurry."

"Oh, I wish I could come with you." There was real

enthusiasm in her voice. "What a marvellous way to see America!"

Silky did not take her seriously. "You're welcome if you want to. There's plenty of room. Only two of us going, me and my buddy."

"Two men? No girls?"

"No girls. That's right."

"Oh, I would just love to come! Do you think your friend would mind? I could cash in my air ticket and fly home from New York. Are you sure? Are you serious, I mean?"

Silky was taken aback. He had figured she was just kidding, talking of things she wanted to do. She did not look like the type to make such big decisions on the spur of the moment. "Sure I'm serious." What else could he say?

"What time are you leaving? Could you pick me up?"

The situation tickled Silky. Jake would fall out of his tree. Here was Silky, the guy who could never make a pickup, bringing a woman on a seven-day safari.

"Where're you staying?"

"At the Fergusons. They have a big, white house, back from the main highway, halfway between here and Mount Casino. Their name is on the gatepost. You can't miss it. What time are you leaving?" she repeated.

"No special time. Maybe ten or eleven."

"Please," she was really excited now, "can I come? Promise?"

"Sure. I promise."

She fished in her handbag and took out a pen and a small notebook, scribbling out her number. "Call me there," she tore a sheet off and handed it to him, "half an hour before you leave. I'll be ready. Incidentally, I'm a good driver."

"Well," Silky said, standing up, holding out his hand for her glass, "I guess this calls for another drink, to celebrate. By the way, what's your name?"

"Renata Dalmain. Rena for short."

"O.K. Rena. My name is Silky. Sit tight while I go replenish the glasses."

When he got back to the staircase, he found a stocky man in dark glasses standing over Rena. They seemed to be quarreling.

The man was dressed in a charcoal-gray tuxedo and frilly shirt, very expensive looking. He wore a big diamond ring on his right forefinger and was squeezing the frame of his glasses in a kind of nervous twitch. Silky guessed it was Nick Diamado.

Nick turned to Silky, standing there with the two drinks. "She's coming home with me," Nick said menacingly.

"Anything you say, captain." Silky shrugged. It was hard to see why the guy was so uptight.

"She said that you were going to drive her home." Nick seemed to be issuing a challenge.

"She did?" Silky was genuinely surprised. "Well, then, I suppose I am."

"No, you're not. I told you. I'm driving her."

"Listen, sonny." Silky made a show of stubbing the man in the chest with his amputated finger: it was his favorite put-down. Nick stared at the hideous stump of flesh in revulsion. "I'm not usually in any great demand as a chauffeur," Silky continued prodding. "It's not a big thing in my life. But I don't like people telling me what to do. Particularly little sawn-off runts like you. Now let's just ask the lady again nicely, what d'you say?" Silky suggested.

Rena was standing up now. She looked at Nick with contempt. "Come on, you jerk," she said to him, the German accent seeming to add an element of depth to her scorn. "You've ruined my evening anyway. Take me home —now." It was an order.

Nick glared at Silky. "I'll get to you later," he said.

"You and who else?" Silky laughed.

Nick pulled Rena roughly toward him and turned on his heel. Sonofabitch, he was thinking. No respect.

Rena awaited the arrival of her two escorts with some trepidation. As Silky had rightly surmised, she was not in the habit of making decisions impulsively and she was nervous.

The prospect of a week alone with two entirely strange men gave rise to all sorts of embarrassing and even dangerous possibilities. What if one, or even both of them forced his attentions on her? What if she quarreled with them and they decided to leave her somewhere along the road? What if? There was no point in worrying about it now. She was going ahead, whatever the risk.

Nellie Ferguson had been very surprised, but was reassured when Rena insisted that her companions were close friends. It was indeed a golden opportunity for Rena to see something of the country.

Rena's reasons for the sudden decision were hard to rationalize, even to herself. Ostensibly, the chance to see more of America than Lake Tahoe and the Los Angeles air terminal was the prime factor. Coming from a tiny country, she was intrigued by the vast distances and vivid contrasts of the American continent.

Getting away from Nick's attentions before he became any more serious was another consideration.

The prospect of a leisurely drive across the United States—a few days of suspended animation—gave her more time to adjust to an empty future. The transition from her present environment, a relatively happy one despite Nick's over zealous attachment, would be less traumatic than if she were to take a transatlantic flight.

The cross-country trip would be a temporary respite.

From the moment that she had met Silky on the chair lift she had felt an extraordinary affinity. It had nothing to do with sexual attraction; she had a feeling that he was reliable, trustworthy—someone who would be a loyal friend. Intuitively, she was sure that he liked her, and she was equally certain that he would never lay a hand on her. She desperately needed a friend like that.

She watched the car turn into the driveway and park in front of the house. It was a sporty-looking red Pontiac with manual gearshift—a man's car. Silky jumped out to help her with her skis and suitcase, while Jake eyed her from the rear seat. She kissed Nellie quickly and took her place beside Silky, fearful that one of the men would say something that would disclose to Nellie the brevity of her acquaintance with them.

She felt elated now. She was on the way and there was no going back. Whatever the future brought, it would be exciting, a completely new episode in her life.

Silky introduced her to Jake.

"Hi, Rena," Jake said, looking her over with a grin.

Instinctively she was cool to him; he did not give off the same brotherly vibrations as Silky did.

53

She glanced at Silky. My God, she thought, I hope I was right about him. Two like Jake and I'd have my hands full.

The tape deck was under the dash on Rena's side, there were a dozen tapes in a plastic tray beside her. "Can I play some music?"

"Sure," Silky said. "Pick what you like."

The stereo system filled the car with music. Jake seemed to be dozing in the rear, Silky content to drive in silence. She relaxed, enjoying the passing scene, catching sudden vistas of the lake. They moved on through the outskirts of Reno and then into the desert, heading for Salt Lake City.

They stopped for lunch at a roadside diner. Jake seemed to be tired and hung over. Apart from making it quite obvious, in rather a braggart way, that he had spent a strenuous night with a girl, he was very polite and pleasant to Rena. One thing that impressed her was the extraordinary rapport between these two men, the obvious depth of their friendship and respect for each other. It gave her confidence.

"Can I drive after lunch?" she asked. She wanted to establish her equality in the partnership, demonstrate that she could do her share.

Silky explained the gearshift positions to her and she listened patiently. She snapped the seat belt, swung out onto the highway and got under way. Moving expertly through three gears, with her eye on the tachometer, she flashed past a big semi-trailer, shifted into top and eased into the right lane at eighty-five.

"For Christ's sake," Jake dragged himself up to peer over the front seat, "where did you learn to drive like that?"

"My husband was a racing driver. Pierre Dalmain," she answered.

"Pierre Dalmain? French? He won at Monte Carlo." Silky followed motor racing fairly closely. He also remembered that Dalmain had been killed at Nurburgring.

"You still married?" Jake knew nothing of the Grand Prix circuit.

"No," she said.

They had soon settled down to a regular routine, each taking about three hours behind the wheel. The men took

54

turns sleeping in the back, but Rena refused to close her eyes for a moment. She was too interested in everything about her, the surging traffic, the neon signs, the ever-changing landscape. By mutual consent they let her stay up front all the way, like a contented child gazing rapturously at the passing scene.

Silky liked her. She did her share, never asked for any special treatment.

He had felt a bit of a jerk when he had first explained the setup to Jake. But now he was glad that she was along. It was a diversion.

At first she had been very quiet. She was strange somehow, moody, as if she nursed a secret sadness. But now she seemed at ease, ready to chat about anything.

"You are very lucky," she said suddenly. "You both seem to enjoy life so much. And you live it so carelessly. I wish I could do that."

"Why can't you, then?" Silky asked. "What's your hang-up?"

"Lots of things."

They were into their third day, moving through the bleak cornfields of Nebraska. Silky was at the wheel and Jake was snoring in the back.

"Name them." Silky challenged her.

"I think life has to have a point, a goal. Mine does not seem to have any, since Pierre died. There is nothing that I really want to do. Everything now is an anticlimax."

"This trip, for instance?" Silky asked, feeling a stab.

"Oh, no. Of course not. I haven't been happy like this for . . . I don't know. But this is an episode. It has to come to an end soon. It's just going to make it all the harder to return to reality."

"Why go back to Switzerland if you don't want to?" Silky asked. He remembered how she had talked of going home at the party in Tahoe.

She shrugged. "Where else would I go? It's where I belong."

"What are you going back to?"

She told him about Kurt and his Belgian wife. How she did not feel welcome. She felt at ease with Silky and spoke frankly. "I suppose I will get some sort of job in Zurich."

"I don't see why you are so depressed, Rena. Let's face it. You had a beautiful marriage, even if it was very short. Most beautiful things are very short. Don't you see? Flowers, views, sunshine, parties, the ski season. How would you know they were beautiful if you had them all the time?"

"But there is another season next year."

"Yes. A different one. There can be another marriage for you, too. A different one."

"Oh, no," she said fiercely.

"Back up a minute, Rena. You say that you envy Jake and me. You also say that life must have a point. The whole point in life is to enjoy it. To grab it. You want a goal? Make happiness your goal."

"That's totally selfish."

"What the hell's wrong with that?" Silky laughed. "It's your life. Your own private gift. Who are you helping if you don't set out to enjoy it? And who are you hurting if you do?"

"Are you as happy as you seem, really?" she asked.

"Yes."

"Why? What have you got that I haven't got?"

"Contrast." Silky smiled. "I have seen more death, more misery, more pain, more discomfort, more ugliness than you will ever see. I left too many friends lying dead in Vietnam to complain about being alive."

"I'm sorry," she said.

"You're a real nice person. But you're not very nice to yourself."

She shrugged. He was right. There was something deep inside her, a resentment against life for what it had done to her.

They reached Chicago in the afternoon of the fifth day. They were firm friends by now, three musketeers.

Jake and Silky decided to take Rena out to a formal dinner, to give her a chance to get out of her jeans. She was very touched, but, as the evening wore on, she decided that they should take her home. "I think you boys should go on a stag. Get—how do you say it?—the dirty water off your chests?"

They protested, laughing.

"I insist," she said. "For my safety and your sanity. Five days platonic relationship with a girl is enough for you. You are both getting irritable. You two sleep in—or whatever—tomorrow. I'll get up early and take a bus tour."

It was funny. Left to their own devices, they made Rena the sole topic of conversation. They checked a lot of bars and drank a lot of bourbon, but somehow all the local women looked shabby after Rena.

Around two in the morning they found themselves in a smoky little strip joint.

"I was thinking." Jake was drunk, speaking very deliberately to get his tongue around the words. "What about bringing Rena into our act?"

"What the fuck for? As the getaway driver? You're drunk." Silky was full of booze, too, but figured that he held it better than Jake.

"No!" Jake gave Silky a vacuous kind of grin. "Just to hold the money."

"I don't get it," Silky said. The whole conversation was like a slow-motion movie. "What d'you mean—hold the money?"

Jake tapped his nose, full of conspiracy. "Alright, I'm a bit smashed. But I've been thinking about this a long time. Shut up and listen, O.K.?"

"Shoot," said Silky, lighting up a cheroot and sitting back. "You're pissed out of your mind, but you're a nice guy. I'm ready to listen . . . but," he pointed the cheroot between Jake's eyes, "I'm not in any condition to make decisions. O.K.?"

"O.K." Jake nodded. "Look at it this way." Jake began with a big sigh, pulling himself together with an effort and trying to look solemn: "What gets in must get out. Right?"

"Right," said Silky, not having the faintest idea what Jake was talking about.

"What I mean is this." Jake was quite fuzzy, searching his mind to reach the beginning. "You get inside . . . say in a bank for instance, and you pick up a load of money. Right?"

"Right." Silky swayed back in his chair to simulate a nod.

"Now the problem is . . . how do you get out? Right?"

"Right." So far, Silky had no problem following.

"The point is," Jake was becoming more intelligible as he warmed to his subject, "you can only get out through an exit. Right?"

57

"Right." There was no arguing against such logic.

Jake speeded up the presentation as he began to find his stride. "But the police know that, you see. The police *know* that you have to come out of one of the exits. So they block the exits. Understand?"

Silky nodded. He found the atmosphere in the bar very stuffy. And the girl wiggling her fanny on the small stage seemed to have two pussies, side by side.

"Now, say," Jake reached over to tap Silky on the shoulder, "say that you could *leave* the money right there in the bank . . . come out of the exit clean, nothing incriminating." He stumbled over the last word. "And say that you could come back to the bank, maybe two, three months later and pick up the loot, then what?"

Silky shrugged. He had lost the point and felt like going for a leak. Jake held him down.

"Don't you see, Silky, for Christ's sake, we leave the money with Rena right in Lake Tahoe. We just drive out of town—through the police roadblocks—clean—nothing, no money. And we come back to pick it up later—when the whole panic is over! It's perfect!"

Silky brushed Jake aside. "I'm going for a piss. Tell me again tomorrow."

They left Chicago after lunch the following day, Rena at the wheel. Silky was in the back. Jake dozed next to Rena. After a desultory conversation mostly concerned with getting on the right road, silence descended. They were heading in the direction of Washington, having decided that Rena must see the White House before she went home.

Jake woke up around five o'clock but was in no condition to do his stint of driving. He sat quietly, thinking about his plan. Now that he had managed to put it into words, it had crystallized in his mind. He was sure that it was the missing link. If she would go for it. The thing to do was to put her through some preliminary tests.

"You got a place lined up to stay in Lake Tahoe next season?" he asked her.

"Yes. They have promised me one of the condominium apartments right at Mount Casino," she replied.

"What date you coming back?"

"I'm supposed to report for work by November 15. Costa is arranging my permit."

He wanted to probe a little deeper.

"Everyone has a price," he began. "What's yours for taking a big risk?—for instance, would you do a double back flip or a moebius for twenty-five grand?"

Rena looked at him quizzically. "Well," she said after a moment's thought, "I would not do it right now, because I don't know how. I mean, I would kill myself for sure. But if I was allowed to take some lessons first, sure. I would do it for ten grand, even."

"What kind of risk would you take for a hundred grand?"

She laughed. "Almost anything, I suppose. Why do you ask?"

"I'm just interested. You don't seem to value your life very highly. I just wondered what your price would be for gambling it."

At first Rena said nothing. Then suddenly she started again. "I think the price for which I would risk my life would have to be high enough to make an appreciable difference to my happiness if I won." She paused. "I mean, my problem is that I cannot get free. Free from the past. I would risk my life," she was very deliberate now, "if someone offered me sufficient money to buy a whole new one. Enough that I could make a clean break and start entirely afresh. Total independence, absolute freedom. But it couldn't happen."

"It might." Jake was intrigued now. "How much would that be, do you think?"

She shrugged. "Oh, I don't know, Jake. Half-a-million. A million. That should do it." She giggled. "It depends on what I'm asked to do."

That night they went to bed early. Jake engineered it that way because he wanted to talk to Silky. He was obsessed with his new plan, sure that he had solved the getaway problem.

He explained it to Silky again. "Don't you see? The police will have roadblocks everywhere. They'll guard the airports too. They're not stupid, for Christ's sake. One phone call and the whole country will be on alert."

"I don't see what they can do if we take hostages with us."

"They will wait us out. We have to let the hostages go sometime—unless we kill them. The police will just wear us down, waiting for us to make a mistake, just like you said. But if we use the hostages to keep them from tailing too close for the first fifteen minutes—that should not be too difficult—and we stash the money right in Tahoe in that time—then we walk out free. It's beautiful!"

Silky mulled it over. The roles were reversed now, Jake doing all the pushing, Silky acting as the devil's advocate. "How do we know we can trust her? What if she tells the cops? Or what if she takes off with the entire bundle?"

"A little piece at a time," Jake said. At least Silky was on board with the general concept. "As to whether she tells the cops we would have to take that risk. I don't think she would. That's just a gut feeling. As to whether she takes off with the entire proceeds—well, I agree, we need more than gut feel to cover that one. We need insurance."

"Insurance? You going to buy a policy on her life?" Silky asked sarcastically.

Jake ignored the crack. "I have been puzzling that one ever since Omaha, when I first got the germ of the idea. And I think I've got it figured out." He enjoyed keeping Silky on tenterhooks.

"Come on, then," Silky said impatiently. "What's the insurance?"

"The insurance is," he paused for an imaginary roll of drums, "a confession."

"A confession? What does that do?"

"It ensures her cooperation. That's what it does."

"Spell it out. I don't get it."

"It's simple. She signs a detailed confession implicating herself in the complete hijack operation. We hold the confession. If she delivers, we tear it up. If she doesn't, we get to hell out of the country and send her confession to the police. How's that?"

Silky went through it again step by step in his mind. "It's fucking brilliant."

They had agreed not to approach her right away. "Let me get used to the idea of her as an accomplice," Silky said. "We still have plenty of time."

It was their last night together. They were really attached to one another now. Rena made no attempt to disguise her misery. Tears rolled down her cheeks as they shared a final toast to friendship.

Both Silky and Jake were ready to offer her anything to cheer her up.

"Shut up crying," Silky said passing her a napkin, "and go and wash your face. We have a proposition for you."

"A proposition?" She stared at him red-eyed. "What kind of proposition?"

"A half-million-dollar proposition. It'll cheer you up."

They did not tell her what the caper was. There was no point. She did not have to know. Jake just explained her part of it.

"All we are asking is this," Silky repeated Jake's proposal. "If one of us arrives at your apartment with a suitcase full of money—and, of course, we won't show up unless we are completely clear of the police—will you hold it for perhaps three months—nothing else, understand? For that you get half-a-million dollars."

"You're crazy." She was still sobbing, perhaps some of it was shock. "I would probably do it for nothing—just for the joy of hanging around you both, you idiots."

The atmosphere was fairly lighthearted as they drove her out to the airport. Their secret set them apart from the rest of the world, gave them a sense of shared destiny.

Rena's mind was in turmoil. It was hard to believe what had happened, harder to avoid asking questions. But she sensed that questions would make them nervous. Finally, she summoned the courage to offer a suggestion.

"Once you get the money, how do you get it into circulation? I mean I can't just walk into the bank and deposit half-a-million dollars. Not in this country. They would suspect me at once."

"Let's get the money first," Silky said guardedly. "We'll figure something out."

"What about Switzerland?" she suggested.

"What about it?" Silky retorted.

Jake got the point at once. "Rena, I love you!" he exclaimed excitedly. "Of course, numbered accounts. No trace. Perfect! The girl is a genius!"

She was really one of them now, a full-fledged conspirator. Jake leaned over from the back seat and gave her a big kiss.

"Fair shares for everyone." She laughed, snuggled up to Silky at the wheel, and pecked him on the cheek.

They drove directly to Kennedy Airport with an hour to spare before her Swissair flight. Having checked her in at the counter, Silky and Jake took Rena for a final drink and conference. It was agreed that she would not contact them again; they did not even exchange addresses. They would get in touch with her in Tahoe sometime shortly after November 15. If either she or they did not show up, the deal was off.

There were no more tears when they parted at the gate. She had not felt so happy since the day that Pierre had won the victor's crown at Monte Carlo.

Once they had seen Rena safely on to her plane, a pall descended. It was hard to believe how completely she had infiltrated their brotherhood.

"Quite a lady," Silky said as they drove back to the motel.

"Yeah," agreed Jake. "She's a good luck charm. Everything is beginning to fall into place."

Until Jake had come up with his idea, they were like two men floating around in a battle cruiser with no way to land. Jake had suddenly provided the all-important gangplank.

They now got on with the basic purpose of their trip. The first item on the shopping list was artillery.

Silky had an ex-army buddy, a young black called Tupper, who lived in Harlem. He apparently could put his hands on a small arsenal. Silky called him on the phone, arranging to meet him at noon the following day at Buzzy's, a small bar.

Jake watched Silky replace the receiver. "That finger," he said, "could point right at us."

Silky looked at his right hand unconcernedly. "Don't see why."

"Because it's in your army records, isn't it?"

"So?"

"So, let's give the cops credit for not being stupid. When they find the gondola towers neatly packed with explosive, they're going to put two and two together and guess that it's the work of an army vet. Ten to one they will try Special Forces first. They will check the records—you know, that's what they always do on the TV. Now, if they know that they are looking for a guy with nine and a half fingers, it sure narrows down the choice."

Silky shrugged. "It's a good point. But we will be wearing gloves. I could just stuff the glove with paper."

"You could. Seems to me it would be better to do the job properly. We are going for the jackpot. We have all the time in the world to do our planning. The only way to win a play like this is to be perfect in every detail. No chances. No traces."

"What do you suggest? A falsy?"

"Sure."

"Aw, come on. That's overdoing it a bit."

"No it isn't. And you know it. You're not alive today because you were slipshod about your preparations in 'Nam. You've got an obvious identifying feature. That's death in this kind of occupation. No good sticking it up your ass and pretending it isn't there. Get it fixed, man. Here, give me the yellow pages."

Silky was reluctant. It seemed such a queer thing to do. A false finger!

Jake thumbed through the directory. "There see. ARTIFICIAL LIMBS, there's four of them."

Silky looked again at the offending digit. "Could be just as dangerous," he said, stalling. "The guy will have a record."

"Well, we'll just have to make sure that he has the wrong record, won't we?"

A middle-aged lady in a white coat smiled from behind the counter as they entered. They were both wearing dark glasses, and Jake had disguised his facial scar with Pan-Cake makeup. "Good morning," she said.

The place was full of merchandise, wheelchairs, canes, and other contraptions around the walls. The counter had a glass top, beneath which was a neat array of hands, feet, glass eyes, and even a couple of ears. Standing on the counter at one end, displayed on a raised dais, were a metal leg and arm.

Silky was in a complete funk. "Do you have fingers?" Jake asked.

"Fingers?" the lady said. "We don't have much call for fingers. Occasional special order for a lady. Cosmetic, if you see what I mean." She looked at him rather superciliously.

"It's not for me," Jake hastened to assure her. "It's for my friend here. He's an actor."

Silky shot him a look of astonishment.

"Yes. You see"—Jake was enjoying himself hugely. He had prepared this little skit in his mind but had not forewarned Silky. "I'm his manager. We're just about to make a movie and," he grabbed Silky's sleeve and pushed his right hand down on the counter, "he plays a pianist. He has to have ten fingers."

The lady looked at Silky's stump. "I don't know about playing the piano," she said dubiously.

"He doesn't *actually* play the piano." Jake swept her hesitation aside. "He just has to look as if he could."

"I see," she said, reassured by this explanation. "It will be a special order, of course."

"Don't you have anything in stock?" Silky asked.

"Oh, no, dear me, no. We have to get a match. I will have to take a lot of measurements."

"Really?"

"Of course. Color match, length, thickness, so on. Just put your left hand down here." She laid it on a white towel.

She went to a cupboard in the rear and brought out a color chart, matching it first to his left hand, then to his right, taking notes as she went. Then she measured his left forefinger between knuckles. "Is this about regular length for your nails?" she asked.

Silky nodded.

"How long will it take?" Jake asked.

"Three weeks to a month for the fitting."

"Fitting?" said Jake, taken aback. "I'm afraid a fitting is out of the question. We are making the film in Africa and he is leaving in two weeks. Couldn't you get a rush order?"

"Do you want hair?"

"Hair? How d'you mean?"

She pointed to the fine black fluff on the back of each of Silky's existing fingers. "Like this," she said.

"Is that extra? Does that take more time?"

"Of course."

"Could you do it without hair in two weeks?"

"I can try."

"How much will it be?"

"Three hundred dollars."

Jake whistled. "As much as that, eh? I wouldn't have believed it." He looked at Silky. "What d'you say, then? Do you want it?"

"Not much," said Silky frankly.

Jake turned to the woman. "We'll take it. Two weeks, though. That's very important."

"I'll try." She would not commit herself. "What is the name and address?"

"Fred Carr," Jake replied. "The address is the Grand Hotel, Nairobi."

She looked mystified. "Don't you have a local address?"

"No," he said. "We have let our apartment. We'll be away two years."

"Oh." She seemed to find this rather irregular, but filled out the order nevertheless. "I will have to have a deposit then," she said plaintively.

"Of course." Jake pulled out his wallet and peeled off five twenties. "How's that?"

"Fine, sir." She handed him his receipt. "Call in about ten days, and I will let you know when to pick it up."

"Two weeks," Jake insisted.

"I can't promise," she said, looking exasperated.

"By the way," Jake said, winking at the lady, "Fred Carr is not his stage name. You'd be surprised who he really is."

They had some trouble finding the place. Someone had thrown a rock at the neon sign, knocking out the two zs. It now read BU YS.

It was a dingy little joint that smelled of fried potatoes, stale garbage, and rank sweat. Silky lit up a cheroot and ordered two beers. The beer was lukewarm.

There were a couple of young blacks playing pool at a half-sized table in the middle of the room and a moth-eaten whore was listlessly swinging a skinny leg at the bar. A small box radio strained to squawk some music against the crackle of its own static and the click of the pool balls.

They sat at a booth in the far corner of the room and waited. Tupper was late.

Jake grew impatient.

"He'll show," said Silky.

Tupper appeared in about twenty minutes, all smiling white teeth under a wide-brimmed maroon hat, with a yellow band around it. He slapped hands all round and waved at the barman who shuffled over with a double rum and coke. "What you need, man? Hash, coke, pot? Artillery? Name it. I'll get it for you."

"Artillery," Silky said.

"Got a shopping list?"

Silky pulled a piece of paper from his shirt pocket and handed it to Tupper. Tupper unfolded it, pressing out the creases with his dirty thumbs. He looked up. "Quite a nice order. You going to knock off Fort Knox or sumthin?"

"Right." Jake did not like the cocky little bastard. "Want to come along?"

Tupper stared at Jake for a moment, then grinned at Silky. "Your man's a comic," he said. "Always take a comic to a holdup." He looked back at Jake. "The fuzz enjoys a good laugh."

Silky ignored him. "How much?"

"Twelve grand." It was just a figure. He made no attempt to calculate the list, item by item.

"Five," Silky said. Jake had reckoned five as tops.

Tupper laughed, rolling about and making a big show of his mirth. "I'll get you half-a-dozen water pistols and a B.B. gun for that."

Silky nudged Jake and they both got up to go. "Thanks for the beer, Tupper," he said.

"What beer?"

Silky turned his empty glass upside down. "The one I should have poured on your fancy hat," he said.

Tupper looked up at him sad-eyed. "C'mon, Silky, let's not shit around. I gotta right to make something on this." He put his hand on the shopping list, as Silky reached for it. "That stuff's not for knocking off old ladies. You got a big caper here."

"None of your fucking business what we've got." Silky snatched the list off the table. "We're buying merchandise, not a goddam partner." He folded the list and slipped it in his shirt pocket.

Tupper gave him an injured look. "Ten?" he suggested plaintively.

Silky put the paper back in his pocket. "Five."

Tupper mustered a smile. "Listen, man. I'm losin' on the deal. Eight."

Silky turned to Jake. "Tupper's buying. Want another beer?"

Jake considered. "O.K. then, just to be polite."

Silky waved at the barman for another round. "Seven," he said, "that's tops."

"Seven." Tupper was all white teeth again. "Done. Let's see the color."

Silky peeled off ten bills and held them in his fist. "No serial numbers. No traces. Right?"

"Sure, man, sure."

"One now," Silky said, "six on delivery."

Tupper feigned outrage, appealing to Jake. "How's that for trust, then? I fought side by side with this man. Trusted him with my life."

"You're one lucky sonofabitch, Tupper. Without me, you'd be feeding worms in a rice paddy."

"O.K." Tupper shrugged. "Give me the one, then."

Silky held it. "What about delivery?"

Tupper looked around in a great show of conspiracy. "It's dangerous, man." He paused. "This is how it goes down. You rent a car for me. I drive it away. I come back tomorrow with the merchandise in the trunk. You pay me and drive the car away."

"In whose name? The car, I mean?" Jake asked suspiciously.

"Yours, man."

"No dice."

"Tell you what," Tupper suggested. "You've got four phony licences on your list. Use one of them."

"O.K." Silky said. "But we don't do the switch here." He was not going to transact the business on Tupper's home ground. "I'll phone you tomorrow to tell you where the switch is going to take place."

Tupper considered. "O.K. Let's go."

"Don't forget to pay for the beer," Jake reminded him.

They had picked a deserted corner of the parking lot at

Shea Stadium for the trade. They watched Tupper drive up in the rented Ford.

Jake got out and leaned against the car window, waiting for Tupper to roll it down. "Park it back to back to ours," he said.

"Sure man. Anything you say."

The two cars were close up to a wall, the Ford's trunk open. Jake and Tupper stood guard, holding the trunk down loosely, while Silky crouched inside checking through the artillery, piece by piece, using a flashlight. It took him twenty minutes.

"Alright?" Tupper asked when Silky emerged.

"Not bad," Silky acknowledged.

"Good," Tupper grinned. "Let's scramble then. Got the money?"

"Of course." Silky handed him an envelope.

"I'll count it in the car." Tupper smiled, making to get into the Ford.

"Not that side." Jake steered him away from the driving seat, stepping in himself. "Want us to drop you off somewhere?"

"No man, I'll walk." Tupper counted the money, then strode quickly away in the direction of the subway. "See you guys," he said. "Bring me back a souvenir from Fort Knox. A gold brick or something."

After Tupper had gone, they transferred the merchandise to the Pontiac and drove both cars to the agency to return Tupper's rented Ford.

The transaction was complete. Satisfied, they headed back to their motel, Jake at the wheel.

After about six blocks, Jake turned right, then first left. He was watching the mirror. "I think we are being followed," he announced flatly.

"Shit," said Silky.

"Let's not panic," said Jake. "I'll pull up at a liquor store and buy a jug. It's the blue Impala. See if he stops."

Sure enough, the tail pulled up fifty yards back.

Jake swung out into the traffic again. "I've been thinking," he said. "It's no good trying to race them. That would just draw attention to us and put the police on our tail."

"Maybe it *is* the police," Silky said apprehensively.

"If it is, we're fucked. On the other hand, if it's some of

Tupper's assholes aiming to steal their merchandise back, or maybe a rival gang, we'd better play it cool. I'll move out of town, where we have more room to maneuver."

They cruised slowly out in the direction of Plainfield, New Jersey. The tail was fairly sloppy, making little attempt to take any evasive action. The farther they went, the more Jake and Silky recovered their spirits, convinced that their company was not the police.

"Try the shopping center up ahead," Silky said. "We'll see how wide awake these monkeys are."

They turned off the highway into a big retail complex. There was a giant Sears building back to back with a J.C. Penney, occupying maybe ten acres of real estate, with retail stores around the perimeter.

They parked near the entrance and watched the tail pull up three rows behind them. Silky stepped out and walked in a leisurely fashion through the big glass doors, giving the tail plenty of time to observe him.

He sauntered through Sears looking at the merchandise. He bought a brown felt hat and a gray sports jacket, which was on sale at 25 percent off. It was a good fit.

From men's clothing, he moved over to hardware, picking up a nice sharp ice pick. Then, wearing his new clothes, he strolled the length of the store to the exit farthest from where he had entered.

Coming out of the mall, he walked rapidly in the direction of the largest group of parked cars and ducked behind them. After waiting two or three minutes, he moved out, using stationary cars as a shield and gradually circling back to come up behind the blue Impala. Keeping low, he waved his hand and waited for Jake to answer him by touching his brake lights.

From there on, it was a just a question of speed. He jabbed the ice pick three times in each of the Impala's rear tires, then took off at full tilt for the street exit.

Jake was waiting there with the door open. Silky jumped in and they were gone. Taking a circuitous route, they returned to their motel close by Kennedy Airport, checked out, and headed north on Highway Seventy-six.

Silky opened the jug that Jake had purchased when they first spotted the tail, offering it to Jake. He took a good pull at it. "You've got some assholes for friends," he said to Silky. "I didn't trust that sonofabitch, Tupper, from the moment he came walking in wearing that piss-pot of a hat."

"So what?" Silky shrugged. He was in high spirits now. He had thoroughly enjoyed the game of hide and seek with Tupper's accomplices. "We got what we came for, didn't we?"

CHAPTER FOUR

RENA had phoned ahead from Kloten airport and spoken to her brother, Kurt, doing her best to seem lighthearted. He had not offered to pick her up in Chur, pleading the presence of a small convention of businessmen from Grenoble in the hotel that demanded his full attention.

Arriving in Lenzerheide by bus, she found her worst fears confirmed; every room in the hotel had been let to the paying customers, and no mention was made of the spare room in the proprietor's living quarters. Instead, Kurt had reserved a room for her at the exclusive Waldhaus at a daily rate which made her blanch.

What hurt Rena the most was their evident conviction that she had come home to sponge off them. At dinner the first night, when Kurt and his wife invited her to eat with them in the hotel dining room, they went through an obviously well-rehearsed pantomime of solicitous advice. Rena found their transparent self-interest sickening, and it was as much as she could do to avoid losing her temper and telling them both to go to hell.

There was one thing for sure. To them she was a liability, an unwanted burden. Her brother and his wife were afraid of her, did not even have the grace to credit her with enough sense and self-respect to evaluate the situation for herself.

She checked out of her hotel the next morning, leaving no messages and no forwarding address, and took the bus back to Chur. From there, she rode a train to Zurich and checked into the first *gasthaus* that she found.

Friendless and penniless in a strange city, she found herself between black despair and dogged determination to survive. Only her commitment to Silky and Jake, only the vision of her two strange accomplices and their trust in her—a half-million-dollar trust—sustained her.

Her immediate problem was to get a job. With no special training or experience other than ski instruction, she approached the task with trepidation. But finally, when she was close to giving up, she landed a job in the American Express office.

At last she was able to support herself and she began to acquire a new sense of purpose. Her confidence increased as she soon discovered the market value of her fluency in French, German, and English.

By midsummer she was comfortably installed in a pretty little apartment in the Augustinergasse district of the old town; it had a quaint carved balcony window looking out over the narrow street.

She still kept very much to herself. Now she only looked forward to her return to Mount Casino, her reunion with her confederates and the prospect of a new life.

For Jim O'Malley, the summer at Mount Casino was a welcome break.

Not that there were no chores to keep him occupied: maintenance work on the lifts and vehicles, overhaul of the sewer system, repairs and painting of the buildings and, toward the fall, brush-cutting the undergrowth from the trails were some of his tasks. But this summer they were not cutting any new trails or installing any new uphill equipment. Alfredo had, as predicted, turned down his recommendation for a snow-making system. One of these days they would have a snow-drought, like they'd had in the East for the past two seasons and Alfredo would rue his decision. But Jim did not let it worry him.

Jim usually spent the morning at the office and the afternoon playing tennis or golf. Evenings he sat around his apartment reading or listening to music. Oddly enough, since Rena had gone home he found himself less interested in casual affairs.

He had really liked Rena, although he had not known

her for much more than three weeks and he had had to share her with Nick Diamado.

Long after she had gone home to Switzerland, her image kept popping into his mind at the most unexpected moments, some times when he was with another woman.

Ever since the breakup of his marriage, he had developed a plural attitude toward women. He enjoyed their company, he flirted with some, he slept with a few, but he always thought of them as a group. There was a place in his life for female company and that place was the bedroom.

Unattached women were not uncommon in Mount Casino. Apart from the ski crowd, there was the local talent around the casinos. The blackjack dealers, waitresses, Keno girls, and showgirls were all chosen in part for their looks, so that the percentage of attractive women in the town was well above average. A surprising number of them were young divorcées, many of them with small kids, attracted to gambling by the high wages, the tips, and the opportunity to earn a living in an exciting atmosphere. By and large they were not one-night-standers or whores, rarely accepting dates with the gambling customers. On the other hand, their bodies craved a man once in a while and sometimes the man was Jim.

It was a pleasant, uncomplicated kind of existence, one that Jim had no reason to want to change.

And now Rena. Why did he think of her as singular, individual, particular? What the hell had she got that was so special? Was it just the fact that she presented more of a challenge, that she would be more difficult than the average woman to talk into bed?

Was it that voice? That strange, sensual German accent?

He shook off the daydreams and brought himself back to matters in hand. He had a date to play tennis with Jack Norman, the hotel pro, in half-an-hour. It was time to get ready.

Pat Costa sat in the glassed-in spectators' box watching the action on the court directly below her. There was something mildly erotic about the two beautifully conditioned athletes moving about the court with speed and symmetry, fighting for supremacy. She wished that she was the prize for which they competed.

She compared the two opponents, wondering about their prowess in bed. Jim—tall, muscular, smiling, black hair at the throat of his shirt-collar, a big bear of a man. Jack—blond, slim, and serious, his shoulder-length mane tucked under a dashing red bandana, all grace and youth.

She smiled to herself: she would have liked to have had them both.

She had been bored since Pepi had left to return to Austria for his summer holiday. Pepi had been a perfect lover, skilled and sensous in bed but not possessive between assignations.

Pat enjoyed a variety of sexual experience; it was a diversion, an excitement, a game. But she had no wish to let it interfere with her happy marriage to Alfredo Costa.

She was very fond of Alfredo and acknowledged him to be the perfect husband. He was kind and generous, he had position and wealth, and he provided her with an exciting life. Moreover, he still rated amongst the top ten sexual partners of her total experience.

On no account would she contemplate the sort of affair which would involve her in any obligation outside the bedroom. She wanted no jealous or infatuated admirers.

Jake finished the set with a cannonball service down the center line.

"Good shot," Jim called, careless in defeat.

"A lucky one." Jack remained solemn, embarrassed by Jim's praise.

She watched them come off the court and slipped out of her seat, intending to encounter them in the bar. They would still be at high pitch, glistening with perspiration, chests heaving.

Jim would be the best, she determined. Jack would be too meek. She had wanted Jim for a long time now. She had to find a way to get him.

While the ski area dozed in seasonal recess, the hotel and casino continued to hum with summer tourists.

Nick Diamado, as busy as ever, was in an expansive mood. His father had promoted him to executive vice-president at the spring board meeting and doubled his salary to a hundred and twenty thousand.

Just the fact that he now rated a six-figure salary was sufficient cause for rejoicing. But also, to his intense satisfaction, he now had a powerful say in the operation of both the hotel and the ski area.

Understandably, Alfredo Costa was not enthusiastic about the appointment. But Salvatore smoothed his feathers by making a very flattering speech to the board about the great contribution that Alfredo had made, underlining that he was still the final boss. "We are getting older, my friend," he said, "and we have to think of the future. I think we should give the young fellows a chance while we are still here to guide and control them."

"I want you to watch our interests, Nicolo," his father had said to Nick privately. "This place is becoming more and more useful to the family as a front. But don't antagonize Alfredo. Do you understand? Never cross him up without consulting me first, whatever you do. Costa is what makes this place legitimate. On no account can we afford to lose him."

Nick shrugged. It was little enough to ask. There were some changes that he wanted to make. For instance that goddam cocky mountain manager, Jim O'Malley. Still he knew O'Malley was tops at his job, one of the best in the country, and he also had to admit that part of his antipathy to Jim stemmed from his "insolence" in continuing to take Rena out after Nick had so obviously put his stamp of ownership on her. He could afford to wait. In any case, Rena was past history. She had been a mental aberration for Nick, a side-trip. He was over that now. With his new position and salary he was all the more determined that any serious attachment that he made would be restricted to the upper class. Perhaps a European girl. Maybe the daughter of a titled Englishman or a French countess. He must get to Europe more often. Maybe he would go over and ski there this year.

He recalled now that Jim O'Malley was full of praise for Skip Langdon's annual ski tours; he'd been ecstatic about his recent jaunt to Kitzbühel. Maybe Nick should try that. Not that he relished Jim's company over an extended period, but he could easily take care of that by making Jim change the dates of his annual vacation. On more mature consideration, Nick liked the idea of going with a group, so long as it was classy; it saved a lot of hassle and it would be more convivial, especially if Skip lived up to his reputation as an intimate of the jet set.

He'd talk to Skip Langdon next time he saw him.

Their last call was to pick up Silky's new finger. It was extraordinarily lifelike, made of some kind of rubbery plastic material, presumably reinforced inside with a skeleton of steel wire. It was slightly bent, at a very natural angle and fitted over his stump like a condom.

"Better wear it all the time," Jake suggested. "Get used to it."

"My itchy finger," Silky laughed, wiggling it around, then scratching his nose with it. "Not bad. Not bad at all."

The rest of their buying trip had been uneventful. They did their shopping, item by item, at a series of country stores and supermarkets. Among their purchases were snowmobile suits, four face masks, flashlights, spotlights, jack knives, fatigue boots, a razor-sharp machete, and several pairs of leather gloves. Everything to be used in the operation was to serve once only, then be discarded.

"Christ, even my jockey shorts?" Silky complained.

"Everything. It's a matter of discipline. It stops us getting careless."

Another major purchase on their way back through New York was a radio-controlled model airplane.

Returning home by the southern route, for a change of scenery, they holed up in Flagstaff, Arizona, while Jake spent a couple of days adapting the plane controls to the detonation of explosives. They went out to the Painted Desert and after enjoying themselves with the plane for an hour like a couple of schoolboys, they blew some small explosive charges to test the system.

"Well, at least you did something in the war," Silky said approvingly when they had completed the exercise without a single misfire.

Silky dropped Jake off in Boise at the end of May, then drove on through to San Francisco. They agreed to meet regularly through the summer to review the plan, intending to lock every detail by September 1. After that, they planned to do a few full scale rehearsals.

Jake's return to Boise was none too soon. It seemed that his stepmother had taken on a lover in his absence. This in itself did not bother Jake much, but the more he observed the new lodger, the more he became convinced that he was more interested in a piece of the business than he was in a piece of Mona's ass.

Jake played it cool for a while, making up to Mona, helping with the chores around the motel, keeping out of trouble and generally giving the impression that he was home to stay.

The more the lodger tried to pick on him, the harder he worked, so that when the fight started, Mona took his side. After all, he reasoned, if all Mona needed was a good screw once in a while, she did not have to import a stranger to screw up the business into the bargain. She was not a bad-looking woman, so why not keep the whole thing in the family, he reasoned. Laying his stepmother could create some long term complications, but, in the short term, it solved the dilemma. When the lodger discovered he had been cuckolded, he raised all sorts of shit about the immorality of it, finally barricading himself in the bar and refusing to leave. The upshot of it was that Mona called the police and had them shove him in the drunk tank and see to it that he never came back.

Diana Mitchell was watching Peter Mallory with mild amusement. It did not bother her in the slightest that Peter, who had brought her to the pool party, was making sheep's eyes at Nicole Gareau. Diana had planned it that way.

Nicole Gareau was Diana's best friend. Diana had planned that, too. Nicole's father was Phillipe Gareau, a Montreal millionaire industrialist, and, as far as Diana was concerned, that was enough to open a very special place in her heart for Nicole.

Billy came over to ask Diana to dance.

"No thanks, Billy." She was offhand with him. Billy was not cool. "You could get me a drink, though, rum and coke."

Most of the kids at the party were dull—awkward and adolescent—especially the boys. She preferred college men, guys with a little more poise and experience.

But even if the crowd was boring, the setting, the luxurious Gareau pool-house, was ample compensation. The quadrophonic hi-fi, the well stocked bar, the glass wall opening to the gently lighted pool, the suspended peacock chair in which she lolled, wrapped in a huge, soft yellow bath sheet—these were the touches of luxury that appealed to Diana.

She preferred to be here on the Gareau estate alone with Nicole, riding the horses, playing tennis on the all-weather court or lying around the pool in the sun. The rest of them were way out of their league. Of course, Nicole had to be humored; one did not get to be best friends with Nicole Gareau unless one could contribute something. She had wanted a party, so Diana had organized it.

At seventeen, Diana was a woman of the world. She did not drift aimlessly. She knew exactly what she wanted out of life and how to get it.

She had an uncanny understanding of people, how to manipulate them, how to give them what they wanted.

Her parents, for instance. They wanted to be proud of her. She took pains to give them what they wanted. Intelligence. She got good grades at school without much effort. Poise. She treated her parents as equals and it flattered them, made them feel young. Popularity. She was a natural leader, always surrounded by kids of her own age even if, secretly, they bored her. Thoughtfulness. She did little chores around the house for her mother. It really was not much of an effort in return for her parents' good humor.

They doted on her and she took full advantage of it.

She was really a little ashamed of her parents. They were very nice but—so ordinary. Her father was a fairly successful consulting engineer, her mother just a housewife and not a very good one at that.

Jacques Leclerc was eyeing her from across the room. Jacques was not bad—at least he was going to college this fall. He had obviously been hot for her all summer, but she hadn't given him the time of day while she had been going steady with Peter. Seeing Peter make a play for Nicole, he was probably calculating his chances. She smiled at him, commanding his presence.

"Would you like to dance, Diana?" He seemed a little tense.

"Alright," she said, "but I want to go and change first. Wait for me."

She did not like to dance in a bathing suit. Her most erotic feature was her ample bosom. It was not quite as

78

firm as she would have liked and dancing without a bra embarrassed her.

Once she had got over feeling awkward, she had come to appreciate the value of her glandular assets. She looked so much more grown-up than the other girls. A good pair of breasts seemed to make up for almost any other physical deficiency—which was a good thing, because her stupid parents had never been able to afford to have her teeth straightened. "You're all tits and teeth," a boy had once said to her in anger and she had never forgotten it.

Passing Billy on the way to the changing cubicle, she said, "Everyone has to be out by eleven-thirty, Billy. Mr. Gareau said so. Be a good boy and pass the word, will you? Don't worry about Peter and Jacques. I've told them already."

It was not true. But the hangers-on had overstayed their time. She wanted a quiet tête-à-tête with Nicole and their dates. Jacques would do for tonight.

The thought of going back to school depressed her. Both Peter and Nicole went to boarding schools, so she would not see them again until Christmas. If they were going to make plans for the December holiday, they had to start thinking now.

She was sitting on the chesterfield next to Jacques, making it obvious to Nicole and Peter that she held no grudges. "Why don't we all go skiing at Christmas?" she said. "I mean at a posh resort somewhere, maybe out West? Brent Mountain is such a bore."

Brent Mountain was the centerpiece of a development where they all spent their weekends. The Mallorys had a huge ranch house at the top of the chair lift, the Mitchells a more modest A-frame at the base. The Leclercs had a pretentious fieldstone near the tenth tee of the golf course and the Gareau Estate ran the length of the eighteenth fairway.

Nicole seemed uncertain. "I guess my parents will want to go to Florida."

"Florida again?" Diana had been there last year as Nicole's guest. "It's so gauche. Such a nouveau riche crowd at Christmas, all the excursion people. Anyway, Christmas should have a festive setting. It's just too banal to spend Noël on the beach!"

"It could be fun," Peter said. "I agree with Diana. I'm

79

sick of Brent Mountain. I've always wanted to ski. West. Aspen, maybe, or Vail."

"Mount Casino," Diana said. "It's the best. Terrific mountain and they have indoor tennis. And gambling and discotheques—imagine the four of us there. What a time we would have!"

"My father doesn't ski much." Nicole was hesitant.

"But he's crazy about tennis," Diana reminded her.

Jacques was thinking about two weeks in the same hotel as Diana. He knew that she screwed, because Peter had told him. "I think it would be a super idea," he said.

"There," Diana appealed to Nicole. "Everyone wants to go. All you have to do is talk your parents into it."

"I don't know if my father can afford it," Jacques said.

"Don't be silly, Jacques. Your father has the Gareau advertising account, doesn't he? If Phillipe Gareau goes and suggests it to Mr. Leclerc, he won't be able to refuse. What a chance to entertain his biggest client! He'll probably write off the whole trip."

"That's true," Jacques agreed.

"And Peter, if your father thinks that you're dating Nicole"—Peter gaped at Diana—"he'll go, for sure. You know what a social climber he is."

Nicole shrugged. Diana followed through for the kill. "I'll help you. Everyone is depending on you, don't you see, Nicole? If your father agrees, then everyone goes. Surely he can't be that selfish?"

"Alright, I'll try. I suppose that if I really press him— make it sound terribly important . . ."

"Of course," Diana clapped her hands. "He adores spoiling you. And don't forget to tell him about the tennis."

Everyone could afford it except the Mitchells. But they would go. Diana would see to that.

The week following Diana Mitchell's masterful orchestration of the Brent Mountain junior sophisticates, Philippe Gareau sat at his desk on the twenty-third floor of the huge Place Ville Marie building in downtown Montreal. At thirty-six, he was young to be the president of a powerful corporation with controlling interests in various shipping, construction, and food-processing companies. Of course, it hadn't hurt to have started near the top, as comptroller, after marrying Lise Frenette, eldest daughter of the founder. He had simply stepped into the old man's shoes after his death, two years ago. He was a healthy, good-looking man, perhaps twenty pounds overweight. He spoke now in French, though he could also speak English with reasonable fluency.

"You understand, I am sure, Armand. Whereas I will of course have the final say, it would not be right for me to turn down the proposal. The man is tops in the food business and I paid a lot to get him. It would not be smart to clip his wings before he gets started."

"Of course, Philippe." What else could Armand Leclerc say? They were discussing the corporation's advertising account. Armand's advertising agency had held it for ten years now, all six divisions. It was by far his largest account, the core of his business, billing nearly two million. Without it, he would have a problem surviving.

Leclerc and Bellechasse was the biggest French-Canadian agency in Canada. They prided themselves on knowing the Quebec market and creating original campaigns in French; most of their competition used translators, doing little more than adapt their English campaigns. But the damned Americans were giving him tough competition. They were setting up complete French-speaking branch offices. Backed up by the research and marketing depth of their New York offices, these new hybrids were becoming very effective.

Philippe had recently hired a new marketing vice-president, an American who had had his basic training in Procter and Gamble. He felt that agencies should be kept sharp by being forced to present for the account once every few years against open competition. Not only that, he believed in different agencies for different divisions, rather than putting all his eggs in one basket.

"It's just a question of making a formal presentation. You know so much about our business, Armand, so much inside stuff that you are bound to win—at least keep a major portion," Philippe continued suavely. He always did his job calmly, even the dirty chores, like firing people. He just did whatever had to be done.

"Sure, Philippe." Armand passed his hand over his graying hair, surreptitiously wiping a veneer of sweat from his brow. He was ten years older than Philippe, exquisitely groomed, but a little florid, the penalty to be paid for a lifetime of two or three martini lunches.

"Well, that's fine then, Armand." Philippe was glad to leave the subject. "Whatever happens, we will not make any changes until next spring so it's clear sailing for you for at least six months."

Six months, thought Armand, inwardly groaning. Six months of anxiety and fear. He doubted that his ulcer could stand it. It was a death sentence.

"Now," Philippe said with a broad smile, offering Armand a cigar from the silver box on his desk, "to lighter things. I understand that the kids have cooked up a little adventure. Lise tells me that we are all going skiing at Christmas. That so?"

"I heard about it." Armand was noncommittal, hoping to God that Philippe was going to veto it.

"Well," Philippe continued expansively, "my little Nicole is growing up. Pretty as her mother already. Same sort of temperament, too. Knows what she wants."

"She's a lovely girl," Armand agreed, pessimistic about the direction in which Philippe was leading.

"As you know," Philippe went on, "we usually go to our house in Florida for Christmas. But I can see that it's a little dull for Nicole. I like to have a good rest, loaf about on the beach, that sort of thing. She doesn't get to meet many boys." He grinned. "At her age, boys are important. She's growing up, Armand."

I can't afford it, thought Armand. How can I stop him?

"Lise thinks that it would be very good for Nicole to stay at a big hotel. Give her poise, you know, variety of food, new people, sophisticated atmosphere, that kind of thing. Better to teach her now than have her swept off her feet by the first young man she meets.

"I agree with Lise. Give Nicole her head, but under close supervision, right?"

Armand forced a smile. If it had not been for the danger of losing the whole account, he would have said no to the imminent question. But he had to keep in with Philippe. Philippe was the only man who could save him.

"I understand that you've already committed yourself to going. That's what Nicole says. Mount Casino, I believe? Right?"

"Yes, that's right." Armand was quite emphatic. My God, who got us all into this? He was sure it was not Nicole's idea. She had probably never heard of Mount Casino. It must be that precocious little hussy, Diana Mitchell. The goddam social climbing little bitch!

"Arthur Mallory called me about it yesterday," Philippe continued. "His boy, Peter—nice young fellow— and very good for Nicole's English—he is kind of sweet on Nicole, you know. Arthur says that Peter is mad to go as long as Nicole goes, too. Arthur thinks it would be fun."

Arthur would. He was as bent as little Miss Lolita Mitchell on ingratiating himself with the Gareaus. Armand only hoped for Arthur's sake that his wife, Jane, would behave herself. She was on the wagon now, but given a plethora of cocktail bars and a soupçon of Christmas spirit, she might fall off with a resounding crash.

"What about the Mitchells?" asked Armand.

"Oh, I expect they will come. Diana will, for sure. She's Nicole's best friend."

There it was, then. There was no escape. Five grand minimum, if the gambling did not go against him. Armand suppressed a sigh.

"I'll get my secretary to make the reservations, then. Alright by you, Armand?"

"Mine can handle it if you prefer," Armand suggested. At least he could get some sort of control on the room rates.

"No, no," Philippe said grandly, "my treat."

I wish to Christ it was, thought Armand.

It was the third morning after Rena's return to Tahoe.

There was a knock at her door, making her heart leap. She had waited two long days for them.

"Hello, Rena."

She recognized Silky by his voice before she could adjust to his unexpected appearance. He had shaved off his beard, retaining only a neat black moustache. She was startled by his handsome appearance.

"Silky!" She ran to hug him. "Oh, God, I'm glad to see you!"

He closed the door behind him with one hand, with

83

the other he held her full weight as she clung to him. He waited patiently for her to calm down.

She bubbled with questions. "Will you have a beer? Or a coffee, or something? Where's Jake? What did you do all summer?"

Finally she calmed down. "I was so scared that you were not coming, Silky, that maybe something had happened."

Silky smiled but still said nothing. •

"It's still on, isn't it, Silky? The operation, I mean?"

"Of course," he grinned.

She sighed. At last she sat down.

"There are three things that I want to do on this trip," he said. "I can't stay long, so we had better get on with it.

"First,"—he pulled an envelope out of his pocket, carefully unfolding the contents—"the confession. Remember? Sorry to look as though we don't trust you but, well, it's our insurance."

She glanced at it quickly. "Of course." She signed it, making a show of not reading it in detail.

Silky gave her a sideways look. "You ought to read it, you know. It could get you ten years in jail."

She shrugged. "I trust you," she said, "even if you don't trust me."

"It's just a precaution. You will be holding the full amount, you know. If you were tempted . . ." She looked so hurt at the suggestion that he didn't complete his sentence. "Let's get on with the rest," he said, smiling encouragement.

"We have the whole plan," he continued, "worked out in detail now. However, the more we have checked it, the more it seems that we need to involve one more person."

She could not hide a look of disapproval.

"He only has a tiny part," Silky went on. "Just driving the getaway car. We calculate a fifteen-minute drive, that's all. He will know nothing more about the operation. We figure to pay him ten grand."

She felt better now. Silky seemed predetermined that it would be a man and obviously he would not rank as a coconspirator. For some reason, which she could not explain, she did not want any interlopers to share their close-knit camaraderie.

"Alright," she said, "what do you want me to do?"

"Well, we have two or three people in mind. There may be others. We ought to decide, be sure that the last link is in place, by December first. That's two weeks.

"Our prime choice is a guy called Charlie Potts. He is the number one vehicle driver at Mount Casino. Do you know him?"

"Yes. A bit." She had seen him around, knew that Jim O'Malley thought a lot of him. "Do you want me to ask him?"

"Christ, no!" Silky laughed. "We'll handle that. No. All we want you to do is to find out what you can about him. Judge whether he would be the type to go for this kind of proposition. And keep a lookout for any alternatives. It's something we can't do, because we don't want to be seen in this area."

"Sure." She could get information discreetly from Jim.

"Good. Give me your phone number here. I'll call you in ten days. Better use a code. If Charlie is O.K. say 'The hotel is full of people.' If he is no good say 'The hotel is half empty.' Understand?"

"Yes. But if he is not acceptable, do you want me to give you another name?"

"Not on the phone. If you have an alternative, say, 'I have a friend who drives a bus.' Then I'll drive up to see you. O.K.?"

"O.K." She was impressed at Silky's careful precautions. It made her feel safe.

"Well, all we have to do now," Silky said, lighting up a cheroot, "is to find a good hiding place for the loot. Let's look around the apartment."

They were inspecting the bedroom wardrobe, when the buzzer sounded. They froze.

"What's that?" Silky whispered.

"Front door."

"Who?"

"I don't know."

"I'll hide here," he said quickly. "Check the living room before you open the door. My beer glass. Things like that. Quick."

She opened the door to Jim O'Malley. "Hullo, Rena.

I heard you were back. I had an urge to take you to lunch. What d'you say?"

She thought quickly. The smell of Silky's cheroot smoke in the living room decided her. "I would love to," she said. "Just let me get my coat."

She left Jim on the threshold and ran to the bedroom. Silky said nothing, just nodded approval and gave her a goodbye hi-sign.

On the spur of the moment, she gave him a peck on the cheek. "Call me soon," she whispered.

Charlie Potts got the stamp of approval from Rena and duly received his summons to an interview.

He was thoroughly enjoying himself. He had won three straight hands of blackjack and was sipping contentedly at the free scotch-on-the-rocks that the waitress had brought him. He put his original stake on one side and started to bet with the house's chips.

He did not frequent the Sahara very often. When he had first arrived in Lake Tahoe, he had tried the casinos, attracted more by the nice class of chicks than by the urge to gamble. However, he had soon discovered that there was nothing free in the casinos. They always took your money in the end.

This visit was kind of special, though. Weird, really. He had received an anonymous telephone call. The message was brief and cryptic. He had been told that if he wanted to pick up ten thousand dollars, to get over to the Sahara, sit at a certain blackjack table, and wait for further contact.

With no reason to pass up the opportunity, and greatly intrigued by the mystery, Charlie did as he was told.

All of a sudden, a red-coated bellhop stood at his elbow, patiently waiting as Charlie calculated the chances on the blackjack hand in front of him. He decided on a twist, made twenty-one and collected another ten dollars.

"Mr. Potts?" the bellhop inquired.

"Yes, that's me." Charlie grinned at the flunky. "What do you want, man?"

"I have a message for you, sir." There was a small piece of pink paper lying in the middle of his silver tray.

Charlie glanced at it. "Call room 514." He read it without picking it up. "Where's the phone?" he asked.

The man pointed over to the corner, by the check-in counter. "Over there, sir."

"O.K." Charlie picked up his chips and unwound himself from his stool, ignoring the still proferred tray. He was not going to tip any monkey just for bringing a message.

He strolled across to the cashier's desk and turned in his chips, thirty bucks profit. It was a good omen.

A voice answered the phone, a man's voice. Too bad. Charlie had had a faint hope that maybe some old bag just wanted him to give her a good time.

"Come up to 514," the voice said. "The door's open."

Arriving at the fifth floor, he pushed the unlocked door, and found himself in the living room of a large suite. As he entered, the voice from the adjoining room told him to close the door and sit down.

The voice went on in quite a friendly, matter-of-fact tone, which took a lot of the scariness out of the strange situation, to tell him that he had been recommended for a particular job. "Sorry about the dramatics, Charlie," it said. "It's just safer for both of us if we never meet face to face."

"There's an outside chance," the voice continued nonchalantly, "that someone could get knocked off in this caper. If you knew too much about it, you would be an accessory after the fact and could be forced to plea bargain to save your skin. This would put us all in danger. But, if all you know is your part of the operation, then the risk for everybody is greatly reduced. All you have to do is drive a car for a few blocks."

Charlie was enjoying the whole thing, especially when the voice told him to help himself to a scotch, from the table by the window.

Next, he was told to look carefully at a map of Lake Tahoe, lying open on the coffee table in front of him. A route was marked in red pencil, starting from a big X, in the parking lot behind the Sahara.

"Look out of the window," the voice said, "and you will see a car with its lights on, directly below us. Get that spot fixed in your mind. It is absolutely critical."

He could tell exactly which parking spot it was, just

87

by studying the map, but he stuck his head out of the window, as he was told.

"Now go down there. Find that spot. Stand in front of it for ten seconds, holding your hands high above your head. You won't see anyone, at least not anyone to do with this particular job, but someone will be watching you, to see you have it right. Then come back up here."

So he found the spot and did as he was told. Then the plan was explained to him. Something was going to happen during the Christmas vacation. Two people would need to make a very hasty getaway. He was to be parked in that special spot, from four-thirty to ten on the evening of the job, with the engine running. The two people would appear suddenly and give him a password: "Fishhook. Remember that: Fishhook." All he had to do was drive them exactly along the short route indicated by the arrow, drop them, and then go straight home.

"Simple, isn't it?" The voice laughed.

"Seems easy. What's the catch?"

"There isn't one," the voice said. "We don't get caught."

He was told two more things. First, if he talked to anyone, he would be killed.

"Sorry about that," the voice apologized, "but you can see how it is."

Then he was told to look at the map again for ten minutes and ask any questions. Meanwhile, he helped himself to another drink.

"Now, if you're in, open the drawer of the desk, the middle drawer, and you will find an envelope addressed to you. It's your advance, one thousand dollars. Don't flash it around, or you'll cause suspicion. You get the other nine thousand, on the spot, when you drop your two passengers."

He took the envelope, looked inside, but did not bother to count the money.

"One more thing, Charlie, before you go. You need an alibi. You will use the old standby, the movie trick."

"The operation is set for the week between Christmas and New Year. Whatever you do, don't leave town at all during that week. Get it?"

"Sure. No problem."

"Good. I'll phone you two days in advance. Now,

make sure you understand this because your safety will depend on it. . . ."

"Shoot, man." The intensity in the other voice amused Charlie. He was quite cool himself.

"O.K. The day before the job, go to the movies. Make sure nobody sees you. Go alone and really watch it—make sure you remember the story. Got that?"

Charlie smiled. It sure was old hat. Christ, he had used this one to two-time a broad. "Yeah, I know," he said in a bored voice, "then I go back the day of the stickup—or whatever it is—buy a ticket and make sure that the chick in the box office recognizes me, right? Then I sneak out of a side entrance and go to the job, right?"

"Good boy, Charlie. You're a pro." The voice was relaxed now. "That's it, then, Charlie. Any questions?"

"Yeah," Charlie drawled. "How d'you get my name? Why me?"

"I just told you, Charlie. Because you're a pro. That's why."

They were down to the short strokes now. Setting up the transportation.

Getting the vehicles was one of the critical phases of the plan. They would be leaving them behind, so it was imperative to make it as difficult to trace them as possible.

The job called for a van and a station wagon, the van to be of quite a special type. Jake wanted one of those square type vans, the sort milkmen and bakers use. Not big, but a cargo area of perhaps fifteen by eight. It had to be possible to enter the cargo space through the driving compartment, but there also had to be a sliding door between the driving compartment and the cargo space, so that the two sections could be separated at will. The rear entrance had to be capable of being locked. Not the most common van, this type would usually be on a Ford or Chevrolet chassis, with the bodywork made to order by a custom body shop. It was not going to be the easiest thing to find, but a second-hand one should be available at a decent-sized truck dealer's.

One of the problems to be solved was the storage of the van. If Jake went back to Boise with it, obviously people would ask questions. Same with Silky, if he parked it outside his apartment. It was not that there was anything wrong in that. But, after the operation, and after the police started asking questions about the van which had been left at the scene, then people might start to remember.

They could rent a garage. But this was risky in its own way. People who rented property usually remembered what you looked like. Often you had to sign a lease. Jake discarded this idea at once.

"We'll leave it at an airport," he told Silky. "People going on vacation leave cars in the long-term parking at an airport for months. Nobody is going to worry about a van for a couple of weeks."

It was decided that they would buy the van in mid-December. That gave them fifteen days to locate one and park it. The longer they took to find it, the shorter the time they would park it.

Phoenix, Arizona was selected as the place for the buy.

"Why Phoenix?" asked Silky.

"No reason. That's why. It's an absolutely random choice, big enough to have a decent truck dealer or two, totally unconnected with anyone or anything else in the caper."

They flew down to Phoenix, using, as usual, separate planes. Jake looked over the truck and car lots and found what he wanted. It was a dark blue Ford van, 1971, with thirty-two thousand miles. He inspected it carefully, told the salesman he was not interested and left. Next day Silky bought it for cash, using another of their forged driving licenses. Jake drove it in leisurely fashion up the California coast while Silky worked in the cargo space building a heavy wooden locker secured with double padlocks along each side.

It was the day after Christmas when they finally parked the van at Sacramento airport.

After one ritual drink in the airport bar, they parted, moving to the final steps of preparation. It was good to be in the countdown phase at last. They both felt confident and elated.

Silky went back to San Francisco to pick up all the equipment. He was to drive everything back to Sacramento, switch it to the van, park his car and drive the van to Reno airport. As an additional precaution they had decided to use Reno as a base rather than Lake Tahoe and had made room reservations at separate motels under false names.

Jake flew on to Salt Lake City to rent a station wagon, using one of the phony licenses. He would drive it back to Reno.

They were to meet again in three days' time. The operation was set for New Year's Day.

CHAPTER FIVE

THERE WERE not sufficient first-class seats on the flight to accommodate everyone. Christmas was one of the peak seasons for airline travel.

There were sixteen in the party altogether, only ten of whom could be accommodated up front. Economy seats had been allocated to the two thirteen-year-old youngsters, Serge Gareau and Tim Mallory, Jacques Leclerc's twenty-two-year-old sister Danielle, her friend and Montreal roommate Suzanne Lavoie, and the Mitchell parents. The Mitchells had been the first to be drafted, in recognition of the obvious strain that such a trip would put on their financial resources, a kind gesture engineered by Jeanette Leclerc with Armand's strong disapproval. An exception had, of course, been made for Diana so that she could sit with Nicole in the first-class cabin.

Armand's annoyance was considerable when, within half an hour of take-off, the women decided to play bridge and he became the reluctant volunteer who had to change places with Kay Mitchell; paying a first-class fare for the privilege of sitting with the plebs was not his idea of economy. He leaned back in his seat with a large scotch and a small show of petulance.

The other economy passengers seemed perfectly satisfied with their lot. Danielle and Suzanne, two pretty girls on the threshold of romantic adventure, were too excited to care where they sat, and the two young boys were totally captivated by the thrill of being airborne.

Lise Gareau dealt the cards and studied her hand. She was a better-than-average bridge player.

An intelligent woman, Lise Gareau handled her inheritance with a sense of responsibility. She was very conscious of the gifts her late father had bestowed on her in lifting his family from obscurity to the ranks of the Montreal elite in one industrious lifetime. He wanted her to be a lady and had deprived himself in order to provide for her. She was determined to live up to his hopes for her.

She had taste—in clothes, in cuisine, in the decoration of her homes, and in her choice of husband. She maintained a loose rein on him in the disposal of the family fortune, but, generally speaking, he handled their business affairs with a great sense of dedication.

She had a strikingly beautiful daughter and a fine son and heir, both strictly brought up. Unlike many North American children, Nicole was only now, at sixteen, being allowed her first taste of freedom, while Serge was still treated as the child that he was.

Lise made the very best of herself, despite rather ordinary features, with charm, elegance, common sense and "force de poignet."

She made her three no trumps exactly as contracted.

Kay Mitchell picked up the newly dealt hand, racing to get her cards in order. She never seemed to be able to accomplish this as fast as the others, so that she usually had to beg for more time to make her bid.

The sight of three aces and a bevy of other court cards, as she riffled through, caused a small spasm in the pit of her stomach. Damn, she thought, I am probably going to have to play this hand. She had no confidence at all in her ability to make a contract and far preferred to sit on the fringe of the game as dummy or as a defender. She only played bridge to be amenable because Diana felt that it was an essential social grace, and the sight of more than ten points intimidated her.

Jeanette Leclerc was not afraid of men. But somehow she always found herself strangely nervous when she was close to Philippe Gareau. He was so sure of himself, so strong, so dominating. She liked men who demanded, who possessed, who dictated the terms of a relationship.

This holiday was a stroke of genius, and, of course, it

was Philippe who had organized it while Armand, in his old fashioned way, had grumbled about the expense. She half-regretted having vamped Armand away from his first wife. At the time, he had appeared so sophisticated, so worldly, always wining and dining people on his apparently inexhaustible expense account. His life seemed filled with glamorous people and fabulous places. As a junior secretary in the media department her infatuation had been tinged with envy.

But it was all a sham. Armand was a weakling. He was scratching and clawing to hang on, convinced that he was doomed to failure. He fawned on Philippe. There was no question in Jeannette's mind: she preferred the master to the slave—my God, she did.

Philippe caught her eye and held it; her loins seemed to melt.

"It's your bid, Jeanette," said Lise.

Jane Mallory was sure that the other girls had refused drinks in deference to her. Silly, patronizing bitches, she thought.

She had given up drinking for the sake of her son Peter. Only for him. To be able to retain his love and respect, to be able to live with him the joys of growing up.

The rest of them, the whole goddam lot, men and women combined, meant nothing to her. Except for Lise. Lise was the only human being in the whole bunch.

She hated flying. She needed a drink. She hated her husband. She needed a drink. She loved Peter. She would go without, fight down the fear, the insufferable atmosphere, the pounding headache.

A workaholic and an alcoholic, a marriage kneaded together like a plastic explosive bomb. It was Arthur's insatiable appetite for money, his singleminded pursuit of success in business, that had driven her to drink.

He had no thought of leisure, no time for diversions. Simple family affairs such as playing with his young sons, even casual conversation at mealtimes, interfered with his concentration.

He went to bed with other women—mostly whores—who would meet his limited needs.

He did not make love. He banged. No ceremony.

"Jane!" Her partner, Jeanette, was staring at her in horror. She looked down at the four cards before her.

"What?"

"Clubs are trumps, Jane," Lise said quietly.

Silky was waiting at the side entrance when Jake pulled up at Reno airport in the station wagon. They loaded his bag, boots and skis and two pack sacks. They still had a lot to do; they had to make the Mount Casino gondola lift before it closed.

Jake concentrated on the road. He felt the urge to make speed, but this was no time to get a ticket.

"Any problems?"

"No."

"Did you wear gloves?" The whole operation could tumble on one lousy fingerprint.

"Hell! I don't even take my gloves off to masturbate." Silky laughed, holding out his hands.

"Good. Is the tank full of gas?"

"Yes."

"Is all the equipment inside?"

"Everything. Except what we've got in here."

It was Silky's turn. "Did you call Rena and Charlie to give them the date?"

"About an hour ago."

"Everything O.K.?"

"Seemed like it. I feel confident about him."

"Did you book me a room?"

"Yes. City Motel."

"What's my name?"

"Cranston." He spelled it to be sure. "Charles Cranston."

"How's Mona?" He grinned. Jake had told him the story.

"I was only home two days. But I gave her enough to keep a smile on her face for a while. She's no chicken, but she sure is a grateful woman in bed. She'll do anything."

They pulled up in front of the Mount Casino hotel. Jake, with his usual caution, had realized that someone might be suspicious of a car left in the ski area park until past midnight. It was not far to walk the extra distance and they had plenty of time, half-an-hour before the gondola closed. Each of them donned one of the pack sacks.

"Got a knife?" Jake asked.

"In your pack."

"Flashlight?"

"In mine."

"O.K. Let's go."

They walked over to the ticket office and bought a single ride each. The girl looked at them a bit quizzically, not expecting to sell tickets at this time.

"We've just got in from Chicago." Jake smiled at her. "Got to get one run in today, after all that flying, to blow away the cobwebs."

There was not much lineup, so they got a gondola to themselves. The attendant glanced at their pack sacks, but said nothing. There were no rules against carrying them.

"Long way down," Silky said as they swung up the mountain, "I hope it's safe."

At the top, they put on their skis and turned down the Roulette trail. It was fairly narrow, with woods on both sides. Halfway down, Silky stopped on the side nearest the gondola, Jake pulling up a few yards above him.

They watched the skiers for a few moments, then Jake ducked into the woods. Silky waited for a group to go by and then, spotting a lull in the traffic, followed in behind Jake.

They skied slowly between the trees, across the fall line, until they judged themselves to be about in the middle of the wood. Then they took off their skis standing them solidly in the snow, hanging their poles over them. Silky started unpacking one of the pack sacks, threw a kapok sleeping bag to Jake and laid out one for himself. It was going to be a long wait, so there was no point in freezing to death.

Jake switched on the walkie-talkie. He had stolen it out of one of the grooming vehicles, on one of the earlier trips over from Squaw. By listening in on the drivers, they would have a fair idea where the vehicles were grooming tonight. It was another aspect of Jake's master plan.

They both got into the sleeping bags and lay absolutely quiet. The ski patrol would be doing a last sweep within the next hour. It wasn't likely they would come looking in the woods, but there was no point in taking chances.

They heard the first shift of grooming vehicles coming up the cat track.

"We've got company," Silky whispered.

After a while, they could see the flashers and headlights at the top of Thunderbolt. One of them swung off and started grooming Roulette. It was something to look at for a while.

The sun had set quickly, leaving a cold, clear, starlit night behind. It was a practically new moon; Jake had planned it that way, just in case. He would have preferred snow to reduce visibility, but the risk of being seen was very low if they took reasonable precautions.

Silky enjoyed the waiting. It was exciting to be back in action again, alone under the stars in enemy territory. Waiting was a test of guts. Any fool would get a shot of courage when the flak started flying, if only in self-defense. But it was the waiting, the wondering what was going to happen, the self-control needed to stay calm when there was still time to run away that separated the men from the boys.

Jake was going over everything once again. If there were any flaws in it, he had better find them now. Time was running out.

He started thinking about the telephone. The plan called for him to slash the line in order to cut the other side off from any two-way communication. He reconsidered. It was unlikely, but it could be that if something unforeseen happened, he and Silky might want to call out. Maybe they should keep the line open, just in case. He made a mental note of it. He would just take it off the hook, stuff it with a rag, and tape it. They had plenty of tape with the explosives.

Much better. Christ! Was there anything else like that —something he had overlooked?

Jake turned his mind deliberately to the subject of killing, visualizing the liquidation of a hostage in his mind. To make it more realistic he selected a real victim, the desk clerk at the motel in Reno. He pushed him down to the floor and shot him in the back of the neck, aiming the bullet at an upward angle, as Silky had told him, so that the bullet would perforate the brain.

It was not his first dummy run. He had thought about it a lot, practicing on innocent strangers in his imagination. When he had been up to Salt Lake City to rent the station wagon, he had spent a whole evening in a crowded bar, mentally executing everyone in the room.

It was a fascinating exercise. He found it was easier to execute old people than young ones, ugly people than pretty girls. Fat people seemed to be easiest of all. The barman was fat and ugly and had body odor. If Jake had had a gun with him, he might have waited outside for him and plugged him in a back alley, just for the experience.

Silky was right. No use being squeamish about it or worrying about the consequences if they got caught. They were into a deadly game and commitment to kill was what would win it.

Only maniacs and sadists kill in cold blood, Silky had said. That was what the police would bet on. So what did that mean? Only maniacs and sadists got to be successful hijackers? That was stupid. It took brains and planning to pull a heist like this one; guts, not psychosis, to see it through.

He was sure of himself now, impatient for the action.

He glanced at his watch. It was getting on toward ten o'clock. The grooming vehicle was over the other side of the run, still plodding up and down. The walkie-talkie was fairly quiet, except for an occasional wisecrack between vehicles.

"What do you think?" he said.

"We could go and have a look."

"O.K. Let's go."

They rolled the sleeping bags and packed them. They put on their skis and started off through the wood. They moved directly across the fall line; it was too dark to try downhill between the trees.

They came out on the side of Thunderbolt, just below the gondola. They could see the cars above them, suspended on the cable, like prehistoric birds hovering over their prey.

"Go and check."

Silky slid off noiselessly to one of the towers, on which the gondola cable was suspended. The towers were numbered in big white numerals, so that if anything went wrong, the base could pinpoint the problem according to the number of the tower.

He came back. "Number Five."

"Good." They had decided to put ground charges under the upper ones, Number Five and Number Three, and top charges on Two and Four.

They both skied back to the tower, one at a time. Fortunately there was no grooming on Thunderbolt, at least not on this shift. But the vehicles usually used Thunderbolt for their final descent. That would not be until about eleven-thirty.

Silky unpacked the second backpack, handing Jake a collapsible shovel. Jake started digging round the base of the tower. It was not hard work. Much of the snow was relatively new. It only took him about twenty minutes to go down three feet, in a circle round the base of the tower.

Meanwhile Silky worked methodically on his charges. He unpacked his bed roll, laying his tools, explosives, and detonators in neat order, so that he could grab what he wanted in the dark, without looking.

"O.K. Go ahead," Jake panted.

Silky laid his charges slowly, double checking as he went. Then he switched on a pencil light, taking care to aim it uphill, and went over everything again, in a final run through. "O.K. fill it."

Jake refilled the hole to twelve inches from the top. Then Silky went through the same process, with an identical charge. They were fairly sure that some explosives experts would be called in. They would analyze the tower bases as being the likely target, and they would find the first charge. They would disarm it, and, if the ruse worked, they'd move on to the next tower, leaving the lower charge still in place.

When Silky was finished, Jake refilled the hole to the top, while Silky repacked his equipment. Then, putting on their skis, they stepped up and down over the hole, tamping the snow into place. It was eleven-fifteen.

They moved on down opposite Number Four tower. Jake wanted Silky to wait for the vehicles to go by, but he wouldn't. "There is no way they will be looking up there," he said.

Silky selected what he wanted and walked over to the

tower, sinking deep in the snow with each step. He should have brought snowshoes, he realized.

There was a steel ladder on the side of the tower. This was used, in normal circumstances, for running repairs. He shinned up the ladder to the top and waited. He could hear the vehicles on their way down. In a few minutes they came by, six of them. They reminded Silky of tanks rumbling into battle. What a beautiful target, he thought.

He waited until they had all passed, then started packing a charge on the inside of the big crossbeam. Again, this was a backup charge. If the explosives experts did find the lower charges, they would be sure that they had disarmed the lot. They would not expect charges on the top as well; in fact, they simply would not have time to find them all.

Jake had figured all this out. In any case it would not really be that much of a disaster, even if they did find all the charges, because they would still have the hostages as a trump card.

"It's a question of psychology," he explained. "At the start we will have the entire initiative. They will bust their guts to break our advantage. When they find the first charges, they will figure that the initiative has swung to them. They will feel smug. Then we will shove them right back to square one. They will lose their cool, they will have used up a lot of time, and the advantage will swing right back to us. That's the way we want it."

"It's good. I have to hand it to you. But it adds to the time that it will take us."

"The longer it takes to set the charges, the longer it will take them to disarm them."

Silky came down the tower again and trudged back to where Jake was waiting.

They decided to take a short break while they watched to see if another shift was coming back up. They saw the first machine move off, going toward the cat-track.

It obviously was safe to go on down to Tower Three. They followed the same routine of double charges, one deep and one shallow, then moved down to Tower Two, where Silky set another top charge. It took him a bit more time than the first. His hands were getting painfully cold. When he returned to Jake in the wood, he suggested a ten-minute break.

As soon as his fingers had thawed, Silky took off. He felt like letting fly, relying on his reflexes to keep him from falling in the dark. But this was no time to get a broken leg. So he snowplowed down, like a beginner, with Jake about fifty feet behind him. They headed for the far corner of Thunderbolt, to the Number One chair lift. They were going to lay bottom charges on the two lowest towers; only one charge each, this time.

This was the most dangerous part. They were much closer to the lodge. They were on open hill, with no wood cover. Also, they were much nearer the garage. They could see the lights. Someone was working overtime on a vehicle in the workshop. But they were becoming more proficient with practice. The towers were much smaller, so it took Jake less than ten minutes to dig his hole. They finished Tower Two in less than half-an-hour, then moved down to Tower One.

Just as Jake was finishing his last hole, they heard the garage door slam. The lights had been switched off. A second later the beam of car headlights swept across the hill. They fell flat on their faces. The car was doing a back and forth maneuver, obviously turning around. For a moment that seemed an eternity, Jake stared straight up the beam from his position, flat in the snow.

"Holy shit," he said.

"Stay down. He can't see you." Silky spat the words out.

The car immediately took off down the hill, winding below the lodge buildings, and disappeared.

Silky went back to work laying his charges. Jake watched him, taking a minute or two to recover his composure.

"That's it," said Silky making a last pencil-light inspection. "All ready for the fireworks."

They gathered together all their equipment and shouldered the pack sacks. They skied down, past the lift line and into the car park.

"Wait here," Jake said. "I'll get the car." There was no need for two men, loaded down with skis and luggage, to walk about in an open invitation to questions.

Silky stacked the skis in a narrow lane, between two buildings, and waited.

He heard the car coming, got the equipment ready, but stayed in the shadows until he was sure that it was Jake and not the man from the garage returning. They loaded the station wagon quickly and swung out of the lot, back down to the highway.

"I'm hungry," said Silky.

"So am I. We should be able to find an all-night diner."

"Well, that went pretty well. The car from the garage scared me, though," Jake continued.

"You scare too easily. Remember, people tend to see what they expect to see. Even if the driver had seen two people by the chair lift, he would've thought he was dreaming. Or he would've decided it was none of his goddam business."

"I guess you're right."

"I know I am."

It was well after three in the morning, and they had to drive all the way back to the outskirts of Reno before they could find anywhere to eat. They both ordered steak and fries. "I just thought of something," Jake said between mouthfuls. "From now on we should practice using our own code names. I'm Andy and you're Tim. Get that fixed in your head, Tim, my boy, because, if something goes wrong during the operation and you suddenly yell out, 'Hey, Jake! Look out!,' the ball game is over. One slip like that and we're nailed."

"O.K., Andy." Silky laughed. "I always thought Jake was a shitty name, anyway."

They topped up with some apple pie, and Jake drove Silky back to his motel. On a whim, he dropped into Harold's, drank a large scotch and put seven-and-a-half dollars in one of the slot machines. Despite all his planning, a little superstition inside him kept saying, "If you are lucky now, you will be lucky all the way." He hit a thirty-five dollar jackpot with his thirty-first quarter and went home thoroughly satisfied with the night's work.

Saturday morning was cold and gray. It looked as if there was more snow on the way. The mountain was already crowded with skiers, arrayed in a fanfaronade of vivid colors. Red and yellow boots, gold and silver poles,

102

harlequin jackets, striped gloves, pink tuques, and polka-dotted pants defied the achromatic setting.

Pepi Mueller was up early for a change. The promotion of Nick Diamado to executive vice-president seemed to have acted as a stimulant. He made his final check at the ski school desk. It was going to be a busy day, with a hundred-and-sixty-two people taking group lessons; many of them charter groups from Montreal, New York, and Miami. He hoped that the full complement of instructors would turn up.

He left Donna in charge of last-minute registrations, and went down to the instructors' locker room to get everyone moving. Ski school was at ten o'clock, but Alfredo liked to see all the instructors out at least ten minutes early, standing in a circle, each alongside his or her flagged positions. It was good for business, Alfredo said; it caught the attention of the impulse buyer, and gave a professional appearance.

Pepi counted heads. Eleven. There were supposed to be thirteen. It seemed that Jerry and Kathy had not shown up.

"Please guys," he fussed. "It's ten to. You're supposed to be outside now. Please!"

By ten o'clock, everyone was in place. Kathy, the last one in, had shown up just in time. Out of spite Pepi decided to give her the beginners. Nobody wanted beginners on a cold day, because you did not get the chance to move around enough.

Rena waited patiently at her regular position, flag number five.

A big man with a French accent stepped up to her, puffing from his climb up the gentle slope.

"Are you Rena Dalmain?"

"Yes, sir. I expect you're Mr. Gareau." She smiled. She always took the trouble to check at the desk for the names of the people in her class.

"That's right." He beamed, pleased at her deference. "We have a whole group in your class. All friends."

"Good," she said brightly, "I hope that I will be a friend, too."

"Of course, Mademoiselle." He grinned again. She watched the rest of them as they gathered together, making last-minute adjustments to their equipment. It was nice to have a group of people who knew each other. It did away with the early shyness and nervousness.

She studied them with a practiced eye. She could tell their prowess by the way they stood on skis. The kids were all good, the women adequate. Two of the men, Philippe Gareau and the tense-looking one, were out of their class. They should be in Beginners. Perhaps, when she got to know them better, she would be able to suggest it without insulting them. "O.K.," Rena said. "Good morning, ladies and gentlemen. I'm your instructor, Rena Dalmain. Now, this is an intermediate class. We will be skiing all the intermediate terrain and later in the week some of the expert. Are you all fairly experienced? Do you all ski parallel?" No one demurred. "Good then," Rena continued, "we'll go up the chair lift. If you will follow me up, I'll wait for you at the top of Thunderbolt." With that, she skated over to chair Number One, getting into the lift line.

She rode up on the double chair with Danielle Leclerc, whom she surprised by talking easily in French.

Finding herself with a kindred spirit, Danielle wasted no time in asking Rena where the action was. "Suzanne and I are quite independent as a rule. As a matter of fact we share an apartment together in Montreal. We don't want to spend the whole vacation with the young kids or," she giggled, "with all the parents. We would like to branch out a bit. You understand?"

"Of course," Rena said with a smile, "you want to know where the boys are."

Danielle nodded coyly.

"Try the Whi-Ski bar at around four o'clock when the lifts close," Rena suggested. "There's usually a lively crowd at that time. I'll watch for you and gladly introduce you around."

"Oh, thank you so much. You're very kind."

"It's nothing." Rena was pleased to do it. She found Danielle's frankness refreshing.

The group assembled at the top. She watched Danielle and Suzanne chatting together excitedly.

Despite the dull day, it was a breathtaking view, with the lake below surrounded by huge peaks as far as the eye could see. Even now, they were not at the top of the mountain. They were on a plateau, about halfway up, around sixty-five hundred feet above sea level. People skied down to the right and to the left, in the opposite direction from Thunderbolt, to connect with chairs to the summit.

As though guessing what they were thinking, Rena pointed up to the left. "The highest point of the mountain for skiing is at eleven thousand feet. You take that lift there, Number Three, then ski down Roulette and pick up Number Five to the top. You can see both sides of the mountain from up there. We'll do it later in the week."

Guessing that the teenagers were the best skiers in the group, she asked Peter Mallory to lead off and the others to follow him down. "Just ski normally," she said. "Let me see you in action. I don't intend to stop you every few minutes with lectures. That way we'll get cold. I'll catch up with you one at a time during the morning and give you some hints."

As she had foreseen, Philippe Gareau and Arthur Mallory skied far below the intermediate standard. Philippe was on his butt before he had gone fifty yards and Arthur only just missed making it a double disaster.

Well, she had other charges. She took off, overtaking the slower ones and judging them as she passed. Lise Gareau, Danielle, Suzanne were quite competent, Jeanette Leclerc and Jane Mallory hesitant, and the rest, the young gang, had already reached the bottom.

When they returned to the top she decided to work on some of the ladies first. She took the five women aside. "You're all inclined to turn your upper bodies too much. Let me see you anticipate your turns. Turn your hips, legs, knees, but not your upper bodies. Now. Just pretend that you have a big billboard on your chests and everyone in the lodge down there wants to read what is written on it. So you must keep the billboard facing the lodge all the way down, still turning with your hips, legs, and knees. Get the idea?"

Everyone nodded. It seemed a good way to explain a difficult maneuver.

"O.K. Down you go. Let them read the message now."

By the time the two hour session was over, she still had had no time to talk to the kids. But she had the impression that the class might be smaller tomorrow. Phillipe and Arthur had quit at the end of the second run.

Nick Diamado was in his office checking credit approvals. It was an idea of his own that had contributed to a nice increase in gambling turnover. Every guest who booked at the hotel was checked out with a credit agency and given a maximum limit for credit at the casino whether he or she asked for it or not.

It was a matter of record that most gamblers would spend more than the money that they had brought with them, if credit was available. So instead of having to refuse them or make time-consuming enquiries when they were in the mood to spend, he did the documentation in advance. Those whose credit was good and wanted it were surprised to receive immediate approval. They were flattered and he was covered.

"Philippe Gareau?" He looked at his card. "One hundred-and-fifty grand without reference," he said to the clerk who was taking notes, "another hundred with my approval if required."

"Arthur Mallory?" He hesitated. He had the money but he was a slow payer. "Hundred grand, tops."

"Armand Leclerc?" He squeezed nervously on the frame of his glasses; it was a risky one. "Five grand on his own. Up to thirty-five, with Gareau or Mallory as guarantor."

"Sam Mitchell? A dud. No privileges." He went on through the list of about seventy names, amounting to a total credit of one million, seven-hundred thousand dollars, a nice additional take if they all spent it. All the cashiers would have a record of the information. There would be no fuss other than the signing of a simple demand note.

Rena spotted Danielle and Suzanne at the entrance of the Whi-Ski bar. She waved them over to the big table where she was sitting with a group of instructors, patrollers, and other assorted ski-freaks.

The girls were welcomed by a bunch of leering male

faces. When they opened their mouths and began to talk with the accents of Catherine Deneuve in a perfume commercial, the leering turned to unabashed lust.

In spite of this sexual attention, the girls handled themselves well, amusing everyone but encouraging no one. Whatever happened, it seemed they would be kept busy for the rest of their vacation. So, having assured herself that they had a suitable selection of escorts, Rena excused herself. She had a seven o'clock date with Jim O'Malley.

Rena took more than usual care with her appearance: she was making herself up to please Jim. He was special. He was nice, she decided. Very nice. He was a manly man, strong, athletic, hardworking. And a gentle man, intelligent, charming, humorous. A well-rounded man with a commonsense philosophy. He enjoyed his life and transmitted that enjoyment to the people with whom he shared it.

It was a long time since there had been a particular man in her life. She was not in love with him—not yet, at any rate. But she was attracted to him.

She had been going out with him fairly steadily since she had returned, and she knew very well that he had a lot of girl friends and was not in search of a serious attachment. Neither was she. But he did treat her with respect, as though she was special to him. He made her feel important.

She was thinking now about her part in another affair. In three days, Silky and Jake would put their plan into action. In three days, her life would be entirely transformed for better—incredibily, irrevocably better—or worse, hideously, horribly worse.

What to do with Jim in three days? Cool him down, protect herself against remorse? Clutch the opportunity to spend pent-up emotion, to taste the elusive joy of loving and being loved? Which should it be?

Three days. The last three days in the life of Rena Dalmain. After that she would be a different person.

She stood before her mirror, staring at the last of Rena Dalmain, long blond hair above a blue gray suede pantsuit and handmade gaucho boots.

She swept up her fur coat and strode over to meet Jim in the hotel cocktail bar.

The groups-within-the-group-from-Montreal were settling down.

Danielle and Suzanne had run in to change, then taken off to eat their dinner at the local McDonald's in company with two ski instructresses and a couple of carloads of men.

The younger group, six of them, were sitting at a table presided over by Diana Mitchell, who had ordered a bottle of Taitinger Blanc de Blanc and sampled it with great solemnity.

The older group sat together drinking a good Vosne Romanée with a selection of steaks, roast cornish hens, and one poached turbot. Kay Mitchell had ordered the fish, and Philippe, after making a gracious gesture of offering her a half bottle of Chablis to herself, had ordered the red Burgundy, convinced that she had not the slightest taste for wines anyway.

"I don't think I'm going to ski-class tomorrow," Philippe announced. "It's too strenuous. I shall take a private lesson in the afternoon. What do you say to tennis in the morning, Arthur?"

"Good idea. I'm with you on the private lesson, too. I'm a bit rusty."

Jane Mallory lifted her glass to her lips. "I'll drink to that," she said, giving Arthur a cold smile. The wine tasted pretty good. She held out her empty glass in front of Philippe so that he could not refuse to refill it without making a scene.

"Jane, watch it," Arthur commanded peremptorily.

She ignored him, her eyes wandering to Peter at the other table. He seemed so content, so totally captivated by Nicole. He had no eyes for any other woman—certainly not his mother. She was happy for him, but she could not share his happiness. She was alone again. She sighed. To hell with the wagon! What was the point of sharp wits and senses if all they served was to accentuate one's sensitivity to pain?

"Excuse me," she said, "I'm going to powder my nose."

"I'll come with you," Jeanette said. Silly bitch. They walked across the dining room in Indian file.

"You go first," Jane said to Jeanette, not waiting for an answer. As soon as Jeanette closed the powder room door, Jane stepped up to the bar, swigged a quick double scotch and made it back just in time to fall into step behind Jeanette for the march back to the table.

Everyone looked more cheerful now. Even Arthur.

Nicole came across to the grown-ups' table to talk to her mother. "We are going to the discotheque, maman. Is that alright?" Peter danced attendance on her, straining to give the impression that, if Madame Gareau would entrust Nicole to his charge, he would defend her with his life.

Lise smiled at them both. "Of course," she said. Then to Peter she added: "But I want her in bed by midnight. Is that understood?"

"Oh, yes, Madame Gareau. Thank you very much." Peter shone with delight.

Kay Mitchell watched with amusement. How quaint, she thought, this regal expression of parental authority. Diana would never dream of going through such a humiliating performance. But then, of course, Diana had so much more poise than Nicole.

Dutifully, Serge came up for his instructions. "Maman," he said, "Tim and I are going to play table tennis in the games room, O.K.?"

"Yes, darling." Lise gently brushed back his untidy hair. "Ten-thirty bed for you. Is that a promise?"

"Yes, maman."

"Same for you, Tim," Jane Mallory added belatedly.

Tim nodded, giving his mother a quizzical glance. Perhaps he had noticed the slight slur in her speech.

"Well, what are the old folks going to do?" Jeanette said brightly. Coming from by far the youngest woman left at the table, this remark did not go unnoticed by Jane Mallory.

"Well I'm all for trying the casino," Jane said. "But maybe you," she gave Jeanette a sparkling smile, "would rather go and dance with the kids."

"Oh, no." The remark was lost on Jeanette. "I just adore gambling. What do you say, Philippe?"

"Why not?" Philippe said expansively, between puffs

at the cigar that he was lighting. "Anyone got a better idea?"

Nick Diamado saw them come in from the window in his office. He had a man at the door whose job it was to signal him when big money walked in.

He immediately slipped on the jacket of his maroon tuxedo and descended to welcome them onto the gambling floor.

"Good evening, Mr. Gareau. Welcome to our casino." A cashier stood at his elbow, summoned by a single flick of Nick's fingers. "Carlo here will arrange to get chips for you, if you would like to play."

"Oh!" Philippe was mildly surprised. "That's fine, then. I think we will play a little roulette." He looked at the others, as he peeled off five one-hundred-dollar bills. "Is that alright with everyone?"

Another flunky appeared magically at Nick's side. "Open up table ten for this party," he commanded. "The other tables are very crowded," he said to Phillipe. Then, turning to Lise, he bowed. "Please, madam. Jack, here, will show you to your table."

As they moved off, Nick sidled up beside Philippe again. "May I have a word with you, Mr. Gareau?"

Philippe looked at him amiably. "Sure, what's the problem?"

"Oh no problem, sir, no problem at all." Nick smiled smarmily. "I would like you to know that your credit is arranged. Just refer the cashiers to me if you have any problem. The same goes, of course, for Mr. Mallory and —in a much more modest amount, you will understand —Mr. Leclerc."

Philippe said generously, "He's good for his debts."

"Really? My information was that . . ." Nick trailed off purposely.

"Nonsense. I guarantee Armand Leclerc. He's one of my best friends."

A flick of Nick's fingers and Carlo was standing beside them again.

"Carlo. Mr. Gareau will guarantee Mr. Leclerc's credit. Is that right, Mr. Gareau?"

"Of course."

"Thank you, Mr. Gareau," Nick made a small bow.

Everything was in order; Carlo was a witness. "And what about Mr. Mitchell, sir?"

"Ah-ha," Philippe laughed, "I don't know what your credit policies are. But between you and me," he said, winking, "I don't think my credit manager would risk too much on him, if you know what I mean."

"Yes, sir. Thank you sir. Now, a drink for your party? Champagne perhaps?"

"Perhaps for the ladies. I'll have a scotch."

The discotheque was a constellation, a stunning light show of flashing colors and reflections, turning the dancers into weird galactic creatures, a science-fiction microcosm of scene and sound.

Hardly conscious of her partner, Jacques, Diana writhed in ecstasy on the painted glass floor, letting the music consume her.

The music crashed into silence, leaving her suspended in another aeon.

"Wow!" She sat down in a kind of trance. "What a place! I mean, this is living!"

"Oh, it's wild," agreed Nicole. "It really was a brilliant idea of yours, Diana, to come to Mount Casino."

Diana accepted the compliment with a shrug. She was on another planet. Thank God she had thought to bring some grass.

She pulled the red leather case from her handbag and lit up a joint, taking a couple of deep pulls. "Mm, that's good," she said, "anyone want a hit?"

"What is it, Diana? Grass?" Nicole asked in awe.

"Right. Want some?"

Nicole glanced at Peter in confusion. "No," Peter said firmly for both of them. "Don't be such a jerk, Diana. You can smell it a mile away. You will get us thrown out—or worse."

Diana gave him a scornful look. "Haven't we suddenly become a bit goody-goody, Mr. high-and-mighty Peter? Trying to impress Nicole, are we? Or her mother?"

"Shut up, Diana. Go smoke in your room, but not here. Or I'm leaving with Nicole."

"O.K., Peter dear, whatever you say." She took another drag and proferred it to Jacques. "What about you, Jacques? Before I put it out?"

Jacques hesitated. He had never tried it, but did not want to look unworldly in Diana's eyes. He took a puff, then stubbed it out for her.

The music started again. Diana was up at once. "Come on, Peter," she said, looking boldly at Nicole, "for old time's sake."

The eight of them had all the seats at the table. There were other players standing around from time to time, but Nick had arranged the seating to discourage them.

They were getting into the second phase. They had started very casually, just a diversion, "keeping the girls amused." Only Armand Leclerc had done any heavy betting, and he was over five hundred ahead. His tactics had been to plunge and see whether he was lucky or not. If he lost two hundred, he would quit. If he won, he would play with the house's money.

Now, they'd become envious of Armand. Philippe decided it was time to show him up. Kay was betting a dollar at a time, using quarter chips, while Sam looked on, smoking his pipe. Lise was betting calmly and sensibly, ahead perhaps fifty dollars.

Arthur returned from the crap table down the aisle and put four thousand dollars, in hundred chips, in four neat piles on the table.

"All profit," he said smugly. "Give me some tens." He passed half a stack to the croupier.

Jane Mallory pushed the rest of the stack to the croupier. "Same again," she said.

Arthur looked at her sharply, but said nothing.

The waitress brought a tray of drinks, placing one beside each player.

"What's that?" Arthur asked her, pointing to the glass beside Jane.

"A drink, silly," Jane snapped. He made to pick it up. Jane beat him to it and took it at one swallow. The waitress saw her chance to escape and left. "Ginger ale," Jane said.

Philippe was down three thousand quickly. He laughed, waving for Carlo. "Give me ten grand," he said. Carlo signalled the cashier's desk and the money was at Philippe's disposal in a few seconds.

"You play for me, Jeanette," he said. "I need a change of luck."

Jane was betting on zero, fifty dollars at a time. It seemed appropriate. It came up. Seven-hundred-and-fifty dollars. Things were looking up. It called for a drink.

"I'm going to powder my nose," she said, rising from her seat. "Be back in a minute."

Arthur eyed her menacingly. "I don't believe you," he said in a half whisper.

"Come and watch then," she said out loud. "Kay, keep an eye on our chips, will you? Arthur wants to come and watch me pee."

There was a hush. Even the croupier lost the rhythm as he swung the wheel.

"You're drunk, Jane. You're making a fool of yourself."

"You're a pompous old fart and you're making an exhibition of yourself," Jane retorted in a slow, deliberate drawl.

He followed her a few steps, grabbing her hand. "Jane. Stop this. You'll regret it."

She shook him off. "Oh, no I won't. I'm enjoying myself. First time in ten years." She turned, swaying very slightly. "Come on. We're going to the john, aren't we?"

"You're disgusting," Arthur said, leaving her to return to the table.

She actually did want to go to the ladies' room but it did not stop her having a double scotch on the way back. That one did the trick. No pain anymore.

She returned to her place at the table. "Where're my chips?" she asked the croupier.

"Your husband turned them in, madam," the croupier said guardedly. He did not like the situation at all and had sent word for Nick Diamado to come to the rescue. He wished that he would hurry up.

"He did, did he?" She looked at Arthur.

He ignored her. He was busy, up seven thousand now, stacked in neat piles of hundred-dollar chips.

"Well," a mischievous smile spread across her face, "titty for the ol' tatty, so to speak." With that, she grabbed a pile of Arthur's chips in each hand and hurled them into the air as far as she could throw them. She'd gotten rid of a third stack before he grabbed her.

"Leggo, you sonofabitch!" she snarled.

Lise was at her side. "Leave her alone, Arthur. Go and find your chips."

O.K., so I'm bombed, Jane decided. Can't accomplish any more here. Even at her worst, she had never been an argumentative drunk. Better go with Lise. Lise would make sure that Peter did not see her.

She picked one more hundred-dollar chip off a remaining stack and threw it to the croupier. "Buy yourself a drink, sonny."

"Let me go ahead," Jim said. "I know where the lamps are." He set them dim before he switched them on, so as not to make it obvious. He took Rena's coat.

"Now we should have the prescribed awkward moment: we have a drink, which neither of us needs, and work up on some necking. I suggest a sauna instead."

There was no arguing with this man. He took you to the point of departure smoothly, if a bit unconventionally.

"Sounds good."

"O.K. The sauna is in there, next to the bathroom." He opened the door and switched the sauna on. It had two benches, one above the other. "Upper or lower?" he said.

"Lower."

"O.K. You undress in the bedroom. Here's a towel." He handed her a huge yellow bath sheet. "I'll undress in here and go in first. You come in when you are ready."

When she entered, he was lying on the top bench. He did not embarrass her by looking at her nakedness. He made nothing of the situation, as though it was the most natural thing in the world for two friends, a man and a woman, to take a sauna together at two o'clock in the morning.

He hung his hand down, wiggling his fingers. She took it for a moment, kissing it impulsively.

"Nice," he murmured.

They stayed about twenty minutes. "It's all I can take," she said.

"O.K. Let's go."

What now, she thought.

He opened the sliding glass door. "Out here," he said. "This is the proper way." He led her to a chair. It must have been twenty below, still, starlit, the lake lapping below them.

He left her, switched on the record player. It was Mozart's *Jupiter* symphony. He brought her a glass of champagne.

They sat for ten minutes, absolutely silent, enjoying the music, the peacefulness, the prelude to love. She wanted him now. Union, connection, passion, flesh against flesh, reality. An escape, a cleansing, an erasure of everything in her mind. A farewell to innocence, before she gave her soul to the devil. Three days. She shivered.

"Go in and have a hot shower," Jim said. "Call me when you're finished."

She got into the bed and waited. She felt no qualms. She was completely committed, allowing sensuous desire to flood right through her.

He put the rest of the bottle of champagne next to the bed. "It's been a long time," he said, "waiting for this kiss." He came to her slowly, gently, kissing her eyes, her nose, ears, cheeks, all small warm breaths of him.

Then her lips. Not hard at first, then opening his mouth to let his tongue chase hers in circles.

Now, everything, now, don't stop, she thought. He kissed her breasts, then down her belly, between her long legs.

She let him play, feeling only sensual, mind bursting with longing, all reason gone.

She was abandoned to him, and let him do as he pleased.

She climaxed almost as soon as he was inside her. He realized it, becoming a little rougher, now that he only had himself to satisfy.

She felt his strength, his moment of animal brutality, his explosion within her, almost coming with him a second time.

He lay beside her stroking her hair.

"Alright?"

She nodded. "Alright."

He passed her a glass of champagne, spilling some on her breast and licking it off.

"I think I am in love with you," he said.

"Better not."

"Why not?"

She dipped a finger in the champagne glass and drew a cold circle round his navel. "I'm a witch."

"What are you going to do?" Jim laughed. "Turn into a pumpkin?"

She dipped again, continuing her caress. "What's the time, darling?" she asked.

Surprised, he looked at his watch. "Three o'clock. Why? You planning to go somewhere?"

After midnight, she thought. Only two days, now. "Not yet," she said.

Diana reached the top of the stairs leading from the disco to the gambling floor. Lise and Jane were passing the entrance arm in arm.

"Hello, Mrs. Gareau," Diana smiled her most charming, innocent smile.

At that moment, Jane Mallory stumbled and fell forward, nearly dragging Lise with her.

"Stop Peter," Lise said quickly to Diana. Diana took her cue, like a born actress. Shoving Jacques forward with a "Quick. Help Mrs. Gareau," she ducked back down the steps to where the other two were dawdling.

"I just saw your mother, Nicole. She said that you could stay another half hour."

"Oh?" Nicole appeared puzzled. "What do you think, Peter? I'm a bit tired, really."

"No. Let's go. We want to be fresh for skiing tomorrow." Peter was firm.

"Come on Peter." Diana grabbed his hand and dragged him down two steps. "You owe me a dance. Let Nicole go up alone if she is such a baby."

Nicole stared at Diana, looking wounded.

"Let go, Diana." Peter shook himself free. "For Christ's sake what's the matter with you tonight?" He climbed back beside Nicole.

Diana dropped her handbag, having taken care to open the clasp. The contents spilt down the staircase.

"Now, look what you have done," she glared at Peter accusingly. "Pick it up for me."

"You stupid pothead," Peter said resignedly, bending to his knees to recover her trinkets. "You're the one who needs to go to bed."

Thoroughly proud of her performance, Diana figured

116

that she had done all that was expected of her. She had delayed Peter close to five minutes. She would explain the scenario to Nicole tomorrow. "I'm sorry," she said.

Jacques came back down to give the all-clear. "Come on, you guys," he said. "What're you waiting for?"

Well done Jacques, Diana thought.

They reached the door of Diana's room. Jacques made a clumsy grab for her and she granted a kiss. "Come in a moment," she whispered. "Someone will see us out here."

She switched on the lights, putting a finger to her lips. "My parents are next door." She brushed his cheek with her lips. "Undress in the bathroom," she said.

Jacques was breathing hard, goggling at her as though in a hypnotic trance. She pushed him into the bathroom leaving the door ajar. "Don't come out till I tell you," she said.

Throwing her clothes carelessly on the armchair, she undressed as quickly as she could and dived into the bed.

"Jacques," she called quietly.

"Yes?" He peered self-consciously round the bathroom door.

"Come on out," she said, "slowly."

Jacques walked self-consciously out of his hiding place and stood before her, stark naked, his penis sticking up like an antiaircraft gun.

"Come over here," she commanded, "slowly."

He slithered over to the bed like a zombie, eyes dilated, chest heaving, arms outstretched, penis throbbing.

"Stop, there," Diana commanded. He was right beside the bed. She lifted a hand from the covers and stroked his hardness, watching his face as he began to groan in ecstasy.

She felt the first dribble of ejaculation. "That's all for tonight, Jacques," she said quietly.

Jacques grabbed her hand. "No. Please, Diana. Please."

"I said that's all, Jacques," she said firmly. "You wouldn't like me to start screaming, would you?"

"Please, Diana, please," he begged.

Her voice was cold now. "Get your bloody pants on and get out, Jacques."

"But I know that you do," Jacques argued desperately.

"Do what?"

"Screw."

"I screw when I feel like it," she said. "And I'm not screwing tonight. Now get out before I start hollering." She switched out the light.

"You bitch," he said, taking a swing at the pillow and catching her on the side of the face.

"Jacques!" It was not that loud, but in the silence it sounded like a crash of cymbals. "I'm warning you, for the last time."

He turned in panic and ran for the lighted bathroom. She heard him struggling back into his clothes.

Silly bastard, she thought. If he had any guts, he would have raped me. That might have been fun.

"Where the hell have you been?" Jake greeted Silky angrily, "I've been trying to get you on the phone."

It was early evening and Jake was sitting in his room watching TV. He jumped up as soon as Silky was inside, switching off the set.

"The movies," replied Silky, unconcerned.

"The movies! Jesus Christ!" Jake exclaimed.

"What's eating you?" Silky grinned. "Got the pre-op jitters?"

"Well we're not exactly getting ready for a tea party."

"Take it easy, Jake. We've been planning this thing for nine months and it's as perfect as it will ever be. Now, everything depends on our performance, our ability to act and think clearly. You're going to screw it all up if you start getting uptight. The way you are now, if I gave you a gun, you would probably shoot your own fucking foot off."

"I'm nervous, I don't mind admitting it. It's going to be the hell of a caper for two guys to pull off. If we screw it up, it's going to be jail for life. I don't care for that."

"We are not going to screw it up. Shit, I've done fifty operations more dangerous than this one."

"Well, I haven't."

"Look, Jake. If you go on like this, you're going to stay awake all night worrying and, by the time we are ready to get started, you'll be about as much use as tits on a bull."

"I can't help it. I wish I could."

"What you need is a good piece of tail, maybe two, half-a-dozen full shots of bourbon and a few hours of sleep."

"You're crazy."

"I'm serious."

"I don't think it is good policy to go out. You never know, someone might remember us."

"Together, maybe you are right. But there's nothing wrong with one at a time."

"Maybe." Jake was bending a little in sheer desperation.

"Tell you what. I'll drive you out to the Stardust Ranch."

"The what?"

"The Stardust Ranch. It's only three miles out of town. The best whorehouse in Nevada. It's famous. It's even legal. And it's guaranteed clean; the girls have a weekly medical inspection by a doctor as a condition of the license."

"You're kidding!" Jake started laughing.

"I'm not, man. It's gospel."

"We couldn't go together." Jake was mellowing a little.

"I'll drive you. But I won't go in."

"What's the matter? You give it up?"

"You're the one with the butterflies. As far as I'm concerned, getting you laid is insurance. You can take two girls, one for each of us."

Jake poured himself a bourbon, passing the bottle to Silky. "Let me think about it."

He sipped his drink, letting his mind fantasize a little, picturing a good, slow blow job. It sure took his mind off the hijack.

He slapped his knee. "O.K. Doc," he said, "I give you my permission to operate. Let's go to surgery."

They drove about three miles out of town then turned off on a narrow winding road. They did not pass a single house until suddenly, going over a short incline, they found themselves in a courtyard in front of a low ranch house. There were maybe eight or ten cars parked. It was the end of the road.

Jake got out and rang the bell at the front door. It did not open at once. He waited, feeling a bit stupid, Silky watching him.

All of a sudden the door opened and he was inside a large square room, looking at maybe a dozen or more naked broads standing in a semicircle. There wasn't any hallway or anteroom or anything like that. It all just happened—boom!—one minute he was outside waiting at a closed door, and the next he was standing there looking at these chicks. It was enough to make a guy blush.

No one spoke.

Jake grinned. They all smiled at him simultaneously.

"Hi," he said. He was beginning to warm to the situation.

"Hi," they replied, not in unison this time, some more quickly than others.

He looked them over with the air of a connoisseur. Four black and ten white. All real good young stuff. Well, might as well have a mixture.

He looked the blacks over first, picked a tall well-built one with big tits.

"You," he said to her. The others all smiled. There seemed to be no jealousy between them. The semicircle began to break up.

"Hold it," Jake commanded.

They stared at him with interest. Something new.

"And you." He pointed to a fluffy, little blond thing, real blond, with fair hair on her pussy.

They all giggled, unsure now what to do. Maybe he was going to have half-a-dozen.

"Come on, greedy boy." The one called Lena grinned at him with huge, mischievous eyes and held out a pale palm at the end of a sinuous arm, like a long black eel.

Jake lost interest in the others. He got the impression that his request for a double helping had caught this one's imagination, adding a pinch of zest to her otherwise grinding routine. It made him feel horny.

Zelda, the blond, led the way, wiggling a cream-white bum as she opened the door to one of the rooms.

Zelda flopped on the bed, while Lena helped Jake out of his clothes and led him into the bathroom. She completed the ablutions with a snaking lick of her wicked tongue.

She looked up at him prankishly. "Got any special routine in mind for this party, honey?"

Jake hadn't given it a thought. He had only gone for

the double at Silky's suggestion. It was for the extra laugh they would get in reminiscence rather than for the orgiastic value. "No." He shrugged helplessly. "It's for my buddy."

She was squatting on the john. The black eel pulled at the toilet roll and slithered between her legs to wipe her pussy. "Some buddy! You do all his fucking for him?"

"No. We're just close. He'd do the same for me."

"Man!" Her deep-throated laugh mingled with the gurgle of flushing water. "Greater love hath no man"— she struck an exaggerated thespian pose—"than to lay a girl for a friend!"

CHAPTER SIX

ARMAND LECLERC sat at the window of the ski lodge cafeteria drinking black coffee. It was the only restaurant open at seven in the morning.

He had been up all night.

He laid his head down on his fists, hunched over the table, letting his agony eke out in sobs of desperation.

Just one stupid impulse.

At around three in the morning, he had been nearly fifteen thousand ahead. He had been betting a system of twelve numbers, his longest losing streak all night being four consecutive bets. It was like taking candy from kids.

He was just about to cash in his chips when the thought struck him. Why not one big bet on a practically fifty-fifty chance, just red or black? Double the money in thirty seconds. What a coup! What a laugh he would have about it with Philippe! Smart fellow, Philippe would say.

He put twelve thousand five hundred on black. If it went wrong, he would still have three thousand profit left over.

There were just two of them, himself and the croupier. The croupier met his eyes with the shadow of a smile.

Armand watched with confidence as the little ball bounced on its merry way around the wheel. It was his lucky night. He could still hear it now, in his head—the tap–tap–tap of the ball as it slowed to its final resting place.

"Zero," said the croupier without emotion, sweeping up the chips with three sharp pulls of his rake.

"Zero?" Armand could hardly believe it. Zero, the house number, the only one that could spoil the odds on his nearly even bet!

From then on his memory was hazy. He did not want to remember. He had drunk a lot of scotch at a crap table and beer at a dawn poker game. He had been in a kind of daze. He remembered the dealer's voice.

"I'm sorry, sir. There is no more credit. You are over the limit."

"Limit? What limit?"

"The thirty-five thousand guaranteed by Mr. Gareau."

"Thirty-five thousand?" Armand was stupified. "I've lost that much?"

"Yes, sir. That's right."

"Oh, my God! Oh, my God!" He had reached the end of the tunnel and he was out of breath. "A drink," he said hoarsely, "give me a drink."

"The cafeteria at the ski lodge, sir. They open for breakfast at six-thirty."

Armand paid for his coffee with loose change and walked back from the lodge to the hotel. The bitter morning air froze the tears on his cheeks.

"Where the hell have you been?" Jeanette asked sleepily, as he closed the door of their room.

"In the casino."

"By yourself? All night?" She looked at him suspiciously. "You've been with that little whore, Diana."

"I wish I had."

"Armand! What's the matter with you?" She flung off the bedclothes and stared at him.

"I'm tired," he said, falling on the bed, fully clothed.

"You're disgusting," she said, slamming the bathroom door behind her.

Well, that decides it, she thought. I am not going skiing. I am going to watch Philippe play tennis. And after tennis, who knows?

Rena found the Sunday morning class sadly depleted. But, it seemed that most of the dropouts were the duds. She decided to take advantage of the situation and put them on the more difficult terrain at the top.

There were only nine in the class. Jacques was the

sole representative of the Leclerc family. His father, mother, sister, and her girl friend were missing. She was a little surprised about Danielle and Suzanne until Jacques told her that they had been invited over to Heavenly Valley for the day by a couple of young men whom they'd met the previous evening.

Only Sam Mitchell represented the men. As far as Rena was concerned, the loss of Philippe and Arthur Mallory was no calamity. The other truant was Jane Mallory; perhaps she had gone to watch her husband play tennis.

Rena led the group to the gondola, riding up with Lise and Serge Gareau. She felt a touch light-headed from lack of sleep, but otherwise she had no regrets about her night with Jim. She felt calmer than she had done for a long time.

This morning, they went to the very crest of the mountain, moving from the gondola up Number Three chair to Roulette, a considerably steeper trail than Thunderbolt, but with some graceful plateaus, like steps, to give respite between the pitches; then on to chair Five to the summit, almost two miles up.

It was a brilliant sunny day, matching her mood, a day of all days to be at the world's top-gallant. They were above the tree line, a sprinkling of new night powder, unblemished, cotton woolly, crunching under their skis. Pristine, virgin, untrodden, chinking and giggling with a thousand lights, each tiny flake catching its own timid wink at the sun.

To the north, cruel black crags and canyons, rock shapes all sizes, blacks, blues, grays all deep and menacing, proud peaks, jutting from a million miles of stark white snow. Like the walls of a giant's castle, impenetrable, guarding the sleeping lake below, cold, deep, unruffled, reflecting the azure blue sky.

To the south lay flat green and brown desert, another world, shapeless, thirsty, arid testimonial to nature's chameleon powers.

"My God, it's magnificent," Peter exclaimed, his arm around Nicole's shoulders.

Rena waited for them to gather themselves. "Nicole," she said, "would you like to lead off behind me. Try to follow in my tracks. O.K.?"

Nicole shrugged shyly. "Sure. I'll try."

Peter smiled encouragement.

The challenge of Blackjack soon brought Nicole out of her daydreams. It was considerably narrower than Thunderbolt or Roulette, covered in moguls. There was no question of making turns at will, shifting weight when she was good and ready. This hill commanded the skier, forcing action and reaction, challenging reflexes, compelling decision, demanding her full concentration. She swept into it fast, following Rena and trying to maintain her easy rhythm over the bumps, moving in shortcuts across the fall line, to keep her speed under control. Halfway down Nicole missed her timing on the top of a mogul, twisted out in the trough and, heart beating fast, began gathering speed. She had lost the rhythm now, began fighting the slope, struggling to keep her balance, flexing her knees for all she was worth, as the angry mountain beat against her with bump after bump. She could not win, was too exhausted, surrendered before it broke her, falling sideways, sliding nearly another hundred feet before she came to a stop. She lay still for a moment, her lungs bursting, head pounding. For an instant she wondered why she had such a dizzy, breathless feeling; then she quickly realized that it was the air at eleven thousand feet that was causing her distress.

Peter pulled up beside her. "Jeeze," he panted, fighting for breath. "You alright?"

"Thanks, Peter, yes. Just a bit breathless. That's all."

"Wow, aren't we all." He collected her ski pole from ten feet below her, panting like a puppy dog as he climbed back up. "Thin air," he gasped, "but it sure beats Montreal smog."

Nicole, none the worse for wear after a short rest, picked herself up and reset her safety binding.

Diana swept by, going fast, drawing attention to herself with a wild war-whoop.

Rena was much happier with the restricted class. They were more of a level standard now, and she could make a more effective contribution, giving them little hints and correcting their individual faults. Watching them from the top of Thunderbolt as they made their last run ahead of her, she felt quite proud of what she had been able to achieve.

Jim moved on down the passageway to the bar, checking the daily ticket sales at the main ticket booth on the way.

He ordered a Bloody Mary, heavily spiced. Holding a mouthful before he swallowed it, letting the hot Tabasco burn the scale off his tongue, he moved over to the big window, glass in hand, watching for her.

He spotted her at once. Funny. Yesterday he would have had to scan the whole mountain for her, uncertain whether he could identify her at long range. Today, he picked her out of the crowd of skiers right away, somehow knowing the flow of her movements, even at that distance. He watched her all the way down, experiencing a new-found sense of pride in the flawlessness of her technique.

He moved over to meet her at the top of the steps, as she came across the sundeck. She smiled and waved as she saw him, pulling off her tuque and shaking out her hair. She was tanned, bubbling with health and good spirits.

I'm afraid it's true, he said to himself. I am in love with her.

There was no doubt that Philippe and Arthur were better at tennis than skiing. Philippe, in particular, although ponderous and out of shape, played with strong, graceful strokes. Arthur gave him a game, but there was no question who was going to be the eventual winner.

Jeanette was watching Philippe—not his style, just the power and strength of the man. He had everything. Good health, good looks, money, position, and character. He was all the things that Armand longed to be. Poor Armand. So phony, so afraid.

She wondered about his story of last night. It seemed inconceivable to her that anyone could play at that silly wheel for nine or ten hours. It must have been a woman. Sex would certainly be the only diversion that would ever keep *her* out all night.

She had watched the way Diana looked at Armand. She was bold, that one, the type that liked older men.

126

She wouldn't go for Philippe—the father of her best friend—for fear of losing all the luxuries that Nicole's friendship provided. And no one would go for Arthur; he was sexless. No. It was Armand she wanted, for sure. She was welcome. If Armand arranged a little something on the side, then the coast would be clear for Jeanette. Of course her stepson, Jacques, had a permanent hard-on for Diana. But Jacques was not Diana's style. I know, Jeanette realized suddenly, because I am like Diana myself, when it comes to men. We *play with* the easy ones, the ones who drool over us. It's the strong ones, the secure ones we *want*. And it's all the more exciting if we have to take them from someone else.

Arthur and Philippe were coming off the court now. Jeanette went down to join them in the bar.

Arthur had a quick orange juice. "I'd better go and see how Jane is," he said sullenly, "before she starts up again."

Philippe nodded, sipping his gin and tonic. It made him feel young again to get a bit of exercise.

"Do you know what time Armand came to bed, Philippe?" Jeanette said. "Eight o'clock this morning!"

"God! What was he doing?"

"What d'you think? Maybe another woman, would you say?" She smiled suggestively. It was a simple ploy to get around to the subject of sex and to show that she had a modern view about extramarital affairs.

"I don't see why he would look at another woman when he has you, Jeanette." Philippe rose to the bait like a hungry salmon. "I'm sure you don't leave a man unsatisfied."

"Sure?" she said. "You can never be sure of anything until you have tried it."

Philippe laughed loudly. "You are very blunt, Jeanette. You're a dangerous woman."

"Blunt?" She smiled. "Perhaps. Not dangerous. Very —discreet, I assure you."

Philippe gauged her carefully. "You have some ideas in the back of that pretty head, Jeanette?"

"Ideas, yes. But that's all. Perhaps a little champagne would stimulate them."

"I'll change first," he said.

"No, Philippe." She touched his bare thigh below his

127

shorts, leaving her hand there, caressing gently. "Don't leave me just yet. Order the champagne first."

Philippe waved for the waiter, ordering Veuve Clicquot. "But I'm all sweaty," he said.

"I like it." She smiled. "You smell of man."

The waiter brought the bottle and Philippe signed the chit.

"Don't open it yet," Jeanette said to the waiter. "Let it get cold."

"I thought you wanted it now?"

"I do." Jeanette gave his remark a double meaning. "And I want you to do it to me."

"You mean . . . ?" Philippe had never been seduced before. He was used to making the advances himself. He grinned at her sheepishly.

"Of course."

"But where?"

"Your room of course. Lise won't be back until noon. You need a shower, don't you?"

She took the bottle and stood up. "You coming?"

"But my clothes—in the changing room."

"You won't need them, cheri. Come back for them later."

Armand woke up in a cold sweat. He had experienced a terrible nightmare. He was locked in a black coffin, suffocating. He could hear the desperate tap–tap–tap of someone trying to get in. The tapping got slower and slower and he knew that, when it stopped, he was going to die.

His head was throbbing and his mouth was parched. His mind cringed from the truth, tempting him to stay in the twilight zone, not fully awake.

"Oh, my God," he sighed aloud. Thirty-five thousand dollars! What the hell was he going to do?

He would have to tell Philippe first. Philippe had apparently guaranteed him although he really did not know how or why. Yes, why? If Philippe had not gone surety for him, they would never have let him draw that much on credit.

He got up and stumbled to the bathroom, turning on the shower while he swallowed a couple of glasses of water. It was all Philippe's fault. He would tell him so. Why the hell was Philippe always so goddam patronizing?

My God, what would Philippe say? How would he pay Philippe back? He would have to sell the house at Brent Mountain. Jeanette would leave him, for sure. And what about Peter's college fees? And Tim just going to Bishop's private school?

He got into the shower, holding his face up to the stream, letting it run into his nostrils, symbolically drowning himself, only to break into a paroxysm of coughing.

If only his brain would stop torturing him. What about the business? What about Philippe's account? The presentation?

He brushed his teeth, eyeing himself in the mirror. Nothing seemed different. He was the same man as yesterday—less thirty-five thousand dollars.

Well, I had better find Philippe, he decided. Confession was good for the soul. It would give him some relief to share his terrible news with someone, anyone, just to get it out, so that it would stop the pressure inside his head.

The management would surely tell Philippe. Armand must get to him first. He remembered that Philippe had arranged to play tennis. Perhaps he was still there.

He dressed quickly and went down to the lobby, looking for the way to the tennis court.

"Can I help you, sir?" There was a small bar in a recess off the lobby. It was the barman who addressed him. Armand turned to him absent-mindedly. "Yes—er—the tennis courts."

"Yes, sir. You go down to the end of the gambling floor and . . . " Armand looked in the direction in which the man pointed. He could see the roulette table, empty now. Tap–tap–tap. Zero.

"Give me a drink. Double Bloody Mary." His hand was shaking; he could not face Philippe like this.

He saw them coming across the floor, Philippe in his tennis clothes. He heard Philippe's laugh and Jeanette's high-pitched giggle.

Not both of them together. He could not face that. Jeanette would scream at him, make a fool of him in front of Philippe.

He slipped back into the shadows of the little bar, turning his head to stare at the Chartreuse bottle at the far end of the shelf.

He stole a glance as the elevator door closed, just a glimpse of their hands. They were clasped together around a bottle of Champagne.

It took his mind a moment to shift gears. Even then—it was silly. He was hallucinating.

He finished his drink, signed the chit and gathered himself for the meeting with Philippe. He would just go to his own room first, see Jeanette and tell her that he had business with Philippe—to go down to lunch and he would meet her later.

"Jeanette?" He tapped on the bathroom door. No answer. She must have gone into Philippe's room. Damn her! He wanted Philippe alone.

He let himself out of his room, leaving the door ajar, unsure what he was going to do. He walked to Philippe's room and waited.

What the hell is she doing in there, he thought. He could not believe it. It was just too much for one day.

He put his ear to the door and listened. He heard it distinctly. That high pitched wail of ecstasy which she used to emit, when they had first made love, before he married her.

He moved away from the door, feeling sick, clinging to the opposite wall. He felt his way back to his room staggered into the bathroom and threw up into the basin.

Throwing water over his face, splashing carelessly over his shirt and tie, he pulled himself together.

Making a supreme effort, he returned to the elevator and walked over to the reception desk.

"The key to eight-one-four, please."

"Yes, sir? Your name, sir?"

"Gareau. Philippe Gareau."

The man looked in the pigeonhole. There was a key there. He handed it to Armand.

He moved like an automaton now, drawn by some irresistible force to spring the trap which he knew would destroy him.

He turned the key in the lock and just stood there, groaning and whimpering like an abandoned puppy.

Nobody spoke.

Silky and Jake turned up at Mount Casino after lunch to iron out a few final details. They were well pleased

130

with the radio weather report, forecasting snow. Another eight or ten inches of snow would be additional concealment for their explosives.

They got into the gondola lineup separately, studying the behavior of people in the base and watching the loading routine. Jake purposely got out of the line and moved to the back of the room, pretending to re-buckle his ski boots. No one paid the slightest attention to him, as he expected. No one watches for the first signs of an earthquake when none is expected.

Each of them skied the line of towers individually, stopping for a breather at strategic points, just to see that everything was in place.

Jake felt an enormous sense of power as he looked up to see the gondola cars sailing quietly above his head, full of happy, carefree people. The stillness added to the atmosphere of security and calm. Quietness was one of the beautiful things about skiing, he thought. No yelling crowds, no roaring engines, no applause, no bawling play-by-play announcers; three thousand skiers sliding soundlessly over the silent snow.

"Boom!" He yelled at the top of his voice, as he did a spread-eagle jump from the crest of a big mogul. No sooner uttered but the sound disappeared on the wind in his wake.

Just wait a couple of days, he chuckled to himself.

At quarter-past three they rendezvoused at the sundeck of the lodge. They did not talk to each other, just exchanged glances, then Silky took off in the direction of the garage.

This was their final walk-through. They had changed out of their ski boots and put on fatigue boots, to get the time simulation absolutely right. Time was of the essence at the beginning of the operation.

Silky walked up the hill at a measured pace, a steady speed, which he could duplicate without hurrying.

Arriving at the garage, he saw five vehicles parked in the yard. This surprised him slightly, since he expected six. He decided to walk right up to the bays and take a peek through the glass door at the side-entrance.

There was a vehicle in each bay. He went in, nodding to the mechanic who was working on the first vehicle, and walked down the line, acting businesslike.

He noticed that the Bombardier had its differential down and the far Thiokol, an old Spryte, had the engine out of it.

Those two will be down for a few days, he thought. He turned back, still looking very purposeful in the hope that no one would stop him, but he saw he was going to get caught.

"Can I do anything for you?" a burly, bald man with a German accent asked him, barring his exit.

"Not really. I'm with Tucker Sno-cat sales. Just wanted to check your fleet for my records."

"We don't have a Tucker."

"I know."

"We may trade that old Spryte at the end of the season. I would consider a Tucker, if you gave me a good price for it."

Silky wanted to get the hell out of here. But he did not want to do anything that might be remembered later as unusual.

"O.K.," he said, "I'll ask head office. Excuse me now. I have to catch a plane."

The man smiled at him. "Come again."

He closed the door. Shit. That had really screwed up his timing. It was ten to four. He did not reach Jake, standing at the entrance of the gondola base, until four minutes to four.

Jake looked at him questioningly and moved off to the station wagon. He said nothing until they were out of the car park.

"What the hell happened to you? You were over five minutes late. You would have blown the whole deal." Jake was quite upset. After all the planning, he did not expect such a total breakdown of the time plan at this stage.

Silky explained what happened.

"Stupid fucking thing to do," Jake said.

"I don't know. If eight machines suddenly appeared when I expected six, that could really knock my schedule for a loop."

"You should not have exposed yourself." Jake was obsessed with secrecy, whereas Silky, who had practical experience behind enemy lines, believed that the more natural you acted, the less suspicion you aroused. He had a kind of basic bravado, enjoyed the excitement of going to the brink of danger.

"No harm done." Silky grinned. "Maybe I should sell him a Tucker to cover our expenses."

"Shit," was all Jake would say.

"Anyway," Silky said seriously, "I think the schedule is too tight. Anything could happen to slow me down up there. It's very exposed. I think it would be smart to allow another five minutes."

"I think you're right. I'll buy that."

Jake pulled up alongside a roadside phone booth. It was time to call Charlie.

He checked over some of the important details. Charlie had everything pat.

"O.K. We will be in a dark blue delivery van when we get to you. Understand? A dark blue van." A thought struck him. "You got time to run over to Reno tomorrow? Yes? O.K. Why not go out to the airport and take a look at it? It's in the parking lot. Then you will be sure."

He got back into the car, well satisfied. Charlie seemed to be a reliable guy.

There was nothing left to do now but wait.

Monday morning's ski class was a full one. Rena congratulated them on their punctual attendance. "Incidentally, before I forget, tomorrow's class will be in the afternoon. Out of consideration for those who celebrate a little too hard tonight."

It was New Year's Eve, the old year almost expired, a time to consign the past to the past and to make resolve for a brighter future.

The two gamblers, Armand and Philippe, eyed each other cautiously as they waited to move off. By now, Nick Diamado had informed Philippe of Armand's indiscretion. Armand had gambled and lost. Thirty-five thousand dollars.

My God, thought Philippe, I wish that was all that I had gambled. I have gambled my position, my wife, my children, my entire fortune. And for what? At least Armand had a fifty-fifty chance of doubling his money. But what did I have as a prize? A piece of ass! An ejaculation inside a pretty woman's body! What a dumb bet!

There was still a place for human misgiving behind Philippe's autocratic facade. He had not risen to the top of business by the normal means of stealth, manipulation, treachery, deceit, and flattery. He had got there by marriage. Lucky perhaps, but at least some of his moral values were still intact.

Like most busy executives, he lacked the time to look into his own heart. He tended to accept the North American business ethic which made human compassion an intolerable weakness in a top executive. At the altar, he had been presented with a role to play and mode of behavior to adopt; it went with the job.

Now for the first time in years, he took stock of himself. Away from the trappings of his office, he saw himself as he really was, contaminated by power. Without power he was nothing—and Armand, the fawning servant whom he had patronized for so long, held the key to his retention of it. If Armand told Lise about Jeanette, Philippe would be ruined.

Philippe reviewed his options. He could hold Armand to ransom, pay off Armand's debt and keep his I.O.U. as a guarantee against his silence. The power option.

Or he could admit to Armand that he had behaved treacherously and inexcusably and beg for his forgiveness. Then, as a gesture of friendship but not in any way conditional, he could pay his gambling debt. In return, he could hope that Armand would have sufficient compassion not to tell Lise. The human option.

Interesting. Both options had the same result. His choice depended on how much he valued Armand's friendship.

Rena led the group over to the chair lift. She had decided to work them on Interstate for a change. She was going to give special attention to the two laggards, Arthur and Philippe, hoping that their private lesson with Pepi had had the desired effect.

The grown-ups played musical chairs as they boarded the lift, avoiding the embarrassment of a forced tête-à-tête with their formal partners. Philippe went up with Rena, Arthur with Armand, Lise with young Serge. Only the Mitchells seemed unscathed by the happenings of the previous night.

134

Jane Mallory brought up the rear with Jeanette, each engrossed in her own thoughts.

Jane Mallory did not try to kid herself. She realized that she was an alcoholic and that it was a test of her willpower not to drink. The problem was that no one else realized it—that the test was hers alone! They all treated her, especially Arthur, as though she had no willpower, as though they were her benevolent jailers, dutifully standing on guard to prevent her from slitting her own wrists.

My God, it was Arthur who had driven her to drink! Couldn't he understand that by standing over her like a sadistic male nurse, ready to snatch every glass out of her hand, he was driving her even harder?

I got drunk and I am glad I got drunk, she thought. I haven't had a drink for twenty-four hours now because I haven't wanted one. Tonight I will drink, and whether I get drunk or not depends on how Arthur and the rest of them behave. Can't they understand that? They are the cause, I am the effect. If they would just goddam well leave me alone, maybe I could control my own destiny. I am tired, Arthur Mallory, of you running my life. From now on it's mine, totally and exclusively mine.

Jeanette Leclerc felt rather smug. She was the center of a drama of catastrophic proportions and even if she wanted to do anything about it, she had little power to influence the outcome.

She had achieved what she wanted, the seduction of Philippe, and the only pity was that, with all the potential uproar, she would probably have a long wait before it happened again.

Whether Armand told Lise or not was up to him. In some ways she hoped he would, because, in that case, she would set her cap seriously for Philippe on the rebound. Meantime she would keep her mouth shut. She prided herself on her discretion in these matters.

Armand had apparently lost a lot of money gambling and he talked insanely about selling the house at Brent Mountain. He couldn't because it was in her name. Anyway, as she pointed out—any idiot could see it except that fool Armand—he now had the power to blackmail Philippe for a lot more than a few measly gambling debts. He ought to thank her for what she had done.

135

As the class came down to the bottom of the last run, everyone was the better off for the exercise, the company and the fresh air. And all, including Rena and Jim O'Malley, had been invited to the first frolic of the New Year's Eve celebrations, a cocktail party in the Mallory suite starting at six o'clock.

It was nearly midnight and the festivities were in full swing.

The Montreal group were all at one big table for the occasion, their number swelled to twenty by the addition of Jim and Rena and two young navy ensigns on leave from their nuclear submarine in San Francisco. The navy types were escorts for Danielle and Suzanne and were named Dave and Dick but, of course, it was too late in the evening for anyone in the party except the girls to remember which was which.

Jane Mallory had remained strictly on champagne throughout the evening. She was a teensy bit high but rather proud of herself, having been objectionable to no one at the party—other, of course, than Arthur.

Armand and Philippe had excused themselves from the Mallory party for a few minutes and seemed to have settled their differences. Certainly Lise seemed in blissful ignorance of all that had transpired the previous day. Much to Jeanette's annoyance both Armand and Philippe were ignoring her and, as she'd predicted, Armand was making a rather clumsy play for Diana whenever he could get her away from Jacques.

Rena was drinking a lot of champagne, trying a little too hard to catch the spirit of the occasion. Deep in her heart she was the war mother, aching with anxiety, unable to influence events, but knowing that her two sons were going into action tomorrow. Whatever Silky and Jake had in mind to do, tomorrow was D-day. Even though she was indirectly involved, her concern and her prayers were for their safety alone. Please God, she said silently, I know that they plan something bad. But they are good. Remember that.

Jim O'Malley was amused to watch Danielle's undisguised efforts to seduce one of the young naval ensigns. There was nothing indecent about it, she was just a viva-

136

cious, warm-blooded French girl with an expressive body. It had been obvious all evening that she was quite infatuated with the young man, ready to give him anything he wanted at a snap of a finger. But he simply did not have the poise to handle the situation. He was very reserved and shy and, although he was obviously deeply attracted to Danielle and flattered by her attention, he was simply too awkward to be able to respond to her advances. This, of course, only served to stimulate her desires. Right now she had herself draped around him so close and tight, eyes closed and pretty little bottom wiggling in and out in time to the music, that an orgasm appeared inevitable. Yet the ensign seemed to have all his attention on the dance, erect but obviously erectionless, steering her around with studious precision, as though entered in a ballroom dancing competition.

Perhaps Sam Mitchell was one of those people who only rise to the most commonplace occasions. Possibly his prosaic understanding of etiquette established for him a few festive affairs at which it was considered *de rigueur* to get a little smashed. At any rate, judging by his behavior, New Year's Eve was a five star event on his calendar. Emerging unexpectedly from behind his pipe, he blazed into action like a camouflaged armed merchant ship suddenly disclosing its hidden armament.

He danced the samba with Suzanne, the cha-cha with Lise, a waltz with Kay, and a rather gymnastic jive with his daughter Diana. The nearer it came to midnight, the more keen he was to celebrate the demise of the old year. Maybe it had been a particularly lousy one for him and he was glad to see the last of it.

He took to the floor with Jane Mallory at the very moment when she was teetering between inspired insobriety and drunken crapulence. Together they pranced around the dance floor in a bacchanalian mazurka, stopping unexpectedly from time to time to kiss anyone who came within reach, old ladies, waiters, the pianist, the hirsute drummer. "Might not be here at midnight," Sam confided in them. "Might pass out. Happy New Year."

At last the drum rolled, the balloons came tumbling down from the ceiling, toy trumpets blew, rattles whirred, Sam and Jane collapsed in a heap, and the band struck up "Auld Lang Syne."

Everyone kissed each other, some perhaps with more sensuality or more sadness than others, and a tired old year was consigned to memory.

It was New Year's Day.

Rena kissed Jim, then crossed her fingers for Silky and Jake.

CHAPTER SEVEN

SILKY tapped on the door of Jake's motel room at eight o'clock sharp.

This was the day. A cold morning, bitter cold, just about perfect.

Jake let him in. He looked a bit tense and bleary-eyed. "Ready for the party?" Silky was cool as ever.

"Almost." Jake double-checked his room for the slightest trace of any telltale items and wiped it clean of fingerprints. "Did you wipe yours?" he asked Silky anxiously.

"Yes."

"You're sure?"

"Yes."

Silky packed the station wagon while Jake checked out and they were on their way. They grabbed a bite of breakfast at a drive-in, bought a good supply of sandwiches to last the rest of the day, then drove out to the airport. Silky put on his raincoat, dark glasses, and slouch hat and checked the van out of the parking lot. He followed Jake, in the station wagon, along the road to Lake Tahoe.

About ten miles out, they pulled into a rest area, and cleaned the van of fingerprints from end to end. As usual, they were both wearing gloves. Then they cleaned the station wagon, just in case.

Next, while Jake kept watch, Silky opened the locker in the van, checking all the hardware. He had oiled the submachine guns and revolvers before he put them away, but firearms were temperamental things, needing regular nursing and attention. Silky's life had depended enough times on the absolute reliability of his armament for him to treat his weapons with a respect akin to love.

By eleven o'clock they were on the road, this time running independently, not in convoy.

First stop for Jake was the Heavenly Valley Ski Area, where he purchased two all-day tickets. This was another example of his methodical planning, a precautionary alibi. If they were ever called upon to prove where they had spent the day, what could be more convincing than a ticket with a place and date stamped right on it? From there, he doubled back through town to Harrah's parking lot, picking an inconspicuous spot, close up against the building, in the middle of a bunch of other cars. He locked the car, double-checked the exact spot in relation to other landmarks, and walked casually up to the main street. Silky swung by with the van and pulled up momentarily. Jake jumped in.

Shortly after noon, they arrived at Mount Casino.

The parking lot was almost full. Silky cruised it slowly, finally selecting a suitable spot, and backed in, so that the cab faced the mountain. They sat in silence for a few moments, both of them involuntarily drawn to watch the gondola cars sailing serenely up the mountain, one after another at regular intervals, as though they were being stamped out by a machine. There was an orderliness and immutability implicit in their flow. Like a slothful giant too benign to scratch the playful insects off the vast expanse of his white belly, the mountain presided over the scene.

Jake slid open the door between the front and the cargo space and stepped into the rear. Silky followed, closing the door behind him.

They opened the locker and set to work, each systematically packing his own gear and laying out his operational kit and equipment, snowmobile suits, face masks, fatigue boots, and the skis, which Silky had stolen at Boreal Ridge on the way up.

Everything checked.

There were more than three hours to go; nothing to do, now, but wait. They munched their sandwiches.

It was a chilly afternoon, about eight below zero and

getting colder; there was a northwest wind, nothing much but enough to add sting to the chill factor.

Rena stood alone at her flagged position waiting for her ski class. She was the first instructress on duty, twenty minutes early in fact, which would have pleased Alfredo Costa if he had been watching. But her punctuality was not motivated by enthusiasm as it might seem; she just wanted to get it over with as soon as possible.

She had not got to bed after the party until past three in the morning and had slept soundly thanks to the anaesthetic effect of a skinful of champagne. She had quite deliberately had too much, partly to ease her mounting tension, and partly to give her an excuse to fend off Jim O'Malley's advances. He had made it clear at the start of the evening that New Year's day was one of the few occasions when he could lie in until noon and that this offered an opportunity for lovemaking which they should enjoy to the full.

Despite the temporary refuge of sleep, she felt the cold grip of panic as soon as she awoke, even before her mind began to function. There was no escape, no chance even of postponement. Today she was to become a criminal; tomorrow she might be in prison.

She had sat alone in her apartment searching for things to keep her mind occupied, washing a sweater by hand, cleaning the oven and preparing a brunch for which she had no appetite. Finally, unable to bear the strain any longer, she had taken the lifts to the top of the mountain and skied the Blackjack moguls fast and recklessly, relieved at last to have found an activity which demanded her full concentration. Then, as though trying to speed the passage of time by conscious effort, she had taken a flat-out run to the bottom, arriving almost twenty minutes early for her ski class.

Surprisingly, when the group eventually gathered, it was a full class, not a single absentee despite the New Year's celebrations. Even the two naval officers, Dick and Dave, had signed on for the afternoon.

Judging by the high spirits of some of the grown-ups, it was obvious that most of them had enjoyed a relatively liquid lunch. Taking this into account as well as the cold weather, Rena decided to spend the afternoon on the wide and easy Thunderbolt trail close to the gondola

141

which offered protection from the elements for the uphill run.

Philippe was a little subdued but at least he had attended to the more pedestrian details of his problems with Armand. He had gone over to see Nick Diamado and paid Armand's gambling debt immediately before the Mallory cocktail party. He had then taken the first opportunity to draw Armand aside to discuss it.

"No Armand," Philippe had said, "the whole situation was my fault. It was patronizing and meddlesome of me to arrange a line of credit for you without even discussing it with you. Let's face it, just because I am fortunate enough to be able to afford to lose that kind of money it does not follow that all my friends can."

"But I lost the money, not you." Armand's pride made him unwilling to accept charity.

"I created the opportunity for you to lose it," Philippe answered. "Gambling is a disease which softens our brains. In the heat of the moment, we lose perspective. I provided the poison and you swallowed it. If I had not interfered they would have stopped you—at five thousand tops."

"Let me pay back five thousand, then."

"No, Armand. Five thousand means little to me, a lot to you. I do not want to buy back your friendship, but if I can regain it, despite my disgraceful behavior in the other matter which concerns us, it would give me pleasure to save you and your family from any suffering that such a debt might cause."

Then they talked of Jeanette.

"Look, Philippe, this is not something that a discussion will solve," Armand said. "It was unforgivable. The only hope is that it is not unforgettable. It happened. We must just try to forget it, that's all."

Armand did not want to dwell on the details, searching for extenuating circumstances. Intuition told him that Jeanette had certainly played a less than passive role. But the hurt could not be shaded by apportioning the blame. If he was to continue his marriage to Jeanette, it was a question of blotting the whole subject from his mind. Whether he could do this or not remained to be seen. For the moment he could not even bear to talk to her.

Meantime, Jeanette remained unconcerned, almost disappointed that the battle over her body seemed to have fizzled out. She still held a trump card. If Armand tried to make things tough for her, then she would put the pressure on Philippe. They could keep their little secret if they wished, but not at her expense.

Rena did not work the class too closely, spending the majority of her time with the two who still needed the most instruction, Philippe and Arthur Mallory. Following them closely in line to the gondola for the last run she was reasonably gratified with the improvements in their style.

She glanced at her watch as she waited with the others for a last ride of the day on the gondola. It was nearly five minutes to four. She wondered about Silky and Jake, where they were now, whether they were safe, whether they had done whatever they were going to do. She looked round to see Philippe talking to a man in a white ski mask. Then they all began to file into the gondola base.

Silky walked up the hill to the garage at a steady pace. He felt tight, tense, excited, high-pitched. Not afraid. He had trained himself to react to danger aggressively, using it to sharpen his alertness and tune his reflexes. No need to hurry, no cause to be stealthy. Just a nice steady pace.

He looked at the vehicles parked in a semicircle in the yard. Six of them. That meant that they were almost certainly still working on the other two. Good.

He stood about fifty feet away, watching. He was wearing a black one-piece snowmobile suit and a white face mask, with blue trim around the nose and eyes.

A man came out of the garage and walked over to one of the machines. He moved slowly around it, looking at the track, as though checking the tension. Silky didn't move, just watched him. If the man stayed more than three minutes, or if anyone else came out to interfere, the operation was off. It didn't bother Silky. They could pull this caper any day for the next three months. It didn't have to be today. It should be possible to cancel any well-planned operation, up until the very last second. A good general did not get impatient and launch the offensive despite unfavorable conditions, unless he had to. If the conditions weren't right, you called it off.

The man kneeled down to check something. Silky looked at his watch. Then the man stood up, blew on his hands and, putting his gloves back on as he went, sauntered back into the garage, slamming the door behind him.

Silky walked deliberately over to the first machine, put his duffel bag down and took out the machete. He kept the vehicle between him and the garage, but he did not act furtively. The last thing on earth that the people inside would suspect was that someone was slicing up their tracks. You start creeping around like an Indian brave and maybe someone wonders what the hell you are doing. You act normal and no one notices you are even there.

He had cut the tracks on four vehicles, when he heard the car coming up the road. He did not look up. The job was started and it had to be finished. He moved over to the fifth vechicle and started cutting. The car pulled up in front of the garage door and two men got out. Silky moved to the sixth machine, glancing up as he went. One of the men was looking straight at him. Silky waved and the man hesitated, then waved back, turning to enter the garage.

Silky cut the last track, put his machete in the bag, slung it over his shoulder and strolled off across the snow toward the gondola.

Jake was scared. Not scared enough to run away or panic; more overwhelmed by the enormity and finality of the situation, and the loneliness of it. It had begun—there was no stopping it now—and no matter how well they had planned it, it just did not seem possible that they would get away with it. He felt as though he was in a play, acting a part, but knowing deep down inside that the real world was not like that. He seemed paralyzed, sweating, looking for Silky. He needed Silky to get him started. He glanced at his watch, nine minutes to four. "Come on, Silky, for Christ's sake. I've got to move."

Maybe twenty people were waiting for one last ride

before the tow closed. On a good day there would have been a hundred or more, but the cold deterred most of the crowd. He still had time.

Two young people, coming fast, swung off Thunderbolt, skating toward the gondola. Soon, he thought, soon. His heart and head were pounding; he thought for a moment that the blood was going to come gushing out of his nose.

Then a group, apparently a ski class, appeared together, laughing and shouting, their breath coming in clouds. Now. If I don't move, I've blown it.

Then he saw Rena. Holy shit! What the fuck was she doing here? Her class was supposed to be in the morning —Oh, Christ, if she calls my name, we're dead!

She seemed not to recognize him. Then he remembered he was wearing a ski mask!

Where the hell was Silky? Would he want to call it off now that Rena had stumbled in? He was beginning to panic, a sour taste in the back of his throat. Why the hell hadn't they told Rena to keep away from the gondola? Of all the stupid . . .

"You going in?" The man next to him in the lineup startled him.

Jake turned. There was no one between him and the open door to the gondola base.

"Yes, sorry." Jake slung his skis over his shoulder, stumbling clumsily over to the entrance. The man must think he was nuts.

Well, there was nothing he could do now. The drill was that if Silky didn't show up, Jake would just take the gondola to the top and ski down.

There was still time, he told himself. There were about thirty people in the base, separated into the four roped-off aisles as they approached the loading ramp. Jake took the farthest aisle, nearest to the emergency switch, according to plan. He held back, letting others move ahead of him.

The man who had spoken to Jake was now beside him. He noticed white frost marks on his cheekbones.

"Smart man," he said to Jake. "I wish I had one of those face masks on today."

Jake nodded, unzipping the front of his jacket and groping for his automatic. "It wouldn't have done you

145

any good," he said. They were past the point of no return. He had spotted Silky, calmly unpacking his duffel bag, over toward the rear wall.

Two people, young kids, boarded a car, and the attendant slid it shut. This is it, thought Jake, glancing one final time toward Silky, now leaning nonchalantly against the wall, with a submachine gun crooked under his arm.

One of the attendants moved down to the entrance door to close it; he seemed unperturbed when he found it already locked.

Jake ducked under the rope and pushed the emergency switch. A gondola had just gone out, another ready to roll. The motor cut, creating a sudden eerie silence in the almost empty room.

"Hey you!" The attendant made to grab Jake. "What the hell d'you think you're doing?"

Jake stuck his automatic in the man's open mouth with a force that smashed his upper lip against his teeth; it squirted blood. "I'm going to blow your fucking head off, that's what."

The man's eyes popped. He gurgled unintelligibly. Silky fired a short burst into the wall opposite him.

Rena gasped. She knew it was them, but she couldn't believe it.

Jeanette screamed and only stopped when the man in the mask slapped her hard across the face.

"Shut up and lie down," he said.

Lise Gareau felt the creep of terror as it slowly displaced surprise. It was hard to accept the reality of what was happening.

"This is a holdup," one of the masked men announced. That made it real.

Everyone was sprawled on the floor where they had dropped in response to the shots. Skis and poles lay strewn all over.

"What the hell's going on? Are you guys crazy?" Philippe was sitting up looking angry.

One of the masked men spun round aiming his gun at him. "I'm going to shoot at your head, man." He fired a burst as Philippe dropped flat. Everything happened so quickly, that it was hard to tell whether Philippe had been hit.

"Philippe!" Lise screamed.

"I'm O.K." Philippe said in a hoarse whisper.

The other man was dismantling the roped-off aisles. "O.K." he said when he had finished. "One at a time crawl over here and lie on your backs with your hands over your heads." He poked Jane Mallory with his gun. "You. You're first. Move it!"

Kay Mitchell was still in a daze, shivering with cold and fear. She had taken her place against the front wall directly below the opening through which the gondola cars entered and exited. There were four empty cars in the base. The masked man who was giving the orders sat in the open doorway of the nearest car, his gun resting on his knees, watching them as they moved obediently into place, side by side on the floor.

As soon as they had settled down, Jake got up and moved among them deliberately poking each one in the side of the face with his gun, holding it there for ten or fifteen seconds, then on to the next. He felt a surge of excitement. He was intimidating them, building his power over them. He made no exception for Rena, so that she was hardly less afraid than the others.

"That's better," Jake said when he had completed his tour. "Everyone seems to have gotten the idea. You just lay there and keep quiet. We are holding you and everyone on the gondola for ransom. The gondola has been mined and we can blow it from here by radio.

"Now, I want absolute silence. Understand? Absolute silence. Anyone who moves gets their head smashed in or a bullet in the gut. We don't need this many hostages so we can afford to waste a few."

Jake walked across to the rear wall where Silky was waiting. "Rena's in here," he whispered.

Silky stared through the narrow eye-slits of his mask. "Get her out with the first message. Don't make it obvious."

Sam Mitchell glanced cautiously around the room at the others. At least all the kids had gotten out in the last cars before the holdup. Otherwise, everyone else in the group was here. Plus a few other people. He looked down the line of the bodies. He lay next to Kay at the end of the line. On his other side were Jane and Arthur Mallory, then Armand, then the Austrian ski school director, whatever his name was, and a blond woman—Mrs.

Costa, the president's wife, he was almost sure. Further down he could see Lise and Philippe Gareau, Jeanette and another man—the manager of the casino. Finally, over near the door, were the two gondola attendants.

Jake walked over to the end of the line. "You," he gave one of the attendants a prod. "Pick up all the skis and poles and stick them over there." He pointed to the wall behind the empty cars.

The man hopped to his feet and started to clean up the mess, while Jake followed him with the muzzle of his gun. When he had finished, Jake directed him back to his place on the floor.

"Good," Jake commented when everything was in order. "Now, we are going to send one of you out with a message to the management. It contains our ransom terms."

He made a show of walking among the hostages. They were all eyes—terrified, pleading eyes.

He stopped over Rena. "You," he said gruffly, "get up."

Rena rose slowly. She gave him a glint of recognition, but played her part as though she knew the script.

He handed her the package.

"This is a tape," he addressed Rena, loud enough for everyone to hear him. "The lives of all these people depend on this tape being delivered to Mr. O'Malley. Understand? It contains our ransom conditions. Tell him there are five of us; the others will be in in a minute. O.K. Now move it."

Jake escorted her to the door and locked it behind her. Then, on a signal from Silky, he took the intercom telephone off the hook, stuffing a thick rag over the mouth piece and binding it tight, with insulation tape. "Don't call us, we'll call you." He laughed.

It was getting dark now and Silky got busy with the spotlights. He set two of them up side by side, trained directly on the hostages. The lights had a dual purpose, to allow them to keep watch on the prisoners and, at the same time, to give him and Jake cover from the windows. There was always the chance that a police sniper might try a shot at them through the windows along the front of the base, but the spotlights would dazzle anyone who tried it, making it impossible to see the targets.

Meantime, Jake pulled his radio equipment out of the duffel bag and set it carefully on the floor, switching it on to warm it up. He wanted to time the explosion of the chair lift as close as possible to their prediction, as stated in the tape. The tape said fifteen minutes. Give them an extra three minutes to get listening. Eighteen minutes from now should be about right.

"Everything O.K.?" asked Silky.

"Right." He looked at the luminous dial of his watch. "I'm giving them another seventeen minutes. Four thirty-three."

The silence was oppressive. Just the breathing of the hostages, not another sound.

Suddenly, the putter of a snowmobile, then another. They had obviously received the tape and were patrolling, as ordered, to see that there was no one in the danger zone. It was all going like clockwork.

They heard the snowmobiles run to the top, then slowly down again. The whole exercise took about eleven minutes. Three minutes to go.

Jake was building up a little nervous tension again. He was sure his radio switch would work and yet there was always an element of uncertainty. The whole idea was to capture a psychological advantage, absolute control of the situation. But if it didn't blow . . .

Shit. It had to.

He watched the bright needle of the sweep second hand creeping around the watch dial for the last time before blast-off.

Lise Gareau took stock of the situation. Her first thought was for the kids. Thank God they were all out of the base. She had seen Serge and Tim get into a gondola car just before the holdup. They must be hanging just outside the base now. Pray God that they did not do anything silly like trying to jump. The attendant should not have let them go alone, should have insisted on filling the car. But on the last run of the day, when it was not busy, they couldn't care less.

Nicole was with Peter, thank God. Lise liked Peter. He was very reliable. Did they go out alone, just the two of them or were they in the same car as Diana and Jacques?

149

She could not remember. I hope they are all together, she thought.

Who else? She recalled seeing Danielle and Suzanne with their two naval officers. Yes, they were all in one car. She was sure of that.

She glanced around. Most of their group was there as far as she could see. She recognized one or two others. Mrs. Costa, the president's wife. Pepi Mueller, the ski school director. And another young man, dark, quite handsome—oh, yes—she remembered—the man who had greeted them when they went to gamble the other night—he had an unusual name. What was it? Diamant—diamond, she was thinking in French—no, it was Italian. Diamado, that's it. Nick Diamado.

Jim O'Malley was waiting for Rena in the Whi-Ski bar. It was Bloody Mary time. He needed a few after last night's party. So would Rena. Booze did not seem to agree with her. She had drunk a lot last night, yet instead of being relaxed and flirty it had seemed to make her silent and reserved.

He looked out of the window. The gondola had stopped. That was normal. It was after four o'clock. They ought to be on their last run down. But there was no one on Thunderbolt, not a soul. Funny. I hope it's not an accident, he thought. It wouldn't be her—she was too good. But some of her class were rather clumsy.

"Jim!"

He heard her yelling at him from the other end of the cafeteria. She was running, distraught, as though something was terribly wrong.

"They've hijacked the gondola!" she blurted out.

"What?"

"Hijacked the gondola. Five of them." She pushed the little package at him. "This is a tape. Ransom demand. They let me go. Told me to bring it to you." She was panting, looking scared to death.

"Come to my office." He grabbed her by the arm. Some people were staring at them and Jim didn't need to broadcast it to the whole ski area. Not yet, anyway.

He pushed her down in a chair. Mavis was just leaving. She looked at the two of them in amazement, waiting to see what was going to happen next.

"Mavis, call Alfredo. Call Greg. Tell Alfredo there's an emergency and I'm coming up to his office. Tell Greg to join me there. Then call the senior personnel, including Hans at the garage, and tell them not to leave their offices until they hear from me."

"Are you alright, darling?" He turned to Rena.

"I'm fine." She forced a smile.

"Tell me about it—quietly. O.K.? Go ahead."

She recited all that she knew. She had decided that it was the best way to protect Silky and Jake. Whoever they would have let out with the tape would have done the same. If they had wanted her to say anything special, except for the explicit instructions about there being five of them, they would have told her in advance. She had to remember. She was a victim, not a coconspirator. She must act like a victim. Otherwise she would create suspicion.

Jim listened to her story without interruption. "O.K., darling. Relax now. Would you like a drink or something?"

"Yes. Scotch. Double. Thanks."

"O.K., I'll get it for you. Then, if you feel up to it, it would help if you could repeat your story upstairs in Alfredo's office. So everyone can get the picture. Alright?"

"Of course."

Alfredo was sitting behind his big mahogany desk, set at the far end of the room. It was a large office, about forty feet long by thirty wide, with a picture window along one wall, overlooking the slopes.

There was a boardroom table against the wall, alongside the door. The room was furnished with deep calfskin armchairs and sofas, on a beige Indian carpet.

"What's the new emergency, Mr. O'Malley?" There was a slight note of sarcasm in his voice. "It must be something unusual, if you can't handle it yourself." He was eyeing Rena curiously, wondering why Jim had brought her in. He knew that the two of them were going fairly steady together.

"It's unusual, alright." Jim laughed uneasily, not quite sure how to deliver a bombshell. "The gondola has been hijacked!"

151

Alfredo's eyebrows shot up, his eyes glinting with anger. "Mr. O'Malley, don't play the fool, please."

"I'm serious. The gondola has been hijacked by five men."

"When did this happen?"

Jim looked at Rena.

"Just before four o'clock," she said. "They told me to bring this tape to Mr. O'Malley."

"They mentioned him personally?"

"Yes."

He took the tape, inserting it in the recorder in the right hand drawer of his desk.

Jim thought, "I bet he tapes everything that goes on in here, including his phone calls."

Alfredo snapped the top shut and pressed the play-back key.

They waited tensely.

The voice was strange, a bit muffled. He is disguising it, Alfredo thought to himself. Maybe the man is not a fool.

"Here is the situation," the voice began. They had really done a job of masking the voice. Rena could not tell if it was Silky or Jake. "We have laid a number of explosive charges on the gondola lift and on Number One chair lift. We can detonate this explosive from anywhere within a radius of ten miles by radio control. We are heavily armed and we are holding hostages in the gondola base.

"Here are your instructions.

"First. Clear everyone away from Number One chair. We will be blowing it up in fifteen minutes. This is just to show you that we are not bluffing. Do this at once. It will be your fault if someone is killed.

"Second. We want two million dollars for the release of the hostages in the gondola and the base."

Alfredo whistled through his teeth and snapped the pencil he was holding in two pieces. The voice continued in a slow deliberate monotone.

"The money is to be paid in hundred-dollar bills. That is twenty thousand one-hundred-dollar bills.

"The bills are to be in stacks of two hundred, each stack bound with a rubber band.

"All the bills are to be used bills, with random serial

numbers. There is to be no marking with visible or invisible ink or any other substance. They will be chemically checked before we leave, and tested for radioactivity. Any attempt to trick us will result in people getting killed.

"The money is to be delivered as soon as possible, with two hours the outside limit. Don't forget that the people on the gondola are slowly freezing to death.

"It is to be delivered, in two canvas bags, personally by Mr. O'Malley. We know what he looks like, so don't send any brave cops as substitutes. He is to come to the side door, bare-headed, and hold a flashlight to his face as he approaches. He will wait while we test and count it and will then be given further instructions.

"Third. Do not try to contact us or to negotiate our terms. They are not negotiable. If you break this rule, we will assume that you are not cooperating and we will shoot a hostage.

"Fourth. We will kill a hostage at six sharp if Mr. O'Malley has not delivered the money by then. We will then kill one at a time until we run out, finally blowing the gondola. The lives of a large number of people depend on you doing what you are told and doing it fast.

"Do not waste time wondering if we are serious. If you still have misgivings, watch Number One chair."

Greg had come in at the tail end.

"Make sure Number One chair is clear, Greg," Jim barked an order. "It's going to be blown up at any minute. Call the top on the intercom and tell the operator to stay clear. Call Hans, tell him to run a couple of skidoos up, but make sure they stay away from the towers. Get the ski patrol to insure no one goes near the lift line. It's twenty past, so there shouldn't be anybody, but we'd better be on the safe side."

Alfredo turned to Rena. "You saw the men?" he asked.

"No, not really. They were wearing face masks."

"They were armed?"

"Yes. Pistols and machine guns."

"Did you recognize any of the people, the skiers who were being held hostage?"

"Of course. Most of them were in my ski class."

"Most of them? Who else? Did you recognize any of the others?"

"Yes." Rena lowered her eyes, feeling guilty, then forced herself to look back and hold Alfredo's gaze.

"Pepi was there and Nick too. And Mrs. Costa, I'm afraid."

The phone rang shrilly. Jim picked it up.

At the same moment, there was a flash outside the window, followed by a muffled explosion. The window seemed to bend inward, vibrating, but it did not collapse. The coffee cup on Alfredo's desk rattled and the teaspoon spilt on the glass top with a tiny tinkle.

"They're not fooling." Alfredo turned to look at everyone, his face white with rage.

Hans came through on the phone. "I guess that was the chair. I'm afraid I have some more bad news. They have slashed the tracks on six vehicles. The other two are down. The engine is out of one and the differential is out of the other. It would be four or five hours before I could get one mobile. Do you want me to start?"

"No. Forget it."

Jim reported to Alfredo. He said nothing. His hand crept unconsciously to the silver paper knife in front of him. His fist tightened around it, as though he was throttling someone, his eyes fixed on the blade. Then, on an impulse, he swung it above his head and smashed it on the desk top, shattering the glass.

"Leave me alone," he said quietly.

Suzanne had suffered from vertigo since she was a child. It made her feel dizzy to look down from the window of her parents' sixth story apartment, or even to climb a few rungs of a ladder. When, at the age of eight, her parents had taken her to the lookout in Mount Royal Park, overlooking the city of Montreal, she had stubbornly turned her head, and when her father had held her on his shoulders and walked to the edge, she had kicked and clawed him in a paroxysm of terror, drawing blood on his cheek.

As she grew older she had learned to control the phobia by keeping her eyes level, never looking down. And when she took up skiing with a group of friends, she had to make the decision whether to continue with the sport, or be ruled by fear. Love of skiing had made her persevere, and gradual familiarity with the feeling of midair travel had enabled her to bring the problem tolerably under control.

This afternoon, when the lift stopped suddenly, an awful feeling of helpless fear engulfed her, closing her off from her companions with a terrible pounding and buzzing in her ears.

"I feel sick," she moaned.

She felt Dave's arm tighten around her shoulders. It helped, the sensation of something solid to hang on to.

"She suffers from vertigo," Danielle explained. "We've got to take her mind off it."

"I have just the thing," said Dick, the other young ensign, feeling in his pocket and pulling out a flask of brandy. "This is good for vertigo, ulcers, chilblains, and hangovers. Have a shot."

Suzanne looked at him wanly. He helped her to take a sip.

She leaned her head back and felt the comforting warmth of the liquor in her churning stomach.

BOOM! There was a flash, followed immediately by a muffled explosion.

"Mon Dieu! Strong stuff." Danielle's humor was always at the tip of her tongue. "Let me have a shot."

"What the hell was that?" Dick said.

Dave was staring out of the window. "An explosion of some kind. Over by the chair lift. I don't know."

"Are you sure it wasn't us? The gondola, I mean?"

"Quite sure. I only saw it for a second, but it was at least half-a-mile away."

Dick retrieved the flask from Danielle and offered it back to Suzanne. She made no reply. She had fainted.

Alfredo was on the phone to Salvatore.

"Pat too?" Salvatore was incredulous. "It must be an inside job. With Nick and Pat in there, they've got us by the balls."

"Could be," Alfredo agreed. "But I don't see how anyone could have known Pat was skiing. Even I didn't."

There was a long silence. Alfredo deliberately swept a big chip of glass from his desk to the wastepaper basket. "What about the police, then? Do I call them?"

"Yes," Salvatore said. Godammit, it was like calling in the Russians to settle an American strike riot. But Mount

Casino was a legitimate front and he had to try to think like a legitimate businessman. "Don't let them see the books, understand. I'll send Sol up right away. And I'll put in a fix at the top. What's the local county sheriff like?"

"Stupid. Completely incompetent."

"Good. Everything's normal then. I'll get to him as fast as I can, but it will take time. Meanwhile, go ahead and call the police. And play ball with the hijackers. Give them the money. We'll get it back," he said confidently, "and we will fix those sons-of-bitches so they'll wish they had never been born."

The two youngsters, Tim Mallory and Serge Gareau, had caught the last gondola car to leave the base; their cab was not more than twenty feet from the building, maybe thirty feet in the air, when the lift came to a sudden halt.

They were not especially concerned. It was not the first time for either of them to be stopped on a lift. More often than not, in the case of chair lifts and T-bars, it just meant that someone had been clumsy getting on or off and that the operator had pushed the emergency button.

Premonition of evil had no place in their young minds and they accepted the delay without comment. When the man on the snowmobile called up to say that it was a technical breakdown, they sat back patiently to wait. It was their last run of the day anyway.

The explosion of the chair lift was so sudden and unexpected, was over so swiftly, that they did not know what to make of it. A huge flash lighting up the sky, an ominous rumble, then silence.

"What was it, Serge?" Tim asked.

"I don't know. An explosion of some sort. But it wasn't on this lift. It was over there," he pointed, "about half-a-mile away."

"What about us? Do you think our stoppage has anything to do with it? Maybe there is some big electric failure or something. I'm frightened."

"Could we jump?" Serge asked Tim's opinion. "We're not very high."

156

They looked out, judging the distance to the ground. "I don't think we should." He looked out of the front window. He could see his elder brother, Peter, in the next car up ahead with Nicole. "Let's wait and see what Peter does," he said. He had confidence that Peter would know what to do.

They remained relatively calm, much calmer than most of the little groups dangling silently in the sky like holidaymakers on a broken Ferris wheel. The innocence and discipline of youth.

Peter and Nicole sat together in the gondola car so engrossed in each other's company that they hardly noticed they had stopped.

Nicole had become the epicenter of everything in Peter's life. His final year at school, his college career, his future employment had all suddenly taken on a new degree of importance. They were all steps on a long journey to a predestined goal, his eventual marriage to this adorable girl.

Two things for sure. He would never soil her virginity until the wonderful day that she became his wife. He would never look at another girl as long as he lived.

BOOM! They both stared out of the window together. "What was that?"

Peter saw the tower of the chair lift lying crumpled on the ground. He did not want to scare her, was sure she had not noticed it. "I don't know," he lied, "probably someone blasting rock somewhere. Maybe they're cutting a new trail. On the top of the mountain."

"Why're we stopped, d'you think?"

"Malfunction, I expect." Peter moved across the car to sit beside her. He put his arm around her shoulders. "Come on, snuggle up and keep warm. It may be a while before we get started again."

The last ride up the mountain was Jacques's first chance to get Diana to himself since the episode in her bedroom two nights ago. She had hardly spoken to him all day and she had spent half the New Year's Eve party dancing with grown-ups, some of the ski pros, even his father.

"Can I come to your room again tonight?" He blurted out the question.

She looked at him patronizingly. "You're too greedy."

"I'm just crazy about you, that's all. I can't help it," he whined.

"You're a typical little Frenchman," she said. "Oversexed."

"Christ, Diana. You're driving me mad. I know that you're not a virgin."

"Oh? How do you know that?"

"Peter told me."

She considered whether to deny it. There was no point. "I'm more choosy now."

"Oh, come on, Diana. I know you like it."

"It? What do you mean—*it?* I'm not a goddam whore, you know—I just, well," she shrugged, "sometimes—very rarely, of course—I may like someone enough to go all the way."

"Oh, alright, then." He pouted. Then he started again. "What about the same as the other night?" He was ready to settle for half measures if that was all he could get. "Only keep going until . . ."

BOOM!

Diana roared with laughter.

"What the hell was that?" Jacques asked.

"I don't know," Diana was howling with laughter, "I thought it was you going off in your pants."

Carl Svenson, the county sheriff, sat down heavily in one of the calves leather armchairs and pulled out a cigar. He was a jowly, florid-faced, porcine man with small, piggy eyes. A tough cop, but not a smart one.

Alfredo took charge at once. He was not going to allow this fool to play with his money and his wife.

"We are going to have to pay, Carl," Alfredo opened.

"Well, sir, I don't know about that. That's for me to judge. I have a duty . . ."

Alfredo cut him off. "You have a duty not to get us all killed, Carl. The money can be raised and that's what we are going to do. You can catch the thieves after they leave Mount Casino. But while they are on this property, there will be no shooting."

Carl let out a lot of air, almost visibly deflating.

"Now, I can get some of the money," Alfredo continued, "but I can't get it all, in the time limit, without some police authority. I will handle the casinos, which should account for a million, maybe a million two, but the rest must come from the banks.

"The banks are going to waste time, want to call head office for authority, need papers filled out. All of which will take twice as long today, because it is a public holiday.

"I want you, personally, to pick up the managers of all the banks, arrest them if you have to, get them over to the station, and explain the situation. Our comptroller, Mr. Cambetta, will go with you.

"It is ten-to-five, so we have seventy minutes to deliver. Telephone me as soon as you have a commitment from the banks, because we have to let the kidnappers know that we are paying. Ask for a million-and-a-quarter, to be on the safe side, and if they are short, get them to call on reserves in Reno. Finally, sign nothing other than a simple receipt for the money."

"Now see here, Mr. Costa. My place is here at the scene of the crime. I have to deploy my men, intercept the getaway and so on. And the FBI should be here soon. They are going to want a say in this."

"Mr. Svenson. People, maybe one hundred and fifty of them, are freezing to death, *literally* to death, on that gondola. A dozen or more people are being held at gunpoint in the base. The first thing to do is to save those people. You can play cops and robbers after you have done your duty to protect human lives. Get your deputy to take over the ground forces. Now stop wasting time!"

"I will have to put this in my report, Mr. Costa. It is not regular."

"Put what you please in your report, Svenson."

Mavis bent down to pick up Carl's hat and handed it to him. "Come on, sheriff." She smiled encouragingly at him.

"O.K. I'll give it half-an-hour. Burton can lay out a plan of action for my approval while I'm gone."

As Carl moved toward the door, Alfredo made a sweeping gesture with his hand. "Everyone out. Now. I have to make some phone calls. We will meet here again at five-fifteen."

Jim had excused himself from Alfredo's office as

159

quickly as he could, signalling Rena and Mavis to go with him.

"There must be bedlam in the lodge and the hotel," he called over his shoulder, as he ran along the corridor to his office. "Mavis, patch me through on the main intercom."

He had no time to prepare anything. He just ad-libbed an announcement stating the bare facts, stressing the danger of being caught in crossfire or wounded by an explosion. He then appealed to all those who did not have a close friend or relative involved in the hijacking to leave the area as soon as possible. It was vital to everyone's safety to clear the building and the parking lot quickly.

Finally, he asked all those with reason to believe that someone close to them was on the gondola to find a seat in the cafeteria. Staff members would contact them there shortly.

Next he called Paul Mullins.

"Paul, will you handle the P.R. problem, please?—good man. Do what you have to do. You will surely think of more points than I can, but be sure to cover the following. One, get the names of everyone waiting for a friend or relative. Get two lists, people here and a full inventory, if possible, of all gondola passengers.

"Two, call the hospital. Talk to someone in charge and organize emergency service, you know, doctors, nurses, blankets, and so on. We'll bring everyone into the cafeteria. Use the instructors' locker room for emergency.

"Three, have the cafeteria staff lay on some hot food and drinks. Keep tabs on what is going on and get it going as soon as you see the gondola move."

"What about the press?" Paul asked. "They'll be on to a thing like this in a few minutes. We should initiate it. They will be a lot more cooperative if we do."

"Hold it until I get an O.K. from Alfredo. But you can get started typing something up for approval. Stick to the facts, no cover-up, or they will print something worse than the truth."

He turned to Rena. "Look, I am going to be very busy now. Why don't you go back to your apartment and relax?"

Relax! she thought. If only he knew. She felt a pang

160

of remorse watching Jim working to break out of a trap that she had helped to set. She was a double agent with friends and lovers in both camps. But her loyalty did not waver. It remained with Jake and Silky. For their sake, she would be better out of the way. Less chance of making some fatal slip.

"Alright, Jim," she said, feigning exhaustion. "Phone me when it's over."

Two hours, they had said. Two hours with everyone's life on the line. It would be excruciating to be completely cut off from any news. Maybe she would sneak back later, just as an observer, to see how everything was working out. Oh God, she prayed, please keep them safe. And please don't let anyone get killed.

Jim paced his office, chain-smoking. "Anything else you can think of, Mavis?"

"Nothing, cool boy. You are running through it just as though you had rehearsed it."

He stared at her. "What d'you mean?"

"Just that you are right on top of the situation as usual." She smiled.

Burton came in without bothering to knock. He was the deputy chief of the Lake Tahoe police force.

"What's the situation, from your point of view?" Jim asked him.

"The sheriff is on his way over. He has alerted the FBI and there should be a bomb squad coming in by helicopter any minute. The State Police officials are on their way from Carson City with reinforcements and I expect the Governor's office will get involved too. This is a big one. There is going to be a problem sorting our jurisdictions. Anyway, we're in charge until further notice."

"Are my arrangements satisfactory?"

"More or less," Burton said. "We've closed the bar. And we're putting a tight control on the people in the cafeteria. I would rather have everyone right out of here really, but I don't want to countermand your instructions for the moment. At the far end of the cafeteria they are quite safe. We'd better make sure they don't get in our way."

161

"What about the ransom? Can we get it? Will you pay?" Jim asked.

"I don't see much option at the moment. We have to assume that they will carry out their threats. The sheriff will have to decide that."

"He had better decide damn quick. We haven't got much time."

The phone rang. It was Alfredo. He wanted everyone back in his office in five minutes.

He turned to Burton. "We might as well go on up. You too Mavis."

There was an eerie silence in the gondola base, broken only by the sound of human breathing. The spotlights, focussed on the huddled group of hostages, threw ghostly shadows on the wall exaggerating every small gesture into grotesque silhouettes. It gave Jake the creeps.

"Watch 'em," Silky whispered. "Things are going too well."

Suddenly the tension was broken by the sound of snowmobiles, maybe two or three of them, cruising the gondola line. That was fine. It meant that none of the big vehicles was mobile; the two in the garage must still be under major repair. So there was no way they were going to be able to try to evacuate the gondola cars. The trap was closed.

They heard a loud hailer, quite close at hand, someone talking to the people in the gondola cars, telling them that there was a technical malfunction—absolutely no danger —and insisting that, on no account, should anyone try to leave his car.

Jake counted the hostages. He felt a sudden clutch of panic. "There's thirteen of them, including the two lift attendants."

"Unlucky for them." Silky smiled behind his mask.

CHAPTER EIGHT

RENA stood at the window of her apartment, looking out at the mountain.

Until now, she had never really had to come to terms with the stark realities of the operation; since she had not been privy to the plan, it had always remained slightly in the realm of fantasy. It was a drama in which she played a shadowy, minor part. Now, all of a sudden, it was a nightmare in which she had become the female lead. Left alone, she found it almost impossible to cope with the enormity of it.

The sheer daring of it! Her two young, happy-go-lucky confederates were suddenly transformed into cold-blooded terrorists pitted against society. The stakes were enormously high: it was their lives against those of perhaps two hundred innocent people! And she was a part of it!

Her mind was in turmoil. Visions of prison, of innocent people maimed, of impending disaster intruded into her prayers for the success and safety of Silky and Jake.

But how could they expect to get away with it? It did not seem possible. The whole world was ranged against them. The plan was surely doomed from the start.

Utterly dejected, she gazed out of the window, wondering what to do. She could see the gondola cars, somber shapes against a dark sky. Two narrow shafts of light, snowmobile headlights, were creeping up the mountain, like angry eyes straining to find an escape from the black trap. The flashers of a dozen police cars swirled in the parking lot.

She could stand it no longer. She must get some information—any news, good or bad, to relieve the tension. She decided to return to the ski lodge.

"Sons of bitches," Nick Diamado muttered under his breath. My God, when Salvatore caught these bastards he would make them scream for mercy. He knew that his father would never let them go unpunished. If necessary, he would track them to the ends of the earth.

Poor slobs, he sneered to himself, they didn't know who they were up against. They might think that they could beat the police, but they would never escape the vengeance of the family.

Why did they have to go and blow up the chair lift? The wanton destruction infuriated him. A hundred-thousand dollar chair lift gone, all because of a couple of vicious maniacs.

If they made a mistake, maybe he would get a chance to outmaneuver them. Watch their every move, he said to himself; better check the lay of the land.

Philippe Gareau was on one side of him, a scared blonde woman on the other. Gareau, at least, might back him up if he got a chance to jump one of the gunmen. It could be worse.

Funny thing about Gareau. You would think he would have been pissed off about his friend blowing thirty-five grand on his guarantee. He might be wealthy, but nobody kisses that kind of dough away for somebody else.

Yet he had come knocking at Nick's office door positively begging for a chance to pay off the debt.

"Don't worry, Mr. Gareau, your credit is good way over that," Nick had said.

"I want to pay it." He handed Nick a check. "I don't want my friend to worry about it."

Jesus! Some kind of friendship! The other guy, Leclerc, had to have some hold over Gareau or something.

If Nick had sent out a call for volunteers amongst the captives to mount a counteroffensive against the two masked men, he would have been sorely disappointed with the turnout. All of them, including Nick, had their lives on the line. But none of them, other than Nick, had any other interest at stake; after all, they were not being asked to make any personal contribution toward the ransom. The best way for each to protect his own skin was to do exactly as he was told—to lie completely still.

Even though there were thirteen of them huddled together on the floor, the rule of silence, which had been enforced since the very outset, allowed no discussion of their predicament. Each one was imprisoned alone with his thoughts. Such solitary confinement was not fertile breeding ground for heroes.

They are really gamblers bargaining for high stakes Philippe mused wryly. Men with the imagination and skill to plan such a daring stratagem were hardly likely to be sadistic murderers. Very possibly, they would shrink from the act of killing, even if it were in their own interests to do so. However, he had no intention of putting them to the test. What, he wondered, was the size of the ransom they were demanding? In their position what would he ask? As much as the market would bear, of course. He considered this for a moment, reviewing the potential sources. The banks. The casinos. These men were no fools, they had obviously selected their target with care. A million at least. They should not be asking less than a million. Was the enormous risk justified by the potential reward? He discarded the idea of asking them. The less attraction he drew to himself, the better. They might find out what he was worth and decide to sweeten the pot with a personal contribution from him. It was ironic really: had they known about him and Arthur Mallory, they could easily have picked up enough to double their kitty!

As things now stood, he was being held to ransom, but somebody else had to pay it.

He glanced around. Lise seemed calm. Both the kids were out. They were probably cold and scared, but they were safe. Nicole was alright if she was with Peter. Serge? He'd be okay as long as he didn't do something stupid, like try to jump.

He caught Nick Diamado's eye. There was something disconcerting about the look that Nick gave him; aggressive, angry, like a wild animal about to spring.

Philippe shook his head, at the same time trying to increase the distance between them.

"Keep still, you," Silky barked at Philippe. "One false move and I'll stick a grenade in your pants."

Pat Costa had never been so cold in her life. She was seriously afraid she would freeze to death if she were not allowed to move soon. It was deep inside her body, an excruciating pain that penetrated her bones and muscles.

Christ, how did she get into this? Well, at least, when Alfredo found out that she was involved, he would pay the ransom. The others had her to thank for that. If she weren't a hostage, he would probably let the police fight it out with the hijackers, preferring a few nameless people to be killed or wounded.

She had to move soon. Should she tell them who she was? If they knew that she was the president's wife, they would surely consider her the prime captive. And they would not want to kill her because she would be worth more to them alive.

Then another thought struck her. When the hijackers made their getaway they would surely take some of the hostages with them, probably only a few. In that case they would take the ones through whom they could exercise the most leverage.

Perhaps it would be wise to keep quiet a little longer. She gritted her teeth. The pain was beginning to ease. Her arms and legs were slowly going numb.

They had been suspended in midair for over an hour now and had gradually accommodated themselves to the circumstances. Despite the extreme cold outside, the temperature inside the cab was maintained at a reasonable level by their body heat.

Suzanne had succumbed to an intense fit of shivering immediately after regaining consciousness. However, a few more good slugs out of the flask had succeeded in making her a little drunk, anaesthetizing her nerves, so that now she lay quietly in a sort of semiconscious limbo.

They had all taken off their ski boots, tucking their toes under the armpits of the person opposite, legs intertwined across the narrow aisle. Each man hugged a girl close, like two couples bundled at opposite ends of a huge double bed. Given their warm outerwear and liberally brandied insides, they were relatively comfortable.

Out of concern for Suzanne, Dave had only taken a

couple of quick nips at the flask, leaving the rest for Dick and Danielle. A fatalist by nature, Danielle saw no point in dwelling on the danger of their predicament. They were here, they were alive, they were powerless to alter the situation. The best thing to do was to be cheerful. Having helped Dick empty the flask, she was teaching him to sing a well-known French-Canadian folk song. The strains of "Alouette" floated incongruously on the cold night air, like a bright feather blowing across a silent battlefield.

Despite the fact that twelve other poor souls were sharing his discomfort, Armand took this infuriating holdup as a calculated assault against him personally. Some vacation!

Having been the one voice of reason raised against this ridiculous holiday, he was now its most injured victim. He had dropped a fortune at the tables, had lost his wife to his best friend, his business was in jeopardy, and now what? Here he was, grovelling on the ground, his very life in danger.

This is the last straw, he thought. My nerves are shot, my ulcer is killing me, and I'm freezing to death. I might just as well charge at these two bastards and let them put an end to my misery!

He gave the idea of a hero's death some consideration. By God, it would damn well make Jeanette contrite. At least, he would have that satisfaction.

He eyed the two masked bandits, sizing them up.

Jake seemed to sense his mood. He gave him a poke with the snout of his gun. "Don't get any ideas, man," he said menacingly.

Armand stared at the black steel barrel, an inch from his nose. He began to tremble. There was no satisfaction in death.

The five-fifteen meeting in Alfredo's office was brief and businesslike.

They reviewed the situation.

Alfredo reported that the casinos would come up with at least a million. They would send a man over with it as soon as possible. There was no word yet from Svenson on the contribution from the banks.

Burton reported that all available police were being

concentrated in the area. He should have at least thirty men in position by five-thirty, including a couple of trained sharpshooters. He went on to say that the FBI had been alerted. They were sending up some agents by helicopter, accompanied by a team of demolition experts.

Greg was directed to help Burton to set up a temporary police communications center in the accounting office. "And bring the plans and drawings of the gondola," Jim went on. "The bomb squad will need them."

"Anything else we can do at this stage?" Alfredo asked.

"Yes, sir. The press has been alerted, but I was awaiting your approval before releasing anything. I got Paul Mullins to draft this statement." He placed it in front of Alfredo among the slivers of broken glass. "I would like your approval to let it go. There are already some reporters on the premises."

Alfredo picked the release up and moved to one of the armchairs. "Perhaps you would not mind cleaning up the mess, Mavis." He indicated the splintered glass on his desk. The request was made quietly and gently; it was typical of Alfredo's courteous consideration of women under even the most trying circumstances.

He read the release carefully. "Good." He nodded. "Go ahead." He returned it to Jim.

Snatching it up, Jim strode quickly to Paul Mullins's office at the end of the passageway.

There were half-a-dozen reporters crowded together in the room, fighting over the telephone, scribbling in notebooks, yelling questions at Paul Mullins, clamoring for information and interviews.

Jim's entry into the room was a signal for even more vociferous pushing and shoving. Microphones were shoved into his face as he pushed roughly through the mob to the chair behind the desk. Holding up both his hands, he shouted, "Shut up! For Christ's sake, shut up! I only have five minutes."

Given some semblance of order, he started, "Look, gentlemen—ladies and gentlemen," he corrected himself, spotting a spectacled girl with long, black hair in the group, "we want to cooperate as much as we can. But I must ask you to be patient. There are a lot of people in very grave danger, and our first concern must be for their safety. I realize that you want to talk to some

168

of the key people like Mr. Costa, the police chief, and myself. But we must be available, for the moment, to make the decisions required to protect the hostages.

"As soon as the hostages are safe, which should be in about one hour from now, we will hold a short press conference. We will hold another one tomorrow at ten o'clock in the morning. In the meantime, I will try to keep Paul informed as to what is going on.

"For the moment, I must ask you to be patient and to use the press releases, as they are issued.

"I can add a few things at this time. First, the ransom demand is two million dollars. Second, we intend to pay it. Third, the deadline is six o'clock. Fourth, the hijackers have cut off the intercom system with the base and refused to communicate with us except by pre-dictated tapes. At this point we have no further information."

A storm of angry voices greeted this announcement. Ignoring the commotion, Jim fought his way to the door. Somehow the black-haired girl twisted out of the throng to accompany him.

She grabbed his arm. "Now listen, mister," she protested, "I have a right . . ." He swung his hand out, involuntarily knocking her hard against the wall, and turned back up the passage to the communications center.

Jeanette Leclerc had been watching Nick Diamado for an hour. He was a good-looking young man, stocky and strong. She noticed the monogram on his custom-made red ski suit.

He seemed more alert than the others, watching every move that the hijackers made. He had looked at her from time to time and she got the impression that he wanted her to help him in some way.

It was all rather exciting. But what coud she do?

Then it dawned on her. Create a diversion, of course.

She thought about it for a while. Gradually a plan formed in her mind.

"Please?" she said aloud.

The plaintive sound of her voice broke the oppressive silence like the blare of trumpets. Everyone stared at her in amazement.

169

The two machine guns lifted as if by reflex. "What?" snapped Silky.

"I have to go to the bathroom."

Jake laughed involuntarily. Jesus, he thought, we forgot to plan for this. "Do it in your pants, lady."

"I can't," said Jeanette weakly.

There was a long silence. Everyone relaxed. Philippe looked at her in disgust. That moth-eaten little pussy of hers got into more trouble . . . His mind froze in horror at what he saw. She had deliberately winked at Nick Diamado—oh, God.

"Please?"

What the hell could Philippe do to stop her? The silly bitch was going to get them all killed.

"Fuck," Silky said. He got up and walked over to where she lay, nudging her in the belly, with his machine gun.

"Does that help?" he asked.

"Please," she groaned pitifully.

"O.K. Piss in the corner over there."

Deliberately, she squatted on her haunches, dropping her pants. Philippe watched in petrified fascination as Nick Diamado grabbed for Silky's ankle.

There was a crash. Silky hit the concrete floor and his machine gun fell at Jeanette's feet. She made a lunge for it at the same time as Jake delivered a flying kick which caught her flush in the mouth.

Nick jumped on Silky's back, grabbing both his wrists. Silky rolled over in a cold fury and brought his knee up into Nick's crotch. As Nick released his grip, Silky gave him a backhand chop across the ear with his left hand. Forced on the defensive, Nick caught Silky's right hand from above and, summoning all his strength, started bending it back. He felt Silky's forefinger break at the first knuckle.

Then the butt of Jake's machine gun came crashing down on the back of Nick's head.

Silky got up and retrieved his gun. Jeanette lay beside it, blood trickling down her chin. She still had her pants down. He gave her bare bottom a resounding thwack.

"You little bitch," he snarled.

The tension was electric as Silky and Jake moved back

170

to their position against the far wall. Silky waited to recover his breath before he spoke.

"See if he's dead," Silky panted loud enough for everyone to hear. "If he isn't, I'm going to shoot him."

Jake prodded the motionless body with his foot. It groaned. The hands began clutching, knees slowly flexing. Jake watched the signs of recovery in disgust.

"Pull the sonofabitch over against the wall," Silky commanded.

Jake clenched his teeth. The bastard was going to get what he deserved. He dragged Nick over beside the door.

"Watch the others," Silky said. "This one's mine." Slinging his gun over his shoulder, he reached inside his jacket for his Beretta automatic. He grabbed Nick by his collar. "Stand up, you bastard," he said, swiping him across the face.

Nick rose slowly, propping himself againt the wall. He seemed more dazed than afraid.

Silky clicked off the safety catch. He took deliberate aim at pointblank range. A shot rang out, the noise singing and clanging in huge echos, like church bells in an empty cathedral. Nick slumped to the floor.

Only Jeanette's muffled sobbing punctuated the horrified silence which followed.

Silky stood over the body for a moment as he put the automatic back in its holster. "He's not dead," he said contemptuously, "I plugged him in the shoulder."

Jake gasped. "Christ! Why?"

"He's not in the contract," Silky said firmly. "We don't kill anyone till six o'clock. That's our deal."

"But the bastard disobeyed orders," Jake argued.

"So. He won't do it again."

Nick began to show signs of life; he was making gurgling noises. Hoisting him to his feet, Silky slapped his face to get him fully conscious.

Nick cowered, looking plaintively at Silky. His left hand went slowly to his shoulder, feeling the warm blood.

"Now listen to me," Silky shook him. Nick puked right there, spewing some vomit over Silky.

Silky waited.

"Okay, you gutless asshole. You listen to me. You're not dead. You're simply bleeding a bit. You just about got everyone killed. Now, you're going to run a message

171

for me, understand? Go and find Mr. O'Malley. Tell him to get a move on with the money. Tell him we mean business. Got it?"

Nick nodded.

Silky opened the door, taking care to stand at the side. He gave Nick a kick in the ass. "Now fuck off!"

He strolled back to where Jake was standing. Their eyes met through the slits of their masks.

"You should've wasted him," Jake snapped.

"No," Silky answered deliberately. "We aren't going to break our conditions. We kill if the ransom doesn't show by six o'clock. Not before."

Jake said nothing. It was no time to argue. He watched Silky peel off his right glove, false finger and all.

Silky inspected the finger critically, but could see no damage. It had simply twisted off the stump under pressure. He slipped the finger back in place and drew on the glove.

He was sure he had been right about Nick. He had felt a sudden explosion of rage. But it would have been an act of reckless provocation to have killed him.

Jim O'Malley was in the communications center when he heard the shot.

They all moved to the window overlooking the base.

"My God!" said the FBI man, "there is going to be a blood bath if they are shooting hostages already."

"Maybe someone has jumped the hijackers," Burton said hopefully.

Suddenly the door to the base was flung open and a figure stumbled out. Jim caught a glimpse of the red ski suit. "It looks like Nick," he said, turning on his heel to run downstairs.

Nick leaned against the window of the cafeteria, clutching at the glass as he slid slowly to the ground.

"Christ!" Jim leapt through the door. "Give me a hand," he called to a burly cop as he passed him.

They carried Nick down to the locker room and laid him on a table. There was a doctor already there and other medical personnel from the hospital.

Nick was still conscious, staring up in bewilderment, as a couple of orderlies quickly cut off his bloodstained jacket. "The bastard shot me," he said.

172

Jim watched anxiously as they bared his chest and stemmed the flow of blood from his shoulder. Then they pulled off his pants and checked for any further injuries.

"Doesn't look too bad," the doctor reported as he worked. "Flesh wound. Bad contusions on the back of the neck. Deep shock. He'll be alright. Keep him warm and dress the wound. Then move him out. I'll call the hospital."

"Better come to the communications room," Jim suggested. "Best place for a phone."

Just as he was going out of the door, Jim heard his name called. It was Nick croaking at him, "Jim!"

He turned and came back. Nick mumbled something. "I didn't get it, Nick," Jim said.

Nick lifted his left hand, weakly motioning him closer. Jim bent down, his ear at Nick's mouth.

"I busted his finger," Nick whispered.

"Which one?" Jim asked.

There was no reply. Nick had passed out.

The bomb squad men were in the communications room, two of them, pouring over the technical drawings of the gondola lift.

"How's it going?" Jim asked Greg.

"A bit of a hitch," Greg said, nodding at one of the bomb men. "You explain it."

"Why in the name of Christ didn't someone tell us about the radio detonation?" The bomb man said in obvious disgust. "We could have brought a jammer."

"Hell!" Jim answered. "I suppose no one thought about it. Can't you do anything?"

"Oh, sure. We can go up and disarm the charges—if we can find them. But a jammer would have wiped out any chance of explosion. It's too late to bring one in now."

"Can't be helped." The other bomb man seemed less inclined to waste time with recriminations. "Let's get on with it."

"I had better leave you to it," Jim smiled encouragement. "I've got to let Alfredo know what's going on. He'll be wondering about the shot."

The bomb squad returned to their drawings. "Must be the towers," one of them said, "probably the top ones.

173

We'd better get on with dismantling. How do we get up there?"

"I'll take you up," Greg volunteered. "But I'm afraid that our grooming vehicles have all been knocked out. It will have to be by snowmobile."

"That's it, then. Perhaps you would come with us to get our gear. It's in the squad car."

"Sure," said Greg. "Got any warm clothing?" They were both in light overcoats.

"Afraid not. By the way, could you bring some shovels?"

"Okay," Greg said. "You go ahead to get your gear. I'll call the garage and get a couple of snowmobiles over. I'll ask Hans to bring some shovels and see if I can rustle up some parkas for you. You got flashlights?"

"Sure."

"I should be there in five minutes." He looked at his watch. "Christ, it's nearly five-thirty and we're supposed to deliver at six. Not much time."

Alfredo was standing at his office door looking apoplectic. "My God!" he said angrily to Jim. "Where have you been? Doesn't anyone think to let me know what's going on here? Who got shot?"

"Nick. It's nothing serious. Just a flesh wound. They have taken him to the hospital."

"Nick? Jesus, I'll have to phone Salvatore!"

"I wouldn't," Jim ventured. "Wait till the party is over. There's not much time. Don't bother his father until we have a full report from the hospital. He's not going to die or anything."

Alfredo ignored him, turning on his heel.

As Jim made his way back to his own office, he found police everywhere; they had taken over virtual control of the parking lot and building. Two armed and helmeted men guarded the main entrance and, looking past them, he could see perhaps fifteen or twenty squad cars parked outside.

It was like an armed camp. The bar, in fact the complete lodge, had been entirely cleared of civilian personnel. A group of friends and relatives of the gondola passengers, had been herded into the far corner of the cafeteria, away from the windows, under the watchful eye of two officers.

Burton had also posted the two sharpshooters and three of his best shots in strategic positions, overlooking the gondola base. Each had a high-powered rifle at the ready, but had been given strict instructions not to fire, on any account, without a direct order from Burton himself. One of their main duties was to watch the base and to report at once on any suspicious activity.

Suddenly Jim remembered something. He called Burton on the intercom.

"Burton?"

"Yes?"

"O'Malley here. Maybe we have got something to help us catch these bastards. Some identification. Nick said that he busted the finger of one of them."

"Good," said Burton. "That could be just what we need. Thanks, Jim, I appreciate it." Then, as an afterthought, "Did he say which finger?"

"Afraid not. But when he has recovered a bit more, he may be able to tell you. They took him to the hospital."

"O.K., Jim. Thanks for the help."

Jeanette's sobbing had subsided, and everyone had settled back to the silent vigil.

Suddenly they heard the staccato roar of snowmobile engines, close at hand, then charging up the mountain at full speed.

Jake looked at his watch, five-thirty-five.

"The bomb squad," he said to Silky with a shrug. "They're too late to be a problem, so long as we are out of here shortly after six. They're going straight to the top, which makes sense. They're not stupid."

"How many of them d'you figure?"

"Doesn't sound like more than two snowmobiles. I doubt that they are driving themselves, so that makes only two of them, with a driver each. It's not enough."

"What d'you mean?"

"Well, if they had more than one team, they would probably start on Towers Five and Six at the same time. But with only two of them, chances are they will work together on Tower Six first. It is going to take them half-an-hour to draw a blank there before they even get started on Number Five."

"I hope you are right."

"It's immaterial. No matter what they do, they can't be sure that they've cleared everything in under an hour. It's physically impossible. And they can't put any pressure on us until they're sure."

"I guess you're right. But it settles one thing. If they ask for more time, we can't go past six-fifteen."

"Agreed," said Jake. "Maybe we'd better decide who we are going to kill if they don't show up on time."

Silky looked over the hostages with disdain. "Go ahead," he said. "Pick one of the women. It will throw a scare into them."

Jake walked slowly along the line of hostages, thinking about the selection formula that he had established in the bar in Salt Lake City. He stopped opposite Jane Mallory. She wasn't fat or ugly, but she was the oldest of the bunch. "Get up!" he said, prodding her with the barrel of his gun.

She looked up at him in panic, drawing herself slowly to her knees. Jake grabbed her arm impatiently and dragged her over to the nearest gondola car, pushing her inside. She lay huddled on the floor of the car, sobbing and staring up in terror at Jake's expressionless mask.

Jake turned to the group. "This dame goes first," he said. He saw Arthur straighten up. "And anyone who moves goes with her. We're giving them five more minutes to contact us about the ransom. If they don't show, we're blowing this lady away."

"You bastard!" Arthur could not hold it back.

"You're next, uncle," Jake retorted. "Or are you in some special kind of a hurry?"

Jane was sobbing quietly, thinking about Peter. She didn't care anymore except about him.

Silky had the door to the base ajar, waiting for O'Malley to show up. At last, he saw him approaching holding the flashlight to his face as he had been instructed. Silky knocked the door wide open and stood back covering Jim from an angle. "Take it easy!" he shouted. "Stop when you get to the door."

Jim stood at the entrance, flashlight up to his face, looking straight ahead.

"O.K. Come in," Silky said. "And close the door behind you."

Jim waited for someone to speak.

"Well?" said Jake.

"We'll pay the ransom," Jim said flatly. "We should be on time. But give us to six-fifteen."

"Why?"

"It's taking time to get the money together. It's a lot of money."

"We said six o'clock," Jake said. "We're fixing to shoot the bag in the car," he pointed over his shoulder, "at six. Why should we wait till six-fifteen?"

"I told you," Jim argued. "We are going to pay. But six is too tight."

"Yeah?" Silky cut in. "What's going on man? We heard the bomb squad going up. That's right, isn't it? The bomb squad is working to dismantle the charges, right?"

Jim nodded. "Yes. But you and I know they won't make it by six-fifteen."

It was true. What the hell? Jake had never really expected them to meet the deadline. "O.K. then," he said. "Six-fifteen yes. Six-sixteen too late. Understand? One minute late and the lady croaks. Make sure they understand that. We shoot her at six-sixteen, if you haven't shown up with the money."

"I understand." Jim was convinced.

"Better check watches then. I'd hate to kill someone just because we weren't synchronized."

They compared and agreed.

Silky handed Jim a tape. "Here are some more instructions," he said abruptly. "Now beat it."

It was nearly a quarter-to-six.

Alfredo had recovered his composure and was sitting at his desk.

He pressed the switch of the tape recorder. They all listened in absolute silence.

Carl Svensen was sitting in the same armchair, chewing a cigar. He seemed jittery.

That's all we need, thought Jim, a nervous cop. He is going to do something stupid if he gets a chance.

The two FBI men stood together, like two soldiers at ease on a parade ground. One of them was in his fifties, with bushy gray sideburns. The other was much younger, straight-haired, in a dark suit and bright red tie. The younger one, Granger, turned out to be the spokesman when they were introduced.

Paul Mullins was sitting on the sofa with the doctor on one side and Burton on the other. Burton appeared to be much more in control of himself than Svensen.

Cambetta, the comptroller, was hovering behind Alfredo.

Jim and Mavis were leaning against the wall near the door, and Greg stood over by the window, peering out from time to time.

It was the same flat voice.

"You have agreed to deliver the ransom. O'Malley will deliver it personally, using the same approach as before, lighting his face with a flashlight, and coming alone. I suggest that you replay the previous tape, to make sure that you follow the delivery instructions to the letter.

"If you have tried any tricks, like marking the bills, you still have time to reconsider. It will cost lives if you do not do exactly as you are told.

"O'Malley will stay with us this time. He will become a hostage. In exchange, we will release one other hostage with a third tape. This third tape will tell you how we are leaving.

"You will only have ten minutes to obey the third tape. To save time, I will give you some of the instructions now.

"First of all, do not be tempted to shoot when we come out. We will be taking hostages with us and will have no compunction about killing them. Don't forget, we can still blow the gondola at a range of ten miles.

"Now, the police are going to want to follow us, naturally. *Don't.* If we spot a vehicle, marked or unmarked on our trail, everything goes. Figure the odds for yourselves. We will have the money, the hostages, and the radio switch to blow the gondola. We will still have the advantage, so long as we keep two hostages alive. That gives us a lot of dead people to bargain with if you try any smart tricks.

"Get that straight. If someone follows us or tries to stop us, we will kill one hostage at a time for five minutes and then blow the gondola."

Alfredo switched it off.

"Well, gentlemen," he said calmly, "it seems to me that they have us by the balls."

It was an unusual expression for Alfredo. He rarely used coarse language.

"Not so fast, Mr. Costa," Carl Svensen said, pointing the chewy wet end of his cigar at Alfredo.

Alfredo ignored him. "Doctor," he said, "could you explain the situation of the people in the gondola?"

The doctor cleared his throat self-importantly. "There is almost no danger. Their body heat will keep them relatively comfortable for many hours. The only harm that can come to them is from panic or shock. This is one item," he continued pompously, "where your hijackers seem to have miscalculated."

"I agree." Carl Svensen leaned forward with the cigar again, about to make a point.

Once again, Alfredo cut him off. "I wonder, doctor. I wonder if they did not calculate exactly the opposite. If they had held up a chair lift, then there would have been a real danger of death or injury from exposure in the open air. What advantage would that be to them? If they are going to blow up the lift, they want to blow up live, warm people, not cold, dead people."

"Of course," said Jim.

"Alright, now," Alfredo continued, "we have ten minutes to consider our options —if we have any."

The wet cigar was not to be silenced this time. "No sonofabitch murderer is going to dictate to me," Svensen said, glaring around the room for support. "No, sir. We are going to get those bastards."

"How?" Alfredo looked at him cynically.

"Well, I have to make a plan."

"You have five minutes to do it."

"See here, Mr. Costa. I have my duty. Kindly stop interrupting me." He turned his attention to Burton.

"Have you got sharpshooters out?"

"Yes, sir."

"How many?"

"Five, sir."

"Are they in radio communication?"

"Yes. They are all on walkie-talkie."

"Good." He wiped his wet lips with the back of his puffy hand. "Then, if we get a clear shot, we are shooting." He glared around the room again. "That's final."

Jim glanced over at Granger, the FBI man with the

red tie, wondering whether he was going to intervene. Surely he was not going to let Svensen bungle his way through this situation. But Granger remained expressionless, a credit to the silent service. Obviously he was not the talkative type. Jim fervently hoped he would put Svenson in his place after the meeting.

Alfredo shrugged. There was nothing he could do but hope that Pat would not get caught in the crossfire.

"There are only two of them," Jim announced. "We should have a good chance."

Everyone stared at him, Carl nodding approval as though he had known it all along.

"Are you sure?" Alfredo asked quietly. "Rena said five."

"I only saw two," Jim said. "I am pretty sure that there were no more of them."

"Good," said Carl. "We knock off one and the other one will panic soon enough. We've got 'em," he added with an air of triumph, which seemed to denote that everything could be solved by positive thinking. He felt in charge of the situation at last. It was time to give some instructions.

"Burton," he barked, "get the State Patrol to post roadblocks—at least fifteen miles out of town." The hijackers said they could blow the gondola up to ten miles. He did not believe it, but there was no point in taking any chances.

"Post an unmarked car at the bottom of the road. Tell them to keep out of sight, just report movements. Post one a mile east and one a mile west, same orders.

"Take an unmarked car—commandeer one in the parking lot—and get down to the McDonald's hamburger joint. Watch for them from there and tail them. Understand, *tail* them. But don't let them spot you."

"For Christ's sake, don't," Alfredo cut in.

"I'll be careful," Burton said with assurance, "but I don't know what I'm looking for yet."

"Take a squad car with you and keep the radio open. I'll stay by my car during the getaway and I'll broadcast everything that goes on. I'll give you a description of the getaway car." Carl had his counteroffensive in full swing now. "That's it then." He got up. "Let's go down and talk to the sharpshooters. Then we will take up positions."

"Mr. Svensen," Alfredo spoke with resignation, "you have planned a fine defense. But you do not yet know when or how the attack is going to be launched. There is still another tape to come."

"Call me when you get it. The instant, you hear?" Then with a wave of his hand he swept out of the door, followed by Burton and the FBI men.

"Christ," Jim sighed, "he's crazy. He could get a hundred people killed."

"If I thought," Alfredo said deliberately, "that the hijackers were as reckless as he is, I would be very, very afraid. Fortunately, I have a feeling that they will be a match for him and, once they've got their money, they will avoid needless bloodshed.

"Now, O'Malley, you'd better go down to the main entrance and wait for the money to arrive. If I know the police, they will refuse entrance to the couriers. We only have eleven minutes before the deadline expires."

"You're right, sir." Jim jumped up. He had not thought of this complication.

He was just in time. A big Cadillac limousine pulled up at the door just as he reached it. Two heavy-set men, bareheaded and without overcoats, stepped out and ran up the steps. A canvas bag dangled from the arm of one of them.

"That's the ransom money coming," Jim said to the cop. "Let them through."

"Sorry, sir. Nobody comes through here. Orders."

Jesus! Jim thought. There were only minutes to go.

Jim recognized the man with the bag, a "security officer" from Bailey's club, one of the big casinos in town. He was sure both the couriers were armed and could kill the cops who barred the way without compunction.

"Wait here a minute," he called, running out into the parking lot toward the group of police cars. The first five were empty, but he found a driver in the sixth one, quietly smoking a cigarette.

"Do you know where Carl Svensen is?" Jim was out of breath.

"No, sir. Haven't seen him."

"Shit. I've got to find him quick. Try him on the radio. It's a matter of life and death."

The cop looked at him insolently, considering whether

to do as he was told. The expression on Jim's face convinced him to comply. He picked up his radio mike and called for the sheriff.

"Yeah, what you want?" Carl snarled when he eventually got on.

Jim grabbed the mike. "Carl, your men at the entrance won't let the ransom through, for Christ's sake. We only have four or five minutes left. For the love of God, do something!"

"Keep your shirt on. I'll handle it. Out."

Jim ran back to the entrance. Carl strolled over as if he had all the time in the world. "These them?" He looked at the two big torpedoes with disdain.

"Yes."

"Let 'em through."

Jim made to go with them.

"We know the way," one spoke.

"Good. I'll wait for the others," Jim said. "Carl!" Carl was walking away. "There's another lot to come. From the bank. Will you tell these guys to let them through? Time is nearly up."

"O.K." He took a couple of steps back, looked at each cop. "You got it? Let 'em through—so long as they've got I.D."

"Fuck their I.D." Jim said in exasperation to one of the cops. "I have to get this money to the gondola by six-fifteen or they start shooting."

It was ten after six. Jake took a long look at Jane Mallory. He hoped that she wouldn't squirm. He felt sorry for the old bird. But he had to start somewhere.

Well, they had given her a break. If they had stuck to the rules, they would have knocked her off at six o'clock. By rights they should have done. It was hard to know what to do in this kind of situation. Once you started weakening, the other side had you by the balls. It was the first one that was tricky. If Silky hadn't screwed up on snuffing Nick, this number would've been a snap.

He looked at his watch. Just three minutes to go. What the hell! Maybe he would throw in a couple more—up to five. It would be silly to snuff her out for the sake of two minutes. But that was all he could afford. It would not be his fault after that.

He walked over to Silky. "Better watch the others when I give it to her," he said. "They may go berserk. Especially that one," he pointed to Arthur. "Probably her old man."

Arthur guessed what they were talking about. He summoned all his courage. "I would like to make a proposition," he announced, shattering the long-enforced silence.

Jake grinned at him in amusement. "A proposition? Who the hell d'you think you are, you crazy old fart?"

"Look," Arthur said. "Give her five extra minutes and then take both of us."

Jane was already dead inside, resigned to her fate. Her dulled mind struggled to understand the significance of Arthur's proposal. Then suddenly she started to live again.

Jake looked at Silky's expressionless mask. It wasn't a bad idea.

Silky looked at his watch. "O.K., uncle," he said. "You got yourself a deal. You've got until six twenty-one."

Jim heard the police car coming up the road, siren blaring. This had better be it.

Three men jumped out as it pulled up with a screech at the lodge entrance. One of them carried a canvas bag.

"Let the one with the bag through," Jim yelled. "I don't give a shit what you do with the other two."

The man with the bag followed Jim up the steps to Alfredo's office. He was no athlete and was twenty paces behind Jim when he eventually dumped the bag on the desk.

Jim put on his parka and grabbed the two bags, making for the door.

"Christ," he said in frustration, "these are as heavy as lead. Greg, for God's sake hurry and give me a hand."

He made for the door with one bag, Greg close behind with the other one.

"You've got time, Jim," Mavis said, handing him the flashlight. "Don't forget this. You have two-and-a-half minutes."

They bounded down the stairs together, he and Greg, two at a time.

He hoisted the two bags over his shoulder with Greg's

help and started out of the door, holding the flashlight to his face with the other hand.

The cold wind hit him as soon as he stepped outside. He could see the nearest gondola cars swaying gently as he approached. He had forgotten his ski mitts in the rush and his right hand began to lose grip of the bags.

"Jesus," he said to himself, "this is stupid. I'm going to have to let go."

He could not have hung on, even if his life depended on it. Maybe it did.

One of the bags slipped through his fingers, falling with a thud in the snow, the harsh canvas searing his flesh as he struggled to hold onto the second one. He plodded on, cursing and swearing under his breath, until he reached the door to the base.

It opened.

A man in a face mask stood in front of him, pointing a gun at his stomach.

"It isn't my fault, mister," he began to say, "I couldn't help it. Please."

The man spoke with a chuckle in his voice. "You're a bit careless with *our* money, O'Malley. Please go back and pick up the rest."

Nick Diamado was more angry than concerned about his health. They had dressed his wound, and apart from a nasty throb, he felt very little the worse for wear.

The cop sat at the end of the bed laboriously writing everything he said down in his notebook. He would have done well to learn shorthand. Granger was questioning him.

"Can you recall which finger you broke?"

"Not really. It all happened so fast. But it was one of the first ones, if you know what I mean. The index finger or the one next to it."

"Which hand?"

Nick thought about it for a while trying to reconstruct the fight as it happened.

"The right hand, I think. Yes, I'm sure."

"Good, sir. That's a big help." Granger cracked a smile for the first time since he had come into the room. "Now," he went on, "let's see if we can pin down which joint. Would you say first or second knuckle?"

"Second definitely," Nick answered. "It felt like the whole top of the finger just broke clean off—bent back a hundred and eighty degrees, if you see what I mean."

"Did the man groan, show any signs of pain? I mean, that would be painful, to snap a finger like that, wouldn't it?"

"I don't remember. I got clobbered on the head just as it happened."

"Yes, quite," Granger said, "but the same man, the one you fought with, was the one who shot you. Is that right?"

"Right."

"Well, did he seem to be in pain? Did he hold the gun in his right or left hand?"

Nick was getting a little tired of this third degree. "Christ! How should I know? When a man shoots you at point blank range, you don't look to see if he has clean fingernails!"

"I'm sorry, sir," Granger was contrite, "but, as you can probably understand, every little clue can be of enormous significance."

"I understand." Nick was getting tired now. "Anything else?"

"No, sir. Not for the present. I will get this out on an all-points bulletin. After that I want to analyze the notes for a while. Then I may be back to you, if you don't mind. There's something I can't quite . . ."

"Put your finger on?" suggested Nick.

"Yes, sir," Granger smiled. "That's right."

Rena had not been permitted to return to the ski lodge. There were police at the hotel entrance and all access to the lodge had been cordoned off. She decided to go and have a drink in the lobby bar; maybe she would pick up some information on the current situation from Sammy, the barman.

She was surprised to find the lobby packed with people, spilling over to the gambling floor. Some clustered round the bars, obviously enjoying the excitement, while others milled around, waiting for news. The gambling operation was at a standstill, the tables draped in black cloths and row upon row of slot machines standing in silence like an honor guard at a funeral.

185

"What's happening, Sammy?" she asked.

"They tell me it's pretty bad over there," he confided. "Mr. Diamado got shot and now they have taken Mr. O'Malley hostage. He went in to deliver the money, I believe."

"My God! Are you sure?"

Sammy shrugged. He wasn't an eyewitness but he had got his information from one of the security men, who in turn got it from a cop. "That's what I'm told." he said.

"Give me a brandy, Sammy," Rena said quickly. Oh God! Nick had been shot. She felt physically sick. "Is Mr. Diamado—dead?"

"No. Not that I know of. They took him off to the hospital."

Pray God he's not. And Jim a hostage. Why did they do that? Her loyalties were being tugged in every direction now, like an innocent child in a family vendetta. Please Silky, please don't harm Jim. Oh God, how she wished that she had never become involved.

"Another brandy please, Sammy."

He refilled her glass. "You were sweet on him, weren't you? Mr. O'Malley, I mean."

She caught the implication of the past tense, as though Jim was already dead. He couldn't be. She put the idea out of her mind. "We are good friends," she said emphatically.

CHAPTER NINE

JIM dumped the second sack on the floor. He looked around, searching the faces of the hostages, but in the glare of the spotlights he could make out very little.

Jake picked up the sack and motioned Jim, with the muzzle of his gun, to move to the back of the room where Silky was waiting.

Silky was on his knees, holding a pocket flashlight in his mouth, stacks of bills spread neatly around on the floor. He looked up. "Here. Hold this," he said, taking the flashlight out of his mouth and handing it to Jim. "Keep an eye on the prisoners," he said to Jake.

Jim's first impression of the loot was anticlimactic, much less awe-inspiring than he had imagined. Silky had piled the stacks five up, so that when he had finished, there were only twenty piles. Not much to show for two million dollars. Jim stood there staring at it.

Silky rummaged in the kit bag, pulled out a portable geiger counter, and passed it slowly over the haul. No reaction. So far so good.

Next he selected a stack from each pile, then calmly shuffled them as though he were playing cards, finishing up with five stacks of two hundred bills each.

"Looks like a full house you've got there," Jake giggled. He was getting a little lightheaded.

Silky ignored him. He selected one stack, ripped off the rubber band, and stood up to get closer to the flashlight in Jim's hand. Jim focused directly on the stack.

Pausing from time to time to lick his fingers, Silky then checked the serial number of each of the two hundred bills. It seemed to take an eternity, but he carried on methodically. Finally satisfied that the serial numbers were random, he replaced the rubber band, tossed the stack back into the sack and picked up another one.

"Got change for ten bucks?" Jake asked facetiously. The delay was making him nervous.

To Jake's relief, Silky now changed over to a random check, maybe ten consecutive bills, then a few in the middle and some at the bottom of each stack. Finally, he replaced all the money in the two sacks and wiped his hands on his shirt. "Seems O.K." he said in a flat, businesslike tone.

"What's it feel like?" Jake asked, putting his hand in one of the sacks and pulling out a wad of bills. He slid one bill out and crinkled it through his fingers, looking at it carefully. "Man, that's pretty," he said, grinning at Jim.

"Put it back," Silky commanded curtly, "and let's get on with it. Tie up the sacks."

He turned to Jim. "So what's the situation on the home front?" He posed a number of questions and Jim saw no reason to be evasive. He admitted that, at the time he left, the bomb squad had not yet reported the discovery of any of the explosives.

Silky took the flashlight back from Jim. "Put him down there," he said to Jake, indicating the corner near the door, "and then make an announcement."

"Ladies and gentlemen," Jake proclaimed, "the ransom has been paid. However the party is not over yet. We still have the slight problem of escape.

"You'll all be coming with us. We'll be using some of you as shields, in case anyone gets the notion to do a little shooting. Those of you who are selected as shields should be careful not to struggle. Apart from the fact that we'll shoot you if you do, you'll run the additional risk of being shot by mistake by the police. The more disorderly our exit, the more chance that an innocent person will get hit.

"We'll be leaving in a van, which will be parked at the rear door here." He pointed to the door behind him.

"I'll be giving you individual numbers and you are to enter the van in that order.

"O'Malley, here, will be driving. He'll be wired with a plastic bomb, attached to the back of his neck. So, if you find that he's disappointingly obedient, you'll understand why. If he doesn't do as we tell him, his friends will have a difficult job finding his head.

"Let's not have any heroes. We have the money now, so if we have to kill one or two people to keep it, we will."

Jake then walked over to where the hostages were lying and prodded one of the two gondola attendants in the stomach with his gun. "Get up," he said.

"What are you going to do?" He seemed scared out of his wits. "Please, please don't hurt me!"

"We're letting you go."

"Letting me go? Letting me leave, you mean?"

"Yes. You're taking the last tape. Now get up and get out." He grabbed him by the elbow, pulled him up, and propelled him to the side door. Handing him the third tape, he opened the door. "Get that to whoever is in charge fast. They only have ten minutes to obey the instructions."

The man took one last look, then started running toward the lodge as fast as he could.

"Get up. All of you," Jake said.

For a moment nobody moved. It was as though they had lost the ability. Then slowly the bodies began to stir, bending and stretching their limbs and painfully propping themselves up.

Jake watched them impatiently. He had not bargained on their becoming so stiff, but realized that they couldn't help themselves. "Come on, move it!" he barked. "Line up along the wall."

Arthur Mallory was the first to his feet. He limped over to help Jane out of the gondola car. She met him with a kiss.

Gradually the others managed to heave themselves up, stamping their feet to get the circulation going. Only Pat Costa remained groaning on the floor until Pepi and Jim O'Malley were able to haul her upright and lean her against the wall between them.

Jake reviewed them disdainfully, like a sergeant-major

looking over a bunch of raw recruits. He only had five minutes to knock them into shape for the getaway. Better put the strongest ones at the head of the line.

"You!" He pointed to Philippe Gareau. "Stand here. You're going out number one."

He put Pepi Mueller as number two. "You go straight in the side door of the van then lie down in the back. Don't try any tricks. We will be covering you from here and I'll be right behind you," Jake said.

He looked at Pat. "You're Mrs. Costa, aren't you?"

She gaped at him in surprise. They seemed to know everything. "Yes."

"You'll go out number three with me. You'll be my shield, understand, in case the police try any tricks. So stick close and don't struggle, because I'll have a gun in the back of your neck."

He went on down the line selecting people and putting them into the proper order. When he got to Jane Mallory, he could not help feeling sympathy for her. "You O.K.?" he said, speaking a little more softly than to the others.

"Yes. I'm alright."

"Good. I'm glad O'Malley showed up with the ransom."

"So am I," she forced a smile.

Jake liked her guts. "You're going out with my partner. As his shield. You know the drill. We wouldn't want anything to happen to you now, so don't struggle. You go out last."

Finally he came up to Sam Mitchell. "You're the waterboy. You carry the kitbag. Don't drop it whatever you do. Move up to number five."

Silky was already busy packing. They were leaving nothing behind, except their skis. They were stolen so there was no way of tracing them. He extinguished the two spotlights, stuffing them in the kitbag with all the other equipment, leaving the room pitch dark except for the pencil of light from his pocket flashlight.

He handed the kitbag to Sam Mitchell and laid the two money sacks close by the door.

Together he and Jake fitted the bomb around Jim's neck. "Don't cough," Jake advised him.

After a final check to see that everything was in order,

Silky handed one of the money bags to Jake and took a firm grip on the other himself. Then he opened the rear door a chink and looked out.

"We'll be leaving in three minutes," he said.

Mavis handed the new tape to Alfredo. The group waited in silent anticipation.

"You have ten minutes to follow these instructions. Ten minutes from now we will shoot a hostage if you do not comply.

"There is a dark blue delivery van at the northeast end of the parking lot. The keys are taped under the dash, on the driver's side.

"Bring that van to the rear entrance of the gondola base and leave the engine running. Park it with the doors open and exactly opposite the base door. The distance between the van door and the exit from the base is not to exceed thirty feet.

"Once we are satisfied with the position of the van, we will be coming out. Do not shoot or you will hit a hostage. Do not follow us.

"Now move. You only have eight minutes left."

"Goddam nerve," Svensen exploded. "Telling us to drive their getaway van up to the door."

"Don't waste time," Alfredo said. "Do it."

"O.K." Carl replied grudgingly, "but if I get the bastards in the open, I shoot. That's final." With that, he got up, crammed his hat on his head and strode out of the office.

I'll show these bastards, Carl thought to himself. He didn't do twenty-two years in the Marines to start taking orders from a couple of two-bit punks, or from a goddam wop, for that matter.

He strode down the steps, along the hallway to the front door, picking up a military march rhythm as he went. This was Iwo Jima all over again. Get the objective and to hell with the casualties. You did not win wars by pussyfooting around.

There were half-a-dozen police officers on the entrance steps, all eyes turned on him.

"The action is going to start," he said, with an exultant grin.

"You," he pointed at one of the cops, "and you, come

191

with me." He strode firmly over to his own command car.

He fished in his glove compartment, pulling out a small metal object. He handed it to the first man. "It's a bug," he said.

The cop nodded.

"O.K. Now listen carefully. Lives depend on this." They waited in silence for him to continue. "Find a dark blue van in the northeast corner of the parking lot. The keys are taped under the dash, driver's side. O.K.?"

They both nodded. "Yes, sir."

"Alright then. Put this bug under the rear center of the chassis. Make sure it's well-hidden and secure. Understand?"

"Yes, sir."

"Then drive the van over to that door"—he pointed—"at the rear of the gondola base. Now get this part: park it with the offside door no more than thirty feet from the exit. Got it? Thirty feet. Leave the door open and the engine running. Then report to me for my personal inspection. On the double. You have four minutes to complete your mission."

He dismissed them, then yelled for another cop. Three ran down the steps and he pointed at one.

"You. Get Burton on the radio. Tell him they are using a blue van in the getaway. Call the road blocks and all cars. Tell them that we have put a bug on the van. It will be parked there," he pointed, "in four minutes. Get the make and license number and broadcast it. Got it?"

"Yes, sir."

"Get going."

He strode back to his command car, beckoning two cops to follow him.

"I'll need you to run messages," he said. "Get yourselves automatic rifles and come with me. Pronto."

He opened the door of the car and climbed in. He switched on the engine, put on the headlights and drove very slowly toward the door of the gondola base.

He moved the car back and forth a little, until he was satisfied. He was about eighty feet from where they would come out, his headlights at right angles to the exit. He picked up a rifle off the seat, opened the door, and lowered the window. Taking a position on one knee, with the rifle propped on the window, he squinted down the telescope sight. As he did so, the van pulled up and he watched them maneuver it into position. He had a clear line of fire into the thirty feet between the door and the van. Besides, there was a flight of four steps down from the door to the parking lot, so they would be exposed for at least fifteen seconds.

Next he picked up his walkie-talkie, calling the five snipers. He gave them clear instructions about the getaway plan and told them to pick vantage points to cover that thirty feet and report back.

Satisfied that everything was ready, he doused his lights. "Don't fire unless you hear a direct order from me," was his final instruction.

Silky watched through the chink in the door. He could hear the engine running. He looked the van over carefully. Everything appeared to be in order. He swung the door wide-open and jumped back. Nothing happened. There was absolute silence.

He turned to Philippe and Pepi.

"You ready?"

"Yes," said Philippe. Pepi nodded, too scared to make a sound.

"Put this on." He handed Philippe a face mask, an exact replica of his own. "You too," to Pepi.

Philippe froze. He gasped at Silky, weighing the obvious implications. If the police got trigger happy, they would shoot at the first masked man who came into their sights. "No." He forced it out, more of a croak than a word.

"You don't trust the police?" Silky asked in mock concern.

"No."

"Well trust me, baby." He pulled his revolver out, holding his machine gun in one hand, cocked it, and stuck it in Philippe's nostril, letting him smell the bitter scent of cold steel and oil.

"I'll count to ten, and then I'll blow your fucking head off."

Pepi already had his mask on. Philippe made to put

193

his on, but could not, with Silky's pistol in his face. Silky went on counting up to nine.

"Please," Philippe yelled. "Please!"

Silky moved the revolver to his stomach. Philippe pulled his mask down, searching desperately for the eyeholes. He felt himself urinate in sheer terror. "Give me a minute before we go," he panted.

Silky ignored him. "You go when I slap your back. Twenty seconds."

He started counting again.

Philippe got ready. He prayed.

... eighteen ... nineteen ... twenty!

Philippe felt a slap on his back and ran. As he went through the door a bright shaft of light hit him. He did not hear the shot. He felt an impact against his right thigh, like the kick of a horse, tripped, tried to recover and then fell headlong, with the weight of Pepi on top of him.

He lay there panting. He was not dead. He tried to get up, shook Pepi, yelling, "Get off me, you fool!"

Pepi's face lolled over in front of him. There was no left eye, just a hole with blood pumping out of it.

Lise screamed. Pat yelled, "You fucking bastards!" Jake slapped her. Silky moved to the door and looked out. He calmy slipped the safety catch of his machine gun.

"Charge!" Carl screamed into his walkie-talkie, heading full tilt for the door. He was running on the hot sand now, zigzagging up the beach, dodging machine gun fire. The Japs were on the run.

Silky waited until Carl was about fifteen yards from him. He aimed low, no need to kill him. He put a short burst into Carl's legs, shattering both knees.

Carl saw the flash, felt the pain, refused to believe it.

"There must have been five of them," he said later, when they picked him up.

"Shut up!" Silky yelled above the din in the gondola base. "So help me, I'll kill someone soon. I'm really getting itchy. Now shut up! The police have screwed everything up. Just keep quiet and don't panic."

Jake kept the remaining hostages covered, while Silky went back to the phone. Really, he was quite unperturbed by the turn of events. After all, if he had not half-expected it, he would not have planned for it.

Silky pulled off the tape, stuck the rag in his pants and put the phone back on the hook. Taking his flashlight out, he scanned the sheet pasted above the phone, which indicated various local numbers. Not seeing one for the President's office, he selected one under the title of Operations.

"Greg here," he heard.

"This is the gondola base. I am in charge here. Get me?"

"Yes."

"O.K. The local here is 323. Tell Mr. Costa to call me here at once."

"Right. 323."

"I will wait three minutes. No longer."

Greg slammed the phone down and headed upstairs, running as fast as he could.

Alfredo looked up.

"They called from 323, the gondola base. The hijackers. They want you to call at once—sir," Greg stammered.

Alfredo was still not sure what had happened. He had heard shots and had been waiting with mounting anxiety for Svensen to come back to make his report.

"I should wait for Carl," he said.

"They said three minutes, sir. I think they meant it."

Alfredo made his decision. He opened the drawer, switched on the tape recorder and clipped a suction cup microphone to the earpiece of his telephone. He dialed 323.

"Who is this?" a voice asked.

"Alfredo Costa. President of Mount Casino. Who are you?"

Silky noticed the slight Italian intonation in Alfredo's accent. "I am in charge at the gondola base." He paused. "Do you know the situation?"

"Not precisely."

"Alright, I'll give it to you. It's not very good. You have shot two hostages, one dead. The other looks as if he is still breathing."

Alfredo looked up at Greg, pursing his lips tightly. That fool Svensen, he thought.

"Your wife is alright." Another shock for Alfredo. They knew her identity; but she was safe.

"However," the voice continued, "we'll be using her as a shield, so if you want her to stay alive, call off the sharpshooters. Got it?"

"Yes."

"We'll give you another five minutes to clear the bodies. There is a wounded cop out there too. Then we are coming out. This time, no shooting. No lights. Someone switched on his headlights. That's out. No one follows us. This is it. Any foul-ups this time and the gondola goes. That's a promise. Check back. I have kept all my promises, so far. This time the full stakes are out. The gondola and your wife. Any questions?"

"No."

"Check your watch then. Five minutes." The phone went dead.

Alfredo said nothing. He rewound the tape. "Greg, find Svensen!"

"He's been shot."

"Goddam idiot." Alfredo could not restrain himself. "Who's in charge?"

"Sergeant Lipzke. He's here."

A burly, blond fellow about thirty-years-old stepped inside from the outer office.

Alfredo nodded at him. "You had better listen to this." He pressed the playback switch on the tape recorder. They listened.

"I suggest we do as they say, Sergeant. Do you agree?"

"Yes, sir."

"Is Svensen dead?"

"No, sir. Both legs."

"Do you know who the hostages were, who were hit?"

"Not yet, sir."

"Have someone call me when you do, please."

"Yes, sir."

"Now let's be clear what the plan is. No shooting. No following. Let them go. We will catch them later, when they have freed the hostages. Right?"

"That's the way I see it, sir. But I will have to check with Deputy Sheriff Burton by radio. And the FBI."

"Do it then. And let me know if there is any deviation from the plan."

"Right, sir." Lipzke moved out of the room.

"Fools make brave soldiers but stupid police chiefs," Alfredo remarked to no one in particular.

The phone rang. Alfredo picked it up. "Yes?"

He listened, then replaced the receiver. "Pepi Mueller is dead and one of the others, a Mr. Philippe Gareau, is seriously wounded," he announced flatly.

Poor Pepi, thought Mavis. Just a friendly, foolish good-time guy. What a horrible, senseless way to go. Up until now the whole episode had seemed unreal; she was just going through motions, dictated by her natural efficiency and her loyalty to Jim. But Pepi's death made it real. She felt physically and mentally exhausted; she staggered to the sofa and sat down.

Jake was busy trying to get the hostages back into some sort of order. He held his flashlight on Sam and Kay Mitchell as they worked to comfort Lise Gareau: she finally seemed to have lapsed into a kind of delirium, leaning against Kay, shaking with pitiful sobs.

"Take her with you when we go, understand?" Silky turned to Kay. "We are not leaving anyone behind—alive—so it's up to you."

Kay gave him a look of scorn. "You bastard!"

"Don't you start, lady, or else . . ."

Silky addressed the rest of them. "It's not likely that the police will shoot again," he said. "They have done enough damage for one day. That's no reason for us to change the drill. So let's get out there fast and without any struggling."

He turned to Kay. "You two go out first. I will count to twenty and slap your back. Then go."

They exited without a hitch. Lise and Kay together, then Jim O'Malley, then Jake and Pat, with Jake holding a gun at the back of Pat's head.

Silky watched them all file out, his machine gun trained on Jane Mallory. Then he grabbed her firmly around the throat and she felt the gun barrel pressing into the nape of her neck. She closed her eyes, letting him guide her, a waltz in the arms of the devil.

Jim was sitting in the driver's seat of the van; his

left wrist was attached to the steering wheel with a handcuff. Jake sat beside him, with Pat pressed against him, half on his knee. Everyone else was in the rear of the van.

Silky squeezed in the front, forcing Jane on top of him, banging her knee under the dash. He put out his left hand and pulled closed the sliding door between the driving compartment and the rest of the people in the cargo space.

"Go," he said. "Out of the parking lot, turn right, and down the hill."

Jim said nothing, following instructions. Jane could see the lump of plastic material, the bomb, taped to the back of his neck.

The driving compartment was terribly cramped, with five of them sitting in it. Jane wondered just how far they would go like this. She was crushed and in pain.

They turned right and started down the hill.

"You two ladies will be getting out soon," Silky announced. "You will be free, so long as you move fast. Got it? We stop. You jump. You are on your own. We go on with the rest."

"Why? What are you going to do with the others?" Pat could not help asking the question.

"Never mind, sister," Jake said. "Watch your own ass."

Suddenly she had an urge to pull off his mask, see what he really looked like.

"Stop!" Silky commanded.

Jim obeyed with a jerk.

"O.K., out!" He pushed Jane, made way for Pat and jumped back in.

"Move."

The two girls were left in the middle of the road, watching the van disappear. Jane noticed that there was no rear light on the van.

"Thank God!" said Pat clasping Jane around the shoulders and hugging her. "Thank God!"

Within seconds of the departure of the blue van, the gondola base was swarming with cops. "Don't touch anything," Sergeant Lipzke shouted, "and seal the place off."

Greg ran over as fast as he could, only to be stopped

at the door by an officer. "We have to get the people down, man," he shouted in exasperation, pointing wildly up at the gondola cars. "I'm the operations manager. Get Sergeant Lipzke."

Lipzke had already arrived to check on the commotion. He recognized Greg. "Let him through," he commanded.

Greg pushed his way through the crowd and pressed the button. There was a long whirring sound as the big motor took the load and then, slowly at first, the cable started moving. Ten minutes later, the first passengers entered the base, setting off a cheer from the group of cops.

The first car in brought four smiling young men in their twenties. Although dazzled by the lights, they seemed none the worse for wear, and walked out without assistance. It was a good omen.

"What happened?" one of them asked, staring at all the cops. "Has there been a robbery or something?"

"A hijack," Greg replied. "You must be frozen. If you can just wait a second, we have a hot meal ready for you."

"A hijack? You're kidding."

By now a dozen people had landed safely. One older couple looked dazed and unsteady. Two cops moved in to give them support.

"Let's go," Greg said, leading the way for the first group of people to follow each other for the short walk to the cafeteria.

As soon as they entered, there was a rousing cheer from the anxious waiting friends and relatives who were standing in a semicircle at the cafeteria door.

There was a sudden melee of hugging, shoving people, with the hospital staff fighting to rescue the few who seemed to require medical attention.

Paul Mullins's voice repeated the same message over and over again. "Welcome back. We are glad you are safe. There are blankets on the tables by the bar. Take all you need. We are serving hot drinks and a hot meal at once. Please sit down quickly."

The Montreal group were the last ones in. In order to disembark everyone, the gondola had been run forward so that those who had boarded last, Tim Mallory and

Serge Gareau, had to be routed right to the top of the mountain and down again.

Realizing that this last group of youngsters were the children of the hostages who had been held in the base, Mavis made it a point to go and sit with them to explain why their parents were not there to greet them. She was just wondering how she was going to handle the situation when Pat Costa and Jane Mallory walked in.

"Peter!" Jane rushed to hug her son. "Tim, darling! Nicole! Thank God you are all safe!"

Peter held his mother close, then disengaged himself. "Where are the Gareaus?" he asked feeling Nicole's anxiety. "And the Mitchells? And Dad?"

"They will be here soon," Jane said emphatically. "They had to go with the hijackers—but I'm sure they won't be long." She purposely made no mention of what had happened to Philippe.

"With the hijackers?" Jacques asked anxiously. "My parents too?"

"Yes," Jane said. There was so much to explain. She could not do it in this hubbub. "Listen. They are all safe, I promise you. Now eat your food and then we will go back to the hotel and I will explain exactly what happened." She got up. The only way to escape further cross-examination was to play for time. "I'll be waiting for you in the hotel lobby," she said. Maybe by that time there would be more news.

Mavis was left to deal with the stream of questions from the anxious youngsters. To her relief, Dave, who had taken Suzanne down to the first aid station in the locker room, came to her rescue.

"Look," he said, "why doesn't everyone shut up and let this lady give us an account of what happened?"

Mavis smiled in gratitude and did her best to explain the sequence of events, leaving out, as Jane had done, the episode involving the shooting of Philippe Gareau and Pepi Mueller.

"But how did Mrs. Mallory get away?" Nicole asked.
"The hijackers let some people go—I don't know why."
"What happened to Rena?" Peter asked.
"They let her out with the first tape," Mavis answered.
"What do you think will happen now?" Diana asked.
"I don't know," Mavis answered. "They have got the

money and they have got away. They have no reason to hurt anyone. I am sure, quite sure, because I was at the meetings, that the police will do nothing to endanger the lives of your parents. So don't worry. It's just a question of time. I'm sure we'll get news very soon."

There was no use dwelling on the outcome. Warmed by the food, relieved to have returned safely, their spirits quickly revived excitedly. They exchanged tales of their experiences in the stranded gondola cars.

"We just sat around and talked," Diana said, giving Jacques a knowing look. What they actually had been doing was a bit too kinky to explain.

CHAPTER TEN

THE BLUE VAN wound slowly down the hill toward the highway.

Inside, tension was mounting. They were all conscious of a new dimension of risk.

Now they were out in the open, in hostile territory. The danger had escalated for captor and captive alike.

"Where are they taking us?" Jeanette had to scream to be heard above the eerie whine of the differential gears and the roar of the engine.

Armand stretched in the pitch darkness to find her. "I don't know. Just lay low and keep quiet."

They all had the same thoughts. Where were they going? How long would the hijackers hold them? Would some of them be killed to buy time for the hijackers? What would happen if the police decided to shoot it out?

Isolated and frozen in their cramped black cell, the seven remaining hostages huddled together on the floor, like terrified cattle on the way to slaughter. Lise Gareau lay groaning and sobbing in Kay Mitchell's arms; the others, Sam, Armand, Jeannette, Arthur Mallory, and Billy, the gondola attendant, were huddled together in a desperate attempt to get warm.

Up front, Jim O'Malley steered the van like a man in a trance. Beside him Silky and Jake fingered their machine guns uneasily, peering into the gloom, alert for the first signs of ambush.

"Turn left at the bottom of the hill," Silky snapped out an order. "No speeding. Keep it to thirty."

Jim obeyed like an automaton, nursing the van with exaggerated care and avoiding any sudden movements; the explosive collar around his neck made everything feel fragile.

Silky kept his eyes glued to the rear view mirror as they moved out along the highway, watching for a tail. Nothing. Or just a glimpse of dim parking lights pulling out behind? He lost them as the van dipped over the far side of an incline.

He felt uneasy. Even though he had given strict instructions that the police should not follow them it stood to reason that the van was not going to be allowed free passage. The police *had* to have a counter-plan. Perhaps they had bugged the van and were following at a safe distance.

"Anyone on our tail?" Jake asked.

"No. Must be a bug." Silky replied.

Burton watched the van come down the hill. Everything was operating smoothly and he was getting a strong beep from the transmitter on the van's rear axle.

His plan was to act as a long shadow, just keeping contact with the quarry. Since he did not have a police radio in the private car which he had commandeered, a patrol car would follow him, broadcasting details of the route to outlying cars posted in a ring, cutting off all possible escape routes.

He proposed to keep the van under constant surveillance until it was out of the ten-mile danger zone. After that, the cars would close in on it, but no action would be taken until the hijackers made their expected break. On no account were the lives of the hostages to be endangered.

"Shit!" Burton said suddenly. "They're heading downtown." He hadn't expected this at all. He only had a couple of cruisers in the city area and one parked a mile down the road from the Mount Casino intersection. "Get it on the radio!" he shouted to the other car. "But tell them to lie low downtown until they hear from us." All hell would break loose if a police car confronted the van in a crowded street. "O.K. then, let's go."

Burton switched on his parking lights and pulled out in pursuit. He could not see the van; he had noticed that it had no rear light. But he was getting a strong signal from the bug.

The van covered the four miles to South Lake at a leisurely speed, mixing with the traffic in a strange assumption of normality.

"Better get in the back and check around," Silky said to Jake, handing him the pencil flashlight.

Jake pulled himself up and slid open the door to the rear compartment with a clang. He swept the thin beam of light around the pile of bodies, looking into scared, blinking eyes. Dumping his machine gun out of Jim's reach, he drew his revolver and crawled into the rear.

"Do what you're told," Silky addressed the hostages. "I've got him covered."

"Move!" Jake gave Arthur Mallory a shove. "And you! Move toward the front." He cleared them away from the rear of the van and the left-side locker. He took a small portable detector out of the locker and passed it slowly along the rear of the van. It started reacting directly over the center of the rear axle.

"Fuck!" He groped his way back to report to Silky.

"I heard it," Silky grunted. They had a bug alright.

They were downtown now, weaving their way through the traffic. There was a weird incongruity to the scene— lighted shop windows, neon signs, bustling pedestrians, all cheerfully ignorant of the pirate ship in their midst.

"Take the next left," Silky said to Jim. It gave Jim a start. He should have given him more warning if he wanted him to cross the traffic. He nosed the van out gingerly and swung round into Park Avenue. "O.K., speed it up, now. Not more than fifty."

Jim stepped on the accelerator moving it up gently.

Jake was still busy in the back. He lifted up two loose floor boards across the very rear of the van, disclosing three round holes in the floor cut clean through to the street. A blast of cold air filled the already frozen compartment and the noise of tires on tarmac added to the confusion. The huddled bodies on the floor pressed closer together in terror.

Jake fished three large paper bags out of the locker and placed one in front of each hole.

"O.K.," he yelled to Silky when he was ready. "Anytime." He knelt poised above the center hole with one of the bags in his hands.

"Take the next right," Silky said to Jim, "and gun it when you get around." Then he leaned back into the rear compartment. "We're turning now," he shouted. "Give it a count of five and let it go."

Burton had been following the van on sound alone, judging his distance by the strength of the signal. He had a young cop with him, working the receiver.

As they got into town, he switched on his headlights to make him less conspicuous among the other cars and speeded up, threading his way through the traffic. If the van made a sudden turn, he would not necessarily pick it up until he was past it.

"There she is!" His sidekick pointed excitedly. "I saw them turn up Park Avenue, I'm sure."

"Good man," Burton said, thanking his stars for the young man's sharp eyes. He switched back to parking lights and swung across the traffic in pursuit.

The beep was getting fainter. "They've speeded up," the cop said.

Burton didn't like it. Something was wrong. The hijackers were acting as though they knew they were being followed, and he had the uncomfortable feeling that he was being drawn into a trap.

"Better prepare for an ambush," he said quietly, taking his gun from its holster and slipping the safety-catch. He figured that maybe he was going to come swinging round a corner into a hail of bullets. "Is the squad car behind us?" he asked.

"Yes, sir."

The beep was getting fainter. He put his foot down. "We better not lose 'em," he decided grimly.

They kept going fast for about three minutes but the signal did not improve. "I think they must have turned off," the cop suggested. "Probably on Montreal Road."

"Shit!" said Burton. He glanced in the mirror. He flicked his left-turn signal, yelled "wave 'em down behind!" and skidded around in a one-eighty-degree turn.

"Be ready for it," he yelled as he screamed the car back down Park Avenue. "They're probably waiting for

205

us on Montreal Road. Don't fire unless I tell you. I'm not ready for a shoot-out yet."

Jim shoved his foot down as ordered as soon as he had turned into Montreal Road. The van shot forward with a squeal of churning rubber, throwing Jake off his balance as he crouched over the center hole in the rear deck. Not bothering to count, he pulled himself back into position and emptied the three bags of steel tacks through the holes to the street as fast as he could. The whole job took maybe fifteen seconds.

"Next right!" Silky yelled, and Jim skidded round on Primrose, still going fast. He had his wits about him now, concentrating on keeping the van under control. Seeing the main highway ahead, he made his own decision to slow down.

"That's right." Silky seemed satisfied. "Bring it right down to normal traffic speed. Turn right on to Highway 50 when you hit the junction and make for the Sahara. Keep hustling, but don't pick up a speeding ticket."

Silky watched the rear mirror as they turned the corner. Nothing yet. Only a few minutes to go and they would be home free.

Jake moved back into the front, picking up his machine gun. "What's happening?"

"It looks O.K., man." Silky seemed fairly calm. "I think we've made it." He turned to Jim. "This is the end of the road. We can blow that bomb around your neck at a range of ten miles. We're getting out. We're going to detonate the bomb in 25 minutes. There is explosive in the rear compartment, so everything will blow sky-high—unless you're more than ten miles away. Get it?" He grinned at Jim. "Ten miles, understand? Ten miles and you are safe. So, once we get out, you just drive this rig as fast as you can for twenty-five minutes and make goddam sure you have gone more than ten miles in that time. After that, you can stop and wait for the police. The party will be over."

Jim shrugged. "You're the boss."

Burton took it cautiously as he swung into Montreal Road, peering along both sides of the street. The beep was very weak.

"They're way ahead of us, sir," the young cop said impatiently.

Burton gave it a bit more speed, but he wasn't going to rush into anything, whatever the young fellow said. Then he felt both front tires go flat, almost simultaneously. At the slow speed at which he was travelling, he managed to pull up under control.

"Damn!" he said. "They booby-trapped us. They must've laid some tacks!"

"Look out!"

Burton just had time to brace himself against the steering wheel before the crash. The squad car behind had come round at speed, blown a front tire and spun out of control, side-swiping Burton's car with a grinding crunch. The young cop shot forward, stunning himself on the dash, and the receiving set fell to the floor with a crash. There was an eerie silence. Not even a beep.

Burton kicked open the damaged door. The driver of the other car was unhurt but the radio operator was bleeding like a pig. "Gimme the mike," Burton yelled, ignoring the wounded man. Snatching it from the driver, he leaned inside, pressing the switch. "Calling all cars. Calling all cars. This is Burton. We lost the blue van on Montreal Road. Car Thirty-four get on up here to Montreal Road at Park Avenue to pick me up. Everyone else watch for them and call Thirty-four when you pick 'em up! Get 'em, for Christ's sake, get 'em!"

Silky and Jake started gathering their belongings, the money, the kit bag, the guns. Silky made his usual methodical check. He was not going to get caught because they had left some telltale piece of evidence in the van. Finally he clipped a padlock on the door leading to the rear compartment.

"O.K." He turned to Jim. "You are dropping us in the Sahara parking lot." He could see the big neon sign a couple of hundred yards ahead. "We're getting off just after we go in. Now get this, or there is going to be one hell of a goddam explosion. As soon as we're out, you circle the parking lot, drive out the other exit, and head north on Highway 50 until you're out of range. Got it?"

"Yes," Jim answered. He was not going to try any stunts at this point. The hijackers were getting out and in

207

another half-hour everyone else in the van would be safe. He was cool now, relieved to be able to see the beginning of the end.

"Turn right now!" Silky shouted, opening the door as they turned. They drove fifty yards down the driveway to the side of the building.

"Stop!" Silky jumped out, followed by Jake. "Go!" Silky screamed, waving his gun from the ground below. Jim, who had not even had time to bring the van to a halt, pressed the accelerator as he was told. He drove through the huge parking lot, up the far lane to the highway, and turned north at top speed.

Charlie had been parked in the selected spot for nearly three hours. He had not enjoyed the wait, his nervousness mounting by the minute. He had spent the time looking at his watch, smoking cigarettes, and allowing his imagination to scare the hell out of him.

Even though he had not taken his eyes off the entrance to the car park, it still gave him a jolt when the van suddenly swung round the corner.

He was parked nose against the building, doors and trunk open, engine running, lights off. He watched the van slow down alongside him as two masked men leaped out. They threw a heavy kit bag in the trunk, slammed it shut and jumped in, closing the doors and ducking out of sight.

"Fishhook," the man next to him said. "Now move out, easy."

Charlie backed out cautiously and headed for the exit. Just as he reached the highway, a police car swung into the entrance, causing Charlie to make a quick swerve. He missed it by inches. "Jesus Christ," he said, "was that sonofabitch trying to ram me?"

"Skip it, Charlie. You missed him." What the hell would have happened if he hadn't, God alone knew. "Turn left and get moving," Silky said.

Charlie turned off the highway on Edward, took a right on Michelle, right again on Kahte, back on to Highway 50 going south.

Almost immediately he turned east on Highway 19. The man beside him was watching the rearview mirror and struggling out of his snowmobile suit at the same time.

"Anything?" the guy in the back asked.

"No. We're clear. That cop who nearly hit us coming out of the parking lot must have picked up the van's bug. I hope they're all on their way to Spooner Junction."

Charlie was following the prearranged route, circling back toward Highway 50 again. Eventually he swung into Harrah's parking lot, not so far from where they had started.

"Park it over there, Charlie." Silky pointed to a spot facing the wall. "And keep your eyes front. It wouldn't be good for any of us if you could recognize our car."

"Sure, man, sure. Anything you say."

The man at the back passed an envelope over to Charlie. "Nine thousand dollars for you," he said. "Give me the key to the trunk."

Jake got out of the back and opened the trunk of Charlie's car. He took off his mask and stuffed it in the kit bag, then carried all the luggage over to the station wagon, which had been sitting there since morning. When the job was finished, he returned the keys to Silky, who was keeping an eye on Charlie.

"O.K., man that's it." Silky said to Charlie. "Don't flash that money around. Spend a little at a time, preferably somewhere away from here. Now go back to the movies. By the way, what's playing?"

"*The Godfather.*"

"That's nice. It's worth seeing twice." He handed the keys to Charlie. "Good luck, then. Now get to hell out of here."

Charlie took off without a word, nine grand richer and no wiser as to what had happened.

Silky slipped off his mask and strolled across to the station wagon. Jake was already working in the rear of the wagon straightening everything out. He was dressed in a neat white turtle neck and a denim leisure suit, but he still wore his fatigue boots. He put the two money bags into one of the three matching gray suitcases, the one with a red leather tag on it, so they would know which was which. He changed into a pair of black loafers and shoved his fatigue boots and both the snowmobile suits in the second suitcase. The third one was already packed with his clothes and personal belongings.

Together they stuffed all the armament and Silky's mask in the kit bag, which they threw on the rear seat. Finally they lined the three bags and Jake's boots and skis neatly along the rear deck. After a final check, they were ready.

Silky got behind the wheel, smiling with satisfaction. "I think we made it," he said.

"I think you're right," Jake grinned.

Silky swung the wagon into the driveway of the Sahara and parked in front of the entrance.

A solemn doorman opened the door with a flourish and an inquiring look. "Yes, sir?"

"I have a room booked." Jake smiled at him.

"Yes, sir. Need some help with the luggage?"

"Yes, please."

The doorman signalled a bellhop with a flick of his fingers while Jake got out to open the trunk. "The three gray suitcases and those boots and skis." He pointed, watching the man load them on his buggy.

He glanced around. No police, no commotion, no people.

He walked round to the driver's window. Silky lowered it and leaned out.

They shook hands.

"See you tomorrow," Silky said.

Suddenly Rena felt stifled in the crowded bar. She paid her bill and escaped back to her apartment.

She did not turn on the lights. She just threw herself on the bed, trying vainly to turn her mind to blankness.

It must have been twenty minutes later that she suddenly became alert. Whether it was some telltale noise or whether it was intuition that made her go to the window she did not know.

She peered into the darkness, searching for something. Then she saw it. The gondola was moving! The siege was over!

Anxiety soon overtook her initial elation. What did it mean? That Silky and Jake had gotten away? Or that they had been captured or killed?

210

Oh, God, oh God when will this night be over? she wondered. Now that they were rescuing the gondola passengers, perhaps she might be able to get some fresh news. They might even let her go over to the ski lodge. At least she could try.

The change of engine pitch to a sustained full-speed intensity was reassuring after the preceding series of stops and starts. The van was obviously out on open highway now, heading for some predetermined destination.

There was still no knowing where they were going, but Sam Mitchell reasoned that it was toward safety. The hijackers had said that the hostages would be safe within an hour of leaving the base and he was inclined to believe them. Despite their cold hostility toward those who challenged them, the hijackers had not seemed sadistic. There would be little to gain by killing any hostages now. Sam felt an urge to convey his optimism to the others. "Is everyone alright?" he shouted above the din. "Kay, you O.K.?"

"Yes."

The sound of their own voices seemed to relax the tension.

"What d'you think is happening?" Arthur Mallory called out.

"I think we'll be out soon. They've got a plan, these guys. They don't need us much longer."

"What makes you say that?" Arthur asked.

It was hard to carry on a conversation at the top of their voices, but it made them all feel better. They were anxious to sieze on any crumb of hope. As though by common consent, they began to stretch, relaxing a little, finding more comfortable positions.

Armand put his arm round Jeanette's shoulders, giving her a squeeze of encouragement. "I think Sam's right," he said. "These guys aren't just charging round the countryside in a van with a bunch of hostages. They're too smart. I don't think they are going to hurt us."

"My guess," Sam said, "is they are going to switch to another car soon. As soon as they shake the police."

"I think they already did."

"Who said that? Why?" Arthur asked. It was scary to

hear the voice of a stranger in the darkness, just as they were beginning to regain the comfort of their group friendship.

"Me, Billy."

The gondola attendant! They had forgotten about him. He had been lying alone on the right side locker up against the thin steel wall of the compartment. "I think I heard one of them yell from outside the van at the last stop. He shouted just before we took off."

"Are you sure?" Sam asked.

"Nearly sure," Billy answered.

"Why the hell are we chasing along the highway then?" Arthur Mallory was skeptical.

"I don't know," said Billy, "but I still think they got out."

Jim kept moving along the highway at seventy miles an hour. He looked in the rear mirror, spotting headlights a fair way behind him. He was not sure whether it was a tail or not, but since he was well over the speed limit and the car behind was maintaining a steady distance, he presumed that it was.

He became suddenly aware that he was sickeningly cold. Without realizing it, he had been sweating profusely. Now, he became acutely conscious of his undershirt clinging clammily to his skin, like a damp dishcloth.

In the excitement of the getaway, no one had thought to turn on the van's heater. It was about fifteen below outside and precious little more in the driving compartment.

He switched it on full blast.

His thoughts turned to the others in the back of the van. He wanted to let them know that the worst was over, that they could begin to relax. After all, they did not even know that the kidnappers had baled out and that the van was on its way to safety. Aware only that the van was now travelling at high speed, they must be wondering what new disaster was in store for them.

But the only way he could communicate with them was by yelling at the top of his voice through the closed door. They probably would not hear much above the roar of the engine, and the situation was not one that could be explained in a few words. The best thing to do, he decided, was to keep on going full speed toward safety.

He could see the fork at Spooner Junction ahead and started to slow down. Glancing in the mirror, he watched the car behind react and maintain its distance. He pulled into the driveway of the gas station on his right, switching off his engine. The car pulled up immediately about two hundreds yards behind him, dousing its lights. Pretty clumsy tail, he thought to himself, considering that they had been told not to follow on any account. He spotted a squad car in the shadows, close to the building, probably standing by for orders to set up a roadblock. It was maybe a hundred feet away.

He lowered his window and yelled, "Hey! Police! Help! The hijackers have gone. We're just hostages in here."

Silence.

Well, the news was likely to be confusing to them. They probably suspected a trap. Jim tried again. "Police! My name is Jim O'Malley, the mountain manager at Mount Casino. The hijackers got out twenty-five minutes ago, at the Sahara. We're the hostages. Please radio in. Then come and let us out."

There was still silence. They were probably calling for assistance.

Sure enough two more cars, one a police car and one unmarked, drew up at a safe distance.

Jim banged on the cargo compartment behind him. "Is everyone alright?" he shouted.

"Yes," Sam answered. "Did you say the hijackers have gone?"

"Yes, you're safe now, but better stay put for a little while. The police are rather jittery."

All of a sudden, the car by the building switched on its spotlight, aiming it directly at Jim, making him blink.

"Get out with your hands on your head!" a voice called out.

"I can't. I'm chained to the steering wheel."

Another silence. He did not resent their caution, wishing that Carl had been as careful.

Finally the first car moved toward him, parking broadside to him. The two other cars surrounded the van, all three with their headlights and spotlights trained on it. He heard the police shouting to each other, car doors slamming. He could see the glint of steel. No more shooting for God's sake, he thought.

"Don't shoot!" he shouted. "There's no one here but hostages."

Sam and the others listened intently to what was going on. One thing was certain, the situation was improving. Apparently the kidnappers had skipped and the police were moving in. Billy had been right.

It reminded Sam of stories he had read of miners trapped in a mine disaster. He had heard accounts of them sitting, sometimes for days, in little black tombs, listening to the sound of rescuers searching for them, unable to do anything but hope and pray that they got through in time.

It was hard to be patient. Safety and freedom were just outside that thin panel wall of the truck. He felt like banging as hard as he could and yelling "Let me out."

A policeman was approaching Jim, carrying a shotgun at the ready. He could feel the barrels of a battery of guns, out there in the dark, pointed at him.

"Put your hands on your head and step out slowly," the approaching cop called out. There was no question that he was nervous and would shoot if Jim made a false move.

"I can't," Jim said as quietly and calmly as he could. He wanted to reason with the man, not defy him. "My left hand is handcuffed to the steering wheel. Look!"

The cop came closer, then switched on his flashlight. Jim held up his chained hand as high as he could.

"O.K. I'm coming in," the cop said, reasonably convinced. "Open your door and then sit absolutely still," he commanded.

The cop came right up close, looking up at Jim; he had dropped his shotgun and was holding the muzzle of his revolver maybe six inches from Jim's face. Jim watched a bead of sweat trickle down the side of his nose, then pick up speed as it got caught in the channel of a laugh-line.

He inspected the cab, then stared at Jim's neck.

"What's that?" he said suspiciously.

Shit, thought Jim, here goes the panic button again. "Well"—he wanted to soften the blow, but couldn't think of anything to say without sounding evasive—"it's a bomb."

"A bomb?" The man looked flabbergasted.

"Don't worry," Jim said quickly. "It won't go off. The kidnappers rigged it on me. But they said that they couldn't detonate it at a range of more than ten miles."

"Stay where you are," the cop said and walked back to his squad car.

"What the hell is happening?" Armand yelled from the cargo space. "Why don't they let us out?"

"Keep your shirts on," Jim shouted back. "It won't be long now. They're not quite sure what to make of the situation."

This time three cops came back but only one, the first one, pointed a revolver. They looked at Jim's hand chained to the wheel, then his neck.

A new fellow, older than the first one, spoke.

"Well they sure have got you trussed up." He smiled at Jim. The tension subsided, like air fizzing out of a balloon.

"There are hostages in the back," Jim told him. "They're pretty scared."

The older one turned to the other two. "Let them out of the back," he said.

"How're you feeling?" He returned to Jim.

"O.K. I've felt better."

"I'm afraid we have nothing with us to cut that handcuff. And I wouldn't want to tamper with that bomb." He paused to consider. "This seems to be the best thing to do. I'll send the others back in the cars and I'll stay here with you. I'll have to order up some cutters to get the cuff off and a demolition man to defuse the bomb. Shouldn't be too long."

Jim caught sight of Lise and Kay being escorted to one of the cars. At the same moment Armand appeared at his side. "Jesus, I need a drink," he said looking at the cop. "Got anything in your first aid kit?"

"Afraid not, sir."

"How are you, Mr. O'Malley?"

"I'm alright. What about you? And the ladies?"

"We're alive. And, right now, that feels so good that

215

anything else is just secondary. What happened to our hosts?"

"The kidnappers? They got out at the Sahara. But they had this bomb rigged around my neck and told me to get out of range as fast as possible."

"So that's how they arranged the switch! I knew they would. They were real smart." He made to leave.

"Well, are you coming?"

"I can't." He held up his chained hand. "I have to wait for someone to cut this off. And I have to be defused by a bomb man."

"Well, then I suppose that I'd better not keep them waiting. Good luck."

Armand climbed in the back of one of the squad cars next to Jeanette. Arthur sat up front next to the driver.

Lise was in the other car with the Mitchells and Billy, the attendant.

They took off at once, sirens blaring.

Sam leaned over to the cop next to the driver, speaking quietly. "Do you know what happened to Mr. Gareau? He was one of the hostages who got shot. This is Mrs. Gareau." He pointed to Lise, who was lying in Kay's arms.

"No, sir."

"Could you radio in?" Sam put his fingers to his lips to indicate discretion.

"I'll try, sir."

The cop handled the assignment quietly, telling headquarters that he was bringing in Mrs. Gareau and asking for news of her husband.

The dispatcher told him he'd try to find out. Sam and Kay exchanged glances, but Lise seemed totally oblivious to her surroundings.

The radio crackled and a call signal came through. The cop acknowledged.

"Your party is in hospital. Condition serious. Not fatal."

Kay looked at Lise, then at Sam. She shook her head. At least Philippe was alive, but there was not enough to go on unless Lise asked about him.

The car stopped at the police station and they got out. The two cops helped Lise, who stared at them in a daze. Suddenly she seemed to pull herself together. "My hus-

216

band," she said. "Do you know what happened to my husband?"

"He's alright," said Kay.

"Are you sure?"

"Yes, I'm sure. He is at the hospital and he is alive."

"Thank God! Oh, thank God!" Lise started weeping profusely. "Please," she groaned, "I want to see him. Please."

"Can we do something?" Kay asked the cop who had driven their car.

"Yes, ma'am. I'm sure we can. In a few minutes. Just sit down." Billy joined them.

Sam was just beginning to get really fidgety when a sergeant came over and ushered them into a private office. He was very sympathetic. "I realize you are very tired and upset so I won't keep you long." He addressed Sam. "Where are you staying?"

"Mount Casino."

"All of you?"

"The three of us," he indicated Lise and Kay.

"May I have your names?"

Sam gave the three names.

"And you, sir?" to Billy.

Billy gave his name and address.

"Fine. Now will you all be available tomorrow?"

They nodded.

"Good. Then that's all for the moment." He looked at Lise, who seemed to be somewhat recovered. "Mrs. Gareau, your husband is at the hospital. He has had some bullets removed from his thigh. He is under sedation and is presently sleeping. He is definitely not in any danger. I believe it would be best for you to go back to the hotel."

"I would like to see him. To talk to the doctor. Please." She was in control of herself now.

"Very well." The sergeant smiled. "I'll arrange for a car to take you there."

Kay looked at Sam, then put her arm round Lise's shoulders. "I'll go with you," she said.

Armand, Jeanette and Arthur were waiting for them as they came out of the sergeant's office. They had already been checked through.

217

"Would you believe it?" Arthur greeted them with a broad grin. "I called the hotel and spoke to Peter. All the kids are O.K., and they're celebrating in the bar. They heard we were safe. Jane is there, too, and drinks are on the house. I guess this is one time when she can drink as much as she goddam well likes!"

CHAPTER ELEVEN

FOR THE MAJORITY of the company, actors and spectators, all the drama was over. Most of the gondola passengers had gone home or over to the hotel, the hospital staff had dispersed, the cafeteria staff were washing up and the majority of the squad cars had moved off to the road blocks. Only a few of the players remained for the last curtain.

There were six of them left in the communications center. Sergeant Lipzke and two cops, one on the telephone and one on the radio; Alfredo, Pat, and Paul Mullins working together on a bottle of scotch. They all sat in silence.

At last the radio man spoke. "Message coming in," he said excitedly, conscious that he was on center stage. Everyone watched him.

He listened to his earphones, brow creased in concentration. Then, to everyone's relief, he broke into a broad smile. "They're all safe, sergeant," he said with evident satisfaction. "That was car 27. They have the van. They are bringing in seven people, all uninjured, to the station. There is one person, the driver, a Mr. O'Malley, who has to wait for defusing—something about a bomb around his neck—but he should be coming in in about ten minutes. Any message, sir?" he asked Sergeant Lipzke.

The sergeant looked inquiringly at Alfredo.

"No. I think we have all the news that we wanted to hear. Except that the hijackers have been caught."

"Well, then, if it's alright by you, sir, I think we'll start dismantling here." He looked to Alfredo for approval. "Our job is to get out there and catch them now."

"Go right ahead, sergeant." Alfredo rose to go, putting his arm round Pat's shoulders. "For their sakes, I hope you catch them first."

"First, sir?"

Alfredo just nodded absently. He was too tired to say more.

As soon as Paul Mullins heard the news, he announced it in the ski lodge, then hurried over to the hotel, where he completed his message by announcing drinks on the house. The crowd went wild with joy, laughing and slapping each other on the back. There was a kind of wartime atmosphere, the commemoration of a great victory, strangers sharing the joy of deliverance from a common enemy.

Mavis was just coming in with the young group when the news was announced.

One of the desk clerks waved at her frantically, catching her eye at last.

"This is the group of young people from Montreal?" he asked.

"Yes," Mavis answered.

"Is there someone called Peter Mallory among them? I have a phone call for him."

Peter spoke to his father and then returned to the group. "Everyone is O.K. I spoke to Dad. The hijackers let them all go. They'll all be here soon."

It was all that was needed to set them off. In retrospect the whole episode became an exciting adventure. It was time to get back to enjoying their holiday.

Leaving them in Jane Mallory's charge, Mavis turned her thoughts to Rena. She would surely be anxious about Jim.

She called her apartment. "Jim's O.K., Rena. It's just been announced."

"Oh, thank God. What about the others? They were all in my ski class."

"They're all fine, except Mr. Gareau."

"Yes, I heard about him. That's awful." Rena paused and then it came out involuntarily. "What happened to the hijackers? Were they"—she found it hard to say it— "were they—caught?"

"I don't know," Mavis said. "I don't think so, yet. But I am sure they will be."

A different squad car came barrelling up the highway, beacon flashing, and screeched onto the lot. Two men got out of the rear, one of them in plain clothes, a heavy parka, and woolen cap. They walked quickly over to the van.

The man in the parka got into the van from the passenger side and, kneeling on the seat beside him, switched on his flashlight.

"Well, now," he said. "What seems to be the problem here?" He sounded a bit like a family dentist about to ask where it hurts. He looked over the contrivance around Jim's neck, humming tunelessly to himself as he did so.

"What's this supposed to be?" he said finally.

"A bomb," Jim replied.

"Funny sort of bomb. Doesn't seem to have a detonator. Tell me about it."

"I don't know any more than they told me. They said it was a bomb and that they could blow it at ten miles' range."

He looked, then searched in the tool bag beside him, taking out a small pair of pliers. "Well, let's operate and see what happens." There was a hint of fatalism in his tone, conveying to Jim an uneasy feeling that there was a fair chance that they might both be blown sky-high. He waited tensely.

Snip! A delicious tiny sound.

Snip.

"That's that."

"You mean it's over?" Back at the dentist's office again, this time that nice feeling, when he shows you your tooth in his forceps, just as you are plucking up courage for the long pull.

"That's right." He tore the whole contraption off Jim's neck at one grab. "Never would have gone off anyway."

"Well that's nice to know—now."

The man got out of the van. "O.K. He's safe," he said

to the policeman who had accompanied him. "You can cut him out now."

Silky looked at his watch. He had about ten minutes to go.

According to their reckoning, there would not be any road blocks until Jim had driven for the stipulated twenty-five minutes and the police had realized that he and Jake had slipped out. After that, all hell would break loose. He had to get rid of the hardware, the guns and ammunition, before that deadline. They were the only remaining evidence that could incriminate them.

He headed back up Tahoe Boulevard to Elks Avenue to the end of Hill Street at Elk Point.

Parking the wagon, he reached over to the rear seat. He pulled out the kit bag, hoisted it over his shoulder and started walking along the deserted shore of Marla Bay.

At the highest point above the bay he dumped the bag on the ground. He took each weapon out, one at a time, and hurled it as far as he could into the lake. Finally he shovelled some stones into the bag and threw it in after the weapons.

He stood for a short moment looking down, then turned on his heel, jogging nonchalantly back to the station wagon.

Next, he unpacked his regular ski jacket and donned it after carefully attaching the Heavenly Valley ski ticket, which he had purchased that morning, to the zipper.

Before closing the rear door, he made a final careful flashlight inspection of everything in the car, checking the floor and then the glove compartment. Next he turned out his own pockets and emptied his wallet, laying everything out neatly on the floor. He found the last of the forged driving licenses in the wallet and taped it under the dash.

He was clean.

He lit a cigarillo, slammed the rear door, and swung the station wagon back up Elks Avenue to the highway, turning left and heading for Reno.

After about ten minutes, he spotted the police flashers as he approached Spooner Junction. It gave him a comfortable feeling to find the police acting so predictably.

He pulled up behind a group of cars, maybe a dozen, and waited his turn. It did not take long.

Two cops approached the station wagon, one on each side. He lowered his window.

"Good evening, sir." The cop stared Silky right in the eye.

"Good evening, sergeant. What's the problem?"

"Just a routine inspection. We have had a little trouble in town tonight." He scanned the inside of the car.

"What sort of trouble?"

The cop ignored the question. "May I see your driver's license?"

Silky handed it over.

"Where are you coming from, Mr. Ambler?"

"Been skiing at Heavenly Valley."

"Not Mount Casino, by any chance?"

"No, Heavenly Valley." He pulled the zipper of his jacket and displayed the ticket. It was convincing; the cop didn't bother to look.

"Do you mind if I just look in the back?"

"Not at all. Help yourself." He made to get out, but the cop was accommodating.

"I'll handle it," he said, taking the keys.

He walked to the back, took a cursory look with his flashlight and slammed it shut.

"Thank you, sir." He smiled, returning the keys. "You're on your way."

Silky slipped the key into the ignition and switched it on. All of a sudden the cop started banging a tattoo on the window. Jesus, something's wrong! thought Silky. It crossed his mind to put his foot down and get out.

He lowered the window. "Yes, what is it?" He was ready for an instant getaway if he had to.

"May I have a look at your hands, please?"

My God, the finger! They knew about the finger! How the hell did they know that?

He had to think fast. Play for a little more time. He lifted his hands slowly, eyes concentrating ahead to gauge the fastest escape route.

"Would you take your gloves off please?"

This was it. They had him. Mayday. He had her in second gear, on the point of take-off, when something held him back. "What's this in aid of, officer?" he asked.

"We are looking for a man with a broken finger." The cop smiled apologetically.

Silky spread his bare hands on the wheel. They were trembling too much to do anything else. "I hope you find him," he said.

"Thank you, sir. You're on your way."

Silky changed back down to first and glided away very gently.

Jesus, he had nearly blown it. Thank God for Vietnam, for the cool it had taught him, the steel nerves in a panic situation.

A broken finger? Of course! The fight. The other guy didn't know it was a falsy. He thought he had broken it! That was it.

He laughed out loud, thinking back to that day in New York when Jake had introduced him as Fred Carr, the actor. Did he want hair? Maybe he should have taken hair. If the cop had known the false finger business a bit better, he might have noticed.

Thank God for the itchy finger!

Rena came down to join the crowd on the gambling floor. She had to have news, whatever the cost in emotional strain.

She tried to remain detached, on the periphery just gleaning information, not becoming involved. The sight of Peter Mallory, Nicole, and the others filled her with a terrible feeling of shame and remorse. She slipped into the lobby bar, finding a stool at the far end—alone, afraid.

She plucked up her courage. "Did they catch them, Sammy?" Oh God, what if he said yes?

"No." Sammy seemed somehow to be a kindred soul, on the side of the underdogs. "Real smart cookies," he said in a tone of admiration. "They got clean away. Of course, the dragnet is out now and it's hard to see how they can penetrate that. But I, for one, wish them luck."

"Why?" Rena was curious.

Sammy shrugged. "What do you want?"

"A brandy, please."

Sammy brought the drink, then tried to put his feelings into words. "It's hard to explain. These two guys, they've got courage, imagination, discipline, nerve. This is the kind of exploit you'd get a silver cross, hell, a president-ial citation for in wartime. They have the qualities of heroes. Who says it's more heroic to kill fifty communists who are fighting for a cause they believe in than to knock off this week's gambling profits?"

I love you, Sammy; she almost said it aloud.

"Listen,"—Sammy seemed bound to make his point now—"I've been here three years. Seen hundreds of people sit on that stool there—and they have been look-ing at their own deaths. Gamblers, you know, been in there"—he waved at the room outside—"and lost it all. Not just money. That's what they think they lost until they come in here for one last drink in the dark. That's when they realize that they have lost everything. Wives, kids, home, job, confidence, self-respect—every-thing. You think some of those guys aren't cheering when they see someone walk off with the house's profits?"

Rena smiled. "Are you a gambler, Sammy?"

He grinned. "I've lost some in my time. Enough to be cheering for the hijackers, that's for sure."

She paid for her drink. "Thank you, Sammy," she said with feeling. He would never know how much she meant it.

By the time Silky reached Reno, he was in high spirits. The finger incident at the road block, the hair's-breadth proximity to disaster, acted to pique the spice of success.

Arriving in town, he turned off toward the airport, pull-ing up at the end of the terminal. He unloaded all his luggage, taking it over to the lockers. He put a quarter in each of two contiguous ones, stowed the bags and skis, and pocketed the keys.

He returned to the station wagon, drove it to the Hertz rental return, took the papers from under the sun visor, and walked to the desk.

"Yes, sir?" the girl said brightly.

"I'm returning this wagon." He handed her the keys.

"Rented in Salt Lake," she observed, checking the doc-uments.

"Yes."

"I'm afraid there will be a return charge."

"That's O.K."

"Cash or credit card?"

"Cash."

He paid the bill and thanked her, then strolled out to the main concourse. Typical of Nevada, it was full of slot machines, with a bar running along one wall.

He ordered a large scotch on the rocks, paid with a ten dollar bill, and asked for his change in quarters.

He picked a machine in the far corner and began feeding its appetite. He did not even register surprise when he hit a thirty-five dollar jackpot. He bought another drink.

Twenty minutes passed before they announced a plane coming in from Sacramento. He changed his quarters back into bills, while waiting for the crowd to come off the aircraft. Then he watched them move into the luggage reception area.

He took his luggage out of the lockers and made his way to the taxi stand. The driver helped him stack the bags in the trunk. "Where to?"

"Hillcrest Motel, please."

"Going to do some skiing?"

"Yes."

"Been here before?"

"No, never."

Silky was feeling good. The two drinks had relaxed him and he began to accept the incredible enormity of the day's take. What a pushover!

"Say, driver," he said. "Do you know Reno well?"

"Sure. I ought to. Been driving a cab for five years."

"Ever heard of the—er—something ranch?"

"Sure. Want to go there?"

"Well, I might. What's it like?"

"First class. Whorehouse, you know."

"Is it far?"

"No. No more than three miles. Might fancy a piece myself if you want to go out."

"O.K. Let's check me in. Wait for me. I won't be long."

They drew up at a motel. Silky had booked a room two days ago, telling them he would check in late from the Sacramento plane. Unlike Jake, he used the false name from the forged driving license. Even though the robbery was over, they still felt that Silky's Special Forces record was a potential danger. Better not to leave any trace of him in Nevada at all.

He came back to the driver. "Listen, on second thought,

do you mind waiting fifteen minutes? I've had a busy day. I could use a hot shower and a change of clothes."

"You're paying. Take as long as you like."

It only took Silky ten minutes, but he came out feeling like a millionaire. After all, he was one.

"There they are," Arthur said pointing across the room.

All the kids were there, even Tim and Serge, sitting at a big table alongside one of the bars which lined the walls of the gambling area.

Jane had her back to him as he approached. She turned as Peter announced excitedly. "It's them! It's Dad!"

Arthur went straight to her, hugging her tightly and laughing. He pointed at the glass beside her. "What's that?" he said with a twinkle in his eye.

Jane went cold. Could he never leave her alone? "Scotch," she said sullenly.

"Good," Arthur beamed. "Just what I need." He drank it at one swallow. "Let's get some more. Lots of it!"

For a brief moment everyone was embracing and talking at once. Then, in the silence that followed, Diana asked, "Where's Mom?"

"She's at the hospital with Lise," Sam answered.

"The hospital?" Nicole asked. "Why?" Sam threw a questioning glance at Jane.

"I haven't told them" she said flatly. "There didn't seem to be any point."

"Told us what?" Nicole looked pale and frightened.

Sam hesitated. There was no way to make the news any better than it was, but at least he knew that Philippe was out of danger. "Your father got shot, Nicole. But he is absolutely fine. It happened during the getaway. Your mother and Kay have gone to see him."

Jane had moved beside Nicole while Sam was talking. She put her arm around Nicole's shoulders, holding her close. "Let's go upstairs together," she said gently, "and wait in your mother's room. She's going to need your help when she gets back. She has been through an awful lot."

Jake followed the bellhop with the suitcases to the registration counter and signed in, using his proper name and address. It gave him a nice feeling of mission accomplished to be a real person again.

Oblivious of everything else around him, he trailed the luggage into the elevator. Two people entered with him and the bellhop. He gave them a cursory glance, but his eyes returned quickly to the bag with the red tag. He stared at it.

At the fifth floor, the bags were wheeled out along the corridor, stopping outside room five thirty-two. Jake followed them in a hypnotic trance.

The door opened. The bellhop picked two bags off the truck and stood aside to let Jake enter the room.

"Go ahead," Jake gestured, standing guard over the red tag in the hallway.

The bellhop switched on the lights and stacked the bags neatly at the far end of the room. He put the skis, poles, and boots in the clothes cupboard, checked the temperature in the room, adjusted the thermostat, put the bathroom light on, and looked at Jake. Jake continued looking at the bags.

"Will that be all, sir?" he said.

"Yes, thank you." Jake felt in his pockets and peeled two dollar bills out of his wallet.

"Thank you, sir." The man left.

Jake moved across the room, picked the money suitcase up, and felt it for weight. He walked over to the full-length mirror, bag in hand, and stared at himself, mesmerized.

"Two million bucks," he said aloud to himself. "Jesus!"

He carried the bag back across the room and put it down next to the others. He thought about opening it.

He returned to the door of the room, applied the double lock and the door chain. Then he laid the bag out flat, ready to open, and sat on the bed looking at it.

He couldn't do it. A jumble of conflicting emotions prevented him. Partly superstition—somehow it would be unlucky to tempt fate, the money might suddenly disappear if he unlocked it. Partly self-consciousness—it was silly just to stare at it, like a miser. And partly fear —fear of the two million eyes he felt were watching him.

He picked up the other bag, the one with his clothes in it. It was lighter. He laid it on the low table beside the dresser, unlocked it, and snapped it open.

228

He undressed and had a quick shower, leaving the bathroom door open, then picked out some clean clothes. He dressed and sat down on the bed. He had never felt so alone in his life, alone with two million dollars.

He wanted to talk to someone, anyone. But he could not leave the bag.

He picked up the house phone and called room service, ordering a bottle of bourbon, some ice, and a club sandwich. Maybe that would help. Before the waiter arrived, he took the heavy bag, the one with the money in it, and slid it under the bed, where it could not stare at him anymore.

He ate the sandwich at the table, stealing a glance under the bed from time to time. Then he poured himself a hefty slug of whiskey and sat down on the bed.

He took a big gulp of liquor, relishing the sting of it at the back of his throat.

That's better, he thought.

How does a guy spend his first night with two million dollars? What does he think about? He couldn't do too much laughing, all by himself, or dancing, or celebrating. He could not even brag about it, kid about it, be amazed or enchanted about it.

All he could do was sit with it.

It was going to be a long night.

The peal of the telephone jolted her awake. She grabbed for it in the darkness, knocking the bedside lamp to the floor with a crash.

"Rena? Did I wake you? This is Jim."

"Jim?" In her first flash of consciousness she had hoped it was Silky. "Are you alright?"

"Sure. I just got back."

"Back from where?"

"The hijackers took me for a little ride."

"Did they hurt you?" she asked anxiously.

"No. Not at all."

"Did they catch them? The hijackers?"

"No. Not so far."

She was more relaxed now. "What time is it?"

"Only ten-thirty. I need a drink and some food. And I need you. I was hoping that we might put the three things together."

She considered. She was starving for an account of what had really happened. How Nick got shot. And the others. News of Silky and Jake. But caution told her to lie low. A meeting with Jim now would be too great a strain on her conflicting loyalties. She might make a slip of the tongue.

"Not tonight, Jim. I'm too exhausted. Let it wait till tomorrow."

"Lunch, then?"

"Call me." She did not want any ties anymore. Her past was over; her future had begun.

"What's the matter?" Jim sounded disappointed.

"Nothing," she said. "Just tired. I'm so glad that you're alright."

He did not seem to want to hang up. "Rena." He gave a little nervous laugh. "I thought about you a lot during this thing. It kind of brought things into focus. Made me realize what you mean to me. Did you miss me?"

"Of course," she lied. Lying was going to be part of her new life she realized numbly.

"Alright then." He seemed to sense that he was not making any headway. "I'll call you tomorrow. Goodnight."

" 'Night." She put the phone down. She wouldn't sleep anymore tonight. Anyway, the operation seemed to have been a success. She should be happy. But she couldn't. She did not seem to have any emotions left.

It reminded Silky of a debriefing session after a stint behind enemy lines, slowly accommodating oneself to the absence of danger. A gradual metaphysical decompression, as though someone was turning the burner of one's emotions down one notch, releasing the tension of one's reflexes.

He felt loose and indulgent.

He circled his plate with a chunk of warm bread, sopping up the egg, and chewed on it thoughtfully as he studied the newspaper in front of him.

SKI AREA HELD TO RANSOM
SKIJACKERS HOLD 150 HOSTAGES
HUGE SUM SAID STOLEN

The article covered the whole of the front page. "Po

lice authorities stated that they had not yet completed their investigation and that a statement would be issued later. Meantime, it is understood that statewide alerts have been set up in both Nevada and California. Road blocks are in effect throughout the area and airports and bus terminals are being watched," he read. Another section stated, "The getaway van used by the hijackers was abandoned at Spooner Junction, a few miles north of Lake Tahoe. It is understood that this vehicle is expected to provide important evidence as to the identity of the robbers."

Another chunk of bread cleaned the whole plate. He turned to the sports page.

He finished his coffee, paid his bill and walked over to the Avis rental desk at Harold's.

He rented a Chevrolet with a ski rack, using the last phony driving licence, then drove it back to his motel. He packed the car, checked out, and swung out of the driveway, heading for Lake Tahoe.

Approaching Spooner Junction, he was flagged down by a cop, but when he made to stop, he was waved on. There was a roadblock on the other side of the road, but they were only stopping northbound traffic, while slowing the southbound lane just to prevent accidents.

He pulled into the Sahara parking lot at the rear, left the car and called Jake on a housephone in the hotel lobby.

"What kept you?" Jake sounded jittery.

"Why, anything wrong?"

"No. I guess not. I'm just—well, I'm fed up with my own company, that's all."

"Everything O.K. otherwise?"

"Sure. What about you?"

"Smooth."

"Where are you?"

"Downstairs. I'll be right up."

He waited while Jake slipped the chain off and undid the double lock, peering out cautiously.

"Come in," he said, locking up again behind him. Silky looked around the room, noticing one bag unpacked, one over on the far wall.

"Under the bed," Jake said. "It felt safer there."

"You had breakfast?"

231

"Yeah. Shit. I didn't sleep a wink. Man, I'll be glad to get rid of this stuff. It haunted me all night."

"Seen a newspaper yet?"

"Yes. They brought one up with breakfast. Everything seems nice and quiet. How did it go last night?"

"I had a bit of finger trouble," Silky smirked ruefully.

"What do you mean?"

Silky recounted the episode at the roadblock. He played down the fact that he had almost pressed the panic button.

"Jesus!" Jake said. "It just goes to show. Can't be too careful."

They sat and looked at each other's slowly spreading grins. "Well, we made it," Silky said. "Congratulations."

Jake felt it was a bad idea to start celebrating. It might make them careless. "Let's get going with the rest of the stuff," he said. "I'm going stir crazy in here and I would like to stretch my legs. Why don't you watch the room while I go down for parcel paper? Probably get it from the front desk."

"Better buy it at the store. If a parcel ever came back, they might match the paper with you."

"Guess you're right. O.K. I'll be back in five minutes or so."

Silky switched on the T.V. and sat down.

"I'll knock three times, when I come back," Jake said. "Better lock up behind me."

Jake returned within ten minutes with some heavy brown parcel paper, scotch tape, and labels. Silky switched off the television.

They unpacked the bag with the masks and snowmobile suits. They made two neat parcels, each with a suit and a mask. Jake printed out two labels, placing one inside each parcel. "FROM THE FRIENDS OF THE POOR. SAINT SIMON'S CHURCH," he wrote. Then he addressed the outside labels, one to the Salvation Army in Duluth, Minnesota, and one to the Salvation Army in Burlington, Vermont.

"We can afford to be generous," he said, grinning. "You mind the shop and I'll go mail them."

"Buy some beer while you're out."

"Good idea."

Well, that was goodbye to the last bit of evidence. Another notch down on the burner.

Jake came back with a dozen cold Schlitz. They each took one, drinking out of the can.

"Did you take a look at it?" Silky asked.

"No. It seemed silly."

"Wouldn't you like to?"

"Yeah. I guess. Just to make sure it's there. I started hallucinating last night, suddenly thinking maybe we'd left it in the van in the rush. Or given it all to Charlie."

Silky laughed. "Let's check."

"O.K."

Jake pulled the suitcase from under the bed. He knelt down and unlocked it.

There was a knock at the door.

"Shit." Jake went cream-colored, staring at Silky.

Silky gestured to him to shove it back, but he seemed immobilized. Silky pushed it with his foot, while Jake stayed on his knees, staring at the door.

Silky walked across the room, unlocked the door and looked into the face of a black maid.

"Hi," he said.

"Can I do your room?" she asked.

"Don't worry about it. We're having a business meeting."

"Shall I come back then?"

"Why don't you? Maybe in an hour."

"Sure. In an hour."

Silky closed the door, hanging the "Do Not Disturb" sign on the outside and double locking it. He grinned at Jake still on his knees.

"What would you have done"—Jake was still shaking —"if it had been the cops?"

"I would have been fucking surprised. That's about all I could have done."

They both roared with laughter.

"Come on. Let's have a look," Silky said impatiently.

Jake pulled the suitcase out again. The two canvas bags lay there, side by side, like a couple of oversized pork sausages.

Jake opened one and put his hand inside gingerly, as though he half expected a pair of handcuffs to close on

233

it with a snap. He pulled out a wad of hundred dollar bills.

Silky put his hand out for it and Jake passed it on.

"Nice," Silky said, pressing the wad against his cheek. "From the friends of the poor to my favorite charity."

They laughed and laughed. Jake rolled around the floor, letting it gurgle out of him uncontrollably.

Silky helped himself to another beer, opening one for Jake and handing it to him.

Jake sat down on the bed again. Silky threw the roll of bills back into the suitcase.

"What's next?" he said.

"Nothing," Jake answered. "Just the handover to Rena. I reckon we had better wait until after dark."

Silky looked at his watch and shrugged. "Might as well watch the afternoon movie."

Jake closed and locked the suitcase, pushing it back under the bed. He shrugged his shoulders. "I suppose so. But I sure hope being a millionaire picks up. So far, it hasn't got a thing on being a ski bum."

Jim woke early as usual and looked at the alarm clock. There was no hurry. The police had closed Mount Casino for at least another day.

He just lay in bed luxuriating, eyes closed, pretending that he was going back to sleep

He could not manage it. His mind was racing in circles, thoughts of what he had done competed with thoughts of what he had still to do.

But he put off thinking about the day ahead for another twenty minutes, lids pressed tight.

He looked at the clock again. Eight o'clock. It was the longest lie-in he had had since last summer. It was enough. He had a lot to do. Before leaving the apartment, he called the lodge to tell them to put up posters in the main lobby and to announce over the loudspeaker system that all weekly or other prepaid tickets would be honored at Heavenly Valley. He had arranged this with them last night and they were glad to help, any money transfers to be arranged later.

He called Paul Mullins at home and, getting no answer, found him in the office. Paul had everything under control to keep the guests occupied, including a round robin

234

tennis tournament, transportation to Squaw Valley and various other diversions. It was important to try to prevent a mass exodus.

His first stop was the hospital.

He dropped in to see Nick Diamado first. Nick was dressed, looking pale and sullen, his right arm in a sling; he was just waiting for doctors' rounds and expected to be released around noon.

"Ah, the getaway driver," Nick said sarcastically. "What did they pay you?"

Jim's fists tightened, but he kept his cool. "I didn't have much choice, Nick. They had a bomb around my neck."

"You could have done something," Nick growled.

"I saw what they did to you, Nick—and to Svensen. I figured my job was to protect the lives of the hostages. The police will get the hijackers."

"I hope they don't."

Jim moved on. He had arranged to be allowed a few moments in Philippe Gareau's room. Philippe was pale and obviously under sedation, but he managed a smile and a few words of conversation.

Jim had talked to the head nurse on the way out. Philippe had a fractured femur and would be on his back for at least a couple of months.

He looked in on Carl Svensen, finding him asleep. It was going to be a long time before he was able to walk again.

He went down to the hospital canteen for breakfast, buying a newspaper at the gift shop on the way. It was strange to read about the robbery; it was as though it had happened somewhere else to another group of people. From now on, until some other disaster took over the front page, they would get little peace from the media people.

After breakfast, he went to the ski area. The entrance was cordoned off by police; he was stopped on arrival and kept waiting until the cop received radio approval to let him through.

As soon as he arrived at his office, he called the funeral home to make arrangements for Pepi's funeral, setting it for two o'clock the next afternoon. He got Pepi's personnel file out to check for next of kin and found that he had no relatives in America, his mother in Austria being listed as his beneficiary. There would be a lot to do here, dealing with his personal effects, his estate and so on. He called the company attorneys to ask them to look into it.

He thought about Pepi with a deep sense of guilt. There should have been a way to prevent it. But how could anyone make allowances for a bullheaded lunatic like Carl Svensen? He tried to rationalize the tragedy. Pepi was the kind of man who would have hated growing old. Skiing was all he knew, his charm with women his only other asset. When they were gone, his life would have become meaningless anyway. It was not easy to reconcile oneself to the death of a friend, but it was necessary now to let his mind get back to other pressing matters.

He dropped into Greg's office. Greg had been up all night with the bomb squad.

"Those hijackers were no dummies. One of them must have known a lot about explosives. We found two separate charges at different depths on the towers. They had obviously calculated that one set might be found. The police reckon that they probably were Special Services vets from Vietnam."

"Are they through with the search?"

"Not yet. Now that they know how thorough these guys were, they figure that they may have had some other backup charges. They are searching the tops of the towers right now."

"Did you assess the damage to the chair?"

"Yes. It looks worse than it is. They just blew the bottom two towers. I should get it back into action within a week if all the parts are available. A crew is coming up from the manufacturer tonight. We will start as soon as the police give us clearance."

"Everything under control as usual. I don't know what I would do without you," Jim said. It was always the same with Greg.

Jim went on upstairs to report to Alfredo. He was talking to the FBI man, Granger.

"It looks like we can open again tomorrow, Mr. O'Malley," Alfredo said. "Can you manage that?"

"Yes, sir. But I would like a special advertising budget. People will be wondering about it. I think we should get some newspaper and radio advertising out quick. And I will get the media to carry it as a news item. We should make a point of it at the press conference."

"What about the chair?"

"The crew can clear the debris pretty quick, as soon as the police let them in." He looked inquiringly at Granger. "It would help me a lot if I knew when the area is to be handed back to us."

"It depends on the bomb squad. Let's shoot for four o'clock this afternoon."

"Good. I'll work to that then." He went on to report Greg's estimate to get the chair back in operation and brought Alfredo up to date on the others matters—Pepi's funeral and the injured guests. Alfredo appeared satisfied.

He turned to go. "Anything else?" he asked.

"Yes," Granger replied. "We're using the accounting offices for questioning. Would you please go down there and make a full statement? I'll be along there myself, when I've finished here."

"Sure," said Jim.

He found Charlie outside the accounting office. He was smoking a cigarette, looking distinctly nervous.

"What's the matter, Charlie? You waiting to go in?"

"Yes."

"Pull yourself together then. They have nothing on you."

Charlie had probably been the last person in Lake Tahoe to hear about the robbery. He knew something was going to happen, but he never imagined anything like this.

He had been sitting in the Sahara parking lot throughout the robbery. After he had dropped Jake and Silky, he had gone back to the movie and then gone home to bed. The first he knew of the robbery was when he heard the morning radio news bulletin. He could hardly believe his ears.

"What did you do yesterday afternoon, Charlie?" Jim asked.

Charlie recited his story. It seemed to relax him as he got it off his chest.

"So," Jim smiled at him encouragingly. "What's the problem? Tell it just like that and you're home free."

The cop came out and called Charlie in. Charlie grinned at Jim, looking more confident, and went in.

He came out fifteen minutes later.

"O.K.?" said Jim.

"Fine," said Charlie.

The cop beckoned to Jim.

There were three of them at the table, two State police and Granger, who had joined them. There was a stenographer taking notes in the corner.

"Start at the beginning," one of them said.

Jim recounted the whole episode, as best he could remember it, from the time when Rena had come stumbling in to report the holdup.

The three cops peppered him with questions, so that it took almost two and a half hours to complete the statement.

"Don't you think it strange," Granger asked, "that they called for you by name?"

Jim shrugged. "Yes. I suppose so."

"Why do you think they did that?"

"I guess they wanted to make sure that we didn't send an armed cop in."

"Why did they assume you would not be armed?"

"Maybe they figured that I wasn't that stupid." Jim was getting tired and a little querulous.

"They said they knew you. Did they?"

"Maybe. A lot of the skiers here know me."

"So you figure they were local skiers?"

"I don't know who they were. But they sure knew their way around."

"They certainly did. Exceptionally well, don't you think?"

"Yes."

"Maybe they had some inside help. Or maybe they were employees or ex-employees."

"Anything is possible."

"Right. And anything possible has to be checked."

Jim waited.

"Charlie Potts. What do you think of him?"

"My best driver. First-class employee."

"How long has he been with you?"

"Three years."

It went on for another hour-and-a-half. They went

through the personnel files systematically, including all employees who had worked at the area over the past three seasons.

The meeting finished abruptly.

"Thank you, Mr. O'Malley," Granger said. "Let's take a break for lunch. We will probably want to talk to you again."

Jake went downstairs to pay the bill. "I need a bellhop to pick up the bags," he said as he pocketed his receipt.

He kept his eye glued to the red tag, feeling conspicuous. He was glad when Silky made a grab for it, lifting it into the trunk of the Chevrolet himself and leaving the bellhop to handle the less valuable part of the load.

It was a blustery night, cold and miserable, the banked snow swirling in stinging clouds.

They parked outside Rena's apartment in the row of condominiums. Everything was nice and quiet. "I'll check and see if she's in," Silky said. "Wait here."

He pressed the buzzer and heard her steps inside. She opened the door and put out her arms, squeezing his biceps as though testing to see if he was real. "Oh, Silky," she sighed. "Thank God!"

He beamed at her. "Everything went fine. We're just making the drop. You alone?"

"Yes, of course," she said, pulling him inside. "Oh God, Silky, I'm so happy to see you."

"Hold it," he smiled. "We have to do this quick. We don't want to be seen together, remember? I'll go and get the bag."

He went back to the car. "Everything O.K.?" asked Jake.

"Yeah. She seems a bit tense. I guess she's been worrying. Keep a lookout. I'll get the bag."

Silky pushed the door with his foot; she had left it ajar. He carried the bag to the bedroom and heaved it up on the top shelf in the closet.

"We'll be in touch," he said. "Good luck."

She came at him, throwing her arms around his neck. "Don't go, Silky. Don't leave me alone. I'm afraid."

He looked down at her, kissing her on the nose. "Hey,

239

come on, Rena. Pull yourself together. The party's over. We made it."

"It's hard to believe. All last night I was sure that you had been caught. Oh Silky,"—she hugged him close again—"please stay, just a few minutes. Tell me what happened. Why did Nick get shot? Why did Pepi get killed?"

"The police did Pepi. They thought that he was one of us. Nick tried to jump me." He pushed her gently away. "Listen, it's dangerous for me to stay. We'll pick up the bag in a couple of months. I'll phone you first." A thought struck him. "Did you book your flight yet?"

"Yes," she said. "Jim O'Malley did it for me."

"He going too?"

"Yes. He goes every year."

Silky pondered this piece of news. He and Jake were booked on Skip Langdon's annual ski jaunt to Klosters. Silky had remembered Skip when Rena had come up with the idea of smuggling the money out to Switzerland. It was a perfect cover. No one would be looking for hijack money amongst the luggage of such an exclusive ski group.

He hadn't counted on Jim being along. It wasn't ideal to be travelling so close to one of the victims.

Rena saw the point. "I don't think I could talk him out of it," she said contritely. "It would look suspicious if I changed plans. He'd want a reason." She felt somehow responsible for a silly planning error. "Maybe you and Jake should take another flight."

Silky weighed the options. He considered that Skip's international reputation was an important element. It almost guaranteed that customs inspection would be superficial. That was the key factor. He decided to stick to the plan.

"No," he said resolutely. In a way, the fact that they were travelling with a victim was a kind of double bluff.

The flight back to Montreal was a good deal more subdued than the outward journey. No one had come entirely unscathed through the drama which they had experienced.

Philippe Gareau remained alone in the small hospital. It was planned that his company jet would return him to Montreal in a few weeks, as soon as the doctors allowed it.

Lying in bed, his whole right leg and lower abdomen encased in plaster, he had plenty of time to think.

He was lucky to be alive.

Philippe saw all of life as a huge balance sheet. Every day he was called upon to evaluate opportunities, weigh the consequences of a number of courses of action and make his decision. The balance sheet then told him whether he had been right or wrong.

He was too pragmatic a man to expect to be right all the time. But he had to try for a score in the 90 percent range and this could only be achieved by disciplining himself to admit and to analyze his mistakes. "The only experience that is worth a damn in business," he was wont to say, "is your mistakes. If you forget everything that you ever did right and remember everything that you ever did wrong, you may attain that rare quality, wisdom."

Jeanette Leclerc had been a mistake, a stupid, impulsive mistake. Of course, she was not responsible for the fact that he had been shot.

On the other hand his wound was perhaps fate's way of balancing the ledger. It was an indirect tax penalty. Fortunately, Armand had not betrayed him to Lise, in fact the whole episode was conveniently forgotten. Philippe's experience told him that mistakes never went unredeemed. In the circumstances, the single debit entry, a bullet in the leg, seemed to settle the account quite neatly.

Philippe's family were, of course, shocked by what had happened to him, but they managed to take it in their stride. At least he was alive and would be restored to them almost as good as new. Life had to go on.

Levelheaded Lise quickly recovered her poise as soon as she was assured that Philippe was out of danger. She made whatever arrangements were needed for Philippe's comfort and for the smooth operation of the business. The executive committee would fly out once a week on the company jet, as soon as Philippe was judged fit enough, and Lise would take the opportunity of flying with them for a visit. For the immediate future her mind was on getting the children ready to return to school.

Nicole was in love. She felt bad about what had happened to her father but worse about the prospect of not seeing Peter again until the midterm long weekend.

Serge had had a super time. It was the best Christmas he had ever had. He hoped that they would do the same thing again and again.

To all intents and purposes, Danielle and Suzanne had been virtually independent of the rest of the group, so that their memories of Mount Casino were only incidentally related to the drama of the hijacking.

Suzanne carried the scar of her awful bout of vertigo but, in brandy and Dave, she had discovered a powerful antidote. She felt cherished and contented. She had enjoyed her love affair with Dave, treasuring every moment of it in her mind. She was sad at their parting but not disconsolate. Romance was what girls of her age sought from a vacation and she had got exactly what she had bargained for. There would be other vacations.

Danielle, too, had enjoyed herself. She had adored the powder snow skiing, the glamor of the night life, the shopping, the exquisite food, and the fun of meeting new people. She was fond of Dick too. It had been a new experience for her to go with a clean-cut American boy. But, now that she was homeward bound, she was thinking of Michele and Pierre and Louis; Frenchmen were somehow just a little bit more debonair and gallant than Americans. She would be glad to be home.

There was no bridge-playing on the return trip and Armand sat in the seat for which he had paid, a comfortable armchair in the first-class bar. He was listening to Arthur Mallory discussing his plan to introduce a line of cross-country skis in his furniture factory. "If you look at the popularity of downhill," he was saying, "and calculate the cost—I mean look at the cost of this holiday just for the pleasure of tumbling down a mountain—I think that downhill is reaching market saturation. Same with snow-mobiling, it's getting too expensive. I think people will still want to go out and play in the snow, but they will be looking for something less expensive and less organized."

"I think you're right Arthur." For the first time Armand saw Arthur as a potential client—most of his other business got along with minimal advertising—"in fact I can get you some figures if you like. I know where to lay my hands on a good market survey."

"You do? Yes, I would appreciate that."

You have to keep adjusting, thought Armand. You lose some business, you gain some. Think positive.

When he considered it, the holiday had not been a total disaster. Strangely enough, his friendship with Philippe seemed to have been strengthened by the experience.

Jeannette, at the moment, was more concerned about her face than anything else. The most discomfiting fact was that she would not be able to have the two missing teeth replaced until her puffy lip was entirely healed. It would mean long hours at the dentist's office!

And the stupid doctor in Tahoe! He had completely deformed the shape of her upper lip with his silly stitches. Her features were blemished for life, she was sure.

The worst of it, in a way, was that nobody seemed to give her credit for her act of courage during the hijack. She had done her part brilliantly; it was that clumsy fool, Nick Diamado, who had botched the deal. He had simply been no match, no match at all for that wicked robber. The nerve of the man, whacking her bare bottom like that! The very thought of it made her heart beat with rage. Or was it with excitement?

Damn, it was difficult to drink champagne with a puffy lip! It kept on dribbling down her chin.

Jane Mallory sipped her drink with a new self-assurance. She seemed to have discovered a way to float with alcohol instead of drowning in it. Perhaps she could control it, after all.

Having been the one member of the party closest to death, she now felt the greatest affinity to life. Arthur was a part of her life. Dull and stuffy as he might be, he had come through for her, offered his life to give her a second chance. She was going to grab that second chance and share it with Arthur. Oddly enough, the whole experience of the hijacking and the holiday seemed to have done him good. At least he had relaxed, taken some interest in the people around him, even her.

The truth was that Arthur had actually enjoyed the vacation. For the first time in at least thirty years, he had done nothing other than indulge himself for two solid weeks. At first, he had felt considerable uneasiness at such

243

extravagance, contenting himself only with the though
that it was an opportunity to work on Philippe for tha
seat on the board of Frenette Enterprises, which he se
desperately coveted. But gradually he had found himsel
enjoying the relaxation for its own sake. By God, he ha
never felt sharper in his life!

In retrospect, the hijack seemed to have been a blessing
in disguise. It had brought Jane and him closer together
The tales he could tell about it at his club! Good heavens
everyone who was anyone would want to know about i
and, until Philippe got back, he would be the only source
And Jane seemed so much calmer now. Apart from tha
idiotic tantrum in the casino, she had behaved much bette
than he had dared to hope. It seemed damn silly
he thought, to have to gratify a woman her age witl
pointless little considerations, but if that was what it tool
to keep her from drinking herself into a stupor, he sup
posed that he could find the time for it. He would jus
have to relax a bit more; it wasn't that much of a sacri
fice.

He glanced over at Peter. Fine lad that, real head o
his shoulders. And a great future ahead of him if he mar
ried into the Gareau family.

"Oh, I did enjoy myself so, Sam," Kay Mitchell saic
with a sigh, "despite the dreadful hijacking. And I am s
glad, for Diana's sake, that we were able to help Lis
through her awful catastrophe.

"And I was so proud of you, Sam. You were a rea
tower of strength during the time when we were being
held hostage."

Kay was an addicted good samaritan who loved t
mother and fuss. She was in her element at a charity bak
sale or listening—she never had anything to say—at a
P.T.A. meeting.

Nothing could be closer to her dreams of nirvana tha
fretting over Lise. Such a fine lady and here she was pos
itively dependent on Kay, literally leaning on her! An
so grateful, she was really making Kay feel like a bes
friend. And so nice for Diana, to have her parents reall
accepted, I mean really like equals, she thought, by th
Gareaus—of all people!

And Sam had been such a stalwart! Really when sh
compared him with that Arthur Mallory, so rude and in

244

attentive to his wife, and Armand with his dreadful gambling and even Philippe with his roving eye, well! And how Sam had taken charge and cheered everyone up when they were locked in the van—and, oh, yes, he had been so funny on New Year's Eve! What a lovely holiday it had been!

Diana surveyed them all. Well, it had been quite a lark! There wasn't a lot more you could say.

She felt rather disappointed about her sex life. At least she could have had an affair with an older man or something. She figured for a while that she had Mr. Leclerc on the way until his silly wife got booted in the face, whereupon he suddenly seemed to become all concerned about her.

Jacques, of course, was a total cop-out. From the moment she gave him a whiff of it he had become a kind of libidinous serf, following her around with one hand on his zipper. She enjoyed teasing him. But, instead of reacting with anger and frustration, he had kept coming back for more like a tame puppy. So goddam gutless!

Anyway, the hijack had added a bit of excitement. She only wished that she had been in the base, instead of being cooped up with Jacques in a gondola car. She would have adored to see the robbers at close quarters—they sounded like really super guys. Oh, well, she did have one for the book, although it was a pity that it had to be with Jacques. You could talk of sixty-nine but they would have to come to her to find out how to do it in a gondola car! And in thermal underwear yet!

It had been fun alright. A terrific idea of hers, really. They should all be goddam grateful to her. None of them would have ever thought of going, if she had not organized it. No doubt, they would expect her to organize them again next year, she supposed.

CHAPTER TWELVE

JOE GRANGER was sitting in Bickel's office in Tahoe completing a final review of his notes. He had sent Bickel down directly after the hijack to take over some temporary space as a local field office.

Granger had spent the last three days reviewing three groups of reports; the thirty-two interviews with the hostages and various passengers on the last cars to leave the base before the holdup, the forty-one statements taken from members of the ski area staff and the various official reports from individual police, FBI, and bomb squad members who had taken part in the operation. He was now busy making an inventory of hard data. There was not very much.

This was the kind of case Joe Granger liked, a real challenge to his intellect and powers of deduction. He had always fancied himself more a Sherlock Holmes, pitting his wits against his criminal adversaries, than a gun-toting undercover agent of the television screen.

He had pieced together a workable description of the hijackers. Their height, weight, and approximate ages could be established relatively accurately from the statements of the hostages. However, if his deductions were right, he could put substantially more flesh on the bone than that.

It was a logical assumption that the two men had visited the area during the week before the heist to lay their explosives and to reconnoiter. He had instructed Bickel to try to find out from the witnesses if anything unusual had occurred during the week preceding the holdup. This had produced a reasonably complete description of a blond man with a facial scar and a dark man with a moustache who had arrived late one afternoon from Chicago, purchased half-day tickets and boarded the gondola with large packsacks on their backs. Moreover, the description of the dark one tallied with the man who had visited the vehicle garage professing to be a salesman for the Tucker Snocat company; a check with Tucker disclosed that none of their salesmen had been in the area at the time. A further cross-check with the Phoenix truck retailer from whom the blue van had been purchased was not too productive—the salesman remembered a little about the transaction—but it did nothing to challenge the data on file.

In an effort to narrow the search for his quarry, Joe had made two other assumptions which he considered to be logical; both men were probably keen skiers and at least one of them was likely to be a Vietnam vet with experience in demolition.

Whereas all this information was very useful, Joe was still a long way from being ready to make a concrete move; the current descriptions could fit ten thousand people. Regrettably, the men had been extremely methodical about erasing telltale clues. There were no fingerprints in the van or base, they had left no clues, and it was a safe bet that they had not used their proper names if they had stayed anywhere in the vicinity.

When they had transferred to the car on arrival at the Sahara parking lot, Jim O'Malley had not even bothered to take a look. He insisted that he had been so concerned about driving his passengers to safety that he had been totally oblivious of the men's movements after they left the van.

Granger considered Jim O'Malley's negligent behavior to be highly suspicious, especially in the light of the other factors—the robbers had asked for him by name and they had not bothered to place a detonator in the plastic explosive attached to his neck. He was having Jim watched.

Granger got up and poured himself another cup of coffee; he was so addicted to coffee when he was working on a case that he brought his own electric percolator with him.

His one significant clue, of course, was the broken finger. However, before he got to that, he wanted to reconsider the getaway. How could two men and two million dollars disappear into thin air? How did they get through the roadblocks? Even if they had stashed the loot in such a way as to deceive the police at the checkpoints, how did the man with the broken finger escape detection?

One possible answer, which Granger was more and more inclined to favor, was that the money had remained hidden in Tahoe until the heat was off. It might still be here now, two months after the event. It was this conjecture that led him to speculate that the hijack was an inside job, or, at least, that there was an inside accomplice.

He anticipated that the most likely break in the case would occur when the men began to spend the ransom money. Knowing the underworld's sensitivity to the smell of newly acquired riches, Joe had purposely allowed Nick Diamado to pump him for the hijackers' descriptions.

Confident that the Mafia would circulate the information coast-to-coast in a matter of hours, he had then tipped off his undercover agents to watch for developments. If the men were professional criminals, the underworld would soon run them to ground. Joe's only problem would be to pick them up before Salvatore Diamado did. If they were amateurs, the main hope would be that they would get careless; lack of experience might make them feel that the FBI had given up, whereas, of course, he was only just getting started.

Joe gathered his notes, clipped them together neatly with a paperclip and slipped them into his briefcase. He poured himself another cup of coffee. He was back where he'd started. The broken finger. He'd have to have another chat with Nick Diamado.

It came to him automatically, that familiar mental crouch of alertness which he assumed behind enemy lines. He drove slowly up the road to the condominium, watching the skiers as they came sweeping hurry-scurry down the mountain, then fell neatly into line, two by two, to sail up the Number One chair lift.

Pulling up outside her apartment, Silky sat for a minute or two mesmerized by the calm uphill procession of the gondola cars, glinting in the sun.

Silky had only seen Jake once since the heist. He planned to stay at the motel in Boise the following night, when he delivered the bag with the red tag.

He had spent the two months lying low, covering the last of his tracks. He had regrown his beard and flushed his false finger down a public toilet.

He pulled himself together, glancing cautiously up and down the road. It was deserted. Stepping out quickly, he rang Rena's front doorbell.

"Silky!" She hung on to him tightly. He let her stay there in his arms for a long time, sensing that she needed it. "Oh, Silky! My God, I'm glad to see you."

She looked pretty bad, pale and drawn. He suddenly realized that her end of the deal had not been the picnic he and Jake had predicted.

"I've been so lonely, Silky. It was awful. I never imagined it would be like this. Don't you see? Meeting them all every day, the people we'd robbed, and feeling so guilty! And than coming home to live with that awful bag every night! I nearly went mad!"

"Well, it's just about over now," Silky said, "so cheer up. You're soon going to be rich."

"I don't know if I care anymore."

"Has there been any big police activity? Any problems?" Silky asked.

"Not really. But I think the investigation is still going on. Jim O'Mally told me that he thought he was being watched."

"Jim O'Malley?" Silky was surprised. "I wonder why."

"He says that the FBI think that it was an inside job." Rena answered.

"Have they bothered you?" Silky asked.

"No. Not since the first statement I made. Thank God. I couldn't stand it."

Silky decided that he had come for the money just in time. Rena seemed to be close to the breaking point. He had planned to be on his way as soon as possible, but decided to stick around a while to get her calmed down. She was a real liability in her present state.

He encouraged her to talk about herself, listening to her as she poured out a stream of pent-up emotion. Half an hour of this kind of therapy and she was beginning to regain her spirits. It gave him pleasure to be able to do this for her, just by his presence.

She came over to kneel beside his chair, putting her head in his lap. She was quiet now. "Silky," she said softly. "Oh, Silky, I would have died if you hadn't come soon."

He stroked her hair gently, not quite sure how to reply. His heart went out to her, but he had no proficiency in such situations.

"Listen," he said, trying not to break the spell of intimacy too abruptly, "before I go, we have to straighten a couple of things out. Are you up to it?"

She smiled up at him. "I guess so."

He went over the drill for going through Swiss customs. "And don't forget that we are travelling as strangers. At least when we first meet. Of course, if circumstances allow, we can become casually acquainted on the plane. After all, we are all in the same party."

"Alright," she said simply. "You can rely on me. I'm O.K. now."

She was herself again, a kindred spirit, anxious to play her part.

It was time for him to go. He could feel her willing him to stay just a little bit longer, but he resisted the temptation.

He lifted the bag down from the shelf in the bedroom cupboard.

She watched him. "You will never know how glad I am to see the last of it."

"Did you ever look inside?" he grinned.

"No." She seemed to cringe at the prospect.

Silky flicked the locks. They both stared at the contents.

"My God!" Rena gasped in awe.

Closing it again, Silky hefted it in his hand. "It's on its way to the bank at last," he said.

He carried it out to the car and laid it gently in the trunk. Then he returned to say goodbye.

He held her for a moment, trying to coax the sadness from her eyes with his smile. Then he kissed her on the lips.

Nick Diamado was not surprised when Joe Granger invited him over to the office for another review.

Nick had been staying pretty close to Joe since he had taken up residence locally. It was orders from his Dad, Salvatore. Having an FBI man on the doorstep was not something to be treated lightly. You never knew where he might poke his nose during the course of his investigations.

Salvatore had four men assigned to watch Joe Granger round the clock. They reported his every move to a small staff group headed by Sol Leopold. Sol coordinated with Nick, and together they made a weekly report to Salvatore.

Part of the reason for the surveillance was so they would never be caught off guard. But, more important was monitoring his progress toward catching the hijackers. Salvatore was determined to be first at the kill.

Nick carried out his part of the assignment without protest. He had his own score to settle. Ever since the robbery, his nerves had been on edge. There was an unreasoning anger seething inside his soul, an obsessive hatred of the hijacker who had shot him. The specter of the man in the ski mask seemed to follow him everywhere, even in his dreams, taunting Nick with his crooked finger.

"Would you like some coffee, Mr. Diamado?" Joe asked.

"Yes, please."

Joe nodded at Bickel, holding out his own cup for a refill. Nick watched Bickel as he carefully filled the Styrofoam cups and then sat down at the end of the table with his pencil and notebook. Nick couldn't help feeling that there was little to fear from the Bureau if Bickel was representative of the new kind of agent they were hiring. He looked like a theology student, not more than twenty-four, pale, pimply and tall, with greasy hair, and thick rimless spectacles.

"How's the investigation going?" Nick took pains to appear no more than superficially interested.

"It's coming along," Joe said. To Nick's gratification, he brought him right up to date on the present status of the case. Joe was well aware of Nick's game, but it was one which two could play.

"You've made quite a bit of progress," Nick observed. "Where do you go from here?"

"Back to the finger, I'm afraid," Joe said. "I'd just like to go over parts of your statement again. See if we can jog your memory."

Nick heaved a sigh. "Christ, I've given you a blow-by-blow of the fight about six times. What do you want to know?"

"It's about that finger. You say it broke at the first knuckle. Are you sure of that?"

"Yes."

"Show me, would you, sir?" Joe held out his right hand. Nick pointed to the first joint of the index finger.

"I see," said Joe. He started pressing his own finger back, looking at it carefully. "It's funny. Somehow you would expect the finger to give at the base, at the main knuckle, the root of the finger so to speak. That's what the medics tell me, anyway."

Nick just shrugged.

"Did you hear the bone break?"

"Hear it? Christ, no! We were fighting, man. The place was bedlam."

"And the man showed no pain?"

"I don't know what you are getting at. I hurt him for sure. But he didn't scream in agony any more than I did, when he kicked me in the crotch."

It was Joe's turn to sigh. It was hard to explore hypotheses with a witness who took every question as a challenge. "Mr. Diamado. Believe me I am not impugning your veracity. But it was dark. You were fighting for your life. It is possible that there are other interpretations of what actually happened."

"What, for instance?" Nick asked aggressively.

Joe side-stepped the question. "You say his finger bent back one-hundred-and-eighty degrees. Is that an exaggeration?"

"No."

"You mean the finger broke clean in two?"

"Yes."

"Did it go straight back or to the side?"

"How the hell do I know?" Nick squeezed angrily at his glasses. "Straight back as far as I could tell."

"Perhaps he was double-jointed," Joe suggested quickly.

"The finger busted," Nick said icily. "I saw it. And I felt it."

Bickel suddenly held up the back of his right hand. He had tucked his index finger into his palm so that it appeared to them like a stump. "If the man had had an amputated finger," he said in his high-pitched voice, "that would explain it!"

Both men stared at him.

"Bickel!" Joe exploded in astonishment.

"Don't you see?" Bickel continued excitedly. "He could have been wearing a false finger . . ."

"Jesus Christ!" Nick jumped to his feet and stood over Bickel. "Are you a detective or a screen writer? I busted the guy's finger. If the other bastard hadn't clubbed me, I would have busted his fucking jaw." He turned on Joe Granger. "What's with this stupid monkey? He think I was fighting with a gay or something?" He turned to Bickel. "Listen you! You want me to prove it? Just hold out your hand and I'll show you whether I can bust a finger or not."

"But, Mr. Diamado . . ." Bickel whined.

"Bickel. Shut up!" Joe yelled. He stood up and put a hand on Nick's shoulder. "I'm sorry, Mr. Diamado. Things seem to have gotten out of hand."

"I'll say," Nick answered contemptuously. "I've had enough." He was out of the office in three strides, slamming the door behind him.

Jim found it hard to understand why Rena had taken the episode of the hijacking so deeply to heart. Ever since the morning when she had fainted at Pepi's funeral, she seemed to have become more and more melancholy and withdrawn.

Worst of all, she seemed to have lost her love of skiing, refusing to renew her instructor's contract for the following year. The prospect of not seeing her again was almost more than Jim could bear.

This holiday was just what she needed, Jim thought.

253

It would snap her out of it. He intended to concentrate all his energies on cheering her up.

They arrived at Kennedy Airport in plenty of time for the Swissair flight. Skip Langdon, the host of the party, came over to greet them and offered to steer them through the check-in routines.

"Why don't you go and sit in the departure lounge, Rena?" Jim suggested, indicating that he would stick around to give Skip a hand. "It'll be more restful. You can meet the people later."

"Alright then, I think I will." She was tense now that the final act had begun, glad to escape to seclusion.

She sat in a corner at the window watching the bustle of activity on the busy, lighted runways. There was a blessed air of escape in the sight of the huge planes which roared off every few seconds to their secret destinations, hiding quickly in the expanse of the black sky. If only her escape could be that conclusive, free and safe the moment that she left the ground!

"Hello, Rena."

She looked up with a start. It was Nick Diamado.

She stared at him in undisguised horror. She felt suddenly faint, throat all dry and head pounding.

Nick gave her a quizzical look. "What's the matter? You look scared out of your wits."

She struggled for composure. She felt a threatening aura of menace around Nick. "I . . . I . . . wasn't expecting you," she said lamely.

Nick studied her critically, then broke into an oily smile. "Christ, Rena. It's not that bad, is it?"

Rena struggled with an impulse to flee in panic. She must get a grip on herself. "Buy me a drink," she said.

Nick made an exaggerated bow, sweeping his hand in the direction of the bar. "With pleasure, madam."

Nick led the way to one of the tables. "I'd rather sit at the bar," Rena said, heading resolutely toward it; she wanted them to be conspicuous, hoping that Silky and Jake would spot them when they arrived. It seemed to be the only hope of warning them.

The lounge was filling up now with other groups chartered on the same flight. One noisy crowd seemed to have

254

started its holiday in the terminal lounge several hours before flight time. She envied them.

"How's the shoulder?" Rena forced herself to make small talk, as she searched the swelling crowd for a glimpse of Silky.

"Fine. Good as new." Nick was perched on a stool beside her. "Know any others in the group?"

"No one other than Jim." She had lied so often in the past months that it came to her naturally. She had spotted Jake while they were talking, but he had ignored her.

"Haven't seen you around much lately," Nick said. "Perhaps it's my fault. I've been very busy. How are you making out with Jim?"

"We're good friends," she said.

"I hope he's not going to monopolize you on this trip." Nick smiled at her. "I don't think I should have given up on you so easily."

It was all she needed: renewed attention from Nick.

Finally she saw Silky come in with Skip Langdon. He caught her eye but didn't show any signs of recognition. That was the way they had set it up. But there was a flaw, now that Nick was here. Silky had been with Rena at the freestyle party last year—the night he had got into an argument with Nick about driving her home. So Nick knew that they were not total strangers. She wondered if Silky would remember and play his part right, if it came to a confrontation.

She glanced at Nick. He seemed not to have noticed Silky yet.

Jim O'Malley joined them just as the boarding instructions came over the loudspeaker, and the three of them moved forward together to the entrance ramp.

The plane was an all economy Boeing 727 with double seats on the starboard side and triple seats to port. Jim and Rena settled in a double about halfway down and Nick took the aisle seat in the triple across from Rena. She watched Silky take his place four rows ahead of her while Jake came through with the last to board, giving her a quick glance as he passed her on his way to the rear.

Dinner was served shortly after takeoff and so long as the stewardesses remained busy serving the meal, the passengers stayed pinned in their seats. However, once the trays were removed, it quickly became apparent that the noisy group would live up to its reputation. A dozen of them crowded into the forward serving hatch, pouring drinks and flirting with the stewardesses, while others wandered up and down the aisles shouting and singing.

Jim and Skip Langdon were moving around the plane, greeting members of the group. Rena watched them as they spent a few moments talking with Silky.

"That guy Jim is talking to." Nick leaned over to Rena. "Do you know who he is? I swear that I've seen him before."

Damn, thought Rena, here it comes. Well, at least she was ready for it. "I have met him once, but I can't remember his name."

"Oh, well," he said unconcernedly. "It'll come to me." To Rena's relief, he changed the subject. "I wish these drunks would turn it off," he said. "I need some sleep."

Nick had come up to New York a couple of days ahead of time with the express purpose of getting out on the town. He needed the change of scene. Mount Casino had been getting on his nerves ever since the hijack. He was still haunted by the hateful vision of the masked man who shot him. The slow progress of Joe Granger and his idiot, Bickel, only served to intensify his anger and frustration.

As the son of his father, Nick had received the red carpet treatment from the New York connection. It had been just what the doctor ordered, a continuous banquet of lush night spots, good booze, and beautiful girls. Now he was tired.

He called the stewardess and ordered a large brandy. It would help him to get to sleep. "Can't you get that party to break up?" he asked irritably.

"Yes, sir. We're moving them out now."

He looked down the aisle again at the man with the black beard. There was something about him that put Nick on his guard, a feeling that they were enemies. He turned to Rena again. "That fellow we were talking about, didn't I meet him with you?"

"I don't remember, Nick, honestly." She had supposed that the subject was closed. Her hopes were soon dashed.

"I've got it," Nick said suddenly. "Last year. The party after the free-style championship. He was the bastard who wanted to drive you home!"

256

Rena felt a sinking feeling inside, a premonition of disaster. "You could be right, Nick," she said amiably. "It doesn't seem important. I mean, who cares? It was just a party."

"The guy was goddam cocky. I remember that."

"Come on, Nick." She forced her best smile. "Don't hold a grudge on some perfect stranger. We're on holiday, remember?"

Rena was relieved to see Jim return to his place beside her. She turned to him for respite, trying to switch Nick off.

But he persisted. "What's that guy's name, Jim?" He pointed. "The one with the black beard?"

"Simon Ambler," Jim answered. "Why? Do you know him?"

"Yeah," Nick answered, rising suddenly from his seat, "I think I'll go and shake his hand."

Silky was not as surprised as he appeared. Ever since he had seen Nick in the bar with Rena, he had considered the possibility of this confrontation. The best course was to brazen it out.

"Hello, Mr. Diamado." Silky shook Nick's proffered hand. "Nice of you to remember me."

"I remember you alright." Nick turned Silky's hand over slowly. "You're the guy who tried to steal my date."

"That's right." Silky smiled up at him. "As I recall it, you got a little ugly about it."

For a moment Nick seemed ready to start the argument where they had left off.

"Excuse me," a man with a scar under his eye tapped Nick on the shoulder, "I'm trying to get to the washroom."

Recovering himself, Nick stepped back to let the man pass. He took one more vicious look at Silky and started back to his seat.

Jake exchanged a glance with Silky as he continued forward to the washroom.

"What happened?" Rena had watched the encounter with mounting concern.

"Nothing yet." Nick's seething anger made it hard for her to catch what he said. "But it will."

If Nick had not been so preoccupied with schemes of revenge he might have stumbled onto the connection much sooner. As it was, the plane had already begun its descent to Kloten airport when the coincidence suddenly flashed into focus.

That idiot Bickel! Bickel, with his goddam hand in the air and his high-pitched voice. "If the man had had an amputated finger," Bickel had said, "he could have been wearing a false finger . . ."

Jesus Christ! The man with the beard had a missing finger! He could be one of the hijackers!

His surging mind struggled for a moment to encompass this bewildering new possibility, trying to comprehend it. The man who had shot him sitting right here on the plane? Why? What was he doing here?

He glanced furtively up the aisle, trying to visualize the man with the black beard as his masked adversary in the gondola base. He could have been. He was the right build, for sure. But the false finger? And, if it was, why wasn't the guy wearing it now? And why was he here? Why the hell was he here?

Rena looked out of the window. There was something terrifyingly symbolic about the plane's hurtling descent toward the earth; whether it landed safely or whether it crashed in flames was entirely outside her command. The climax of the whole hijack operation had now arrived; whether it ended in success or utter catastrophe was completely beyond her control.

Events during the long transatlantic flight had only served to intensify Rena's nervous exhaustion. The confrontation between Nick and Silky, adding fuel to an already volatile situation, had filled Rena's mind with such foreboding that there was no question of her getting any sleep.

A gentle bump followed by the roar of reverse thrusting engines proclaimed that one more stage of the fateful journey had been safely negotiated. The big plane sailed gracefully along the runway, throwing up white plumes of snow behind the wide splay of its undercarriage.

Jim O'Malley unbuckled his seat belt at once, despite the stewardess's instructions to the contrary. "Will you excuse me, Rena? I promised to help Skip Langdon with

258

the landing problems. You know—customs, immigration, and things. I'll see you at the bus."

In the circumstances, Rena was relieved to see Jim go; he would only have added another complication to the challenge ahead at Swiss customs.

Moving in mechanical imitation of the group around her, she picked up her flight bag and allowed herself to be bustled out of the plane into the sharp bite of a blowing snowstorm. The freshness was reassuring.

Propelled by the surging crowd, she moved up a long corridor, then emerged into a large room which opened on to half-a-dozen booths manned by uniformed immigration officers. She caught sight of Jim standing next to one of the officers and beckoning her over.

She steeled herself.

The officer looked at her passport. He spoke in German. "You are Swiss?"

"Ja."

"How long have you been in the United States?" His piercing gaze made her flinch.

"Five months."

"What was the purpose of your visit?"

"I was working. As a ski instructress."

He smiled at her. "Thank you, Fraulein. Welcome home."

She moved on into the customs hall. It was familiar ground to her; she had flown in and out of Kloten many times. Today it was inhospitable.

"Come on, Rena. It's going to be alright." It was Jake. He did not look at her, just brushed gently past her. His confidence made her feel ashamed. She stood for a moment watching Silky as he waited nonchalantly at the luggage carousel. She clenched her fists and took a long deep breath. She was not going to let them down.

The moment that Nick saw Silky pick the gray suitcase from the pile of circling baggage, everything fell into place. That was why he was here! He was smuggling the ransom out of the country! Of course!

Nick stared at the bag in fascination. My God, he thought, there is two million dollars in there!

He watched Silky drop the bag at his side and wait, looking calmly around the room.

Goddam, the man was cool! Their eyes met. Then, to Nick's astonishment, Silky began to walk toward him, leaving his bag where it lay. "What's the matter, Mr. Diamado?" he asked. "Lost your luggage?"

"I'll find it," Nick said curtly.

Rena retrieved her suitcase and bag and started to haul them toward one of the long customs tables. "Can I help you miss?" She found Jake beside her—as planned.

Most of the people had collected their luggage by now and those without skis began to move through the customs inspection.

At last the skis came in on two large wagons hauled by porters who dragged them into the middle of the hall. Everyone seemed to pounce on their belongings at once. Jake and Silky waited for the crowd to subside.

Jake picked Rena's skis off for her, placing them at the end of one of the customs tables. He went back for his own, dumping the big canvas carrying case, with its two pairs of skis, next to Rena's. Silky piled his bundle of equipment alongside. Finally everything was lined up in the order in which they had planned, skis first, then Rena's luggage, and finally the three suitcases with the red tag bag in the middle. They were ready for the final scene.

Their act had drawn a critical audience. Nick Diamado stood at the end of the table, staring at the luggage as if transfixed.

"Are you together?" the customs officer asked in English.

"Nein," Rena replied in German.

He switched to her language. "May I see your passport?"

She handed it to him.

"Have you anything other than personal effects?"

"Nein."

He tapped her brown leather duffel bag. "Would you open this, please?"

The officer moved on to Jake while Rena was busy complying with his request. Jake proffered his passport.

"You are with the tour?" the officer asked.

"Yes. With Mr. Langdon."

"Which are your bags?" The officer held his marking chalk poised.

Jake pointed to his ski case and the first two gray suitcases, including the red tag. It was the plan as they had rehearsed it. If Jake got cleared first, he claimed the red tag. If not, he only claimed the first bag. It gave them two chances.

"That's not your bag," Nick said loudly to Jake. "It's his." He pointed to Silky. Ignoring Nick, Silky handed his passport to the officer. "I'm with Mr. Langdon too," he said.

"Anything to declare?"

"No. Nothing."

The officer walked the length of the table, felt inside Rena's open bag, thanked her and began chalking all the bags on the table.

Arriving opposite Nick, he asked, "Which is your bag, sir?"

"I haven't got mine yet," Nick snapped. "I want you to make that man open his bag." He pointed to Silky.

Silky looked at the officer and the officer looked at Nick. "Why?"

"You'll see," Nick said smugly.

Silky shrugged, looking at the officer. "Would you like me to?"

"If you would be so kind," he smiled amiably.

Silky laid the last bag on its side.

Rena was in a daze, staring at Nick. He knew! He was going to get them all caught! "Nick!" she gasped, "what the hell are you doing?"

"Not that one!" Nick commanded as though he was in charge. "That one!"

He pointed to the red tag bag.

A small crowd was beginning to gather, attracted by the commotion. Rena caught sight of Jim striding across toward them.

"Come on, miss," Jake gave Rena a firm shove. "This is nothing to do with us."

He picked up the two big bundles of skis and pushed past her. "Come on, for Christ's sake," he whispered.

Rena stumbled behind him, dragging her bags, her mind numb with terror. Jake barged ahead of her through the glass doors into the crowded concourse. Dumping the ski bags on the ground, he turned back into the customs hall. "Watch this lot," he said to Rena. "I'll go fetch the rest."

"But Silky!" Rena grabbed Jake in desperation. "Silky has been caught. We can't just leave him!" She rushed back to peer in agony through the glass partition.

Silky was standing there with the red tag bag open in front of him. Her heart stopped.

Then suddenly Jake was coming back toward her, grinning from ear to ear!

A moment later Silky followed him out carrying the red tag bag. "Silky!" She threw herself at him. "What happened?"

"Shut up!" She heard Silky say to her. "We're through. Jake will explain."

Rena let go of Silky; she was drained of all emotion, utterly bewildered. She watched as Jake helped Silky to lift the two bundles of skis on to his shoulders. He gave Rena a wink and promptly strode off through the crowded concourse.

"I'll explain in a minute," Jake said. "Just act normal." He called over a porter, who loaded the rest of their luggage on his truck, then moved off toward the exit.

Jake took Rena's arm, falling behind the porter.

"What happened, Jake?" She was still in a state of shock. "Please. I don't understand."

"We've done it," Jake laughed. "We're rich!"

Rena refused to believe it. "We can't have done it. They opened the red tag bag!"

"Yes," Jake chuckled, "but the money was in the ski cases. We decided that it would be safer."

"My God! Why didn't you tell me?"

"What do you care?" Jake squeezed her hand. "The money is on the way to the bank. That's all that matters!"

Jim O'Malley caught up with them just as they reached the bus.

"Hi, Rena," Jim was in good spirits. "Everything O.K.?"

Jake reacted at once, letting go of Rena's arm and trying to seem like a casual acquaintance. "There you are, miss," he said pointedly to Rena, trying to cue her back to her part.

Rena could do no more than force a smile. Events were unfolding too fast for her to adapt to them.

She found a window seat in the bus and Jim sat down beside her. "Did you see all that fuss at customs?" Jim said. "I don't know what was going on. Nick was having some sort of argument with Mr. Ambler."

"I didn't pay much attention, Jim," she answered. "I'm so exhausted that I can hardly think."

He glanced at her anxiously. "Are you feeling alright?"

"Tired. Just terribly tired." She gave him a wan smile. She hoped that he would take the hint.

She closed her eyes, alone at last with the turmoil of her emotions. A door had suddenly been slammed on her past, shutting out everyone and everything on the other side.

She was an enemy of society, a successful thief, a criminal at large. She had defied the law and betrayed her employer. She was counterfeit.

She shivered, suddenly conscious of the cold wall of fraudulence that existed between herself and Jim: he would never know why, but he was on the other side of the door.

She needed Silky's reassurance. He and Jake were the only two people left in her world.

She felt very lonely. Lonely and rich. Would it be worth half-a-million dollars?

She awoke with a start. The bus was parked at the door of the Chesa Grischuna, all crisp white stucco and burnished pine, nestled in the shadow of the massive Parsenn-Gotschna range.

She stepped down from the bus. A cheerful red-coated porter beamed at her, his bald head shining in the sunshine. "Welcome to Klosters, Fraulein."

She took a deep breath of cold, clear mountain air.

"Feeling better now?" Jim smiled at her.

"Oh, yes!" she said, laughing.

Silky was standing there grinning at her through the front door.

CHAPTER THIRTEEN

NICK DIAMADO reread the note that had been waiting for him at the hotel desk. The handwriting sprawled across the mauve, scented writing paper. "Please call me as soon as you arrive. Maria Carlino."

One of his friends in Hollywood had set this up, but Nick had never expected such an instant reaction. After all, Maria was a major Italian film star who could pick practically any man she chose. Perhaps she just wanted to ask him to a party.

Even then, he should follow through. Maria owned a house here and she was the entrée to the local jet-set to which Nick aspired.

He folded the note and sat down on the bed to gather his thoughts. His first impulse had been to telephone his father and put the finger on Simon Ambler. All he could think of, as he came out of the airport, was revenge.

The man had insulted him and made a fool of him. Nobody got away with that. However, gradually his rage had subsided, allowing him to review the facts more coolly.

Could he be sure that the black-bearded man was really one of the hijackers? His only evidence depended on Bickel's wild hypothesis about the false finger, a theory which Nick himself had scoffed at when it was first presented.

Not that any proof of Ambler's guilt was needed. Suspicion, just the breath of it, was enough to set a Mafia

xecution squad in motion. The man with the black
beard deserved to die, whether he was one of the hi-
ackers or not. But there were other considerations.

If the man really was implicated, then the likelihood
was that he had brought the ransom with him. In that
ase it might be better not to take any precipitate action.

If Nick turned the problem over to his father, the
cenario was easily predictable. They would torture the
man until he disclosed the whereabouts of the money and
hen they would kill him. It was as simple as that.

So simple that it seemed rather superfluous to bring in
he muscle. Nick could do the job himself without assistance. No one, not even his father, would know. And he
would have two million dollars conveniently stashed
away in Switzerland. It was almost too good to be true!

But was the man one of the hijackers? He would have
discarded the whole matter, except for one other thing
hat Joe Granger had told him. The second suspect was
a blond man with a facial scar. The man next to Ambler
at the customs table answered to that description. The
wo of them had acted like strangers, but they had
seemed to work together. Nick could swear that the blond
man had picked up the bag which Ambler had put down.

Why he had done it was not clear, since it held noth-
ng but clothes. It did not make sense. The fact remained
hat if they *were* both here, then the money was here
or sure.

He unfolded the note once more and asked for Miss
Carlino's number. He would watch the two men for another twenty-four hours. Then he would decide what to
do. In the meantime . . .

"Hello. This is Maria Carlino." The voice was deep and
ultry.

"Nick Diamado here."

"Ah Neek! I have so much been looking forward to
meet you . . ."

He was glad that he had called her. The way she pro-
nounced his name went right to his balls.

It was a warm-hearted room full of charm and repose.
Rena threw herself down on the feathery red and white
quilt, looking round contentedly at the natural pine decor.
French doors led through cherry curtains to a tiny balcony

265

overlooking the quiet village street. It was good to be alive after all.

She was just beginning to doze off when the telephone rang.

"Rena? It's Silky."

"Yes?"

"I'm sorry about what happened at the airport. I owe you an explanation," Silky said. "When can we talk?"

Tired as she was, she could not relax completely with so many unanswered questions in her head. "Now is as good a time as any. Jim has gone out to arrange life passes."

"Shall I come up?"

"Yes, that's fine."

She let Silky in, then returned to her place on the bed. He sat down in the armchair near the window.

"Well," Silky began, "I guess we had you pretty confused at customs. I'm sorry about it, but I think it was for the best in the end."

"Why didn't you tell me that you had changed the whole plan?" Rena asked. "Didn't you trust me?"

"I didn't change the plan until after the last time I saw you, when I came to pick up the bag.

"I don't know if you realized what shape you were in. I was really worried about you, Rena. You were close to a nervous breakdown."

"So you thought I would let you down." Rena felt hurt.

"No. On the contrary. I underestimated the mental strain of your part of the job. It sounded so simple, until you made me realize what it must have been like to have to live with those people day in day out, knowing what you knew.

"When I was driving home, I decided that I wanted to find a way to get through customs without involving you at all. Your job was to hold the money. You had done it. It was our job, Jake's and mine, to get the money safely out of the country."

"I still don't see why you didn't tell me," Rena argued.

"Because you didn't need to know for the success of the operation. You were not part of it."

"But I thought that I was. I nearly died when you opened the red tag bag."

"I realize that," Silky said. "That's why I came to apol

ogize. But, of course, I didn't know that Nick was going to do what he did. The fact remains that because you were very nervous, it was better that you should be nervous about the wrong bag."

"Why?"

"Because if we had been caught—if they had found the money in the ski bags—you could have walked away scot free. You would not have been part of the conspiracy to smuggle and no one need ever have known that you had been holding the money. You were out. Your part of the job was done."

She suddenly realized that Silky had been trying to protect her. "You mean that you wouldn't have told them about me?"

"Of course not. We would have denied ever having met you—except once at a party," Silky added wryly.

"Oh, Silky"—Rena felt very contrite—"you really are a friend. But of course, I would never have let you take the blame without me."

"What the hell?" Silky laughed. "It didn't happen. The ski bags saved our skins."

"But how did you get all the money in with two pairs of skis? There wasn't enough room."

"Oh yes there was," Silky grinned. "There weren't any skis."

"What d' you mean?"

"Well, there were four long narrow boxes in the bags, each box with the top twelve inches of a ski tip screwed to it. The money was in the boxes."

"Silky!" Rena gasped. "That's absolutely brilliant!"

He shrugged. "It got us through." He got up from his chair. "Anyway, that's the story. Am I forgiven?"

She felt a flood of emotion, a need for this man, a dependence on him. She held out her hand wanting to draw him down close to her. "Of course," she said.

He touched her fingers lightly. "Well, I've got to go out with Jake now to buy some new skis."

Silky strolled down the hill to the main street. He had arranged to meet Jake at the ski shop.

There was still one item of business to attend to, Nick Diamado. How he had stumbled on to the truth and how much he had been acting on intuition rather than specific evidence was hard to gauge. The fact remained that they would never be safe if Nick continued to stalk them.

Silky pondered Nick's possible courses of action. He could turn whatever evidence he had over to the police; fortunately, because of his underworld connections, this seemed an improbable alternative. He could turn the matter over to the Mafia for retribution. In that case the chances of his and Jake's survival, however they tried to escape the net, were nil. Perhaps their fate was already sealed. If it was not, then every minute counted; they had to head him off as soon as possible.

The third possibility was that Nick was greedy enough to covet the ransom himself. If this were the case, he would stop at nothing to get it. Still, of the three alternatives, it was the best chance for them.

In order to lead Nick to select the third alternative, he must be convinced that Silky had the ransom money with him in the hotel.

They had to make a plan and they had to move fast.

It was a continental banquet of Swiss cuisine spiced with Italian passion. Nick had never encountered a woman who played the game of seduction so exquisitely.

They were seated side by side in a corner nook of the dining room. The curved bench on which they sat was overlaid with a deep turquoise velvet cushion; there were matching individual back rests, each affixed to the pine wall by a carved leather clasp.

The nook had its own special romantic personality, *objets d'art* in random profusion around them: a copper vase of fresh flowers, a grandmother clock, a horse brass, a marble statuette, an old violin.

A place for lovers.

There was no doubt in Nick's mind where his evening with Maria would lead. But she was not going to be rushed. The foreplay had to be relished.

"Shall we have coffee and liqueurs in the bar?" he suggested.

She eyed him speculatively, touching his hand. "Perhaps you would like to go to bed, Neek. You must be very tired after your long journey from America."

Nick caught her hand and squeezed it. "I want to go to bed alright, but not to sleep. I'm not that tired."

"Oh Neek, darling." She pouted provocatively. "I think that perhaps you are a naughty boy, yes?"

Silky watched Nick and Maria cross the lobby and go down the stairs to the bar. He followed them at a discreet distance.

The room was full of people. Jake offered his bar stool to Maria, while Nick stood behind her. He ordered a cognac and a Galliano.

Silky pushed his way through the crowd, acting a little drunk. Nick looked at him with distaste.

Silky ordered a double bourbon on the rocks and took a wad of bills out of his pocket. He peeled off a one hundred dollar bill and laid it on the bar.

"I'm sorry, sir," the barman smiled apologetically. "We do not take American money in the bar. You will have to change it in the office."

"Doesn't matter." Silky shrugged. "Gonna change it all at the bank tomorrow, anyway." He picked up his drink and turned to push his way back through the crowd.

"Hey, meester." Silky turned to find Maria smiling at him. "You forgot your money."

Nick watched the bill as it passed from her hand to Silky's.

"Thanks," said Silky seemingly unperturbed. "Careless."

Jake had been watching the performance from the sidelines. It was a dangerous play but he was fairly sure that Nick had taken the bait. All that remained now was to hook him.

It was a majestic day in the Swiss Alps. They sat at long tables on the sundeck of the mountain restaurant eating bratwurst and sauerkraut and drinking German beer from earthenware steins.

The deck sparkled in a blaze of color and bright clothes —glossy people at play. The mountain was a pageant of activity. The perpetual motion of the two chair lifts loading and unloading, the graceful sweeps of the skiers as far as the eye could see, the row upon row of parked skis standing like multi-colored fences while their owners basked in the Alpine sunshine.

They had spent the morning on the lower slopes, limbering up on the broad middle trail, then taking the six kilometer run down to Klosters. After lunch they planned to take the chair to the top and then ski the famous Parsenn all the way down to Davos.

Rena had slept well and was rapidly recovering her spirits. She felt free to mix around the group now and it gave her a natural opportunity to sit with Jake and Silky without arousing suspicion. Jim seemed too busy in his role as Skip Langdon's side-kick to want to try to monopolize her company.

At a signal from Skip, the group began to move toward the ski racks, gradually taking their places, two by two, on the upper chair lift.

Reaching the top, they regathered for the afternoon run. Silky had been conscious all morning of Nick's dogging his footsteps and as he moved off, he was gratified to see Nick follow close on his heels.

Silky remained at the back of the group, moving easily in wide sweeping turns, Nick as always, just behind him. Rena was up front, relaxed now and skiing in her compact, fluid style behind Jim. Jake was the last to move off; seemingly dissatisfied with the fit of his boots, he bent down to adjust the clips. Then, when he was finally ready, he skated after the rest of them, circling the rear like an outrider watching for strays.

Looking down the line of skiers, Silky saw Skip enter the bowl, a wide valley between the two towering peaks, which led down the Parsenn to Klosters. If Silky was going to break away from the group, he had to act very soon, before he became committed to the terrain.

He started a wide turn to the left, shifting his weight to his heels as he moved from packed to virgin snow and disappeared over the ridge which ran along the sky line. He was skiing uncharted terrain now, cutting his own trail across the face of the mountain back to Klosters.

He was in deep powder up to his hips, running a diagonal schuss across the slope toward the canyon, which, according to the mountain maps that he had pored over during the night, should take him safely down to the next level.

He altered course to the right, gathering speed down the fall line, then circled in a slow curve, which brought him across the slope, giving him an opportunity to glance back at the terrain that he had already covered. His quarry had taken the bait. The tiny figure in the red ski suit a quarter of a mile above him was Nick Diamado.

It was a desperately simple plan. He was luring Nick out along an icy tightrope, in the hope that he would fall.

If Nick was to be eliminated, it had to appear to be an accident; any suspicion of foul play would not only attract the scrutiny of the Swiss police—it would also inevitably bring swift reprisal from the Mafia.

Nick had not been surprised when Silky had suddenly peeled off on his own. Having overheard Silky say in the bar that he intended to take the money to the bank today, he had been constantly alert, waiting for Silky to make his move.

He assumed that Silky was doubling back to Klosters to pick up the ransom money. But he had no way of knowing that Silky was flying blind across forbidden terrain; he took it for granted that they were following an approved, if difficult, run. In this respect he was less apprehensive than Silky about what lay ahead of them.

Silky entered the canyon at about seventy miles-per-hour, running almost vertically up the left wall to take off speed and to get a fleeting view of what lay ahead.

Picking his way among the jagged rocks in an uneven slalom of twisting jumps and turns, he hit a sudden patch of glare ice which nearly swept his skis from under him. Almost out of control, he fought his way through a narrow chicane, found himself airborne over steeply falling ground, and crashed out into deep powder again, running uphill over a broad, open hump.

If his calculations were correct, there was a sheer precipice running all along the base of this snowfield. Glancing over his shoulder to check that Nick was still following, he made a wide right turn to draw his unsuspecting prey to the most dangerous point. Ten feet short of the vertical drop, he executed a jump turn to the left and began running along the ridge. Looking back uphill, he saw that Nick had not followed him to the right; instead, he was schussing diagonally across with the obvious intention of heading Silky off. At the speed he was going, Nick would fly straight over the precipice to crash on the rocks below.

Somehow Nick saw the danger at the last moment. Making a superhuman effort, he managed an incredible jump turn and suddenly the two men were running parallel, along the ridge, only a few feet apart.

Pumping on his haunches and curling into an egg-position to reduce wind resistance, Silky gradually managed to draw away, making for the narrow trail at the end of the snowfield.

Both men were exhausted now.

The trail gave Silky a respite. There was a good even powder base and a relatively gentle slope. He relaxed a little, trying to shed some of his tension. If he was where he had planned to be, he could take this trail right across to one of the regular public runs.

Picking up speed, Silky turned to check behind him. At first he saw no one, but finally the red ski suit appeared about two hundred yards above.

Turning back to check his heading, Silky felt a sudden clutch of panic. The trail ahead was coming abruptly to an end!

It was too late to try to stop. He took the jump at full tilt, hoping to God for a soft landing. Fighting to keep his ski tips up against the air pressure and his body perpendicular, he waited for the crash.

The ground seemed to take an eternity to come up to meet him. But at least it was white—it was snow!

The drop must have been fifty feet. He held the first impact, then tried to skid his skis to take off some speed. The steel edge of his right ski caught a jutting rock, his saftey-binding released and he tumbled head over heels down the trail.

As he rolled, he felt the agonizing snap of his shin and ankle.

Nick stood on the edge of the drop looking down. He saw Silky lying sprawled in the snow below, immobile. He hoped fervently that he was not dead: he wanted to find out where the two million dollars was before he killed him.

He looked over the terrain carefully, then moved gingerly over to the right, stepping his way slowly down the side of the trail. He had plenty of time.

Silky wiped the blood and snow out of his eyes and tried to move, but it was hopeless. He watched resignedly as Nick picked his way methodically toward him.

Nick placed his ski poles deliberately in the snow beside him and glared scornfully down at his victim. Then he unzipped his ski jacket, searched inside for a small snub-nosed automatic and pointed it at Silky.

"I owe you a bullet, Mr. Ambler," Nick said calmly. "Whether you get it in the temple or the spleen depends on what you tell me."

Silky had to play for time. "Jesus! I'm all busted," he said.

"You're finished, you sonofabitch," Nick growled. "Where's the ransom?"

"What the hell are you talking about?"

"You know what I want, Mr. Ambler. The two million from Mount Casino. You have thirty seconds to tell me where it is."

Thirty seconds, Silky thought. He had no illusions about Nick's readiness to shoot. He might as well start talking.

"It's in my room."

"Where?"

Silky's eyes searched the trail above in desperation. Jake had cut it fine. He watched him line himself up carefully, fly gracefully through the air, and land with a perfectly executed knee-flex. Nick was only halfway round when Jake hit him, going like an express train. There was a squirt of blood as the point of Jake's ski pole caught Nick in the throat. The two bodies rolled down the slope together.

Silence.

"Jake!" Silky yelled. "Are you alright?"

"I think so," the reply came back. "How about you?"

"Broken ankle for sure. A few other bits and pieces." Silky was stoically cheerful.

Jake unfastened the safety straps of his skis, reset his bindings, and snow-plowed cautiously down to where Nick lay spread-eagled fifty feet below. It was not a pretty sight, red on red; the scarlet-clad body lying motionless in

273

a pool of crimson blood, which continued to pump gently out of the hole in his neck. His glasses lay shattered beside him.

Jake knelt down warily and felt for the pulse in Nick's wrist. He didn't have one. That made it easier. He took one of Nick's aluminum ski poles, worked it back and forth over his knee until it broke in half, then stuck the jagged edge into the wound in his throat. Finally he slipped the strap back over Nick's wrist. It was a messy job, but it looked convincing: accidents where people stabbed themselves with their own broken ski poles were not unknown.

He cleaned the blood off his own pole, took another critical look at the corpse and began side-stepping laboriously up to where Silky lay. He spotted Nick's gun in the snow halfway up. He picked it up and wiped it clean. He would dump it in a ravine on the way back down.

"How's Nick?" Silky asked.

"Dead."

Silky said nothing. They hadn't wanted to kill anyone. But it was him or them.

"You O.K.?"

"I'll live."

"Stay where you are, then." Jake grinned. "I'll go and get the ski patrol."

"Yeah," Silky replied. "Bring one of those St. Bernards with a barrel of booze round his neck. I could use a drink."

Silky lay on his bed staring at the ceiling. He was bored out of his mind.

Official reaction to his accident on the mountain had been one of shock and bureaucratic indignation. Both he and Jake had been severely reprimanded by the local authorities, the police, the ski area management, the mountain guides association, and the press for skiing on an uncharted part of the mountain without, at least, the benefit of a guide. They were variously labelled as reckless, foolhardy, inexperienced, and stupid American tourists. Even Skip Langdon was furious with them for leaving the group without telling him in advance.

Silky and Jake had stuck resolutely to their story that

274

hey were expert skiers, experienced on "wild" terrain, who had considered the easy Parsenn run too tame for their tastes. They did not have the slightest idea why an obviously inexperienced skier like Nick Diamado had followed them; perhaps he had mistakenly assumed that they were just making a small detour. They certainly had been completely unaware of his presence behind them, until he had suddenly appeared out of nowhere after Jake had stopped to assist Silky.

The ski patrol had arrived on the scene in a sullen mood, pulling two sleds; they made little attempt to conceal their opinion that the two injured skiers had received exactly what they deserved.

Silky was taken to the fracture clinic in Klosters where his broken bones were repaired and his right leg was encased in plaster up to his middle thigh. Nick's body was subjected to a local autopsy, following which it was removed to the Zurich morgue. After consultation by telephone with the deceased's father, the body was immediately dispatched by air freight to Los Angeles.

Since then, Silky had been confined to his hotel room. After three days the pain in his leg had subsided, leaving him entirely recovered in spirit and impatient to get out and about.

Given that his skiing was obviously over for this season, he saw little reason to hang around Klosters for another two weeks just to get his money's worth from his tour ticket. He might as well move out as soon as he was mobile and either return to the States or find some alternate diversion.

Yet, despite the cold logic of this conclusion, something was holding him back. Upon reflection he realized that he was unwilling to part from Jake and Rena. They were a trinity, an indivisible trio whose fortunes were now inseparably bound together.

But it was silly, Silky argued with himself. He saw damn little of them as it was; they were out skiing all day and, apart from a couple of hours with them at cocktail hour, they were out on the town half the night. Anyway, for Christ's sake, he wasn't exactly saying goodbye to Jake forever; he would see him again in the States in a couple of weeks, even if he left today.

It was different with Rena. She planned to stay in Switzerland. Once he left her, he might never see her again.

That was it. It had taken him a long time to get around to admitting it, but it was Rena who was holding him here. It was Rena whom he thought about all day, Rena whose evening visits he awaited with impatience. It was the thought of Rena out on the mountain and in the disco with Jim O'Malley and Jake that kept him awake half the night.

Jesus Christ! It wasn't his style to go all soft and stupid over a woman. A woman! He always thought about them in the vernacular, chicks, dolls, skirts. Pretty toys. But this was a lady, a unique, feminine, beautiful, lovable person. Lovable? Him in love? It was unthinkable!

What did he want from her. Marriage? Come on, he said to himself, you don't even have a job—you're a ski bum. Except. Except I now have three-quarters of a million dollars—and, come to think of it—she's got half a million to add to it!

But marriage! His mind recoiled from it.

What would they do? Where would they live? He had to do something, if only to avoid suspicion. If he tried to live on nothing other than the proceeds of the robbery Interpol or somebody would be on to him in no time.

He mused on. Of course they could buy a small hotel somewhere like Klosters for instance. Now that he came to think of it, Rena had been brought up in a hotel. Hell, she would be absolutely terrific in the business!

Turn it off, man, turn it off, his saner half argued. Why would she have you? A beautiful, educated European lady like that getting married to a ski bum? You're crazy.

But a goddam wealthy ski bum, all the same!

He looked at his watch. Just after four in the afternoon. Another hour-and-a-half before she came—if she came.

Well, goddam it, he might not have much of a chance, but he was not going to leave without asking her. Asking her what? To marry him? Something like that. Wait and see.

But when was he going to get the opportunity? He never got a chance to talk to her alone. It wasn't something to be handled at a five-minute coffee break. He had

work her up to it. Goddammit, it required a romantic
tmosphere. How could he propose to a girl lying on his
ack in this crummy room?

He would have to enlist Jake's help—as long as Jake
adn't got any designs on her himself. The idea of it made
is blood run cold. No, he was sure that Rena liked him
etter than Jake. At least, she used to, but Jake could be
aking up for lost time with her now.

And what about Jim O'Malley? It was pretty obvious
at Jim was nuts about her. He certainly dated her a lot.
nd he was a good-looking guy with a steady job. But
omehow, seeing them together, Silky had the impression
at most of the real passion was on Jim's side.

He looked at his watch again. An hour to go. Godammit, if the doctor didn't let him out on crutches tomor-
ow, he'd take the law into his own hands. Jake would
elp him.

Well, it looked as if he would have to stick around this
ump whether he liked it or not. At least until he got a
hance to talk to her—a real chance at the right time and
lace.

Silky had laid his plan with characteristic care, curbing
is impatience to execute it until a propitious moment
resented itself. He found the opportunity two days later,
is first day on crutches, when he was able to arrange to
t next to Rena at the long dinner table with the rest of
e group.

He opened with studied innocence. "What's the name
f that village where you were born?"

She looked at him in surprise. "Lenzerheide," she said.

"How far is it from here? How long would it take to
rive there?"

Her surprise mounted. "Oh, three or four hours I guess.
Vhy?"

"I thought of getting myself a cab and going over to
ave a look at it," he said, as though it was just a casual
him. "You're always saying how pretty it is. I decided
nat I should get out a bit and take a look at the coun-
ryside while I'm here. I'm going stir-crazy sitting around
oing nothing."

"Are you serious?" She searched his eyes.

"Of course."

"Could I come with you? Would I be in the way?"

It brought back memories of the first time that he had met her—that drive to New York. He wondered whether she was conscious of the coincidence. "Of course not. I'll appreciate the company. Maybe we could rent a car and you could drive me, if you felt like it."

"I'd love to," she said, sparkling with enthusiasm. "When do you want to go?"

"What's wrong with tomorrow?" He smiled.

They had made an early start with the intention of reaching their destination for lunch.

The road crept sinuously along the valley of the Landquart River between the towering mountains, threading its way through sleepy villages and isolated farms, their chimneys all puffing in cozy contentment.

Rena was in a scintillating mood, full of lively chatter. Silky had planned to steer the conversation very gently but he soon lost any semblance of control. He just sat back and basked in the joy of her company, suddenly realizing that they had never been alone together long enough to taste this kind of intimacy before. All the time that he had known her she had been under one strain or another. Today she seemed to be beside herself with happiness.

They drove through the lovely old town of Chur with its gingerbread houses, then out into the Engadine, past the frozen Heidsee Lake, creeping slowly up to the Vulpera Plateau.

The day had turned bright and clear as they entered the outskirts of Lenzerheide. Rena pointed here and there excitedly as they went. "That's where I went to school. That's where my best friend lived. Look at the ski runs. Aren't they marvellous?"

Then, gradually her mood changed to melancholy. Finally she pulled up outside a small inn on the outskirts of town, all sparkling whitewash and hand-painted frescoes, an oversized Swiss doll's house. "That's where I was born," she said with a sudden pang of sadness.

"It's lovely," he said gently. "Do you want to go in?"

"No," she answered fiercely. "That part of my life is over. I can never go back." Without another word, she turned the car in the direction of the Waldhaus Hotel.

278

They sat in the stately dining room with its magnificent carved oak ceiling and crisp white tablecloths. Rena seemed quite at ease in the imposing surroundings, while Silky felt overawed. He began to lose his resolve, realizing how far apart their worlds really were. He could feel the happiness ebbing out of her.

"I shouldn't have brought you here," he said. "I thought that it would make you happy, but it has made you sad."

"Did you bring me here? On purpose, I mean?"

"Yes."

"Why?"

"I wanted to see you in your own surroundings, as you really are. We've had a funny relationship, the soldier and the bagman. I was hoping to find that there was more between us than that."

"Well, is there?" She was pensive. "What do you think?"

"I don't know. I can only speak for myself. I like you a lot. You know that."

She studied him in surprise, head cocked to one side, sizing him up.

He endured the silent gaze as long as he could. "What do you propose to do now, Rena? Now, that it's all over."

"I don't know, Silky," she sighed. "I'm so mixed up. I feel so lonely and guilty, so cut off from everybody."

"You've got the money to buy a new life. That's what you wanted," Silky said.

"What's the use?" She gave a desperate shrug. "Whatever life I buy, I still have to live with myself. I don't like myself anymore."

"Well, I like you." Silky grinned. "Does that help?"

"Of course. You and Jake are the only friends I have. Once you're gone, there is nothing left."

Silky took the plunge. At least he could settle one point. "Do you have any preference? Between Jake and me, I mean?"

She smiled. "Does it matter?"

"Yes. Very much."

She toyed with him playfully, making a show of solving a difficult problem. "Well, yes. I have a favorite."

"Come on, Rena," Silky said impatiently, immediately regretting it.

"You're my favorite, Silky. Part of you, that is. You're two distinct people—a cold-hearted soldier and a warm hearted man. If I didn't know the soldier, I could be very attracted to the man."

"The soldier's dead," Silky said vehemently. "The war's over."

"Is it?" She sighed. "Oh God, Silky! I wish I could put wars behind me like you do!"

"It comes from practice," Silky said. "This last thing, the hijack, was a kind of revenge against the world for all the killing it has made me do. I guess it is hard to explain. I spent so long killing people just so I could stay alive— the whole goddam Vietnam thing was so senseless—that anything, even a robbery, seemed more worthwhile." He shrugged. "The hijack made sense then, but it all seems crazy now. I wish I hadn't done it."

"Do you really, Silky?" She grasped his hand across the table. "Do you honestly?"

"Yes. Except that I would not have met you. That's the only thing I don't regret."

"Oh, Silky!" Her eyes lit up with a kind of smile she used to have when he first met her, a long time ago. "Do you mean it?"

"Yes. I mean it."

They did not talk much on the drive back to Klosters. A little spark of hope for the future was glowing between them now, and each was afraid of putting it out with a clumsy word.

It was not until they were parked outside the Chesa Grischuna that Silky decided to take the risk. The flame had to be kindled this evening or else it would die forever. Instinctively, he knew that there would never be another chance.

He switched off the engine and stared straight ahead. It had to be decided cold, no tactile blandishments to undermine her will. "Listen," he said, trying to sound matter-of-fact. "I would like to stick around. Anywhere you want. As long as you want. No strings. I just don't want to leave you. What do you say?"

She turned, reaching to touch him, then checked herself as she fought to suppress her churning emotions. Drawing her outstretched fingers back into a little fist, she waited to find a voice to match his dispassionate tone.

"Alright." She sounded almost casual. "One question, though. Is this relationship supposed to be platonic—or what?"

"Whatever you say."

She pushed open the door of the car and stepped out, looking back at him. "Come on, then," she said mischievously. "Let's go upstairs and find out."

Their lovemaking was tender: but no bells rang for Rena.

Between them lay a gossamer veil of shyness and embarrassment which neither had the hot-blooded sensuality to overcome. Some of Silky's most profound emotions were imprisoned in a cold, black cell in the depth of his soul and even the warmth and fervor of Rena's naked body had not been enough to set them free.

Rena cried softly when it was over. She was not hurt, nor defeated. She was emotionally spent.

Silky was awkward, almost morose, in the aftermath, uneasy with his defenses down. Regretfully, Rena let him return alone to his room to shower and change for dinner.

"Will you tell Jake?" She asked.

"No," he said. "It would spoil things."

She got the message. Nothing must change between the three of them. She consoled herself with the thought it was just the beginning. There was time—plenty of time—for the bells to ring.

They joined Jake for dinner and Rena made a point of playing no favorites. She was soon recounting to Jake a lightly edited version of the day's events at Lenzerheide. Silky sat on the sidelines, feeling edgy; perhaps he still retained a subconscious prickle of guilt for having allowed Rena so near to disarming him. Reflexively, his eye roved the busy dining room. Suddenly he came to full alert.

The girl—it was the Italian actress who had been in the car with Nick Diamado the first night, the girl who had handed him back his hundred dollar bill—dropped her eyes at once. But the man beside her—a dark, predatory-looking man—held Silky's gaze unflinchingly. There was no doubt in Silky's mind that he had been the subject of the other two's conversation.

281

Rena sensed Silky's sudden tension. "What's the matter?" she asked.

Silky reached for his wineglass without shifting his head. He took a measured sip. "I think there's a hit man in this room," he said quietly. "And I'm looking right at him."